# The Land Remembers
# A Hill Country Chronicle

"This book is a work of fiction. While the character and their journey were inspired by the spirit and creativity of a real individuals, the story, characters, and events contained within are entirely products of imagination and are not based on real life. This narrative was created with the assistance of artificial intelligence."

By Richard Dell Schwarz

# Forward

The Hill Country of Texas is more than just a backdrop for
this story—it is a living, breathing character, as complex and
resilient as the people who call it home. *The Land Remembers* is
a tribute to the enduring spirit of those who worked its soil,
endured its hardships, and found beauty in its harshest
seasons.

Set in 1936, amid the suffocating grip of the Dust Bowl and
the widespread despair of the Great Depression, this novel
introduces us to Elara "Ellie" Mae Dawson—a young woman
fiercely connected to the land and to the generations of
strength that came before her. Through Ellie's journey, we
rediscover the value of forgotten wisdom, the quiet power of
nature, and the bonds of family that tether us to our heritage
even as the winds of change threaten to scatter it.

Though fictional, the story is deeply rooted in the emotional
truths and historical struggles of rural America. It is inspired
by the quiet resilience of those who refused to give up, who
found hope in seeds sown in dust, and who believed, even
when the skies gave no sign, that rain—and renewal—would
come.

This book was written with a profound respect for the land,
the legacy of Texas German immigrants, and the healing
knowledge passed from generation to generation, often by
the hands of women who listened to the earth when no one
else would.

May you find in these pages not only a story of survival, but a
celebration of unseen strength and the enduring bloom of
hope beneath the driest soil.

*— Richard Dell Schwarz*
Boerne, Texas

# Table of contents

## Contents

# Chapter 1: Dust and Dreams

The Texas sun, a malevolent eye in a bleached sky, beat down on the desiccated earth of the Hill Country. It was 1936, and the land lay gasping, a parched throat choked with dust. For Elara "Ellie" Mae Dawson, the scent of her family's lavender farm was no longer a sweet, intoxicating perfume, but a ghostly whisper of what had been. The once vibrant purple rows, stretching towards the horizon like a royal carpet, were now a muted, dusty lavender, their delicate blossoms brittle and faded. The air itself was a thick, gritty veil, a constant, suffocating reminder of the relentless drought that had gripped the region, stealing moisture, vitality, and hope with equal ferocity.

Ellie traced a cracked line in the dry soil with the toe of her worn boot. Each fissure seemed to echo the growing despair within her father, a man whose hands, once calloused from the loving toil of the land, now trembled with the weight of impending ruin. The farm, established by her German immigrant grandparents generations ago, was more than just a business; it was a legacy, a testament to their sweat and sacrifice, their enduring belief in the promise of this rugged soil. Now, it mirrored the arid landscape it occupied, on the brink of collapse, its future as uncertain as a cloudless sky.

She remembered her grandmother, a woman whose connection to the earth ran deeper than any well. Grandma Mae, they called her, her fingers stained with the earth's rich colors, her eyes holding the ancient wisdom of the land. It was Grandma Mae who had first taught Ellie the language of the plants, the subtle signs of distress and resilience, the hidden language of roots and leaves. She had shown Ellie how to listen to the earth's whispers, how to find solace and strength in the tenacious life that clung to existence even in the harshest conditions. This deep, intuitive bond was Ellie's inheritance, a precious gift in this time of scarcity, a stark contrast to her father's weary pronouncements of defeat. He saw only the dying lavender, the empty water barrels, the encroaching dust. Ellie saw the stubborn resilience of a thistle, the determined reach of a mesquite root, the quiet promise of dormant seeds waiting for a whisper of rain.

The scent of dying lavender hung heavy, a poignant fragrance that spoke of lost beauty and dwindling resources. It was a scent that clung to the very air Ellie breathed, a constant companion to the dust that settled on everything – the worn wooden fences, the peeling paint of the farmhouse, the very lines etched into her father's face. He would stand at the edge of the fields, his gaze fixed on the horizon where the dust storms brewed, a dark promise on the wind, his shoulders slumped with a weariness that went soul-deep. "We can't fight this, Ellie," he'd say, his voice raspy, like the dry leaves skittering across the parched earth. "This land… it's taken everything."

But Ellie couldn't accept his resignation. Her grandmother's teachings had instilled in her a different kind of understanding, a belief that the land, though unforgiving, also held secrets for survival. She remembered afternoons spent with Grandma Mae, their hands stained with the dark loam as they dug for roots, identifying plants that seemed to mock the drought's severity. There was the scarlet bee balm, its vibrant petals a startling contrast to the muted earth, its leaves known to soothe burns and fevers. And the prickly pear cactus, its thick pads storing precious water, its fruit, when ripe, a sweet, nourishing treat. These weren't just plants; they were allies, part of a complex, interwoven tapestry of life that had endured for centuries before their modern struggles.

The lavender, while the heart of their livelihood, was also their greatest vulnerability. It was a cultivated crop, dependent on water and care, a fragile beauty ill-suited to the relentless onslaught of the Dust Bowl. Her father, a man of practicality and tradition, had poured all his hopes into the fields of purple. He saw the fading blooms as a personal failure, a betrayal of his ancestors. Ellie saw it as a sign that they needed to adapt, to look beyond the familiar, to embrace the wild, untamed wisdom of the native flora.

As she walked the rows, a faint, almost imperceptible sweetness still lingered, a memory of the plant's former glory. It was a scent that tugged at her heartstrings, a reminder of brighter days, of the joy her grandmother had found in nurturing these delicate plants. But beneath the fading fragrance, there was the sharp, dry scent of dust, the earthy tang of parched soil, and the faint, metallic scent of desperation. The farm was a battlefield, and the enemy was the relentless, suffocating drought, a foe that offered no quarter.

Ellie knelt, her fingers sifting through the dry earth. It was as brittle as old parchment, crumbling away at her touch. She looked back at the farmhouse, a sturdy, weathered structure that had weathered many storms, both literal and figurative. But this storm, this drought, felt different. It felt like an ending. Her father's despair was a heavy weight, pressing down on her, but it also ignited a fierce spark of defiance within her. She wouldn't let the land, or her family's legacy, be consumed by this arid tide. She would listen to the land, as Grandma Mae had taught her, and find a way to endure. She would find the unseen blooms, the hidden strengths, the quiet resilience that lay dormant beneath the surface, waiting to be discovered. The sun beat down, relentless, but within Ellie, a different kind of warmth was beginning to stir. It was the warmth of resolve, of a daughter determined to protect her family and honor the enduring spirit of the land.

The scent of lavender, once the fragrant soul of the Dawson farm, now hung in the air like a mournful elegy. It was a perfume tainted by dust, a testament to a dying dream. The Texas Hill Country in 1936 was a landscape etched with the cruel lines of drought, each cracked furrow in the earth a mirror of the despair deepening in Ellie Mae Dawson's heart. Her family's lavender fields, stretching out in muted, faded rows under a sky bleached bone-white by the sun, were on the precipice of ruin. The air itself was a tangible entity, thick with a gritty film that coated everything, a constant, suffocating reminder of their precarious existence.

Ellie traced a pattern in the parched soil with the toe of her worn leather boot, the earth crumbling away like ancient, forgotten paper. This land, her inheritance from German immigrant ancestors who had poured their hopes and sweat into its unforgiving soil, was a living entity, but one that was slowly suffocating. It was on the brink of collapse, a mirror of the arid reality that threatened to swallow their livelihood whole. She remembered her grandmother, Grandma Mae, a woman who had understood the earth's secrets with an almost mystical intuition. Her hands, forever stained with the rich hues of the soil, had taught Ellie the language of roots and leaves, the subtle signs of resilience in the face of adversity.

This deep, almost spiritual connection to the land was Ellie's inheritance, a stark contrast to the growing weariness in her father's eyes. He stood at the edge of the fields, his gaze fixed on the hazy, dust-laden horizon, his shoulders stooped under a burden that seemed too heavy for any man to bear. His pronouncements of defeat were like the dry, rustling leaves that skittered across the barren earth. "We can't fight this, Ellie," he'd say, his voice raspy, choked with dust and despair. "This land… it's taken everything."

But Ellie couldn't surrender. Her grandmother's teachings were a quiet defiance within her, a persistent whisper that even in the harshest conditions, life found a way. She recalled afternoons spent with Grandma Mae, their fingers stained with loam as they unearthed hardy native plants, those that seemed to mock the drought's severity. There was the scarlet bee balm, its vibrant petals a startling splash of color against the muted earth, its leaves known to soothe burns and fevers. And the prickly pear cactus, its thick pads storing precious water, its fruit a sweet, nourishing treasure. These were not mere plants; they were allies, vital threads in the intricate tapestry of life that had endured for centuries, long before the modern struggles of the Dust Bowl.

The lavender, though the heart of their livelihood, was also their greatest vulnerability. It was a cultivated crop, dependent on water and care, a fragile beauty ill-suited to the relentless onslaught of the Dust Bowl. Her father, a man of practicality and tradition, had poured all his hopes into the fields of purple. He saw the fading blooms as a personal failure, a betrayal of his ancestors' legacy. Ellie saw it as a sign that they needed to adapt, to look beyond the familiar, to embrace the wild, untamed wisdom of the native flora that had always thrived here.

As she walked the rows, a faint, almost imperceptible sweetness still lingered, a ghost of the plant's former glory, a scent that tugged at her heartstrings, a memory of brighter days, of the joy her grandmother had found in nurturing these delicate plants. But beneath the fading fragrance, there was the sharp, dry scent of dust, the earthy tang of parched soil, and the faint, metallic scent of desperation. The farm was a battlefield, and the enemy was the relentless, suffocating drought, a foe that offered no quarter.

Ellie knelt, her fingers sifting through the dry earth. It was as brittle as old parchment, crumbling away at her touch. She looked back at the farmhouse, a sturdy, weathered structure that had weathered many storms, both literal and figurative. But this storm, this drought, felt different. It felt like an ending. Her father's despair was a heavy weight, pressing down on her, but it also ignited a fierce spark of defiance within her. She wouldn't let the land, or her family's legacy, be consumed by this arid tide. She would listen to the land, as Grandma Mae had taught her, and find a way to endure. She would find the unseen blooms, the hidden strengths, the quiet resilience that lay dormant beneath the surface, waiting to be discovered. The sun beat down, relentless, but within Ellie, a different kind of warmth was beginning to stir. It was the warmth of resolve, of a daughter determined to protect her family and honor the enduring spirit of the land.

The very air seemed to hold its breath, thick with the anticipation of something terrible. The lavender, once a vibrant wave of color, was now a muted tapestry of purples and grays, each stem brittle, each bloom a fragile memory of life's abundance. Ellie could almost feel the plants' thirst, a silent scream echoing the desperate pleas of her own family. The farm, a testament to generations of hard work, to the unwavering spirit of her German immigrant ancestors, was slowly succumbing to the relentless grip of the Dust Bowl. The cracked earth seemed to yawn open, hungry for the rain that never came, revealing the stark, unforgiving reality of their situation.

Ellie's father, a man whose face was a roadmap of worry etched by the relentless sun and the crushing weight of economic hardship, would often stand at the edge of their property, his gaze lost somewhere beyond the shimmering heat haze. His despair was a palpable thing, a shadow that clung to him like the dust that settled on everything. "It's no use, Ellie," he'd say, his voice hoarse, sounding much like the wind whistling through the dry stalks. "This land's given up. We've given up."

But Ellie couldn't give up. Not yet. She remembered her grandmother, Grandma Mae, a woman whose hands were perpetually stained with the rich, dark earth, her eyes holding a wisdom that seemed as ancient as the hills themselves. It was Grandma Mae who had taught Ellie to see the land not just as a source of crops, but as a living, breathing entity, with its own rhythms, its own secrets. She had taught Ellie about the plants that thrived where others withered, about the deep-rooted resilience of the native flora, the tough, tenacious weeds and wildflowers that seemed to scoff at the drought.

The scent of the fading lavender was a constant, poignant reminder of their vulnerability. It was a scent that spoke of lost potential, of a harvest that would never be. Yet, beneath that sorrowful fragrance, Ellie could detect other scents, subtler ones that her grandmother had taught her to recognize. The dry, earthy aroma of the soil itself, clinging to the air like a shroud. The faint, dusty perfume of the mesquite trees, their thorny branches reaching stubbornly towards the sky. And even, if she closed her eyes and breathed deeply, the ghost of the wild sage that grew on the rocky outcrops, a hardy plant that held its own kind of fragrant defiance.

The farm, a patchwork of fading purples and cracked earth, was a physical manifestation of her father's despair. The lines on his face deepened with each passing day, each empty rain barrel, each unsold bundle of lavender. He saw the farm as a failing business, a betrayal of his heritage. Ellie, however, saw it through her grandmother's eyes. She saw the resilience in the bent, dusty stems, the stubborn life force that refused to be extinguished. She saw the potential in the deep roots that sought moisture far below the parched surface.

Her connection to the land was more than just a matter of livelihood; it was a bond inherited, a deep-seated understanding passed down through generations. Grandma Mae had shown her which plants held medicinal properties, which could be used for teas and poultices, which could offer solace in times of sickness and hardship. These weren't mere weeds; they were vital parts of the ecosystem, offerings from the land itself, meant to be understood and utilized with respect.

As Ellie stood amidst the wilting rows, the sun beat down with an almost malicious intensity. The air was thick, heavy, carrying the fine, suffocating dust that seemed to permeate everything. It was a constant reminder of their precarious situation, a tangible symbol of the forces arrayed against them. The farm, once a vibrant testament to her family's hard work and dreams, was now a landscape of fading hope, its very soil cracking under the strain. Yet, within Ellie, a quiet determination began to bloom, as tenacious and resilient as the native wildflowers her grandmother had taught her to cherish. She would not let the dust claim their legacy. She would find a way to coax life from this dying land, to nurture the unseen blooms that held the promise of a future.

The scent of fading lavender, once a sweet promise of summer's bounty, now carried a melancholic undertone, a fragrance tinged with the dry, dusty breath of the Dust Bowl. It was 1936, and the Texas Hill Country lay parched, its vibrant hues muted under a relentless sun. Elara "Ellie" Mae Dawson stood amidst the wilting rows of her family's farm, the cracked earth a testament to the desperate thirst that gripped the land. The air itself was a gritty veil, a constant, suffocating reminder of their precarious situation, the drought's suffocating hold on their livelihood.

Ellie's connection to this land ran deeper than the shallow roots of the struggling lavender. It was a bond inherited from her grandmother, Grandma Mae, a woman who had understood the earth's language, its whispers of resilience and survival. Her grandmother had taught Ellie to see beyond the surface, to find strength in the tenacity of native plants, in the deep-rooted wisdom that endured even in the harshest conditions. This was a stark contrast to her father's growing despair, a weariness etched into every line of his face, a man whose dreams seemed to wither with the dying crops.

The farm, a legacy of her German immigrant ancestors, was a testament to their enduring spirit, their belief in the promise of this rugged terrain. Now, it mirrored the arid landscape it occupied, on the brink of collapse. Ellie ran a hand over a brittle lavender stem, its once vibrant purple now a dusty, muted hue. The scent that rose was faint, a ghost of its former glory, a poignant reminder of what was being lost. It mingled with the sharp, dry aroma of the soil, the earthy tang of dust that coated everything – the worn wooden fences, the peeling paint of the farmhouse, the very air they breathed.

Her father's despondency was a heavy weight, a constant presence in the quiet, sun-baked farmhouse. He would stand at the edge of the fields, his gaze lost on the horizon, his shoulders slumped with a burden that seemed too great to bear. "We can't fight this, Ellie," he'd say, his voice raspy, like the dry leaves skittering across the parched earth. "This land… it's taken everything." His words were a reflection of the widespread hopelessness that permeated the community, a collective sigh of resignation in the face of overwhelming odds.

But Ellie couldn't succumb to that despair. Her grandmother's teachings were a persistent whisper in her soul, a reminder that the land, though unforgiving, also held secrets for endurance. She remembered afternoons spent with Grandma Mae, their hands stained with the rich loam as they unearthed hardy native plants, those that seemed to scoff at the drought's severity. There was the scarlet bee balm, its vibrant petals a startling splash of color against the muted earth, its leaves known to soothe burns and fevers. And the prickly pear cactus, its thick pads storing precious water, its fruit a sweet, nourishing treasure. These were not mere weeds; they were vital parts of the ecosystem, offerings from the land itself, meant to be understood and utilized with respect.

The lavender, while the heart of their livelihood, was also their greatest vulnerability. It was a cultivated crop, dependent on water and care, a fragile beauty ill-suited to the relentless onslaught of the Dust Bowl. Her father, a man of practicality and tradition, had poured all his hopes into the fields of purple. He saw the fading blooms as a personal failure, a betrayal of his ancestors' legacy. Ellie saw it as a sign that they needed to adapt, to look beyond the familiar, to embrace the wild, untamed wisdom of the native flora that had always thrived here.

As she walked the rows, a faint, almost imperceptible sweetness still lingered, a ghost of the plant's former glory, a scent that tugged at her heartstrings, a memory of brighter days, of the joy her grandmother had found in nurturing these delicate plants. But beneath the fading fragrance, there was the sharp, dry scent of dust, the earthy tang of parched soil, and the faint, metallic scent of desperation. The farm was a battlefield, and the enemy was the relentless, suffocating drought, a foe that offered no quarter.

Ellie knelt, her fingers sifting through the dry earth. It was as brittle as old parchment, crumbling away at her touch. She looked back at the farmhouse, a sturdy, weathered structure that had weathered many storms, both literal and figurative. But this storm, this drought, felt different. It felt like an ending. Her father's despair was a heavy weight, pressing down on her, but it also ignited a fierce spark of defiance within her. She wouldn't let the land, or her family's legacy, be consumed by this arid tide. She would listen to the land, as Grandma Mae had taught her, and find a way to endure. She would find the unseen blooms, the hidden strengths, the quiet resilience that lay dormant beneath the surface, waiting to be discovered. The sun beat down, relentless, but within Ellie, a different kind of warmth was beginning to stir. It was the warmth of resolve, of a daughter determined to protect her family and honor the enduring spirit of the land.

The scent of fading lavender, once the fragrant soul of the Dawson farm, now hung in the air like a mournful elegy. It was a perfume tainted by dust, a testament to a dying dream. The Texas Hill Country in 1936 was a landscape etched with the cruel lines of drought, each cracked furrow in the earth a mirror of the despair deepening in Ellie Mae Dawson's heart. Her family's lavender fields, stretching out in muted, faded rows under a sky bleached bone-white by the sun, were on the precipice of ruin. The air itself was a tangible entity, thick with a gritty film that coated everything, a constant, suffocating reminder of their precarious existence.

Ellie traced a pattern in the parched soil with the toe of her worn leather boot, the earth crumbling away like ancient, forgotten paper. This land, her inheritance from German immigrant ancestors who had poured their hopes and sweat into its unforgiving soil, was a living entity, but one that was slowly suffocating. It was on the brink of collapse, a mirror of the arid reality that threatened to swallow their livelihood whole. She remembered her grandmother, Grandma Mae, a woman who had understood the earth's secrets with an almost mystical intuition. Her hands, forever stained with the rich hues of the soil, had taught Ellie the language of roots and leaves, the subtle signs of resilience in the face of adversity.

This deep, almost spiritual connection to the land was Ellie's inheritance, a stark contrast to the growing weariness in her father's eyes. He stood at the edge of the fields, his gaze lost on the horizon, his shoulders stooped under a burden that seemed too heavy for any man to bear. His pronouncements of defeat were like the dry, rustling leaves that skittered across the barren earth. "We can't fight this, Ellie," he'd say, his voice raspy, choked with dust and despair. "This land… it's taken everything."

But Ellie couldn't surrender. Her grandmother's teachings were a quiet defiance within her, a persistent whisper that even in the harshest conditions, life found a way. She recalled afternoons spent with Grandma Mae, their fingers stained with the rich loam as they unearthed hardy native plants, those that seemed to mock the drought's severity. There was the scarlet bee balm, its vibrant petals a startling splash of color against the muted earth, its leaves known to soothe burns and fevers. And the prickly pear cactus, its thick pads storing precious water, its fruit a sweet, nourishing treasure. These were not mere weeds; they were vital parts of the ecosystem, offerings from the land itself, meant to be understood and utilized with respect.

The lavender, though the heart of their livelihood, was also their greatest vulnerability. It was a cultivated crop, dependent on water and care, a fragile beauty ill-suited to the relentless onslaught of the Dust Bowl. Her father, a man of practicality and tradition, had poured all his hopes into the fields of purple. He saw the fading blooms as a personal failure, a betrayal of his ancestors' legacy. Ellie saw it as a sign that they needed to adapt, to look beyond the familiar, to embrace the wild, untamed wisdom of the native flora that had always thrived here.

As she walked the rows, a faint, almost imperceptible sweetness still lingered, a ghost of the plant's former glory, a scent that tugged at her heartstrings, a memory of brighter days, of the joy her grandmother had found in nurturing these delicate plants. But beneath the fading fragrance, there was the sharp, dry scent of dust, the earthy tang of parched soil, and the faint, metallic scent of desperation. The farm was a battlefield, and the enemy was the relentless, suffocating drought, a foe that offered no quarter.

Ellie knelt, her fingers sifting through the dry earth. It was as brittle as old parchment, crumbling away at her touch. She looked back at the farmhouse, a sturdy, weathered structure that had weathered many storms, both literal and figurative. But this storm, this drought, felt different. It felt like an ending. Her father's despair was a heavy weight, pressing down on her, but it also ignited a fierce spark of defiance within her. She wouldn't let the land, or her family's legacy, be consumed by this arid tide. She would listen to the land, as Grandma Mae had taught her, and find a way to endure. She would find the unseen blooms, the hidden strengths, the quiet resilience that lay dormant beneath the surface, waiting to be discovered. The sun beat down, relentless, but within Ellie, a different kind of warmth was beginning to stir. It was the warmth of resolve, of a daughter determined to protect her family and honor the enduring spirit of the land.

The air inside the Dawson farmhouse was as heavy as the dust that coated every surface, a stifling, oppressive blanket that seemed to press down on their very souls. Ellie's father, Silas, sat at the worn wooden table, his hands spread before him, the callouses that spoke of a lifetime of honest labor now seemed fragile, almost skeletal. The lines on his face, etched deep by worry and the relentless Texas sun, had deepened further in recent weeks. He ran a trembling hand over his thinning hair, his gaze fixed on the faded ledger open before him, its pages filled with numbers that painted a grim picture of their mounting debts. The cost of seed, of fertilizer, of the meager supplies they needed to survive – it all added up, a damning indictment of their current reality.

"Another letter from the bank, Ellie," he said, his voice rough, devoid of its usual warmth. He didn't need to say what it meant. The implied threat of foreclosure hung in the air, as tangible as the dust motes dancing in the slivers of light that penetrated the grimy windowpanes. His shoulders slumped, a gesture of defeat that Ellie refused to acknowledge. He had always been her rock, the steady presence in her life, but the drought, the economic collapse of the nation, and now the failing farm, were chipping away at his strength, leaving behind a man shadowed by a weariness that went soul-deep. He saw the farm as a business, a ledger to be balanced, and when the numbers refused to cooperate, his faith wavered. He couldn't see the quiet resilience of the land that Ellie felt in her bones.

"What does it say, Papa?" Ellie asked, her voice carefully neutral, though her heart hammered against her ribs. She tried to keep her gaze steady, to project a confidence she didn't entirely feel. Her father looked up, his eyes, once bright and full of life, now held a flicker of resignation. "Just… the usual. Payments are overdue. They're giving us a little more time, but…" He trailed off, the unspoken words—*but it won't be enough*—hanging heavy in the silence. He had always been a practical man, his dreams tied to the tangible reality of the harvest, to the tangible reward of hard work. But this year, the earth had offered nothing but dust and despair, and it was breaking him.

Beside him, her younger brother, Thomas, coughed, a dry, rattling sound that echoed the parched earth outside. He was curled in a worn armchair by the hearth, a thin blanket pulled around his small shoulders, though the day was warm. His cheeks were flushed, and his breath came in shallow, ragged gasps. The dust, that ever-present scourge, had settled in his small lungs, exacerbating a weakness that had plagued him since birth. Ellie's heart ached with a fierce, protective love. Thomas was the reason she couldn't give up, the bright spark that fueled her determination. Seeing him so frail, so vulnerable, was a constant torment, a gnawing worry that amplified the fear of what would happen if they lost the farm.

She moved to his side, kneeling to brush a stray strand of sandy hair from his forehead. His skin felt hot to the touch. "Are you thirsty, little bird?" she asked softly, her voice gentle. Thomas nodded weakly, his large eyes, the color of the summer sky before the dust storms, looking up at her with a silent plea. Ellie fetched a chipped enamel cup and poured him some water from the pitcher, her movements deliberate, trying to shield him from the unspoken anxieties that swirled around them. The water itself tasted faintly of dust, no matter how often they filtered it.

"Did you hear?" Thomas whispered, his voice weak. "The Miller boy said they're thinking of moving. Going to California, like the pictures on the wall at the general store."

Ellie's stomach tightened. The Miller family, like so many others, were succumbing to the lure of promises from the West, of green fields and steady rain. It was a siren song that tempted many, a desperate hope in a land that offered so little. But the thought of leaving their home, their legacy, was unbearable. This land was in their blood, in their very bones.

"We're not going anywhere, Thomas," she said, her voice firmer than she felt. "This is our home. We'll find a way to make it work." She met her father's weary gaze across the room. He offered a faint, almost imperceptible shake of his head, a silent message of doubt. It was a look that spoke volumes of the economic pressures bearing down on them,

the crushing weight of poverty that the Great
Depression had brought to every corner of the
country, and amplified here in the isolated Hill
Country by the devastating drought. The farm, once
a source of pride and sustenance, had become a
symbol of their vulnerability, a beacon of their
mounting desperation.

The lavender fields, once a source of joy and
livelihood, were now a haunting reminder of their
struggle. The wilting plants, stripped of their vibrant
color and intoxicating fragrance, seemed to mirror
the dwindling hope within the family. Ellie
remembered the year her grandfather had first
planted the lavender, his immigrant dreams woven
into the very soil. He'd envisioned a future of
prosperity, of a legacy passed down through
generations. Now, that legacy was threatened by
forces beyond their control, forces that seemed
determined to wring every last drop of life from their
land and their spirits.

Her father cleared his throat, the sound a rough rasp.
"It's not just the farm, Ellie. It's everything. Prices
for what little we can sell are down to nothing. Folks
ain't got money for luxuries like lavender these days,
not when they're worried about putting food on the

table." He gestured vaguely towards the window. "And the dust… it's getting worse. Every gust of wind seems to carry more of it, burying what little hope we have left." He looked at Thomas, his voice softening with concern. "And with the boy's cough… we need a doctor, a real doctor, and we ain't got the means."

This was the burden they all carried. The economic devastation of the nation had bled into their lives, creating a suffocating web of debt and despair. The Dust Bowl, an environmental catastrophe of unprecedented scale, was the physical manifestation of their suffering, its gritty presence a constant reminder of their vulnerability. And then there was Thomas, the embodiment of their deepest fears, his fragile health a constant source of anxiety. Ellie felt a surge of anger, a fierce protectiveness that propelled her forward. She wouldn't let this land, this dust, this poverty, break her family. She would find a way, a *real* way, to save them.

She walked over to the small, dusty bookshelf that held their few treasured possessions – a Bible, a worn volume of poetry, and her grandmother's journals, bound in cracked leather. She ran her fingers over the spines, her mind already racing,

searching for an answer, a forgotten piece of
wisdom. Her grandmother, Grandma Mae, had been
a repository of the land's secrets, a wise woman
whose knowledge of native plants and their uses had
sustained their family through leaner times. Ellie felt
a deep connection to that knowledge, a sense of
responsibility to carry it forward. While her father
saw only the dying cultivated crops, Ellie's mind
drifted to the wild, resilient flora that still clung to
life in the scrub and on the rocky hillsides.

"Papa," she said, turning back to him, a new resolve
hardening her voice. "What if… what if we don't
rely solely on the lavender? What if we look to the
plants that *do* survive out there? The ones Grandma
Mae used to talk about?"

Silas looked at her, his brow furrowed with a mixture
of confusion and weary skepticism. "Ellie, those are
just weeds. Folks around here, they don't understand
that kind of thing. They think it's… unnatural.
Superstitious, even." He sighed, the sound heavy
with the weight of community expectations and
ingrained traditions. "We need cash, Ellie. Real
money. Not some wild plants that nobody wants."

"But they *are* useful, Papa!" Ellie insisted, her voice rising with a touch of desperation. "Grandma Mae showed me. The bee balm for fevers, the wild sage for… for all sorts of things. And the prickly pear, it holds water, it's nutritious. If we can find a way to harvest and prepare them, maybe… maybe we can sell them. Or at least use them to help Thomas." She looked at her brother, whose cough had momentarily subsided, his eyes fixed on her with a hopeful intensity.

Her father shook his head slowly. "That's a long shot, Ellie. A very long shot. We're already in deep. I don't know if we can afford to take on any more risks." His gaze drifted back to the ledger, to the stark reality of their financial ruin. The weight of his responsibility, as the man of the house, as the provider, was crushing him. He felt the eyes of his ancestors on him, judging his inability to maintain their legacy.

Ellie felt a familiar frustration welling up. Her father's pragmatism, usually a comforting trait, was a barrier now. He saw the immediate, insurmountable obstacles, while she saw the hidden possibilities, the quiet resilience of the land that her grandmother had taught her to recognize. She knew, with a certainty that resonated deep within her, that the answer lay not in fighting the land, but in understanding it, in working *with* it.

As if on cue, a faint gust of wind rattled the windowpanes, carrying with it the unmistakable scent of dust and something else… a faint, herbal aroma that spoke of resilience. It was the smell of the wild plants, the ones that thrived where cultivated crops withered. Ellie inhaled deeply, drawing strength from that faint fragrance. She wouldn't let her father's despair, or the community's skepticism, extinguish the glimmer of hope that still flickered within her. For Thomas, for her family, for the legacy of her ancestors, she would find a way to make the unseen blooms of Palo Alto Creek bloom again, even in the face of this devastating drought. The burden was heavy, the odds stacked against them, but the fierce love she held for her family, and her innate connection to the land, would be her guiding forces. She would protect them, no matter the cost.

The dust motes danced in the slivers of sunlight that pierced the grimy windows of the Dawson farmhouse, mirroring the agitated particles suspended in the air outside. Ellie watched them, her gaze distant, her mind already a world away from the oppressive confines of the room. Her father's words, heavy with a weariness that seemed to leach the very color from his voice, still echoed in her ears. *"We need cash, Ellie. Real money."* The weight of those words pressed down on her, a suffocating blanket of responsibility. But even as the stark reality of their financial ruin clawed at her, a different, quieter truth bloomed within her, a truth whispered by the parched earth and the tenacious scrub that defied the drought.

It was a truth that had been sown in the rich soil of her grandmother's wisdom, a legacy passed down not through ledgers and market prices, but through calloused hands and hushed conversations under the vast, unforgiving Texas sky. Grandma Mae, as everyone called her, had possessed a knowing that transcended mere knowledge. It was an instinct, a deep communion with the land that allowed her to read its secrets, to understand its language of wilting leaves and tenacious roots. While the rest of the community mourned the loss of their cultivated crops, their predictable yields, Grandma Mae had seen life where others saw only desolation.

Ellie remembered those days with a bittersweet ache. Summers spent trailing her grandmother through the shimmering heat, her small hand clasped in Grandma Mae's weathered one. The scent of sun-baked earth and the sharp, clean perfume of crushed herbs filled the air as they navigated the rocky outcrops and dry creek beds, places the cultivated fields couldn't reach. Grandma Mae didn't point out the lavender first, though its fragrant purple spikes were a familiar sight. No, her eyes would scan the scrub, her fingers brushing against the rough bark of mesquite, the spiny leaves of cholla, the velvety texture of lamb's quarters.

"See here, child," Grandma Mae would murmur, her voice a low rumble like distant thunder. "This is the true strength of our land. It bends, but it does not break. It waits." She'd demonstrate how to identify the drought-resistant plants, the ones that seemed to laugh in the face of the relentless sun. There was the *Fouquieria splendens*, the ocotillo, with its whip-like, leafless branches that seemed to rise from the very dust, drawing sustenance from the air itself. Grandma Mae knew it held a sap that could soothe burns and ease fevers. Then there was the *Larrea tridentata*, the creosote bush, its leathery leaves exuding that distinctive, rain-on-hot-earth scent. It was a powerful antiseptic, a remedy for coughs and colds, and she harvested its leaves with reverence, drying them carefully in the shade.

Ellie learned to recognize the subtle signs of life. The way a certain plant angled its leaves to minimize water loss, the thick, waxy cuticle that protected others from evaporation, the deep, anchoring roots that sought moisture far below the surface. She learned that the thorny branches of the prickly pear, *Opuntia spp.*, were not just a barrier against thirsty creatures, but also a source of hydration and a nutrient-rich food. Grandma Mae would show her how to carefully remove the tiny, barbed glochids before slicing the pads, or *nopales*, into strips to be boiled or roasted. "Nature provides," she'd say, her eyes twinkling, "if you only know where to look and how to ask."

These excursions were Ellie's sanctuary. While her father saw the failing lavender fields as a symbol of their impending doom, and the community saw the parched landscape as a punishment, Ellie saw a testament to resilience. She felt a kinship with these overlooked plants, a quiet understanding that transcended the superstitious whispers of the townsfolk. They viewed Grandma Mae's practices, and by extension Ellie's burgeoning interest, with a mixture of suspicion and disdain. They called it "old country nonsense," the kind of thing best left buried with the immigrants who'd clung to it. They preferred the predictable, the cultivated, the familiar. The wild, in their eyes, was untamed, dangerous, and perhaps even cursed.

But Ellie couldn't dismiss what she felt in her bones. It was more than just learned knowledge; it was an intuition, a deep-seated connection that pulsed through her veins. When she walked the land, it was as if the earth itself was speaking to her, revealing its hidden strengths. She'd often venture out alone, her worn leather satchel slung over her shoulder, a trowel and a small knife tucked inside. The silence of the scrub was a balm to her soul, a stark contrast to the worried murmurs within the farmhouse.

One afternoon, during a particularly stifling week when the sun seemed to beat down with an almost malicious intensity, Ellie found herself drawn to a small, rocky gully where the earth was cracked and dry as an old bone. Most would have turned away, seeing nothing but barrenness. But Ellie noticed a cluster of plants, low-growing and unassuming, with small, leathery leaves that seemed to hug the ground. She recognized it instantly: *Parthenium argentatum*, or silverleaf. Grandma Mae had used its roots, finely ground, to create a poultice for swelling and inflammation. It was a plant that thrived in arid, rocky soils, its silver-dusted leaves a testament to its ability to reflect the harsh sunlight.

Kneeling, she carefully dug around the base of one of the plants, her movements gentle, respectful. She harvested a small section of the root, ensuring not to disturb the rest of the cluster. As she worked, she felt a sense of profound peace wash over her. This was her language, her understanding of the world. It was a quiet rebellion against the despair that threatened to engulf her family, a silent assertion that life, in its myriad forms, could still persist.

Later that week, as Thomas's cough worsened, a persistent rasp that tore at Ellie's heart, she remembered the silverleaf. She meticulously cleaned the root, then pounded it into a fine powder with a mortar and pestle. She mixed it with a little water, creating a thick paste, and, with her father's grudging permission, applied it to Thomas's chest. She didn't expect miracles, but she held onto the hope that this small, earth-born remedy might offer some relief. She watched him sleep, his breathing still shallow, but a subtle calm seemed to settle over his features.

These secret excursions, these acts of communion with the land, were more than just a pursuit of botanical knowledge; they were acts of defiance. They were Ellie's way of refusing to surrender, of finding hope in the very places others had given up. The lavender, so dependent on careful cultivation and ample water, was a symbol of their past prosperity, and now, their present hardship. But the wild plants, the ones that clung to the edges of their world, they were a symbol of a different kind of strength – an ancient, enduring resilience that mirrored Ellie's own.

She would often find herself drawn to the Palo Alto

Creek, or what remained of it. It was a sad, dusty scar across the landscape, a trickle of water in the best of times, and now, barely a memory. Yet, even there, life persisted. She'd find maidenhair ferns pushing through cracks in the dry creek bed, their delicate fronds a startling splash of green against the ochre earth. She knew their delicate appearance belied a remarkable hardiness, a capacity to survive long periods of dryness, waiting for the faintest hint of moisture to reawaken. She'd also find slender, wiry stalks of wild rosemary, *Croton spp.*, its leaves releasing a pungent, cleansing aroma when crushed. Grandma Mae had used it to make a strong tea for digestive issues.

Her father, Silas, remained skeptical, his gaze fixed on the wilting lavender, on the empty bank accounts. "Ellie," he'd say, his voice laced with a familiar weariness, "we need to be practical. This farm is built on lavender. We can't just go digging up weeds." He couldn't see the land the way she did. He saw the dying cultivated crop, the tangible proof of their failure. He couldn't perceive the subtle vitality of the wild, the quiet promises held within the roots and leaves of plants that had adapted over millennia to this harsh, unforgiving environment.

The community, too, watched her with a mixture of pity and suspicion. They'd see her walking the dusty roads, her eyes fixed on the ground, and whisper. "There goes that Mae girl," they'd say, their voices low. "Always with her nose in the dirt. Her grandmother was the same. Strange notions." The fear of the unknown, the distrust of anything that deviated from the established norms, ran deep in their isolated world. But Ellie couldn't let their judgment deter her. Her grandmother's legacy was a beacon, a guiding light in the encroaching darkness. She understood that her knowledge, while viewed with suspicion by many, was also a unique inheritance, a vital connection to the land that might, just might, offer a path to survival.

As she continued her quiet exploration, the scent of the wild herbs—the sage, the rosemary, the subtle, earthy aroma of the creosote—became her constant companions, a reminder of the land's enduring spirit. These plants were not just survivors; they were testament to a different kind of prosperity, one measured not in bushels of harvested crops, but in resilience, in adaptation, in the sheer, unyielding will to live. And Ellie, with every step she took into the parched landscape, was learning to embrace that language, to weave its whispers into the fabric of her own desperate hope. The lavender fields might be dying, but the unseen blooms of Palo Alto Creek were beginning to stir within her, ready to offer their strength when the need was greatest.

The dust had barely settled from the latest gust when a new kind of disturbance rippled through the parched landscape of Palo Alto. It arrived not on the wind, but in a gleaming, olive-green automobile, a rare sight on these rutted dirt roads, its polished chrome glinting defiantly under the relentless sun. The machine hummed with an alien energy, a stark contrast to the weary rumble of farm trucks and the creak of wagon wheels. It pulled up to the Dawson farm, and from its depths emerged a man who seemed to carry the very essence of the East Coast – clean lines, crisp fabric, and an aura of effortless command.

He introduced himself as Cyrus Vance. His voice was smooth, cultured, a melody against the usual grunts and drawls of the men Ellie knew. He was tall, lean, with hair the color of polished mahogany, neatly parted, and eyes that held the sharp, assessing glint of a hawk. His suit, a fine worsted wool despite the oppressive heat, seemed impervious to the dust that coated everything else. He moved with a practiced grace, a stark juxtaposition to the stooped shoulders and sun-weathered faces of the locals who had gathered, drawn by the spectacle. Vance extended a hand, his grip firm and cool, as he met Silas Dawson's gaze.

"Mr. Dawson," Vance began, his smile disarming, "a pleasure to finally meet you. I've heard much about this region, about the tenacity of its people. And I must say," he gestured expansively, taking in the cracked earth and the wilting lavender fields, "it's a tenacity that is sorely tested by our current… atmospheric conditions."

Ellie watched from the porch, a knot of apprehension and nascent curiosity tightening in her chest. Her father, Silas, stood straighter than he had in weeks, a flicker of hope in his tired eyes. Vance's very presence was an affront to the pervasive despair, a vibrant splash of color against the muted palette of their hardship.

"We're in a bad way, Mr. Vance," Silas admitted, his voice raspy. "The drought… it's been unforgiving."

"Indeed," Vance agreed, his gaze sweeping over the fields. His eyes didn't linger on the drooping lavender plants with the same despair Silas held. Instead, they seemed to absorb the contours of the land, to measure its potential, to dissect its suffering with a dispassionate precision that sent a shiver down Ellie's spine. "But despair, Mr. Dawson, is a luxury we can no longer afford. And thankfully, it's a luxury I believe we can help you escape."

He paused, letting his words hang in the air, a tangible promise. The hushed murmurs of the gathered neighbors, the few who had managed to break away from their own pressing concerns, grew louder. Vance was a man who knew how to command an audience, how to make his pronouncements feel like decrees from on high.

"I represent a consortium," he continued, his voice dropping slightly, drawing them in, "that has been developing revolutionary technologies for water management. Specifically, for arid regions such as this. We have devised a system of underground conduits, drawing on deep artesian wells, coupled with an advanced drip irrigation network. It's… efficient. It's modern. It's the future of agriculture in places like this."

He spoke of reservoirs, of subterranean pipelines, of controlled water delivery that would make the land bloom again, regardless of the capricious sky. He painted a picture so vivid, so hopeful, that it was almost impossible to reconcile with the dusty reality surrounding them. He spoke of yields doubling, tripling, of a return to prosperity, of the lavender fields bursting with color once more, their scent carried on a gentle, watered breeze.

Ellie felt a strange duality within her. Part of her, the part that had been steeped in her grandmother's quiet wisdom, felt a deep unease. There was a predatory gleam in Vance's eyes, a calculating nature beneath the polished veneer. He spoke of the land as if it were a problem to be solved, a resource to be exploited, rather than a living entity with its own rhythms and needs. He spoke of technology as a savior, a means to conquer nature, rather than to work with it.

But another part of her, the part that had seen her father's shoulders slump under the weight of debt, the part that had witnessed the quiet desperation in her mother's eyes, couldn't help but be swayed. Vance offered a tangible solution, a way out of the suffocating miasma of drought and debt. He offered hope, dressed in the finest tweed and speaking in the most persuasive tones.

"This system," Vance elaborated, his hands gesturing with an artist's flair, "is designed to be installed with minimal disruption. We handle the logistics, the engineering. All we require is a commitment from the community, a cooperative agreement that ensures the equitable distribution of this vital resource."

He was talking about the land, not as something to be owned, but as a shared commodity that could be revitalized by his company's intervention. The concept of a "cooperative agreement" sounded fair, democratic, but Ellie wondered what the unspoken clauses were, what the true cost would be. Her grandmother had taught her that nature's gifts were not to be bought or sold cheaply, that true abundance came from understanding and respecting the land's own capacity, not from imposing external solutions that could eventually control it.

As Vance continued his discourse, he casually picked up a fallen lavender sprig from the dusty ground, rubbing its dried leaves between his thumb and forefinger. "A delicate flower, lavender. Beautiful, yes, but demanding. It requires precise conditions. This new system," he declared, his voice rising with conviction, "will provide those conditions. It will ensure that your prized crop not only survives, but thrives."

He addressed the assembled farmers, his gaze sweeping across their faces, meeting their eyes with an unwavering, almost hypnotic intensity. "We are not here to dictate terms," he assured them, "but to offer partnership. A partnership in revitalizing this land, in securing your futures. Imagine, gentlemen, seeing the shimmer of water on your fields again. Imagine the scent of lavender, not as a dying memory, but as a promise of a bountiful harvest."

Silas, caught between his ingrained practicality and the allure of Vance's vision, nodded slowly. "It sounds… like a miracle, Mr. Vance."

Vance chuckled, a low, confident sound. "Miracles are merely the results of applied science, Mr. Dawson. And we are here to apply it. We will need to survey the land, of course, and hold a community meeting to discuss the details of the agreement. I believe within a few weeks, we can have the initial stages of the installation underway."

He spoke of permits, of engineers arriving from the East, of a timeline that felt both impossibly fast and desperately needed. Ellie saw the hope bloom in her father's eyes, a fragile sprout pushing through the cracked earth of his despair. She saw it reflected in the faces of their neighbors, the desperation of their situation making them eager to believe.

But she also saw the subtle appraisal in Vance's eyes as he looked at her, a flicker of something unreadable that felt like acknowledgment, perhaps even interest, in her quiet observation. He was a man who saw opportunities everywhere, and Ellie, with her unusual knowledge of the land, with her quiet defiance of the prevailing despair, was an anomaly he might seek to understand, or perhaps, to neutralize.

As Vance packed his belongings back into the gleaming automobile, his parting words to Silas were a final, potent blend of reassurance and subtle command. "We'll be in touch, Mr. Dawson. Prepare your community for progress. The future of Palo Alto is about to change."

And with a final, polite nod to the assembled onlookers, Cyrus Vance drove away, leaving behind him a palpable shift in the air. The dust still settled, but now it seemed to carry the faint, intoxicating scent of possibility, mingled with the unsettling perfume of an approaching storm. The dream of water, once a distant mirage, had been brought startlingly close by a man from the East, and Ellie knew, with a certainty that chilled her, that the true test for the people of Palo Alto had just begun. Whether Vance was a savior or a predator, only time, and the land itself, would tell. His arrival had fractured the weary resignation that had settled over the community, replacing it with a potent cocktail of hope and apprehension, a new kind of dust cloud gathering on their horizon. He represented a force, a power that promised to reshape their lives, and in doing so, challenged the very understanding of the land that Ellie had begun to embrace. The questions he posed, cloaked in the language of progress, resonated with the old wisdom her grandmother had imparted: what was the true cost of control, and who truly owned the water, and the land it sustained? The arrival of Cyrus Vance was not merely the arrival of a man; it was the arrival of a new era, one that would test the resilience of both the land and its people in ways they could not yet fathom.

The olive-green automobile had receded down the dusty track, a shimmering beetle against the ochre landscape, but its occupant, Cyrus Vance, left a residue of unease that settled deeper than the perpetual dust. Ellie watched her father, Silas, from the porch swing, her gaze fixed on the way his shoulders, so recently slumped with weariness, now held a tentative buoyancy. Hope, fragile and potent, had been injected into the heart of their hardship, a foreign substance administered by a man whose words flowed like water, promising to irrigate a land parched by despair. Yet, as the faint scent of exhaust fumes mingled with the dry, herbaceous aroma of lavender, Ellie felt a prickle of apprehension, a deep-seated suspicion that Vance's offer of salvation might, in fact, be a beautifully packaged form of conquest.

Vance's pronouncements had been delivered with such polished conviction, his descriptions of underground conduits and advanced drip irrigation painting a vivid tableau of abundance. He spoke of reclaiming their lost prosperity, of coaxing the land

back to life with the precise application of
technology. He had, in a matter of minutes, offered a
tangible solution to a problem that had been slowly
choking the life out of Palo Alto for years. But as
Ellie replayed his words in her mind, a discordant
note began to emerge, a dissonance that grated
against the ingrained wisdom of her grandmother.
Vance had barely acknowledged the lavender itself,
the delicate, resilient bloom that was their lifeblood.
He'd plucked a dried sprig from the ground, his
touch perfunctory, his assessment clinical. He'd
called it "delicate," "demanding," a plant that
required "precise conditions." He saw it as a
problem to be solved, a challenge to be met with
engineering and infrastructure, not as a living entity
that had adapted, over generations, to this very soil,
this very climate.

Her grandmother, bless her soul, had a way of
understanding the land that transcended mere
observation. She spoke of the soil not as dirt, but as
a living tapestry, interwoven with the roots of
resilient grasses, tenacious wildflowers, and the deep,
seeking tendrils of the lavender. She taught Ellie to
listen to the whisper of the wind through the dry
stalks, to read the subtle signs in the dew-kissed
leaves, to understand that true abundance wasn't
conjured, but cultivated through a partnership with

nature, a delicate dance of give and take. Vance, with his talk of "conduits" and "networks," seemed to view the land as a canvas upon which to impose his will, a passive recipient of his grand design, rather than an active participant in its own renewal.

Ellie's gaze drifted to the edge of the field, where a cluster of native blue sage, its silvery leaves shimmering with an almost metallic sheen, stood sentinel against the pervasive drought. These were plants that thrived on scarcity, that drew sustenance from the very dryness that was strangling the lavender. Vance had not spared them a second glance, his attention wholly consumed by the potential for control, for measurable output. He saw the wilting lavender as a failure, a problem to be fixed with an external solution. Ellie saw the blue sage as a testament to resilience, a quiet reminder of the land's inherent strength, its ability to adapt and endure. Vance's technology, she feared, would not nurture this innate resilience; it would suppress it, smothering the wild, untamed spirit of the land beneath a blanket of engineered uniformity.

The "cooperative agreement" Vance had mentioned also nagged at her. It sounded democratic, a shared venture. But what did it truly entail? Who would set the terms? Who would hold the ultimate authority over the water, the very lifeblood of their livelihood? Vance spoke of equitable distribution, but Ellie knew that power, once centralized, rarely remained truly equitable. Her grandmother had warned her about those who promised the sun and moon, only to demand the stars in return. There was a glint in Vance's eyes, a predatory awareness that seemed to catalogue everything, everyone, with an unnerving efficiency. He wasn't just offering water; he was offering dependence, a subtle form of ownership disguised as a benevolent partnership.

She imagined the disruption Vance spoke of – the digging, the laying of pipes, the relentless imposition of metal and machinery upon the ancient, weathered skin of their land. Vance's system would bring water, yes, but at what cost? Would the delicate ecosystem, honed by years of drought and sun, be irrevocably altered? Would the wildflowers that still bravely bloomed in the sparse shade of the mesquite trees be choked out by the new regime? Would the very character of Palo Alto, its quiet resilience forged in the crucible of scarcity, be replaced by a manufactured, uniform prosperity?

Her father's hope was a thing of beauty, a testament to his enduring spirit. But Ellie couldn't shake the feeling that Vance's vision was a mirage, a shimmering oasis that promised life but delivered something else entirely. He spoke of increased yields, of doubling and tripling their harvest. But what of the quality of that harvest? What of the subtle nuances of flavor and fragrance that made their lavender so prized? Could technology truly replicate the magic of sunlight, wind, and soil, or would it produce something bland, something soulless?

She remembered her grandmother's hands, gnarled and earth-stained, gently sifting through a handful of dried lavender seeds. "Each one, Ellie," she'd said, her voice a soft murmur, like the rustling of leaves, "holds the promise of a new beginning. They carry the memory of the sun, the resilience of the earth. They don't need to be forced; they need to be understood. They need to be loved." Vance seemed to operate on an entirely different principle, one of dominance and control. He saw the land as a problem to be solved, its inherent strengths as mere obstacles to be overcome by his superior knowledge and technology.

Ellie's unease intensified as she considered the possibility of her own role in Vance's plan. He had met her gaze, not with the casual dismissal he afforded the other farmers, but with a flicker of recognition, perhaps even assessment. She knew the land in a way Vance, with his hurried surveys and polished pronouncements, never could. She knew its secrets, its vulnerabilities, its quiet strengths. Was she, in his eyes, a potential ally, someone whose knowledge of the local flora and terrain might be useful? Or was she a potential threat, an anomaly that needed to be understood, and perhaps, neutralized? The thought sent a shiver down her spine. Vance was a businessman, a strategist, and she suspected, he dealt with obstacles with the same efficiency he planned to apply to their drought-stricken fields.

The air, still thick with dust, now seemed to carry the subtle scent of a different kind of dust – the dust of manipulation, of veiled intentions. Vance had presented himself as a benefactor, a purveyor of progress. But Ellie's intuition, honed by years of observing the intricate workings of nature, whispered a different story. She saw not a savior, but a force that threatened to impose a foreign order, to redefine the very essence of their connection to the land. His arrival was a disruption, yes, but perhaps not the kind of disruption they so desperately needed. It was a disruption that could shatter their fragile independence, replacing it with a dependence on systems and technologies they didn't fully understand, and on a man whose motives remained shrouded in the polished veneer of his ambition.

She looked back at her father, whose eyes were still fixed on the horizon where the automobile had disappeared. He was dreaming of water, of rain, of a return to normalcy. But Ellie found herself dreaming of something else – of the resilience of the blue sage, of the quiet wisdom of her grandmother, of a future where progress meant working

*with* the land, not against it. The seeds of doubt had been sown, and in the parched soil of her apprehension, they were beginning to sprout. Vance had brought a promise, but he had also brought a profound question: was the price of survival worth the surrender of their soul? The answer, she suspected, was tied to the very land he sought to control, a land that held its own ancient wisdom, a wisdom that Vance, with all his technology, seemed determined to ignore. And in that ignorance, Ellie found her greatest fear. He was offering a solution that didn't understand the problem, a cure that carried its own, potentially fatal, side effects. The true test, she realized, wasn't just about surviving the drought, but about surviving the saviors.

# Chapter 2: The Unseen Threat

The wind, usually a gentle caress that carried the sweet perfume of lavender across the valley, had turned into a harbinger of a far more sinister scent. It was a dry, rasping breath, carrying not the floral notes of their livelihood, but the acrid tang of desperation. Silas, his weathered face etched with a deeper weariness than even the relentless drought could inflict, stood beside Ellie on the porch, his hand gripping the wooden railing so tightly his knuckles were white. The sun, a malevolent eye in the bleached sky, beat down with an unyielding intensity, mirroring the fiery dread blooming in Ellie's chest.

It had started, as these things so often do in the vast, untamed landscapes of the West, with a whisper. A flicker on the far ridge, barely perceptible against the shimmering heatwaves rising from the parched earth. But whispers in dry country could grow to roars with terrifying speed. A discarded cigarette butt, a spark from an old tractor, a careless hand – the possibilities were as numerous as the dry stalks of lavender that now stood like tinder waiting for a cruel ignition. The thought, unspoken but heavy between father and daughter, was that Vance's emissaries, those men who had been surveying their fields with an unnerving precision just days before, had been less than scrupulous. A careless moment, a forgotten ember, and their fragile hope had been met with a far more immediate and consuming devastation.

The flames, at first, were a distant spectacle, a crimson blush against the pale, desiccated hills. It was the smell that truly announced the horror, a sharp, pungent aroma that clawed at the back of Ellie's throat. Lavender, their delicate, precious lavender, was burning. Not the gentle, sun-dried fragrance that filled their home and their markets, but a violent, stinging perfume, thick with the resins of dry scrub and the very essence of destruction. It was the scent of dreams turning to ash, of years of labor consumed in a matter of moments.

Silas took a step forward, his instincts as a farmer, as a protector, warring with the stark reality of the inferno. He knew, with a certainty that chilled him to the bone, that there was nothing they could do. The wind, that same capricious wind that had often helped pollinate their fields, was now a furious ally to the fire, fanning its hungry maw and pushing it relentlessly towards their precious crop. The carefully cultivated rows, the pride of their harvest, were becoming an undulating sea of fire, each wave a tongue of flame devouring the delicate purple blooms and the tough, resilient stems.

Ellie watched, frozen, as the fire advanced. It was a living entity, a voracious beast that moved with an unnatural speed. The dry grasses and the hardy sagebrush that dotted the landscape offered no resistance, acting as fuel for its ravenous hunger. The heat, even from this distance, was palpable, radiating outwards like a physical blow. The sky, which had been a flawless cerulean blue, began to darken, not with the promise of rain, but with a thick, choking pall of smoke. It billowed upwards, an obsidian plume against the sun, a grim testament to their impending ruin.

The sound of the fire was a symphony of destruction. A low, guttural roar that grew in intensity, punctuated by the sharp crackle of dry vegetation igniting and the occasional ominous hiss as moisture was vaporized from the earth. It was a sound that stripped away all pretense of control, all semblance of human agency. They were witnessing the raw, untamed power of nature unleashed, a power that cared nothing for their sweat, their hopes, or their struggles.

Ellie's gaze fell on the furthest field, the one Silas had been most proud of, the one he had nurtured with an almost parental devotion. The flames, licking greedily at the dry stalks, were transforming the familiar rows of purple into a flickering, incandescent orange. It was a surreal, nightmarish tableau, the very heart of their livelihood being ripped out and consumed before their eyes. She saw the delicate petals, so carefully nurtured, curl and blacken, then disintegrate into glittering embers carried aloft on the fiery wind. The air grew thick with the acrid stench of burnt lavender, a smell so potent it felt as if it were seeping into her very pores, a permanent stain of despair.

Silas finally turned to her, his face a mask of utter devastation. His eyes, usually so full of quiet determination, were hollow, reflecting the emptiness that was rapidly consuming their future. "Ellie," he began, his voice a raw, choked whisper, but the words caught in his throat. There was nothing to say. What comfort could he offer? What solution could he possibly propose when their entire season, their only real chance of recovering from the drought, had been reduced to cinders in a matter of hours?

The memory of Vance's promises, of his talk of conduits and controlled water flow, felt like a cruel mockery in the face of this unbridled chaos. Vance had offered order, efficiency, a sterile, engineered prosperity. But here, on their land, was the stark reality of a different kind of power, a power that could obliterate everything Vance sought to control, and everything they held dear, with a terrifying indifference. Ellie felt a profound sense of loss, not just for the lavender, but for the very idea of a predictable future. The fire was a physical manifestation of the unseen threat Vance represented, a threat that was far more immediate and destructive than any engineered drought. Vance's drought was a slow, insidious enemy, but this fire was a swift, brutal executioner.

She saw her father's shoulders slump, the tentative buoyancy that had briefly returned after Vance's visit completely extinguished. He was a man who had faced adversity his entire life, who had battled the soil, the sun, and the unpredictable whims of nature. But this was different. This felt like a final judgment, a brutal punctuation mark on their long, hard struggle. The fire seemed to feed on their despair, growing stronger, brighter, more insatiable with every passing moment.

The sheer speed of it was terrifying. What had been a distant flicker was now a roaring inferno, sweeping across the fields with an unstoppable momentum. The dry, brittle stalks of lavender, so vulnerable, were consumed in an instant. The smoke, no longer a distant plume, was now a suffocating blanket descending upon them, obscuring the sun and filling their lungs with its bitter sting. Ellie coughed, her eyes watering, not just from the smoke, but from the overwhelming grief that threatened to engulf her.

She thought of her grandmother, of her quiet strength, her deep connection to the land. What would she have said? Perhaps she would have reminded Ellie that fire, while destructive, was also a part of the natural cycle, clearing the way for new growth. But this was not the cleansing fire of renewal. This was a fire of ruin, of absolute loss. It was a fire that threatened to break them, to extinguish not just their crop, but their very spirit.

Silas, galvanized by a desperate, futile hope, turned and started towards the barn, perhaps to gather what little equipment they could save, or simply to feel as if he were doing something, anything, in the face of such overwhelming devastation. Ellie remained on the porch, her gaze fixed on the inferno. She saw individual plants ignite, the purple blooms bursting into fleeting, fiery life before collapsing into ash. It was a painful, intimate spectacle of destruction, each burning stalk a tiny tragedy.

The smell of burning lavender was almost unbearable, a cloying sweetness twisted into something foul and menacing. It clung to everything, a phantom scent that would likely linger long after the last ember had died. Ellie imagined the roots, deep in the parched earth, being scorched, their life force irrevocably extinguished. This wasn't just the surface of their livelihood that was burning; it was the very foundation.

She scanned the horizon, searching for any sign of help, any indication that this was not their solitary battle against the elements. But there was only the relentless advance of the flames, a living testament to their isolation. The distant hills, usually a source of comfort and familiarity, were now a fiery backdrop, framing their despair. The olive-green automobile, Vance's symbol of a different kind of future, seemed impossibly distant, a relic of a hope that was rapidly turning to dust.

The wind shifted, and a shower of hot ash rained down, landing on the porch, on their faces, on the parched earth. It felt like a benediction of doom, a final sealing of their fate. Ellie closed her eyes, trying to block out the sight, the sound, the smell, but it was no use. The fire was an all-encompassing presence, its heat and fury imprinted on her senses.

She thought of the upcoming harvest, the meticulous care that had gone into tending each plant, the anticipation of the fragrant oils, the carefully dried bouquets that would sustain them through the lean months. All of it, gone. Wiped away by an indiscriminate blaze. The thought brought a fresh wave of tears, hot and stinging against her smoke-grimed cheeks.

Silas returned, his face smudged with soot, his hands empty. He looked at the fields, then at Ellie, a profound sadness in his eyes. There was no anger, no blame, only a quiet, devastating resignation. He had fought the drought with every ounce of his strength, and now, this. It felt like a cruel joke played by fate, a final, unbearable blow.

Ellie knew that Vance's offer, while still a point of contention in her own mind, had held the promise of a way out, a lifeline. But this fire had severed that lifeline before it could even be grasped. It had brought their desperate situation to a head with a brutal finality. They were not just facing drought; they were facing utter annihilation of their livelihood. The very earth beneath their feet felt scorched, not just by the sun, but by the consuming flames of their shattered hopes. The delicate balance of their existence, already precarious, had been shattered, leaving behind only the gaping maw of despair and the lingering, suffocating scent of burning lavender. The future, which had seemed uncertain just moments before, now felt utterly obliterated, buried beneath the ashes of their ruined fields. The weight of it all pressed down on her, a crushing, suffocating burden, and she knew, with a certainty that chilled her to the bone, that they were more vulnerable now than they had ever been. The unseen threat, she realized, had manifested itself not in a calculated manipulation of resources, but in a raw, destructive force that left no room for negotiation, no possibility of compromise. It was simply… gone. Everything they had worked for, everything they had hoped for, consumed in a single, terrifying act of fiery devastation.

The acrid scent of smoke, though fainter now, still clung to the air, a persistent reminder of the devastation that had swept through their lavender fields. But for Ellie, a new, more immediate dread had taken root, a suffocating anxiety that coiled tighter with each passing hour. It was Thomas. Her younger brother, usually a whirlwind of boisterous energy, had retreated into a fragile quietude, his small frame seeming to shrink with every labored breath.

It had started subtly, a dry rasp in his throat that she'd initially dismissed as a lingering irritation from the pervasive dust that coated everything in their valley. But the rasp had deepened, evolving into a hacking cough that wracked his slender body, leaving him breathless and pale. The vibrant flush that often colored his cheeks had leached away, replaced by a sickly pallor that mirrored the parched earth outside. Ellie found herself watching him constantly, her gaze tracking the rise and fall of his chest, her heart clenching with each wheezing inhalation. The hardship, she knew, was not confined to the fields; it had seeped into the very walls of their home, and worse, into the delicate lungs of her brother.

Their doctor, a kind but weary man whose own hands bore the indelible marks of rural life, had been by twice in the last week. His visits, once a comforting reassurance, now felt laden with an unspoken gravity. He'd listened to Thomas's rattling breaths with a furrowed brow, his fingers probing gently at the boy's ribs, his pronouncements hushed and filled with caution. "The dust, Ellie," he'd murmured, his voice low, "it's a relentless adversary.

Especially for one as young and… sensitive as Thomas." He hadn't needed to finish the sentence. Ellie understood. The harsh environment, the very air they breathed, was slowly but surely wearing her brother down.

Each time the doctor left, Ellie felt a fresh wave of despair wash over her. She would sit by Thomas's bedside, stroking his damp forehead, her mind racing. The doctor's words echoed in her ears: "sensitive," "adversary," "toll." It wasn't just the lost harvest, the looming debt, or the threat of Vance's encroaching influence; it was Thomas. His fragile health was a constant, agonizing weight. The thought of his suffering, of his small body being ravaged by the same environmental harshness that had decimated their lavender, was almost unbearable. It added a desperate urgency to her already overwhelming predicament.

She remembered the days when Thomas would chase butterflies through the lavender rows, his laughter a bright, cheerful sound that seemed to chase away the shadows. Now, those shadows seemed to have settled permanently in the corners of his room, in the hollows beneath his eyes. He rarely asked for anything, a testament to his quiet fortitude, but his weak smiles and the way he'd cling to her hand spoke volumes of his discomfort. Ellie tried to keep his room as clean and dust-free as possible, but in a place where dust was as ubiquitous as air, it felt like a losing battle. She'd hang damp cloths near his bed, hoping to humidify the air, but it offered only scant relief.

Her father, Silas, too, was clearly worried. Though he tried to maintain a stoic front, Ellie saw the strain etched deeper into his face with every coughing fit Thomas endured. He would often sit by Thomas's side, reading from worn books in a low, soothing voice, his hand resting on his son's feverish brow. But his eyes, when they met Ellie's, held a shared anxiety, a silent question that neither of them could answer. The fire had been a devastating blow, but it was Thomas's fading vitality that truly gnawed at their spirit.

Ellie felt a profound sense of responsibility, a primal urge to protect her brother from the harsh realities that seemed determined to crush them. This wasn't just about survival anymore; it was about Thomas's very life. The doctor's hushed tones had planted a seed of fear that was rapidly growing into a thorny vine, constricting her heart. What if Thomas's condition worsened? What if they couldn't afford the medicine he might need? The questions were sharp, painful, and unanswered.

She found herself replaying Vance's offer, the words he had spoken about modernizing their irrigation systems, about securing their future. At the time, it had seemed like a patronizing, almost insulting proposition, a thinly veiled attempt to seize their land under the guise of progress. But now, with Thomas's health hanging precariously in the balance, Vance's words took on a different hue. They were no longer just about financial security; they were about access to resources, to treatments, to a life that might be less susceptible to the environmental cruelties that plagued their valley.

The thought of accepting Vance's terms, of relinquishing a part of their legacy, of being indebted to a man who seemed to view their land as mere acreage to be exploited, churned in her gut. It felt like a betrayal of her father, of her ancestors who had tilled this very soil. Yet, the image of Thomas struggling for breath, his small body weakening day by day, was a powerful counterpoint. What good was pride, what good was legacy, if it came at the cost of her brother's well-being?

Ellie began to spend more time in the small, sparsely furnished room that served as their makeshift infirmary. She'd fan Thomas with a palm frond, murmuring reassurances, her own anxieties masked by a forced calm. She'd brew him weak herbal teas, hoping their gentle properties might soothe his irritated airways. Each day was a tightrope walk between hope and despair. The financial worries, already immense, were now amplified by the terrifying specter of medical bills and the potential for Thomas's condition to become chronic, or worse.

The fire had been a sudden, violent assault, a visible enemy that, in its own terrible way, was easier to comprehend than this slow, insidious decay of her brother's health. This was an unseen threat, a creeping sickness born from the very environment they depended on. It was a betrayal by the land itself, a land that had always been both their sustenance and their adversary.

Ellie's resolve hardened with every rasping breath Thomas took. She would not stand idly by. She would find a way. She would explore every avenue, however unpalatable. The pride she felt in their self-sufficiency, in their ability to weather hardship through sheer grit and determination, began to feel like a luxury they could no longer afford. Survival, and more importantly, Thomas's survival, was the only currency that mattered now.

She started to research, poring over old books and pamphlets, searching for any mention of remedies for persistent coughs, for the effects of dust inhalation. Her father's library, though limited, held a surprising trove of information, from herbal remedies passed down through generations to more scientific texts on respiratory ailments. She read late into the night, the dim lamplight casting long shadows that danced with her growing anxieties.

The doctor had mentioned the possibility of moving to a different climate, a place with cleaner, more humid air. The suggestion, however well-intentioned, was a cruel irony. Leaving their land, their home, was unthinkable. It was their lifeblood, their identity. But the thought of Thomas suffering in this dry, dusty air, with the scent of smoke and desiccation a constant companion, was even more unbearable.

One evening, as Silas slept fitfully in his chair by the hearth, Ellie crept into Thomas's room. The moonlight cast a pale glow on his sleeping face, highlighting the faint tremor in his lips. He let out a soft, sighing cough, and Ellie's heart ached with a fierce, protective love. She leaned down and kissed his forehead, her touch feather-light. "Don't worry, Tommy," she whispered, her voice thick with emotion. "I'll fix this. I promise."

The promise was a heavy one, and she wasn't sure how she would keep it. But the alternative—watching her brother fade away—was a prospect she refused to contemplate. The weight of their misfortunes, the fire, the drought, and now Thomas's failing health, had coalesced into a single, crushing burden. It was a burden that fueled a desperate, unyielding determination within her. She would face Vance, she would face the world, if it meant a chance at healing for her brother. Her concern for Thomas had transformed their struggle from one of livelihood to one of life and death, and in that terrifying clarity, a new, formidable strength began to emerge. She would not let the unseen threat claim another victim.

The dust, a persistent, gritty specter, seemed to have settled not just on the land but within the very marrow of their bones. Ellie felt its presence most acutely when she watched Thomas, her younger brother, his breath a shallow, reedy sound that scraped against her raw nerves. The doctor's visits had become a ritual of hushed pronouncements and hopeful, yet ultimately unfulfilled, remedies. Each wheezing cough from Thomas was a fresh jab of anxiety, a stark reminder that their quiet suffering had escalated into a battle for survival, a battle that extended beyond the ravaged lavender fields and into the fragile realm of her brother's health.

The air in their small farmhouse, once filled with the sweet, calming aroma of drying lavender, now carried the faint, metallic tang of sickness. Ellie found herself performing a frantic, unseen dance of vigilance, measuring out doses of a bitter herbal concoction her father had brewed, fanning Thomas with a wilting palm frond, and constantly checking the damp cloths she'd hung to offer a semblance of moisture to the parched air of his room. Silas, her father, bore the weight of their misfortunes with a stoic grief, his eyes, once bright with the pride of a successful farmer, now held a perpetual cloud of worry. He would sit by Thomas's bedside, his calloused hand resting on his son's feverish brow, reading from worn books in a voice that, despite its weariness, still held the comforting cadence of their shared history. But the unspoken question hung heavy between them: how much longer could they endure this slow erosion of their spirit, this insidious attack on their very lifeblood?

The doctor's suggestion of a change in climate, of seeking cleaner, more humid air, had landed like a cruel jest. Their land was their identity, their legacy etched into every furrowed acre. To leave it felt like severing a limb. Yet, the alternative – watching Thomas's small body continue to battle the pervasive, suffocating dust – was an even more agonizing prospect. The very elements that had sustained them for generations now seemed to conspire against them, turning their agricultural bounty into a source of slow, creeping poison.

It was in this crucible of desperation that the name Cyrus Vance began to echo with a new, unsettling resonance. Vance, the man who represented everything they had fought to remain separate from – progress, modernization, a predatory form of capitalism that saw their valley not as a home, but as a resource to be exploited. His earlier overtures, dismissive and self-serving, had been easily rebuffed by Silas, a man rooted in principle and a fierce protectiveness of his heritage. But now, with Thomas's labored breaths a constant, piercing reminder of their vulnerability, Vance's "generosity" began to cast a long, alluring shadow.

The fire, a brutal, indiscriminate enemy, had been devastating. It had consumed their livelihood, reducing years of careful cultivation to ash and smoke. But this unseen threat, this slow poisoning of the air and the subsequent toll on Thomas's lungs, felt far more insidious, far more personal. It chipped away at their resilience, not with a single, violent blow, but with a relentless, suffocating pressure. Ellie felt a profound shift within her. The pride she had always taken in their self-sufficiency, in their ability to weather any storm through sheer grit and hard work, began to feel like a dangerous indulgence. Survival, and Thomas's survival above all else, had become the only currency that mattered.

Then, Vance appeared. Not with the swagger of a conqueror, but with an almost solicitous air, his tailored suit a stark, incongruous contrast to the dusty, weathered reality of their farm. He found Ellie by the dry creek bed, tracing the cracked earth with a stick, her mind a chaotic swirl of worry and a nascent, unformed plan. He approached quietly, his footsteps barely disturbing the parched stillness.

"Miss Dawson," he began, his voice smooth, carrying an undertone of practiced sympathy. "A difficult season for everyone, I see."

Ellie turned, her expression guarded. She knew Vance's reputation. He was a man who smelled opportunity in disaster, a shrewd businessman who had been steadily acquiring land on the fringes of their valley, slowly encircling their dwindling acreage. His mills were the source of much of the industrial dust that had begun to plague their region, an unwelcome byproduct of his ambition.

"It has been," she replied, her voice tight. She didn't offer him her hand. "We're managing."

Vance gave a small, knowing smile that didn't quite reach his eyes. "Managing is one thing, Miss Dawson. Thriving is another. And from what I've observed, I don't believe managing is going to be enough for you any longer." He gestured vaguely towards the distant, skeletal remains of their lavender bushes, a silent testament to their loss. "The fire, the drought… it's a harsh hand nature has dealt you."

Ellie felt a prickle of resentment. He spoke of it as if it were some abstract misfortune, devoid of the personal devastation it represented. "We have faced hardship before," she said, her chin lifting slightly.

"Indeed," Vance conceded, his gaze sharp, taking in the weariness etched on her face, the tension in her shoulders. He was a keen observer of human frailty. "But perhaps not like this. Not when the very air itself seems to turn against you." He paused, letting his words hang in the air, knowing he was striking a sensitive chord. He had, after all, heard whispers of Thomas's persistent cough, of the doctor's concerned pronouncements. He wouldn't have been Vance if he hadn't been thoroughly informed.

"I've been thinking," he continued, his tone shifting, becoming more businesslike, yet still laced with an artificial warmth. "About your unique skills, Miss Dawson. Your knowledge of plants, of the natural world. It's a rare commodity, especially in this region."

Ellie's brow furrowed. What was he leading to? His interest in her botanical expertise was as unexpected as it was suspect. Vance was concerned with profit margins and industrial output, not with the delicate art of cultivating herbs or understanding the subtle language of the soil.

"I'm not sure I follow, Mr. Vance," she said carefully.

He stepped closer, his voice dropping to a more confidential level. "My business is expanding, Miss Dawson. I'm developing new product lines, exploring more sustainable sourcing methods for certain botanical extracts. Your family's history with agriculture, and your own specific talents, they've come to my attention."

He was offering her a job, then? Or something more? The thought of working for Vance, of lending her knowledge to his industrial empire, felt like a profound betrayal of everything her family stood for. Their farm was not merely a business; it was a living entity, a connection to the land that ran deeper than any balance sheet.

"I'm a farmer, Mr. Vance," she stated, her voice firm. "My place is here."

"And your brother?" Vance's question was a perfectly aimed dart, striking directly at her deepest vulnerability. "The doctor, I understand, has been concerned about his breathing. The air quality, it's not ideal for a young, sensitive constitution."

Ellie's breath hitched. How much did he know? And

more importantly, what was he planning to use that knowledge for?

Vance saw the flicker of apprehension in her eyes, the subtle tightening of her jaw. He pressed his advantage, his voice taking on a tone of magnanimous concern. "I have the means to help, Miss Dawson. Not just with your farm, but with… other concerns." He paused, letting the implication sink in. "I'm prepared to offer a loan. A substantial one. Enough to see you through this immediate crisis, to purchase necessary supplies, perhaps even to begin the process of rebuilding your fields, if that's your desire."

Ellie stared at him, speechless. A loan? From Vance? It sounded too good to be true, and in Vance's world, nothing was ever truly altruistic.

"In return," he continued, his gaze unwavering, "I would like to propose a partnership. A collaboration, if you will. Your expertise in botany, in cultivating and extracting… I believe it could be invaluable to a project I have in mind. A project that could, in fact, contribute to improving the air quality in this region."

He was painting a picture of a mutually beneficial arrangement, a lifeline thrown to a drowning farm. But the terms felt as shifting and uncertain as the dust devils that danced across their parched fields. She knew Vance. She knew his ambition was as boundless as his wealth. What was this 'greater project'? What was the true price of his 'generosity'?

"What kind of project?" she asked, her voice barely a whisper, her mind racing to decipher his true intentions.

"A research initiative," Vance explained smoothly, as if the thought had just occurred to him. "Focusing on air purification through specialized plant cultivation. Imagine, Miss Dawson, a future where our valley is not choked by dust, but revitalized by the very flora you know so well. I envision large-scale cultivation, perhaps even specialized processing facilities, utilizing your family's land, with your guidance, of course."

He was offering them money, a chance to recover from the fire, and a promise of a cleaner future, all wrapped in the guise of a partnership. The loan would alleviate their immediate financial distress, the crushing weight of debt that threatened to pull them under. It would mean medicine for Thomas, a chance for him to breathe easier, a reprieve from the constant, gnawing fear for his health. The temptation was almost overwhelming.

But the word 'partnership' felt hollow. Vance didn't partner; he acquired. He didn't collaborate; he controlled. She pictured her family's land, the fields that had been tilled by her father, her grandfather, their ancestors, now being parceled out for some industrial-botanical experiment, managed by Vance's cold, calculating hand. Her unique knowledge, honed by generations and nurtured by her own passion, would be reduced to a quantifiable asset, a cog in his profit-driven machine.

"You want to use our land," Ellie stated, not as a question, but as a declaration.

Vance gave a slight inclination of his head. "And your expertise. Think of it, Miss Dawson. A way to not only save your farm but to contribute to a solution for the entire region. A legacy of a different kind, perhaps, but one that benefits many."

The words 'save your farm' snagged in her mind. It was a powerful lure. The thought of losing the land, of being forced to leave it all behind, was a pain almost as acute as her worry for Thomas. Vance was dangling a solution, a way out of the seemingly inescapable trap they found themselves in. He was offering a calculated exchange: a piece of their autonomy for financial salvation and a desperate hope for her brother's recovery.

"A loan," Ellie repeated, her voice still laced with suspicion. "And in return, my knowledge… and our land."

"Think of it as an investment, Miss Dawson," Vance corrected gently. "An investment in a shared vision. A vision that requires your unique insight. I am prepared to be generous. Generous enough to ensure your family's immediate needs are met, and generous enough to provide the capital for this… venture."

He spoke of 'venture' and 'investment' with a practiced ease, masking the stark reality of their situation. They were not investors; they were desperate people facing ruin. Vance was not a benevolent benefactor; he was a predator who had scented their weakness. Yet, the image of Thomas, his small chest struggling for air, flickered behind Ellie's eyes. Could she afford to refuse this offer, no matter how unpalatable the terms? Could she deny Thomas a chance at relief, a chance for better air, simply to preserve a pride that was rapidly becoming a luxury?

She remembered the doctor's words: "sensitive,"
"toll." Vance's offer, for all its undercurrent of
manipulation, did address that very concern. He was
offering a way to potentially mitigate the very
environmental factors that were harming her
brother. It was a Faustian bargain, perhaps, but one
that held the promise of tangible relief for the
person she loved most.

"I… I need time to consider," Ellie said, her voice
hoarse. The prospect of confronting Vance, of
negotiating with him, felt like stepping onto
treacherous ground.

"Of course," Vance replied, his smile widening
almost imperceptibly. He knew he had planted the
seed. "Take your time. But remember, Miss Dawson,
difficult seasons require difficult decisions. And
opportunities, like sunlight, are not always
guaranteed to return." He offered her a thin,
professional smile, a silent promise of further
negotiation, and then turned, leaving Ellie alone with
the oppressive weight of his offer and the
suffocating reality of her family's plight. The air,
heavy with dust and the unspoken threat of Vance's
influence, seemed to press in on her, stealing her

breath just as surely as it was stealing her brother's. The calculated offer had been made, a precise calculation of their desperation against his immense resources, and Ellie knew that the choice before her would define not only the future of their farm, but the very life of her brother.

The words of Cyrus Vance echoed in Ellie's mind, a persistent hum beneath the worried rhythm of her own heartbeat. *Difficult seasons require difficult decisions.* His proposition lay before her, a gilded trap, its edges lined with the desperate hope for her brother's recovery. To accept was to embrace the unknown, to tether her family's fate to the man who, she suspected, was a significant contributor to their current suffering. To refuse was to condemn Thomas to a slower, more certain decline, to watch him wither under the weight of the very air they breathed. The lavender fields, once a symbol of their family's strength and prosperity, now lay as a barren testament to their vulnerability, mirroring the hollowness in her own chest. She traced the cracked earth with a trembling finger, the dust clinging to her skin like a second, unwelcome skin. Each grain felt like a betrayal, a silent accusation of her perceived weakness.

Her father's face, etched with a weariness that went beyond the physical toll of the drought and fire, swam before her eyes. Silas, her stoic father, whose pride was as deeply rooted as the oldest oak on their land, would see this as a surrender, a capitulation to the forces that had been chipping away at their way of life for years. He had always preached self-reliance, the quiet dignity of earning their keep from the earth, of living in harmony with its cycles, not bending it to their will or succumbing to the manipulative promises of men like Vance. The thought of explaining her decision to him, of witnessing the disappointment that would inevitably cloud his already burdened gaze, was almost as painful as the fear for Thomas. It felt like a betrayal of his legacy, of the very essence of their family's identity. Yet, Thomas's rasping breaths were a more immediate, more visceral reality than the abstract principles of ancestral pride. His small, fragile life was a beacon, guiding her through the encroaching darkness, and it was a beacon she could not, would not, allow to be extinguished.

The memory of Vance's unnervingly precise knowledge of Thomas's condition sent a shiver down her spine. He had not merely heard whispers; he had investigated, had factored his brother's very breath into his calculation of her vulnerability. It was a chilling reminder of his ruthlessness, his ability to leverage even the most intimate of heartbreaks for his own gain. He was a spider, spinning a web of calculated generosity, and she was a fly, drawn by the shimmer of false hope. The air in her lungs felt thick, heavy, as if even now, in the absence of Vance's physical presence, his influence was beginning to suffocate her.

She imagined the project Vance had so vaguely described. "Specialized plant cultivation… air purification." It sounded almost noble, a benevolent application of her hard-won knowledge. But the reality, she knew, would be far removed from such idyllic imagery. Vance's mills were notorious for their emissions, great belching smokestacks that spewed a fine, grey powder over the valley, a powder that had a metallic, acrid smell and seemed to cling to everything. Was this "research initiative" a way to mask his own pollution, to paint himself as a savior while continuing to poison their land? Was she to become an unwitting accomplice in his industrial machinations, lending her expertise to sanitize his dirty business practices? The thought curdled in her stomach.

She walked back towards the farmhouse, the familiar path now feeling alien, imbued with the weight of her impending decision. The sun beat down relentlessly, the sky a washed-out blue, devoid of the cleansing promise of rain. Every gust of wind stirred the dust, a constant, gritty reminder of the pervasive threat. She thought of her mother, lost to the consumption years ago, her lungs ravaged by what they had then believed to be the common ailments of the era, but which Ellie now suspected had been an early manifestation of the valley's slow poisoning. Her mother's gentle hands, her soft songs that used to fill the house, felt like distant echoes, drowned out by the harsh coughs of her brother.

The loan. Vance had offered a loan, a lifeline. It was more than just money for medicine; it was a chance to pay off the mounting debts that had begun to accumulate even before the fire, debts incurred from the failed harvests, the dwindling yields. It was a chance to buy feed for the few remaining livestock, to repair the barn roof before winter set in, to simply breathe a little easier without the constant specter of financial ruin looming over their heads. Silas had worked himself to the bone, his hands raw and bleeding more often than not, trying to hold their world together, and even his Herculean efforts were proving insufficient.

But Vance's terms were insidious. Her knowledge, her family's land. It was an exchange that felt deeply unequal, a skewed negotiation where one party held all the cards. He spoke of a partnership, a collaboration, but Ellie understood the true nature of his proposal. He sought to acquire, to absorb, to strip-mine their heritage for his own profit. Her intimate understanding of the local flora, the subtle properties of the indigenous plants, the ancient wisdom passed down through generations – this was not a commodity to be bought and sold. It was a sacred trust, a living legacy. To hand that over to Vance felt like handing over the very soul of their family.

She found her father sitting on the porch swing, his gaze fixed on the distant, scarred landscape. He looked older than his years, the lines on his face deeper, the weight of their misfortunes pressing down on his shoulders. Ellie sat beside him, the familiar creak of the swing a counterpoint to the turmoil within her. She watched his hands, strong and calloused, resting on his knees. They were the hands of a man who understood the soil, who coaxed life from it with patience and perseverance.

"Ellie," Silas said, his voice rough, "you look troubled."

She couldn't meet his eyes. "Vance came by today, Father."

Silas's jaw tightened, a muscle jumping in his cheek. He didn't need to ask what Vance wanted. The man had been circling their property like a hawk for years, waiting for the opportune moment to strike. "And?"

"He… he made an offer." The words felt thick and clumsy on her tongue. She chose her words carefully, seeking to soften the blow, to present the least offensive version of the truth. "He's willing to provide a loan. A substantial one. Enough to help us get back on our feet after the fire, to buy what we need."

Silas was silent for a long moment, his gaze still fixed on the horizon. Then, slowly, he turned his head to look at her. His eyes, usually so steady, held a flicker of something she couldn't quite decipher – was it suspicion, or a dawning, weary resignation? "And what does he want in return for his… generosity?"

Ellie swallowed, her throat suddenly dry. "My knowledge. Of the local plants. He says he has a project… an initiative to improve the air quality. He wants to use our land, my expertise, to cultivate certain things." She hurried on, trying to get the worst of it out. "He said it could help everyone."

Silas closed his eyes briefly, a sigh escaping his lips that seemed to carry the weight of years. When he opened them again, they were clearer, harder. "He wants to own what you know, Ellie. And he wants to own a piece of this land, under the guise of 'helping'. He sees opportunity in our struggle, not a shared cause." He paused, his gaze meeting hers directly. "You know what I think of Vance, and men like him. They build their fortunes on the backs of others, leaving ruin in their wake."

"I know, Father," she whispered, her voice catching. "But Thomas…" The dam finally broke, and the words tumbled out, a torrent of fear and desperation. "He's so weak, Father. The doctor… he says the air is making it worse. Vance's offer, it's… it's a chance, isn't it? A chance for him to breathe cleaner air, to get well. And we need the money, Father. We can't lose this farm. Not now."

Silas reached out and gently cupped her cheek, his rough thumb stroking away a tear that had escaped. His gaze was filled with a deep, abiding love, and a profound sorrow. "I know, child. I see it too. I feel it too." He looked back at the land, his voice low and heavy. "This land has always been our strength, Ellie. It's our history, our future. But if its very air is turning against us, then perhaps… perhaps we must find new ways to survive." He took a deep breath, the effort evident. "Vance is a wolf, Ellie. But sometimes, when you're drowning, even a wolf's teeth can feel like a savior's hand."

His words, though laced with his own deep reservations, gave her a measure of solace. He understood. He knew the impossible choice she faced. And in that understanding, she found a fragile strength. It wasn't forgiveness, not yet, but it was a shared burden, a communal acknowledgment of their desperate situation.

That night, long after her father had retired to his room, Ellie sat alone at the kitchen table, a kerosene lamp casting long, dancing shadows. The house was quiet, save for the occasional wheezing breath from Thomas's room. She felt the weight of her family's legacy pressing down on her, the unspoken expectations of generations. She felt the crushing responsibility for her brother's life, a responsibility that had grown heavier with each passing day. And she felt the chilling certainty that she was about to make a pact that would forever alter the course of their lives, a bargain struck in the crucible of desperation, with a man whose motives were as murky and unpredictable as the dust-laden air.

She picked up the worn leather-bound ledger, the family's farm records, passed down from her grandfather. The neat, meticulous entries documented years of hard work, of bountiful harvests, of struggles overcome. She ran her fingers over the faded ink, a tangible link to the past. This was what she was risking. This history, this identity, this connection to the earth that was as vital to her as her own blood.

But then, her mind's eye conjured Thomas's face, pale and drawn, his eyes too large for his small frame, his breath a shallow, painful rasp. The memory was a physical blow, a stark reminder of what was truly at stake. The lavender fields could be replanted. The barn could be rebuilt. But Thomas's life… that was a resource that could not be recovered once lost.

With a sigh that felt as though it tore from the very depths of her being, Ellie reached for a clean sheet of paper and a stub of pencil. She began to write, her hand trembling slightly, composing the letter to Cyrus Vance, accepting his offer. The words felt foreign, like a language she had never intended to speak. She outlined the terms as she understood them – the loan, her knowledge, the use of a portion of their land for his research. She didn't mention her suspicions, her deep-seated mistrust, or the gnawing fear that she was stepping onto a path from which there would be no return. She focused on the practicalities, on the agreement itself, framing it as a necessary step towards mutual benefit, a way to weather the storm together.

As she wrote, a profound sense of unease settled over her. It was more than just the anxiety of dealing with Vance; it was a deeper, more primal discomfort, a feeling that she was engaging in something fundamentally wrong, something that would stain her conscience and perhaps her very soul. It was a dangerous bargain, a dance with the devil himself, and she knew, with chilling certainty, that the price for this salvation might be far greater than any sum of money, or any amount of land. The air in the kitchen seemed to grow colder, heavier, as she sealed the letter, the simple act feeling like the tightening of a noose, a commitment made in the quiet desperation of a farm teetering on the brink of oblivion. The unseen threat had just become a very visible, very tangible alliance, and the future, once a landscape of familiar challenges, had morphed into a terrifying, uncharted territory.

The air in the farmhouse felt different now, thick with unspoken agreements and the heavy scent of dust and impending rain. Ellie had sent the letter, her brother's fragile breaths a constant, urgent reminder of her compromised position. The agreement, if it could be called that, was a fragile thing, a thread of obligation woven from desperation and Vance's calculated 'generosity.' She had committed to his veiled 'research initiative,' a decision that gnawed at her conscience like a persistent ache. The lavender fields, once her sanctuary and the symbol of her family's resilience, now felt like a battlefield where she had already surrendered crucial ground. The weight of it all pressed down on her, a suffocating blanket woven from the very air her brother struggled to breathe.

Days bled into weeks, each one marked by the slow, steady decline of Thomas's health and the ever-present anxiety of Vance's impending arrival. The loan, when it finally materialized, was a godsend, a tangible relief from the immediate pressures of debt and lack of resources. It paid for the specialist the doctor recommended, for better quality medicine, and for the small comforts that made Thomas's days a little less agonizing. Silas, though still wary, offered a grudging acceptance of the necessity, his stoicism a thin veneer over a deep-seated unease. He watched

Ellie closely, his silent questions echoing the ones she asked herself in the lonely hours of the night. Was this a temporary respite, or a permanent entanglement with a man who smelled of industry and avarice?

Then, one sweltering afternoon, Vance's polished carriage, incongruous against the parched landscape, rumbled up the dusty lane. He arrived unannounced, a familiar, unsettling presence that seemed to drain the very color from the already faded surroundings. He stepped out, impeccably dressed despite the oppressive heat, his smile a practiced curve that did little to hide the calculating glint in his eyes. He carried a worn leather satchel, its contents as mysterious as the man himself.

"Miss Ellie," he began, his voice smooth and unhurried, as if they were old acquaintances catching up over tea. "And Silas, I see you're still tending to your land with the same diligence." He gestured vaguely towards the fields, a dismissive sweep of his hand that seemed to encompass their entire existence.

Ellie met his gaze, her own steady despite the tremor in her stomach. "Mr. Vance. To what do we owe the pleasure of this visit?" She kept her tone polite but reserved, a subtle barrier against his pervasive charisma.

"Just checking in on our little venture," he said, his eyes scanning the farmhouse, the skeletal remains of the barn, and the vast, empty expanse of the fields. "And to discuss the specifics of this… air purification initiative. A noble endeavor, wouldn't you agree? Helping nature heal itself, with a little human ingenuity, of course."

He opened his satchel, revealing not vials of experimental seeds or samples of purified air, but a collection of geological maps, charts, and what appeared to be survey equipment. The air in the room seemed to grow heavier, the scent of dust now mixed with a faint, metallic tang that Ellie couldn't quite place. Vance laid a map across the worn kitchen table, its intricate lines and symbols a stark contrast to the familiar patterns of soil and crop rotation that Ellie knew so intimately.

"My 'project,' as you so quaintly put it, Miss Ellie," Vance began, his tone shifting, shedding the veneer of altruism, "is not about cultivating lavender, or any other plant for the sake of its perfume. Those fields you've so lovingly tended are merely… a suitable place for my operations."

Ellie's heart began to pound. Silas stood beside her, his hand resting lightly on her shoulder, a silent anchor. "Operations?" she prompted, her voice barely a whisper.

Vance's smile widened, revealing a flash of teeth. "Indeed. You see, Miss Ellie, I'm not just a man of industry, though my mills do require a certain… flair. I'm also a man with a keen interest in geology. Specifically, the rare earth minerals that lie beneath this very soil." He tapped a specific point on the map with a manicured finger. "Rumor has it, and my research strongly suggests, that this region is exceptionally rich in a particular deposit. Something quite valuable."

The words hung in the air, heavy and disorienting. Geology? Minerals? It was a world entirely alien to her, a world of rock and strata, a far cry from the delicate dance of roots and soil she understood so well. "I don't understand, Mr. Vance. You said this was about air purification…"

"A convenient narrative, wouldn't you agree?" Vance chuckled, a dry, rustling sound. "The truth is, Miss Ellie, I've been studying geological surveys of this area for years. There are anomalies, signatures that suggest something significant lies buried deep within the earth. But pinpointing it, accessing it, that's the tricky part. These deposits are often intertwined with intricate root systems, hidden by the very earth they nourish."

He leaned closer, his gaze fixing on Ellie, and for the first time, she saw the true intensity of his obsession. It was a predatory gleam, the look of a man who saw not land and life, but resources to be extracted, profits to be made. "And that's where your unique expertise comes in, Miss Ellie. Your family has worked this land for generations. You know its secrets, its nuances, better than anyone. You understand the way the roots of these plants spread, the subtle shifts in the soil, the patterns of growth that even the most advanced technology can't replicate. You can read this land like a book, can't you?"

Ellie felt a cold dread wash over her. Her knowledge, the legacy of her ancestors, the intimate connection she felt to every blade of grass and every whispering leaf, was not being sought for preservation, but for exploitation. Vance saw her not as a partner, but as a tool, a living, breathing instrument to locate his prize. The air purification project was nothing more than a smokescreen, a carefully crafted lie to gain her cooperation, to gain access to the land he coveted.

"You mean…" she faltered, the implications of his words crashing down on her, "you want me to help you find… minerals?"

"Precisely," Vance confirmed, his eyes gleaming. "Your intimate knowledge of the flora, their root structures, the very way they interact with the subsoil. You can guide my surveyors, tell us where to dig, where not to disturb. You can be my eyes and ears in places I cannot see. This 'air purification' is simply a cover story to justify my presence, my activities, and to secure your willing participation."

He gestured to the maps again. "These deposits are sensitive. They require careful extraction. And your understanding of the land's delicate balance, its ecological systems, will be invaluable in ensuring that the process is… efficient. Minimal disruption to the surface, of course, but deep enough to get what we need." He leaned back, a self-satisfied smirk playing on his lips. "Think of it, Miss Ellie. You help me find this valuable deposit, and your financial security, your brother's continued treatment, is guaranteed. And perhaps, just perhaps, a small percentage of the profits for your… consultation."

Ellie felt a wave of nausea. The casual mention of profits, of her 'consultation,' was a grotesque insult. He was asking her to betray the very essence of her being, to turn her knowledge into a weapon against the land she loved, and in doing so, potentially endanger the very air her brother needed to survive. The promise of his "air purification" was a cruel irony. What good was cleaner air if the earth beneath them was being torn asunder?

Silas's grip tightened on her shoulder, his knuckles white. His silence was more potent than any words, a testament to his own dawning horror. He had always distrusted Vance, and now, his worst fears were being realized with chilling clarity. This wasn't about helping a struggling farm; it was about plundering the earth for personal gain, and using Ellie's family's vulnerability as his leverage.

"You lied to me, Mr. Vance," Ellie said, her voice trembling with a mixture of anger and a profound sense of betrayal. The fragile thread of their agreement snapped, replaced by the cold, hard steel of reality.

Vance's expression didn't falter. "Did I? Or did I simply present you with a solution to your problems, a way to secure your family's future? You needed money, Miss Ellie. You needed a way to help your brother. I provided that. The method by which I achieve my own objectives is secondary to the fact that I am solving yours." He spread his hands in a gesture of magnanimity. "It's a mutually beneficial arrangement. You provide the local knowledge, I provide the capital and the expertise to extract what lies beneath. A fair trade."

"A fair trade?" Ellie's voice rose, the quiet farm kitchen suddenly filled with her indignation. "You want to exploit the land, Mr. Vance. You want to turn it into a mine, and you're using my brother's illness as an excuse to do it. My family's knowledge is not for sale, and the earth is not your personal treasury to plunder."

Silas stepped forward, his face a mask of grim determination. "You're wrong, Vance. This land isn't just dirt and rock to us. It's our history. It's our lifeblood. And we won't let you desecrate it."

Vance met Silas's gaze, his own hardening. The amiable mask had slipped, revealing the ruthless pragmatist beneath. "History doesn't pay the bills, Silas. And sentimentality won't save your daughter's brother. I have the resources, the technology, and the willingness to do what is necessary. You have… a unique understanding of the earth's vascular system. You can either cooperate and benefit, or resist and suffer the consequences." He turned his attention back to Ellie, his voice low and persuasive. "Think about it, Miss Ellie. This is not just about your brother anymore. It's about the survival of your family, your farm. With the right resources, we can make this land incredibly productive, in more ways than one."

He gestured around the humble farmhouse, a silent, pointed critique of their poverty. "Your current existence is precarious, Miss Ellie. My project offers stability, security, and a chance to truly thrive. All I require is your… guidance. Your intimate knowledge of this earth." He paused, letting his words sink in. "The delicate ecosystem you cherish will be respected, of course. Minimal surface disruption, as I said. But the wealth beneath… that is a different matter entirely."

Ellie looked at her father, then at the map spread between them, a tangible representation of Vance's avarice. The lavender fields, the symbols of her family's identity, were now mere markers on his geological chart, potential excavation sites. The very air they breathed, the subtle currents and scents that told the story of the land, were to be dissected, analyzed, and ultimately, exploited for a hidden treasure. Vance's project wasn't about purifying their air; it was about a secretive, subterranean excavation, a geological plunder disguised as ecological salvation.

She felt a profound sense of disillusionment. The hope that had flickered when Vance first proposed his "initiative" was extinguished, replaced by a cold fury. He had preyed on her desperation, twisted her family's hardship into a means to his own end, and revealed himself to be exactly the kind of predator her father had always warned her about. The unseen threat was no longer unseen; it was sitting at her kitchen table, his eyes reflecting the glint of avarice as he plotted the dissection of her ancestral home. The decision to accept his initial offer, born of love and fear for her brother, now felt like a pact with a devil who cared only for the riches buried deep beneath the soil, and who saw her own intimate connection to that soil as nothing more than a geological key. The very ground beneath her feet felt tainted, a stage set for a conflict far more profound than she had ever imagined.

# Chapter 3: Beneath the Surface

Vance, unperturbed by Ellie's growing unease, leaned back in his chair, the worn leather of his satchel peeking out from beneath his arm. He tapped a manicured finger on the geological map, his gaze still fixed on Ellie. "You mentioned your lavender. Beautifully fragrant, I'm told. But tell me, Miss Ellie, what else thrives in these fields? Are there any plants that seem particularly hardy, perhaps those that can withstand… unusual soil conditions?"

Ellie felt a prickle of apprehension. His interest had shifted, subtly but undeniably, from the superficial beauty of the lavender to its roots, its very connection to the earth. "Hardy plants?" she echoed, her voice carefully neutral. "Well, the wild chamomile often grows where the soil is a bit thinner, near the old stone wall. It seems to do well with less water, too. And then there are the wild onions, they have surprisingly deep taproots, and they seem to favor certain patches, almost as if they're seeking something specific." She found herself describing the plants almost out of habit, the ingrained knowledge of generations surfacing unbidden.

Vance's eyes lit up. "Deep taproots, you say? Interesting. And the wild onions, you say they favor *certain patches*? Can you describe these patches? Are they in low-lying areas, or perhaps higher ground? Any discernible difference in the soil texture or color?"

Ellie hesitated. She knew the patches. They were pockets where the soil had a different feel, a faint, almost metallic tang she'd always attributed to the lingering minerals from the old quarry that had long since been overgrown. "They tend to grow in the slightly darker soil," she explained, trying to keep her description as botanical as possible, avoiding any mention of the quarry or her vague geological suspicions. "And it feels… denser there. Firmer, somehow." She remembered as a child, digging for the plumpest wild onions, how her fingers would sometimes scrape against something harder than usual, small, dark pebbles that were unusually heavy.

"Denser and firmer," Vance mused, making a note in a small, leather-bound notebook he'd produced from his satchel. "Does the density seem to correlate with any particular moisture retention? Or perhaps a resistance to drying out after rain?" He was meticulously dissecting her observations, turning her intuitive understanding of the land into data points for his own inscrutable purpose.

"The darker soil seems to hold moisture a little longer, yes," Ellie admitted, a knot tightening in her stomach. She was giving him pieces of the puzzle, fragments of her intimate knowledge, and she couldn't see the full picture Vance was assembling. "And there are certain types of mosses that cling to the stones in those areas, a particularly robust variety that you don't see everywhere."

"Mosses," Vance repeated, scribbling again. "Excellent. And these stones… are they part of any exposed bedrock? Or simply scattered erratically?" He was probing, relentlessly, for any hint of geological structure, any indication of what lay beneath the cultivated surface.

"They're scattered, mostly," Ellie said, recalling the uneven distribution of stones in the fields. "Though near the north pasture, there are some larger outcrops, almost like the remnants of a collapsed wall, or perhaps something older. The soil there is always a bit richer, and the ferns seem to thrive, even in drier spells. They have very deep, fibrous root systems, those ferns."

"Fibrous root systems," Vance repeated, a faint smile playing on his lips. "And the richness of the soil… can you describe that richness, Miss Ellie? Is it a dark, loamy humus, or does it possess a different character? A grittiness, perhaps? A certain… mineral sheen?"

The words "mineral sheen" sent a shiver down Ellie's spine. It was precisely that – a faint, almost imperceptible glint that sometimes caught the sunlight in those particular patches of soil. She remembered her grandfather, a man who spoke little but observed much, once remarking on the 'old bones of the earth' that sometimes surfaced after a deep plowing. She had dismissed it as a fanciful saying, but now, Vance's questions made it feel like a coded message she had failed to decipher.

"It's… a deep, dark earth," she said, struggling to articulate the subtle nuances that Vance seemed so eager to quantify. "But yes, there's a different texture to it. It feels… heavier. And when you dig, you often find small, dark pebbles mixed in. They're not like the ordinary fieldstones."

Vance's gaze sharpened. "Pebbles, you say? What color are they? And do they have any particular weight or density?" He leaned forward, his entire demeanor shifting from polite inquiry to intense, focused scrutiny. He was no longer the patron; he was a prospector, and she was his reluctant guide.

Ellie wracked her brain, trying to recall the feel of those small, dark stones from her childhood. "They were dark, almost black, and surprisingly heavy for their size," she explained, her voice growing fainter. "They weren't smooth like river stones, but had a rougher surface. Sometimes they seemed to have a faint, almost greasy feel." She was describing something she hadn't thought about in years, something she hadn't understood the significance of until this very moment.

"Greasy feel," Vance murmured, his pen scratching furiously in his notebook. "Fascinating. And you've observed this in multiple locations where the wild onions and robust ferns are prevalent?"

"Yes," Ellie confirmed, a growing sense of dread washing over her. "It's in those specific areas where the earth is darker and holds moisture better." She looked at Vance, at the avid gleam in his eyes, and the carefully constructed façade of his charitable endeavor crumbled away, revealing the raw, insatiable hunger for profit that drove him. He wasn't interested in the health of her land, or the purity of the air; he was hunting for something hidden, something valuable, and he was using her intimate knowledge of the land as his map.

"Tell me, Miss Ellie," Vance continued, his voice dropping to a more conspiratorial tone, "have you ever noticed any subterranean water sources in these particular areas? Perhaps a stream that seems to vanish underground, or a dip in the land where water collects even in dry spells?"

Ellie recalled a small depression in the north pasture, a place where the grass always seemed greener, even during the height of summer. It was a mystery to her, a small anomaly in the otherwise predictable patterns of the land. She'd always assumed it was a natural spring that had long since dried up, or simply a low-lying area that captured dew. "There's a dip," she admitted, "in the north field, near the old oak. Water seems to collect there for a while after it rains, and the vegetation is always lusher. I've never seen a visible spring, though."

"A dip," Vance repeated, his eyes gleaming with an almost feverish intensity. "And the vegetation is lusher. Excellent. This suggests a possible shallow water table, or perhaps a concentration of… mineral-rich seepage." He paused, then fixed her with a direct, penetrating gaze. "Miss Ellie, your knowledge of this land is truly remarkable. It's as if you have an innate understanding of its very composition, its geological whispers."

The compliment felt like a veiled threat. Her

"whispers" were his signals, her intuition his blueprint. He was mining her mind, extracting information that was as vital to her as the air her brother breathed. The project, the charitable façade, was an elaborate deception, a means to access the hidden wealth that lay dormant beneath the cultivated surface of her family's ancestral home.

"The plants that grow there," Ellie ventured, testing the waters, "do they… have a particular significance in relation to geology, Mr. Vance?" She needed to understand the scope of his interest, the true nature of his "research."

Vance chuckled, a dry, rustling sound that grated on her nerves. "Some plants, Miss Ellie, are quite particular about their environment. Certain species, for instance, have evolved to thrive in soils with high concentrations of specific elements. Their root systems can even concentrate these elements, making them detectable. Others, with deep taproots, can access water sources far below the surface, and in doing so, can bring with them dissolved minerals that subtly alter the soil composition in their immediate vicinity." He gestured to the map again, his finger tracing an unseen vein beneath the earth. "Consider them natural indicators, Miss Ellie. Living seismographs, if you will. And you, with your intimate knowledge of these living indicators, are invaluable to me."

Ellie felt a wave of cold dread. He was not just interested in plants; he was interested in plants as geobotanical indicators, as markers for mineral deposits. Her understanding of botany, her lifelong connection to the flora of her land, was being twisted into a tool for geological prospecting. The lavender, the chamomile, the wild onions, even the hardy ferns – they were all potential clues to a treasure Vance sought to unearth, regardless of the cost to the land or the people who depended on it.

"And these minerals," Ellie pressed, her voice barely audible, "what are they, exactly? What makes them so valuable?" She had to know what she was facilitating, what she was enabling.

Vance's smile was slow and triumphant. "Ah, that, Miss Ellie, is where the real secret lies. This region, my research indicates, is home to a deposit of rare earth minerals. Elements critical for modern industry, for technological advancements that will shape the future. And this particular deposit… it's said to be exceptionally pure, remarkably accessible once you know where to look." He leaned back, the picture of a benevolent benefactor who had stumbled upon a unique opportunity. "And you, Miss Ellie, are helping me find it. Your knowledge of the earth's living tapestry is the key to unlocking this hidden wealth."


Ellie's mind reeled. Rare earth minerals. The words sounded alien, industrial, far removed from the organic cycles of growth and decay that she understood. Her family had always farmed, nurtured the land, worked
*with* its rhythms. Now, Vance spoke of unlocking its secrets, of extracting its hidden wealth, using her knowledge as the key. The implication was clear: her generations of stewardship were merely a prelude to an industrial excavation, a methodical dismantling of the very earth that sustained them. The lavender fields, once a symbol of her family's resilience, were now merely a hunting ground.

"So, the… air purification initiative," Ellie began, the words tasting like ash in her mouth, "that was simply… a story?"

Vance's smile didn't waver, but his eyes held a new, hard edge. "A necessary narrative, Miss Ellie. To ensure your willing participation, and to provide a justifiable reason for my presence and activities. The earth needs healing, wouldn't you agree? And sometimes, the most profound healing requires a… deeper approach. An approach that understands the fundamental elements that lie beneath the surface. Elements that, when properly understood and utilized, can indeed lead to a more balanced and prosperous future for all." He picked up a small, dark pebble from the edge of the map, turning it over in his fingers. "These little treasures, Miss Ellie. They hold more promise than all the perfume in your lavender fields."

Ellie felt a profound sense of betrayal, a cold realization that her desperation had made her vulnerable to a man who saw her land not as a home, but as a resource to be exploited. Her knowledge, her heritage, her very connection to the earth, had been weaponized against her. Vance's carefully crafted plan, his smooth words and promises, were all a smokescreen for a much deeper, more insidious intent. He was not here to help her; he was here to plunder, and she, with her intimate understanding of the land, was his unwitting accomplice. The geological whispers of her home were being translated into a language of extraction and profit, a language that threatened to tear the very heart out of the earth she loved.

Ellie watched Vance's eyes, a disconcerting gleam replacing the practiced benevolence that had initially soothed her. The mention of "elements" and "extraction" hung in the air like an unseen pollutant. Her grandmother's garden, a place of quiet healing and botanical wisdom, felt suddenly exposed, its secrets laid bare to a rapacious gaze. Vance's interest had shifted from the superficial appeal of lavender to the deeper, more potent secrets held within the soil, secrets her family had guarded for generations. He saw not medicine, but minerals; not healing, but harvesting.

"You mentioned your grandmother's remedies," Vance prompted, his tone still remarkably smooth, though a current of something sharp now ran beneath it. "You said she had a particular affinity for certain plants, those that flourished even in the more challenging conditions of the land. Tell me more about those. Were there any plants she relied on specifically, perhaps for their… robust nature, or their ability to draw sustenance from less than ideal soil?" He gestured vaguely towards the map, a silent accusation that her land, her home, was anything but ideal.

Ellie's breath hitched. Her grandmother's knowledge was not a collection of curiosities for Vance's scientific dissection; it was a living legacy, a deep understanding of the interconnectedness of all things. She remembered the small, sun-drenched corner of the garden where her grandmother cultivated plants that seemed to defy the natural order, growing with an almost defiant vitality. There was the feverfew, its daisy-like flowers a potent ally against migraines, a plant her grandmother swore thrived best in soil that had been 'touched by the earth's deeper humors.' Ellie had always understood this to mean soil rich in natural minerals, perhaps enriched by subterranean water flows, but she had never considered it in the terms Vance now implied.

"My grandmother," Ellie began, choosing her words with care, "she understood that the earth provides for us, and that some plants are especially gifted at drawing forth its bounty, even from the harder ground. She cultivated wild thyme near the old well, for instance. It's a plant that loves the sun, yes, but it also seems to prefer soil that is well-drained, perhaps even a little stony. It's hardy, resilient, and its scent is incredibly potent, especially after a dry spell. She would crush the leaves and steep them for a tea that settled the stomach and cleared the head."

Vance made a note. "Wild thyme. Hardy. Prefers well-drained, stony soil. Potent scent. And the tea… a digestive aid? Fascinating. But what about those with deeper roots, Miss Ellie? Plants that might reach further into the earth, accessing… what one might call the 'truer' essence of the soil?" He leaned forward, his gaze intense, as if he could see through the earth to the very roots she described.

Ellie thought of the comfrey. Its rough, hairy leaves and unassuming purple flowers belied its power. Her grandmother called it "bone-knit," a miracle worker for sprains and bruises. The plant's roots plunged astonishingly deep, a veritable anchor into the earth. It thrived in damp conditions, often found near watercourses, and her grandmother always planted it in the lower-lying areas of the garden, where the soil was consistently moist and rich with organic matter. Vance's questions about "truer essence" and "deeper roots" made her skin crawl. He was dissecting her grandmother's sacred remedies, reducing them to their chemical components, their potential for exploitation.

"Comfrey," Ellie said, her voice firming. "My grandmother swore by comfrey. Its roots go very deep, seeking out water and drawing up nutrients from far below the surface. She used it externally, for healing wounds and broken bones. She would make a poultice from the leaves and roots. It's a plant that thrives where the earth is rich and damp, where the water tables are closer to the surface." She paused, a sudden clarity dawning. Her grandmother's favored plants, the ones Vance was now so keenly interested in, often grew in specific geological contexts – areas with higher mineral content, or proximity to underground water. These weren't mere coincidences; they were indicators.

Vance nodded, his pen scratching again. "Comfrey. Deep roots. Used externally for healing. And you say it thrives in damp, nutrient-rich soil, near water sources. This aligns with some of my preliminary geological surveys, Miss Ellie. There are certain areas on your property that indicate a higher likelihood of specific mineral deposits, precisely where such robust, deep-rooted vegetation is known to flourish." He tapped the map again, his finger hovering over a shaded area that corresponded to the northern fields, near the old quarry.

The quarry. A place of scars, of gouged earth and exposed rock. Her grandmother had always warned her away from it, saying the energies there were too raw, too unsettled. But she had also spoken of the rare plants that sometimes pushed through the rubble, resilient life finding purchase where nothing else could. She recalled a specific patch of wild mint, its scent sharper, more invigorating than any cultivated variety, that grew stubbornly near a cluster of unusually dark, heavy stones at the quarry's edge.

"The wild mint," Ellie offered, a cautious attempt to steer the conversation towards her grandmother's more subtle remedies, the ones that spoke of balance rather than brute extraction. "It grows near water, and it's incredibly hardy. My grandmother used it for indigestion, a simple infusion that brought such relief. She said it particularly liked soil that was a little… agitated, perhaps, where the earth had been disturbed. Not necessarily depleted, but… awakened."

"Awakened soil," Vance mused, a flicker of something akin to amusement in his eyes. "An interesting description. And this mint, with its preference for agitated, yet fertile ground, what about its root system? Is it extensive? Does it spread aggressively?" He was mapping the subterranean network, not for its ecological contribution, but for its potential to indicate mineral veins.

"It spreads," Ellie confirmed, picturing the tenacious runners of the mint. "It has a shallow but vigorous root system, spreading out to capture moisture and nutrients. It's a plant that signals a healthy, active soil, even if that activity is a result of past disruption." She met Vance's gaze, a quiet defiance hardening within her. Her grandmother's knowledge was not a blueprint for industrial exploitation; it was a testament to the land's ability to heal, to sustain, to offer gifts of balance and well-being. These were not mere plants; they were living manifestations of the earth's intricate systems, each with its own purpose and place.

"And the 'mineral deposits' you mentioned, Mr. Vance," Ellie pressed, her voice deliberately calm. "What are they? And why are they so important that they warrant such… detailed interest in my grandmother's garden?" She needed to understand the scale of his ambition, the true nature of the "healing" he claimed to offer.

Vance leaned back, a slow smile spreading across his face. "Miss Ellie, the earth beneath us is a treasure trove, far richer than any perfume or herbal remedy could ever convey. Your property, it appears, sits atop a significant deposit of scandium. A rare earth element, vital for advanced aerospace technology

and lightweight alloys. Its extraction and purification
are exceptionally complex, but the potential rewards
are immense. Your grandmother's plants, with their
unique geobotanical properties, are essentially
natural indicators, guiding us to the most
concentrated veins of this valuable element." He
paused, allowing the weight of his words to settle.
"These plants, Miss Ellie, are not just remedies; they
are signposts to the future."


The word "scandium" struck Ellie with a chilling
finality. It was a word utterly divorced from the soil,
the sun, the rain that nurtured life. It spoke of mines,
of machinery, of a landscape irrevocably altered. Her
grandmother's intimate knowledge, her
understanding of the earth as a living, breathing
entity, was being twisted into a tool for the
systematic dismantling of that very entity. The plants
were not merely indicators; they were her
grandmother's allies, her partners in a dance of
reciprocal giving and receiving. Vance saw them as
tools of extraction, unwitting accomplices in a
venture that would scar the land he claimed to be
helping.

"So, the 'air purification' and the 'soil revitalization' were merely… strategies?" Ellie asked, the accusation a quiet storm gathering within her. The carefully constructed narrative of environmental stewardship had dissolved into a naked pursuit of profit.

Vance's smile didn't falter, but his eyes held a steely glint. "A necessary narrative, Miss Ellie. To secure your cooperation and access to your land's unique resources. The earth does indeed need healing, but sometimes, true healing involves a fundamental restructuring, an unlocking of its deepest potentials. And those potentials, in this case, lie not in the fragrant petals of your lavender, but in the mineral wealth that lies beneath. Your grandmother's deep-rooted plants, Miss Ellie, are merely the key to that unlocking." He picked up a small, dark pebble from the edge of the geological map, turning it over in his fingers, his gaze fixed on its intrinsic weight. "These, Miss Ellie, are where the true promise lies."

Ellie's stomach churned. Her grandmother's wisdom, passed down through generations, was being reduced to mere geobotanical data points for Vance's rapacious enterprise. The plants that had soothed ailments, healed wounds, and brought comfort were now viewed as mere markers for a valuable mineral deposit. The intrinsic worth of traditional ecological knowledge, its inherent value in understanding and living harmoniously with the environment, was utterly lost on Vance. He saw only resources to be extracted, profit to be reaped, and Ellie's intimate understanding of her land, her heritage, was the very map he used to guide his plunder. The reverence for nature that her grandmother had instilled in her was now pitted against a greed that saw the land as nothing more than a commodity. The delicate balance of her grandmother's garden, a sanctuary of healing, was now threatened by a modern form of avarice, cloaked in the language of progress and discovery. She felt a profound sense of betrayal, not just for herself, but for the earth, for the generations of women who had tended its secrets with reverence. Vance's ambition was a poison, seeping into the very soil her family had nurtured.

The subtle shift in Vance's demeanor, the barely perceptible widening of his pupils when he spoke of scandium, had been a cold premonition. Now, as he packed his instruments and maps, leaving Ellie alone in the quiet of her grandmother's study, the premonition solidified into a chilling certainty. Her ancestral home, her sanctuary of shared botanical secrets, was no longer just a place of healing but a potential mining site, a resource to be exploited. The knowledge her grandmother had so lovingly cultivated, the intimate understanding of soil and root and leaf, had been weaponized, twisted into a roadmap for avarice. Vance saw not the cyclical abundance of nature, but the linear extraction of wealth. He saw not the earth's living systems, but mineral deposits waiting to be unearthed. And Ellie, armed with the very wisdom he sought to exploit, found herself increasingly isolated, caught between the insidious charm of an outsider and the ingrained suspicion of her own community.

The whispers had started, as they always did in a town like Harmony Creek, as soft as the rustle of dry leaves, but no less insidious. Ellie, with her solitary ways and her grandmother's legacy of herbal lore, had always been an outlier. Her preference for the quiet communion with plants over the boisterous camaraderie of town gatherings, her deep knowledge of remedies that most dismissed as old wives' tales, had marked her. But now, her association with

Vance, the polished stranger with his scientific jargon and his peculiar interest in her land's hidden depths, had given those whispers a new, sharper edge.

"Seen Vance around Ellie's place a fair bit, haven't you?" Mrs. Gable, her voice laced with a manufactured concern, had commented to Martha Jenkins over the fence, her eyes flicking towards Ellie's homestead as if expecting to see smoke rising from the chimney of some forbidden ritual. Martha, ever the town's dutiful echo, had nodded gravely. "Aye, he's been poking about. Asking a lot of questions, they say. About the soil, and the plants. Strange things for an outsider to be interested in, wouldn't you say?"

The implication hung heavy in the humid summer air: Ellie was consorting with strangers, dabbling in things best left undisturbed. Her efforts to leverage her grandmother's knowledge for the family's betterment, to perhaps even revitalize the struggling farm, were being subtly reframed. Her quiet determination was misconstrued as eccentricity, her ecological insights as something bordering on the unnatural. The prejudice, dormant for years, stirred awake, fueled by a potent cocktail of fear, misunderstanding, and a deeply ingrained resistance to anything that deviated from the familiar, the accepted.

Ellie felt the shift acutely. Once, her botanical prowess had been a source of quiet pride, a testament to the enduring wisdom of her lineage. Now, it felt like a liability. The careful cultivation of her grandmother's garden, the meticulous cataloging of roots and herbs, the knowledge of which plants flourished in the mineral-rich soil near the old quarry, was no longer seen as a skilled practice but as an unnerving affinity for the earth's more clandestine properties.

She saw it in the way people's gazes lingered a moment too long when she passed them in town, the way conversations hushed and then resumed with forced heartiness as she approached the general store. Old Man Hemlock, usually so eager to share his own questionable remedies for everything from gout to melancholy, now offered only curt nods and averted eyes. Even young Tommy Miller, who used to trail after her, begging for a tincture to soothe a scraped knee, seemed to shy away, his mother's cautionary whispers undoubtedly having reached his ears.

The isolation was a tangible thing, a suffocating blanket that settled over her whenever she ventured beyond the familiar boundaries of her own land. Vance, with his smooth reassurances and his talk of scientific advancement, was a part of this isolation. His presence, his questions, his underlying agenda— all of it seemed to feed the community's distrust, casting a shadow over Ellie's intentions. She was caught in a tightening vise, Vance's manipulative influence on one side, the community's ingrained prejudice on the other.

Her family, though ostensibly supportive, bore the brunt of the town's scrutiny. Her father, a man of quiet resilience but limited understanding of Ellie's specific pursuits, found himself subjected to knowing glances and insinuated questions. "Heard your Ellie's got some fancy fellow visiting," Sheriff Brody had remarked, his tone casual but his eyes sharp. "Some sort of scientist, eh? Asking about…

the ground you stand on. Hope she knows what she's doing. Folks 'round here don't take kindly to outsiders digging where they shouldn't." The sheriff's words, meant perhaps as a friendly warning, carried the weight of communal judgment.

Her mother, bless her, tried to shield her, offering words of encouragement that felt increasingly hollow against the rising tide of suspicion. "Don't you mind them, Ellie," she'd say, her hands busy with mending a worn quilt, her gaze fixed on the stitches rather than Ellie's face. "They're just jealous. Jealous of your knowledge, of your spirit. Your grandmother was the same way." But the unspoken fear in her mother's eyes, the subtle tightening of her lips when Vance's name was mentioned, betrayed her own anxieties. She saw her daughter's efforts, her very nature, being misinterpreted as something far less innocent or trustworthy.

The pressure was immense. Ellie had envisioned her inherited knowledge as a bridge, a way to connect her family's past with a sustainable future, a means to honor her grandmother's legacy while securing their present. She had seen her grandmother's garden not just as a collection of plants, but as an ecosystem, a source of quiet strength and resilience. The very plants Vance was so keen to catalog – the feverfew that eased her mother's headaches, the comfrey that mended her father's work-worn hands, the wild mint that settled restless stomachs – were testament to a profound understanding of nature's intricate pharmacy. She had believed that by sharing this knowledge, by perhaps collaborating with someone like Vance, she could bring about a positive change, a recognition of the intrinsic value of traditional ecological knowledge.

But Vance's true intentions, revealed with such chilling candor, had shattered that idealism. He saw her grandmother's carefully cultivated knowledge not as wisdom to be respected and integrated, but as a set of indicators, a biological surveying tool for his mineral extraction enterprise. The plants were not allies; they were signposts. Her deep connection to the land, her intuitive understanding of its subtle cues, was not a virtue but a commodity to be leveraged.

The prejudice, therefore, was not just an abstract

societal force; it was a direct consequence of Vance's intrusion and his manipulation of Ellie's perceived "unconventional wisdom." The whispers about her consorting with outsiders were amplified by the fact that the outsider's interest was rooted in a desire to excavate the very earth that sustained their community. Her botanical knowledge, once a source of quiet pride and a potential boon, was now being framed as a dangerous fascination with the unseen, the potentially exploitative.

Ellie found herself retracing the conversations, analyzing every word, every gesture, desperately trying to understand how her genuine desire to help her family had been so spectacularly twisted. She remembered Vance's casual questions about the resilience of certain plants, their ability to thrive in the "more challenging conditions" of the land. At the time, she had taken it as a sign of his genuine interest in ecological adaptation. Now, she understood he was probing for indicators of mineral-rich soil. Her description of wild thyme thriving in well-drained, stony soil, or comfrey's preference for damp, nutrient-rich earth near water sources, were not merely botanical observations; they were geological markers in Vance's eyes.

Her mention of wild mint growing near the old quarry, in soil that was "agitated, perhaps, where the earth had been disturbed," had been a tentative attempt to steer the conversation back to her grandmother's more subtle remedies, those focused on balance rather than extraction. But Vance had seized upon it, his interest piqued by the plant's resilience in disrupted soil – a clear indicator, to him, of potential mineral veins. He'd even pressed her about its root system, its aggressive spread, all data points for his subsurface analysis.

The true sting lay in the community's reaction to this manufactured suspicion. They didn't understand the intricacies of Vance's geological surveys or his obsession with scandium. They understood only that Ellie was associating with a stranger who seemed overly interested in their shared land, and that her own unusual knowledge was somehow central to it. The narrative that began to form in their minds was simple, and deeply rooted in their own anxieties: Ellie, the eccentric botanist, was either being duped by an outsider, or worse, was complicit in some unknown, potentially harmful endeavor.

Her efforts to maintain her family's farm, to introduce more sustainable practices and to perhaps even cultivate some of the more valuable herbs for a modest income, were now viewed with a cynical eye. When she spoke of revitalizing a patch of neglected soil near the northern fields, the same fields Vance had indicated on his map as having high potential for mineral deposits, the whispers would intensify. "She's just digging for minerals herself," some would mutter, their voices low and accusatory. "Got that Vance fellow whispering in her ear, no doubt."

The misunderstanding was a heavy burden. Her grandmother's wisdom, passed down through generations of women who understood the land's delicate balance, was a sacred trust. It was a knowledge rooted in reverence, in reciprocity, in the deep understanding that the earth provided sustenance not for exploitation, but for harmonious living. To have that knowledge twisted, to see it used as a tool for a rapacious enterprise, was a profound betrayal. And to have her community, her own people, turn against her because of it, fueled by fear and misinterpretation, was a wound that cut even deeper.

Ellie felt the walls closing in. She had to find a way to navigate this treacherous landscape, to protect her family and her heritage from both the avarice of outsiders and the suspicion of her own. The challenge was no longer just about understanding her grandmother's plants; it was about understanding the complex, often irrational, currents of human prejudice and fear, and finding a way to emerge from beneath their shadow, not unscathed, but unbroken. The path forward was obscured, much like the mineral deposits Vance sought, hidden beneath layers of suspicion and misunderstanding. Her grandmother's teachings, however, had always emphasized the importance of deep roots, of resilience in the face of adversity. Ellie would need every ounce of that inherited strength now. She had to prove to her community, and more importantly, to herself, that her connection to the earth was one of stewardship, not of exploitation, and that her grandmother's legacy was one of healing, not of harm. The fight, she realized with a sinking heart, had only just begun.

Ellie found herself pacing the worn floorboards of her grandmother's study, the scent of dried lavender and old paper a familiar comfort that now felt like a mockery. Vance had departed hours ago, leaving behind an unsettling quiet, a vacuum that seemed to amplify the insidious nature of his casual inquiries. Her mind, usually so adept at navigating the intricate tapestry of botanical knowledge, felt ensnared in a web of suspicion, each thread spun from Vance's carefully chosen words. He spoke of progress, of innovation, of unlocking the earth's hidden potential, but as Ellie sifted through the fragmented conversations, a far more disturbing picture began to emerge.

It wasn't just a casual interest in the local flora that Vance possessed. His questions had become unnervingly specific, circling around particular geological formations, the resilience of certain plant species in mineral-rich soil, and the historical land usage patterns of the Harmony Creek area. He'd shown a peculiar fascination with the old abandoned quarry, not as a relic of the past, but as a geological anomaly. He'd pressed her about the plants that managed to thrive in its disturbed soil — the hardy wild thyme that clung to the stony slopes, the tenacious wild mint that choked the damp crevices.

Ellie had initially dismissed these as the eccentricities of a dedicated scientist, a man eager to categorize and understand every facet of his environment. But Vance's focus wasn't on understanding for the sake of ecological preservation; it was on understanding for the sake of extraction.

The "discovery" he'd alluded to, the one that had brought him to Harmony Creek with such focused intent, was not just any mineral deposit. As she pieced together the oblique references Vance had made, the subtle shifts in his demeanor when discussing the earth's composition, a chilling realization settled upon her: Vance was after scandium. And not just any trace amounts, but a significant, commercially viable lode. The implications of this were devastating. Scandium, while valuable, was often found in association with rare earth elements, and its extraction was notoriously environmentally destructive. The methods Vance hinted at – large-scale open-pit mining, chemical leaching – were antithetical to everything her grandmother had taught her about respecting the land, about working in harmony with its cycles.

She remembered Vance's almost dismissive comment about the "resilience" of the local ecosystem, how it had "adapted" to the quarry's past disturbances. At the time, she'd interpreted it as a testament to nature's tenacity. Now, she understood. He wasn't praising the ecosystem; he was identifying it as a robust indicator species for his intended operations. The plants that survived and thrived in the altered environment were, in his eyes, simply markers of a mineralized zone. His scientific curiosity was a mask for a rapacious hunger, a desire to exploit the land with a ruthless efficiency that ignored the delicate balance of the Hill Country.

Ellie walked over to her grandmother's worn oak desk, her fingers tracing the faint indentations left by years of meticulous note-taking. Her grandmother's journals were filled with observations on plant cycles, soil composition, the subtle language of the earth. But Vance wasn't interested in the symbiotic relationships of fungi and roots, or the medicinal properties of an herb. He was interested in what the plants
*indicated*. He had asked about the depth of certain root systems, the presence of specific nitrogen-fixing

bacteria, the very things that signaled fertile ground –
or, in his warped perspective, ground rich in valuable
minerals.

He'd spoken about "geological surveys" and
"subsurface anomalies," terms that now resonated
with a sinister clarity. He'd taken soil samples, yes,
but not for ecological analysis. He'd taken them to
test for mineral content, for the very elements that
made the land susceptible to his brand of extraction.
His polite inquiries about her grandmother's
knowledge were a calculated attempt to glean
information that would bypass years of painstaking
geological surveying, information that he could then
leverage for his own gain. He saw her grandmother's
legacy not as a testament to stewardship, but as an
unintended geological survey map, a guide to the
earth's hidden treasures.

The sheer scale of his ambition, and the disregard
for the consequences, was staggering. Harmony
Creek was not a barren, industrial wasteland waiting
to be industrialized; it was a living, breathing
ecosystem, a fragile mosaic of biodiversity that had
sustained generations of families. The rolling hills,
the clear streams, the ancient oaks – all of it was

under threat. Vance's vision for Harmony Creek was one of scarred earth, of poisoned water, of a landscape irrevocably altered. His definition of "progress" was environmental devastation.

The realization hit Ellie with the force of a physical blow. This wasn't just about her family's land or her grandmother's reputation. This was about the very soul of Harmony Creek. Vance wasn't just a businessman seeking a new venture; he was an architect of destruction, his methods poised to annihilate the very essence of the place she called home. The subtle charm he'd initially exuded now seemed like a predator's lure, a sophisticated deception designed to lull his prey into a false sense of security.

She thought back to his eagerness to examine her grandmother's herbarium, the meticulous cataloging of dried specimens. He had seemed genuinely impressed by the breadth of the collection, the variety of plants meticulously pressed and labeled. But his fascination wasn't with the specimens themselves, but with the data they represented. Each labeled plant was a piece of evidence, a clue pointing towards specific soil types, water conditions, and geological substrates. His questions about the provenance of certain plants, their usual habitats, were all part of building his subsurface map. He was a treasure hunter, and the earth's ecological health was merely collateral damage in his quest for riches.

The whispers in town, which had initially felt like personal attacks on her character, now seemed to be a natural consequence of Vance's presence. The townsfolk, with their innate understanding of the land's value beyond monetary worth, sensed something amiss. Their suspicion wasn't born of ignorance, but of a deep, intuitive understanding that Vance's interest was predatory. They saw the stranger asking too many questions, his eyes too keen, his pronouncements too confident. They didn't have the scientific vocabulary to articulate the threat, but they felt it in their gut, the primal fear of an outsider seeking to exploit their ancestral home.

Ellie felt a surge of anger, not just at Vance, but at herself for her initial naivete. She had allowed herself to be blinded by his polished veneer, his talk of scientific advancement. She had, in a way, become his unwitting accomplice, providing him with the very information that would facilitate the destruction of her community. Her grandmother's wisdom, intended to foster life and healing, was being perverted into a tool for exploitation.

The thought of open-pit mining, of the deafening roar of heavy machinery tearing into the earth, of chemicals seeping into the groundwater, sent a shiver down her spine. This was the future Vance envisioned for Harmony Creek, a stark contrast to the gentle, sustainable existence her grandmother had embodied. Her grandmother's garden was a sanctuary of biodiversity, a testament to the quiet, persistent power of nature. Vance's quarry would be a scar, a testament to human greed.

Ellie knew then that she couldn't stand by and let this happen. Her isolation in the community, her perceived eccentricities, suddenly felt less like burdens and more like strengths. Her deep connection to the land, her intimate knowledge of its rhythms and needs, was precisely what was needed to counter Vance's destructive agenda. Her grandmother's legacy was not just about preserving knowledge; it was about protecting the very earth that knowledge sprang from.

The task ahead seemed monumental. Vance was a man of resources, of influence, and his agenda was driven by profit. The townsfolk, while suspicious, were also wary of confrontation, and perhaps, in their own way, susceptible to the allure of promised economic benefits, even if those benefits came at a terrible cost. Ellie, armed with little more than her grandmother's journals and her own growing resolve, had to find a way to make them see the truth, to awaken them to the devastating reality of Vance's hidden agenda.

She picked up one of her grandmother's trowels, its wooden handle smoothed by years of use. It felt solid, real, a connection to a more grounded time. She looked out the window, towards the rolling hills that Vance saw as mere deposits waiting to be mined. They were more than that. They were a living tapestry, a delicate ecosystem, a heritage. And she, Ellie, was their unlikely guardian. The time for passive observation was over. The fight for Harmony Creek had begun.

The depth of Vance's planning was becoming alarmingly clear. His questions weren't random; they were like the methodical probing of a skilled surgeon preparing for a radical operation, meticulously identifying the vital organs to be removed. He had asked about the water table near the quarry, not from an environmentalist's concern for aquatic life, but from a miner's perspective on water management and potential contamination during extraction. He'd inquired about the stability of the soil on the quarry's periphery, information crucial for planning excavation sites and assessing the risk of landslides, a risk he seemed prepared to accept.

Ellie recalled a seemingly innocuous conversation about the best methods for composting, a topic close to her heart as she sought to enrich her own depleted garden soil. Vance had listened intently, nodding as she explained the importance of aeration and the role of specific microorganisms. But then, he'd steered the conversation towards chemical soil amendments, asking about the feasibility of large-scale industrial composting to neutralize acidic conditions. Acidic conditions. The very conditions often associated with mineral-rich ore bodies and the subsequent leaching processes used to extract them. His interest wasn't in making her garden flourish; it was in understanding how to manage the chemical fallout of his proposed operations.

He'd even subtly probed her knowledge of local geological history, asking if there were any documented instances of unusual mineral findings in the area, any old family legends or anecdotes about strange rocks or deposits. Ellie had mentioned her grandmother's stories about the "glimmering stones" found near the old creek bed after heavy rains – small, metallic flecks that her grandmother had dismissed as harmless mica. Vance's eyes had lit up at that, a flicker of intense interest that he'd quickly masked with a casual shrug. Mica, indeed. He likely knew those flecks were indicative of something far more valuable, something he'd come to excavate.

The chilling truth was that Vance wasn't just prospecting for scandium; he was preparing to employ aggressive, potentially ruinous mining techniques. The Hill Country ecosystem, so resilient in its natural state, was not equipped to withstand the brutal onslaught of industrial-scale extraction. The specific geological makeup of the area, while potentially rich in minerals, also meant it was vulnerable to erosion, water contamination, and habitat destruction. Vance's pursuit of profit was entirely divorced from any consideration of the long-term ecological consequences. He saw the land as a resource to be consumed, not an environment to be sustained.

Ellie imagined the seismic surveys he might conduct, the sonic blasts that would ripple through the earth, disturbing wildlife and potentially destabilizing the very ground beneath their feet. She pictured the massive pits dug into the hillsides, the scarred landscapes that would take generations, if ever, to recover. Her grandmother had always taught her that the earth was a living entity, deserving of respect and care. Vance's plans were a profound desecration of that sacred principle.

The weight of this knowledge pressed down on her, a suffocating burden. Vance was not an ally, not a fellow seeker of knowledge, but a wolf in sheep's clothing, his scientific jargon a sophisticated disguise for his avarice. Her initial hope that she could perhaps collaborate with him, that his expertise could be a force for good, had evaporated, replaced by a grim determination to expose him and protect her home.

She knew the whispers in town would only intensify as Vance's presence became more noticeable, his activities more overt. The community's inherent distrust of outsiders, coupled with their deep-seated connection to the land, made them acutely sensitive to the threat Vance represented. But their suspicion, while valuable, wasn't enough. Vance was cunning, and he would likely try to paint her as an obstacle to progress, a sentimental holdout against economic development. She had to gather more concrete evidence, to understand the full scope of his intentions and the specific dangers they posed.

Ellie returned to her grandmother's journals, her touch now firmer, more purposeful. She needed to find anything that might corroborate her suspicions, any mention of geological anomalies or unusual mineral findings that Vance might be exploiting. Her grandmother's knowledge, once a source of comfort and connection, was now her arsenal. Vance saw the plants as indicators; Ellie saw them as allies, silent witnesses to the earth's secrets, and perhaps, to Vance's predatory designs. The true fight, she understood, was not just against Vance, but against the forces of exploitation that threatened to consume the delicate beauty and resilience of the Hill Country. She had to become the voice for the earth that Vance sought to silence.

The air in the study, once a comforting balm of dried lavender and aged paper, now felt heavy, charged with the unspoken anxieties that Vance's visit had unearthed. Ellie paced, her bare feet tracing the familiar patterns on the worn floorboards, each creak a small protest against the insidious thoughts that had taken root. Vance, with his polished veneer and carefully curated scientific curiosity, had left behind a wake of unsettling implications. His polite inquiries, his seemingly innocuous observations about the resilience of local flora in the disturbed soil of the old quarry, had coalesced into a chilling tableau of impending destruction. Ellie now understood with a certainty that was both terrifying and galvanizing: Vance wasn't here to study the Hill Country; he was here to ravage it.

His "discovery" wasn't merely a mineral deposit; it was a lode of scandium, and his methods, hinted at in oblique but increasingly clear terms, promised a level of environmental devastation that made Ellie's stomach churn. Open-pit mining, chemical leaching – these were not practices of stewardship, but of conquest. Her grandmother, whose legacy was etched into the very soil and soul of Harmony Creek, had taught Ellie to listen to the earth, to understand its delicate balance and work in harmony with its cycles. Vance, on the other hand, saw the land as a resource to be exploited, its natural resilience merely an indicator of its mineral wealth. The plants that clung tenaciously to the quarry slopes, the wild thyme and hardy mint, were not symbols of nature's tenacity in his eyes, but markers on his geological map, signposts to the riches he intended to unearth.

Ellie found herself drawn back to her grandmother's desk, her fingers brushing over the smooth, time-worn oak. The journals, filled with meticulous observations of plant life, soil composition, and the subtle whispers of the earth, were more than just records; they were a testament to a life lived in deep reverence for the natural world. Vance, however, had twisted this legacy, viewing these detailed accounts not as a guide to understanding and nurturing, but as an accidental survey, a treasure map of elements waiting to be plundered. His questions about root depths, soil bacteria, and the very things that signaled a healthy, living ecosystem, were, in his rapacious view, clues to mineralized zones. The "subsurface anomalies" he'd spoken of with such detached interest were the vulnerabilities he intended to exploit.


The sheer scale of Vance's ambition, coupled with his utter disregard for the consequences, was staggering. Harmony Creek wasn't a wasteland awaiting industrialization; it was a vibrant tapestry of life, a fragile ecosystem that had sustained generations. The rolling hills, the clear, life-giving streams, the ancient, sheltering oaks – all were now imperiled by his avarice. Vance's vision for this place was one of scarred earth, poisoned waters, and an irrevocably altered landscape. His definition of progress was environmental annihilation. The thought sent a cold dread through Ellie, a visceral understanding of what was at stake. This wasn't just about family or reputation; it was about the very essence of Harmony Creek, its spirit, its soul.

She remembered Vance's particular interest in her grandmother's herbarium, the meticulously pressed and labeled specimens. He had feigned admiration for the breadth and diversity of the collection, but his true focus had been on the data, the ecological narrative each plant represented. He was a hunter, and the health of the ecosystem was merely collateral damage in his relentless pursuit of profit. The whispers that had circulated through town, initially perceived as personal attacks, now seemed to Ellie like an intuitive understanding of the threat Vance posed. The townsfolk, with their deep, abiding connection to the land, sensed the predator in their midst, even if they lacked the scientific vocabulary to articulate the danger.

A wave of anger washed over Ellie, directed as much at herself for her initial naivete as at Vance for his deception. She had been swayed by his polished exterior, his talk of scientific advancement, and in doing so, had become an unwitting facilitator of his destructive agenda. Her grandmother's wisdom, meant to foster life and healing, was being twisted into a tool for exploitation. The stark reality of what

Vance proposed – the deafening roar of heavy machinery, the chemical residue seeping into the groundwater, the permanent scarring of the hillsides – stood in chilling opposition to the gentle, sustainable existence her grandmother had embodied. Her grandmother's garden was a sanctuary; Vance's quarry would be a wound.

The task ahead seemed immense, an uphill battle against a man of resources and influence, driven by the insatiable engine of profit. The townsfolk, while inherently distrustful of outsiders, were also susceptible to the seductive promises of economic prosperity. Ellie, armed with little more than her grandmother's journals and a burgeoning resolve, knew she had to find a way to awaken them, to reveal the devastating truth of Vance's intentions. She picked up one of her grandmother's well-used trowels, its smooth wooden handle a tangible connection to a more grounded, respectful way of life. Looking out at the hills, which Vance saw as mere deposits, Ellie saw a living tapestry, a fragile ecosystem, a precious heritage. She was its unlikely guardian, and the time for passive observation was irrevocably over. The fight for Harmony Creek had begun. The depth of Vance's meticulous planning was becoming alarmingly clear. His inquiries were not random; they were akin to the precise probing of a skilled surgeon preparing for a radical, life-altering operation, identifying the vital organs slated for removal. He had probed about the water table near the quarry, not from an environmentalist's concern for the delicate aquatic life, but from a miner's pragmatic perspective on water management and the inherent risks of contamination during the extraction process. His questions regarding the stability of the soil on the quarry's periphery were equally telling, crucial data for planning excavation sites and assessing the potential for landslides — a risk he seemed prepared to accept as a calculated cost.

Ellie recalled a conversation that had seemed entirely innocuous at the time, a discussion about the most effective methods for composting, a topic deeply important to her as she strove to enrich her own depleted garden soil. Vance had listened with an almost unnerving intensity, nodding sagely as she elaborated on the critical importance of proper aeration and the indispensable role of specific microorganisms in the decomposition process. But then, he had subtly steered the discourse towards chemical soil amendments, inquiring about the feasibility and practicality of employing large-scale industrial composting techniques to effectively neutralize acidic conditions. Acidic conditions. The very conditions frequently associated with mineral-rich ore bodies and the subsequent leaching processes invariably employed to extract them. His interest, she now realized, was not in fostering the flourishing of her garden, but in understanding the intricate science of managing the chemical fallout that would inevitably accompany his proposed operations.

He had even, with a disarming subtlety, probed her knowledge of the region's geological history, inquiring whether there were any documented instances of unusual mineral findings in the area, any ancestral legends or anecdotal tales of strange rocks or deposits that might have surfaced over the generations. Ellie had recounted her grandmother's wistful stories about the "glimmering stones" discovered near the old creek bed following periods of heavy rainfall – small, metallic flecks that her grandmother had casually dismissed as nothing more than harmless mica. Vance's eyes had, at that moment, lit up with an unmistakable flicker of intense interest, a spark he had quickly, and almost too casually, masked with a dismissive shrug. Mica, indeed. He likely possessed the knowledge that those tiny flecks were far more than mere mica, that they were indicative of something far more valuable, something he had specifically come to excavate.

The chilling truth that solidified in Ellie's mind was that Vance was not merely prospecting for scandium; he was actively preparing to deploy aggressive, and potentially ruinous, mining techniques. The delicate Hill Country ecosystem, so remarkably resilient in its pristine, natural state, was demonstrably not equipped to withstand the brutal, unyielding onslaught of industrial-scale extraction. The specific geological makeup of the area, while potentially yielding a rich bounty of minerals, also rendered it inherently vulnerable to rampant erosion, widespread water contamination, and the irreversible destruction of its precious natural habitats. Vance's relentless pursuit of profit, she saw with stark clarity, was entirely divorced from any consideration whatsoever of the long-term ecological consequences. He perceived the land not as a living entity to be sustained and nurtured, but as a finite resource to be consumed with ruthless efficiency.

Ellie found herself conjuring images of the seismic surveys he might commission, the disorienting sonic blasts that would inevitably ripple through the earth, profoundly disturbing the local wildlife and potentially destabilizing the very ground beneath their feet. She pictured the colossal pits that would be carved into the hillsides, the resulting scarred landscapes that would undoubtedly require generations, if ever, to recover their former beauty and ecological integrity. Her grandmother had always instilled in her the profound understanding that the earth was a living, breathing entity, deserving of the utmost respect and meticulous care. Vance's audacious plans, in stark contrast, represented a profound desecration of that sacred, fundamental principle.

The immense weight of this burgeoning knowledge pressed down upon her, a suffocating burden that seemed to steal her breath. Vance was not an ally, not a fellow seeker of knowledge or a partner in understanding. He was, in essence, a predator cloaked in the guise of scientific respectability, his sophisticated scientific jargon serving as a cunning disguise for his insatiable avarice. Her initial hope that she might, in some capacity, collaborate with him, that his considerable expertise could be harnessed as a force for positive change, had utterly evaporated, replaced by a grim, unyielding determination to expose him and protect her beloved home.

She understood with absolute certainty that the whispers that had already begun to circulate through the town would only intensify as Vance's presence became more noticeable, his activities more overt and less easily concealed. The community's inherent, deeply ingrained distrust of outsiders, compounded by their profound, ancestral connection to the land, rendered them acutely sensitive to the palpable threat that Vance so clearly represented. However, she recognized that their suspicion, while valuable and deeply felt, was ultimately not enough. Vance was a man of considerable cunning and strategic acumen, and he would undoubtedly attempt to cast her as a recalcitrant obstacle to progress, a sentimental holdout clinging to the past, impeding much-needed economic development. She had to gather more concrete, irrefutable evidence, to fully comprehend the complete scope of his nefarious intentions and the specific, tangible dangers they posed to Harmony Creek.

Ellie returned to the sanctuary of her grandmother's journals, her touch now imbued with a firmer, more resolute purpose. She was driven by the urgent need to unearth anything that might corroborate her growing suspicions, any mention of geological anomalies or unusual mineral findings that Vance might be attempting to exploit for his own gain. Her grandmother's vast repository of knowledge, once a source of profound comfort and a deep sense of connection, was now her most potent arsenal. Vance perceived the plants as mere indicators; Ellie, with her newfound clarity, saw them as silent allies, unwavering witnesses to the earth's most profound secrets, and perhaps, to Vance's predatory designs. The true battle, she now understood with unwavering conviction, was not merely against Vance himself, but against the insidious forces of exploitation that threatened to irrevocably consume the delicate beauty and remarkable resilience of the Hill Country. She had to become the voice for the earth, a voice that Vance sought with all his might to silence.

# Chapter 4: The Approaching Storm

The horizon, usually a soft gradient of pale blue meeting the muted greens and browns of the Hill Country, began to bleed into a bruised, sickly yellow. It was a hue that Ellie had seen before, not in her lifetime, but in the sepia-toned photographs of her grandfather's youth, images that whispered of times when the sky itself had turned traitor. A tremor of unease, cold and sharp, snaked through her. The air, which had been merely heavy with the unspoken anxieties of Vance's visit, now took on a different texture. It grew gritty, an almost imperceptible abrasion against the skin, a harbinger of something far more substantial.

The wind, too, began to shift. It was no longer the gentle, teasing caress that rustled the leaves of the ancient oaks or carried the scent of wild sage across the meadows. This was a rising, insistent breath, starting as a low moan that wound its way through the eaves of the old farmhouse, a mournful sound that seemed to echo the disquiet in Ellie's own heart. It picked up pace, swirling dust devils in the yard, dancing with the dry, brittle stalks of last season's sorghum. These were not playful gusts; they were the first, angry breaths of a leviathan awakening.

Ellie stepped out onto the porch, drawn by an instinct she couldn't quite articulate. The sky, a mere hour ago, had held the promise of a clear, albeit tense, afternoon. Now, it was transforming with an alarming swiftness. The yellow deepened, taking on an ochre cast, then a menacing brown, as if the very earth were being lifted and hurled into the heavens. Far to the west, a smudge appeared, a stain against the rapidly darkening backdrop. It was a line, impossibly thin at first, then widening, solidifying, growing into a tangible entity. This was not a cloud in the conventional sense, not the fluffy white galleons that sailed across a benevolent blue. This was a wall.

A wall of earth. A black blizzard in the making.

The sheer scale of it was breathtaking, and terrifying. It stretched from one unseen end of the world to the other, a solid, impenetrable mass consuming the horizon. The setting sun, already low in the sky, was being devoured by it, its rays choked and distorted, casting an eerie, blood-red glow on the advancing front. The wind intensified, no longer a moan but a guttural roar, whipping Ellie's hair around her face, stinging her eyes with grit. She could feel the vibration of it in the floorboards beneath her feet, a deep, resonant hum that spoke of immense power.

Panic, sharp and primal, threatened to engulf her. This was the land fighting back, or perhaps, more accurately, the land's suffering made manifest. Vance's talk of mineral wealth, of extraction and profit, seemed pathetically small against the immensity of this unfolding spectacle. The delicate balance her grandmother had cherished, the intricate web of life that sustained Harmony Creek, was facing an onslaught far more devastating than she had yet imagined. Vance's destructive intentions, once a source of cold dread, now felt almost…contained, a man-made threat that could, perhaps, be countered. But this? This was a force of nature, indifferent to human plans and human desires, a wrathful consequence of imbalances far older than any mining operation.

She watched as the first tendrils of the storm reached the outermost fields. The dry soil, pulverized by years of inadequate farming practices, by a reliance on single crops and a disregard for the natural contours of the land, began to lift. It wasn't a gentle scattering; it was a violent upheaval. The air became thick, opaque, the familiar shapes of the landscape dissolving into a chaotic brown miasma. The wind howled, a banshee's cry, tearing at the few remaining leaves on the mesquite trees, ripping them free and flinging them into the churning void.

The town, usually a cluster of resilient structures against the open sky, was now being swallowed by the encroaching darkness. Ellie could almost feel the collective gasp of its inhabitants, the sudden, shared understanding that they were no longer masters of their domain, but subjects to a power far greater than themselves. The dust, fine and insidious, began to seep through the cracks and crevices of the house, a powdery invasion that no amount of sealing could entirely prevent. It coated the windows, blurring the already distorted view, transforming the familiar into something alien and menacing.

A profound sense of helplessness washed over Ellie. She thought of her grandmother, of her quiet strength, her unwavering belief in the earth's ability to heal. But even her grandmother, Ellie suspected, would have found this terrifying. This was not a gentle rain after a long drought, nor a cleansing fire that promised new growth. This was an annihilation, a scouring of the very soul of the land. It was the physical manifestation of the environmental sins being committed, not just here, in Harmony Creek, but across the vast agricultural plains of the nation. Vance's proposed scandium mine, with its inherent destruction, was but a single, concentrated wound on a body already suffering from a thousand cuts.

The storm's approach was a terrifyingly visceral reminder of the interconnectedness of all things. The health of the soil, the patterns of rainfall, the very air they breathed – all were intricately linked. And when one part of that delicate system was broken, the repercussions rippled outwards, manifesting in ways both subtle and catastrophic. Vance, in his pursuit of a rare earth mineral, was oblivious to the larger context, to the fragility of the systems he so carelessly intended to disrupt. He saw only the potential profit, the chemical compounds locked within the earth, and not the living ecosystem that harbored them.

Ellie's personal crisis, her fight against Vance and his destructive plans, felt both minuscule and profoundly significant against this backdrop. The storm was an overwhelming force, a symbol of the larger environmental battles being waged, a visual representation of the consequences of unchecked exploitation. It was a stark, unforgiving mirror reflecting the very dangers she was trying to prevent. If the land itself could be so easily ravaged by natural forces, what hope was there against the calculated, systematic destruction planned by men like Vance?

Yet, amidst the encroaching despair, a flicker of something else ignited within her. The storm, for all its terrifying power, was also a catalyst. It was a wake-up call, a brutal, undeniable demonstration of what was at stake. It stripped away the illusions, the polite veneer of progress, and revealed the raw, unforgiving reality of ecological imbalance. Perhaps, just perhaps, this very devastation would shock the people of Harmony Creek into recognizing the true nature of the threat they faced. Perhaps the sheer terror of the dust wall would be more persuasive than any of Ellie's carefully reasoned arguments.

She remembered her grandmother's words, spoken
not in fear, but in quiet wisdom: "The earth
remembers, Ellie. And sometimes, it shows us what
we have done." The dust storm was the earth
remembering, and its memory was a terrifying storm.

The wind shrieked, tearing at the porch roof, and the
grit intensified, making it hard to breathe. The
darkness was absolute now, a suffocating shroud
that had extinguished the last vestiges of daylight.
Ellie retreated inside, the door slamming shut behind
her with a boom that was quickly swallowed by the
roar of the wind. The house groaned, a living thing
under immense pressure. She stood in the semi-
darkness, the air thick with the taste of dust, her
mind a whirlwind of fear and a dawning, desperate
resolve. Vance's mine, if it proceeded, would scar
this land. But this storm, this elemental fury, was a
stark, terrifying preview of the kind of damage that
could be inflicted when the earth's intricate systems
were pushed too far. The approaching storm was not
just a natural disaster; it was a profound, terrifying
omen, a harbinger of the ecological reckoning that
Vance's ambition threatened to accelerate. The black

dust, clinging to everything, was a stark reminder of what lay beneath the surface, and what would be unleashed.

The roaring in Ellie's ears wasn't just the wind anymore. It was the amplified echo of her own dawning comprehension, a chilling certainty that settled into her bones with the same gritty persistence as the dust now coating every surface. Vance. The name itself, which had once held a sliver of hope, a potential lifeline for her family and Harmony Creek, now tasted like ash. He hadn't seen her as a partner, or even as a knowledgeable botanist with a deep understanding of this land. He'd seen her as a key, a conveniently placed piece on his vast, intricate chessboard, a piece he could maneuver with deceptive smiles and carefully chosen words.

Her botanical expertise, her intimate knowledge of the endemic flora, the delicate balance of the prairie ecosystem, the very things she believed were her strengths and her contribution to understanding the land – they had been nothing more than bait. Vance's interest in the rare lichen found only on the north-facing slopes, his inquiries about the specific root structures of the native grasses that held the soil together, his feigned admiration for her detailed field notes – it all clicked into place with a sickening lurch. He wasn't interested in preservation. He was interested in exploitation. He needed her knowledge to identify what was there, and perhaps more importantly, what wasn't, before his drills and explosives began their destructive work. He had used her understanding of the living, breathing systems of Harmony Creek to map out the veins of mineral wealth that lay dormant beneath.

The betrayal was a physical blow, stealing the air from her lungs just as effectively as the dust storm outside. She had opened her heart to him, shared her deepest concerns for the land, even confided in him about the precarious financial state of her family's farm. She had, in her naive hope, believed he understood. She had believed he shared, at least in part, her reverence for this place, her desire to see it thrive, not merely survive. How foolish she had been. Vance saw Harmony Creek not as a home, but as a resource. He saw its people not as stewards of the land, but as potential obstacles, or worse, as commodities themselves, to be managed and, if necessary, displaced.

His pronouncements about "progress" and "opportunity" were nothing but a thin veneer over a much more rapacious ambition. He wasn't here to build a better future for Harmony Creek; he was here to strip-mine it, to extract its wealth and leave behind a barren wasteland, indifferent to the consequences for the generations who would have to live with the scars. Her family, her neighbors, the very soil beneath their feet – they were all just pawns in his grander game, pieces to be moved, sacrificed, or eliminated as his strategy dictated. The scandium, the rare earth minerals he sought, were merely the prize, the ultimate objective for which he would readily shatter the delicate ecosystem she had dedicated her life to understanding and protecting.

The anger that surged through her was a wildfire, hot and uncontainable, a stark contrast to the cold dread that had permeated her before. It was the anger of being deceived, of being underestimated, of having her passion and knowledge twisted and used against the very things she held dear. Vance had played her, and he had done so with a chillingly effective blend of charm and deception. He had promised partnership while orchestrating conquest.

He had spoken of collaboration while planning annexation.

She recalled the conversation they'd had just days ago, standing by the very slopes where the lichen thrived. He'd spoken of a "symbiotic relationship," of his company's commitment to "responsible extraction." At the time, his words had resonated with a certain plausibility, a careful crafting of language designed to soothe anxieties. Now, they sounded hollow, manipulative. He had woven a narrative of shared goals, a tapestry of common interest, when in reality, he was merely laying the groundwork for his own unilateral appropriation. He had expertly exploited her desire to be heard, her yearning for support, and her deep-seated love for this land.

The dust storm raging outside seemed to mirror the turmoil within her. The land, under siege from the elements, was a stark parallel to how Vance intended to besieve it from within. If the earth could be so violently stripped bare by wind and grit, what chance did it have against the calculated, mechanized assault Vance planned? Her role, as he saw it, was to provide the intelligence, the ecological roadmap that would allow him to bypass the natural defenses of the land, to find the most efficient ways to exploit its hidden riches without undue delay. He didn't need her to protect the land; he needed her to help him dissect it.

A wave of nausea washed over her. She thought of her grandmother, and the stories she told of the land's resilience, its ability to heal and endure. But resilience had its limits, and Vance's intentions seemed designed to push those limits to their breaking point. He wasn't just a prospector; he was an invader, and she, in her earnestness, had inadvertently helped him scout the territory. The realization that she had, in some small way, facilitated his destructive agenda was almost as painful as the betrayal itself.

She felt a desperate need to reclaim her agency, to disentangle herself from the web Vance had spun. Her knowledge was hers, not his. Her love for Harmony Creek was a fierce, protective instinct, not a tool for corporate acquisition. He had treated her like an object, a resource to be mined for information, and now she had to prove him wrong. She had to show him that a pawn could, indeed, move independently, and that this pawn was preparing to strike back.

The implications of Vance's true intentions were vast, far beyond her immediate family or even Harmony Creek. The pattern he represented – the relentless pursuit of profit at the expense of ecological integrity – was a national, perhaps even global, phenomenon. His mining operation, if successful, would be a small but significant contribution to a much larger, more insidious form of environmental degradation. Her fight, which had felt so personal and localized, was now undeniably intertwined with a broader struggle for the health of the planet.

She clenched her fists, the grit between her fingers a tangible reminder of the forces at play. Vance had underestimated her. He had seen her scientific curiosity, her dedication to her work, as a weakness, a vulnerability he could exploit. But he was wrong. That same dedication, that same deep-seated love for the natural world, was now her greatest strength, her most potent weapon. The knowledge he had sought to extract from her was not merely data; it was an intimate understanding of the land's vulnerabilities, and, therefore, its potential defenses.

The storm outside was a terrifying omen, a visceral demonstration of the land's capacity for upheaval when its equilibrium was disturbed. It was a preview of the chaos that Vance's relentless extraction threatened to unleash, albeit on a different, more insidious scale. The dust, the wind, the encroaching darkness – they were all external manifestations of an imbalance that he intended to exacerbate with a calculated, man-made fury. He was not merely digging for minerals; he was disrupting a complex, interconnected web of life, a web that, once torn, might never be repaired.

Her mind raced, sifting through the discarded pieces of Vance's facade. He had been so careful, so practiced in his deception. But in his pursuit of profit, he had overlooked the most fundamental truth about the land: its inherent interconnectedness. He saw scandium; she saw the intricate dance of pollinators, the unseen work of soil microbes, the vital role of native grasses in preventing erosion. He saw a commodity; she saw a living system, a legacy.

The realization of her own culpability, however unwitting, fueled a new, fierce determination. She could not undo what had happened, the information she had shared, the trust she had placed. But she could control what happened next. Vance might have seen her as a pawn, but he was about to learn that even the smallest piece on the board could change the entire game. The betrayal was sharp, but the resolve it forged was sharper still. Harmony Creek, and the land it represented, deserved better than to be a mere stepping stone in Vance's rapacious ascent. She would not let him win. She would not be his pawn any longer. The time for understanding was over; the time for action had arrived. The storm outside was a prelude, and her response to Vance's treachery would be the storm's true reckoning.

The dust, a relentless shroud that had settled upon Harmony Creek, was more than just an inconvenience; it was a physical manifestation of the disquiet Eleanor felt, a gritty, tangible reminder of the storm brewing within her. Vance's betrayal had not just shattered her trust; it had ignited a fierce, protective fire, channeling her despair into a steely resolve. She wouldn't allow him to turn her knowledge, her very connection to this land, into a tool for its destruction. Instead, she would turn to the land itself, to the whispers and murmurs that had always been her truest companions.

Her grandmother's voice, a comforting melody often lost in the clamor of everyday life, now echoed with renewed clarity in her mind. "The land remembers, Eleanor," she'd often say, her weathered hands sifting through the rich, dark soil of their farm. "It remembers who respects it, and it remembers who tries to take more than they give." Eleanor had always understood these words on an emotional level, a poetic expression of stewardship. Now, she grasped their literal truth. The land held secrets, not just of where the scandium lay buried, but of its own intricate vulnerabilities and its deep reserves of resilience.

She closed her eyes, the cacophony of the wind outside fading as she delved into the silent archives of her own memory. She thought of the summer droughts, years when the sun seemed determined to bake the very life out of the prairie. It was during those desperate times that her grandmother had taught her about the hidden springs, the places where the earth's moisture stubbornly clung, sustained by deep aquifers impervious to the surface heat. These weren't marked on any map Vance would carry, no geological surveys would ever reveal them. They were known only to those who had learned to read the subtle language of the land: the particular shade of green in a patch of stunted grass, the way the air felt cooler in a certain depression, the presence of specific, drought-resistant wildflowers that signaled the proximity of life-giving water. She remembered tracing these hidden veins of life with her grandmother, learning to distinguish the subtle indicators, the silent promises of water hidden beneath the parched surface. These were not just sources of water; they were ecological anchors, vital to the delicate balance of the prairie ecosystem, points of refuge for countless species during times of extreme hardship. Vance's machines, designed for surface extraction, would likely never detect these subterranean lifelines, yet their very existence underscored the land's ability to sustain itself, to hold its own secrets close.

Then there were the soils themselves. Vance's surveys would focus on mineral content, on the composition of rock and sediment. But Eleanor's understanding went deeper, to the biological and hydrological properties of the earth. She recalled her studies of soil erosion, the devastating impact of disrupting the prairie's natural grass cover. The native bluestem and switchgrass, with their deep, interlocking root systems, acted like an intricate, living mesh, binding the soil particles together, preventing them from being swept away by wind and rain. Vance's proposed operations, with their heavy machinery and the inevitable disturbance of the topsoil, threatened to unravel this natural protection, leaving the land exposed and vulnerable. She remembered specific areas, particularly on the western slopes, where the soil was thinner, more prone to slumping after heavy rains. Her grandmother had always advised against disturbing those areas, pointing to the hardy little prairie roses and the tenacious yucca plants that managed to find purchase, their root systems designed to anchor themselves in even the most unstable ground. Vance's drills, however, would not discriminate. They would bore wherever the data indicated, heedless of the geological fragility.

Her mind drifted to the lichen Vance had shown such a keen interest in, the one that clung to the north-facing slopes. It wasn't just a rare biological specimen; it was an indicator species, its presence signaling a specific microclimate, a unique combination of shade, moisture, and substrate. But the land held other indicators, too. The flight patterns of certain migratory birds, the seasonal bloom of specific wildflowers, the behavior of the burrowing animals – all these were pieces of a larger puzzle, a complex ecological narrative that Vance was too focused on profit to truly comprehend. She recalled learning about the subtle shifts in the local flora that signaled changes in soil composition, or the presence of underground water tables. Certain sedges, for instance, thrived in areas where the soil retained a higher level of moisture, their presence acting as a visual cue for Eleanor, a natural flag marking the land's hidden hydration. Conversely, the dominance of plants adapted to arid conditions in areas that historically should have been wetter could indicate a deeper issue, a subterranean shift or a depletion of resources, knowledge that could be crucial in understanding the land's overall health and its capacity to withstand disturbance.

These weren't just academic observations; they were survival strategies, passed down through generations of farmers and ranchers who had learned to live in concert with the land, not in opposition to it. Her grandmother had taught her how to identify plants that indicated nutrient-rich soil, and others that signaled depleted or contaminated ground. She remembered mapping out, mentally and in faded field journals, the areas where the native flora flourished most vibrantly, and those where it struggled. These were the ecological fault lines, the places of greatest sensitivity, and paradoxically, of greatest resilience. The land, in its quiet way, was communicating its strengths and its weaknesses, offering up a blueprint for its own protection, a secret language only those attuned to its rhythms could understand.

She thought of the ancient cottonwood trees that dotted the creek beds, their massive root systems reaching deep into the earth, tapping into the water table and stabilizing the banks. Vance's plans might involve rerouting or damming parts of the creek, disrupting the natural flow that sustained these ancient sentinels. But even beyond the creeks, in the higher, drier prairies, there were pockets of resilience. Certain hardy grasses, with their extensive rhizome systems, could regrow even after being severely grazed or burned. Their ability to spread laterally, to find purchase and moisture even in seemingly barren ground, was a testament to the land's tenacious hold on life. Eleanor had spent countless hours observing these plants, documenting their growth patterns, understanding the conditions that allowed them to thrive. It was knowledge that Vance, with his focus on immediate, quantifiable mineral wealth, would likely overlook. He saw the surface, the easily accessible deposits, but he failed to grasp the intricate, interconnected web of life that supported it all, the ancient systems that had evolved over millennia to ensure the prairie's survival.

She remembered a particularly harsh winter, when a sudden thaw and subsequent deep freeze had left many of the shallow-rooted plants decimated. Yet, the native prairie grasses, with their deeper, more extensive root systems, had weathered the extreme conditions, their crowns protected beneath a blanket of snow. It was a powerful lesson in endurance, in the inherent strength of systems designed for longevity rather than immediate gratification. Vance's pursuit of scandium was precisely the opposite: a desire for immediate extraction, a disregard for the long-term health of the ecosystem.

The secrets she held were not just facts and figures; they were an intimacy, a lived experience of the land's cycles and its inherent wisdom. She knew where the best foraging grounds were for medicinal herbs, places where specific soil conditions nurtured their potent properties. She knew which slopes were most susceptible to landslides after heavy rainfall, and which ravines offered natural protection from the fiercest winds. These were not details that would be captured in a geological survey, but they were vital to understanding the land's true vulnerabilities.

The approaching storm, both literal and metaphorical, forced her to confront the magnitude of what Vance intended. It wasn't just about one mining operation; it was about the unraveling of an entire ecosystem, the silencing of a millennia-old conversation between the earth and its inhabitants. But as the wind howled outside, Eleanor found a profound sense of calm settling within her. The land, her silent ally, was not a passive victim. It had endured droughts, fires, and blizzards. It had its own ways of resisting, its own secrets for survival. And she, Eleanor Vance, would be its voice, its protector, armed not with drills and explosives, but with the deep, abiding knowledge of its heart. She would use the very secrets Vance had sought to exploit to confound him, to remind him that the land was not merely a resource to be plundered, but a living, breathing entity with a will of its own. Her grandmother's words returned, a beacon in the encroaching darkness: "Listen to the land, Eleanor. It will always show you the way." And Eleanor was listening, more intently than ever before.

The air in the Harmony Creek Chronicle office was thick with the scent of aging paper, stale ink, and something vaguely metallic, a perfume of perpetually published news. Dust motes danced in the shafts of late afternoon sunlight that slanted through the grimy windowpanes, illuminating stacks of newspapers that threatened to spill from every surface. Old files, their manila folders brittle and yellowed, were piled high on the desk, beside a clattering, ink-stained printing press that seemed to breathe with a life of its own. This was Mr. Abernathy's domain, a testament to years of chronicling the comings and goings of Harmony Creek, a quiet but formidable bastion of local history.

Eleanor stepped over a precariously balanced tower of yesterday's editions, her boots crunching on scattered newsprint. She clutched her worn leather-bound notebook, its pages filled with her meticulous observations, close to her chest. She knew Mr. Abernathy. He was a man who valued facts, verifiable truths, and had a healthy aversion to sensationalism. His skepticism was a shield, forged from years of wading through the exaggerated claims and unfounded rumors that often found their way into print. He'd likely see her, a young woman whose family had recently suffered a public disgrace, as just another voice crying wolf.

"Mr. Abernathy?" she called out, her voice carrying a tremor she couldn't quite suppress.

A head, topped with a receding halo of grey hair, emerged from behind a towering stack of what looked like bound volumes of the Chronicle's own past. His spectacles, perched precariously on the end of his nose, magnified his tired eyes. He peered at her over the rims, his expression a carefully cultivated neutrality that revealed nothing.

"Yes?" His voice was a low rumble, accustomed to projecting over the din of the press.

"My name is Eleanor Vance. I… I need to speak with you about something urgent."

He gestured vaguely towards a rickety wooden chair on the opposite side of his desk, its cushion flattened by years of occupancy. "Take a seat, Miss Vance. Though I must confess, my schedule is rather packed. Deadlines, you understand." He returned to his work, shuffling papers with a deliberate slowness, his attention seemingly riveted to the printed word.

Eleanor sat, the chair groaning in protest. She could feel his gaze, a steady, assessing pressure, even as he pretended to focus on his tasks. She took a deep breath, recalling her grandmother's advice: "When you need to be heard, Eleanor, speak from your heart, but arm yourself with the truth."

"It's about Mr. Sterling Vance's proposed mining operation," she began, her voice gaining a touch more conviction. "And the potential impact on Harmony Creek."

Mr. Abernathy's hands stilled. He slowly looked up, his expression shifting from feigned indifference to something more akin to mild curiosity, tinged with that familiar skepticism. "Sterling Vance? The gentleman who's recently acquired a rather substantial parcel of land out by the old Miller farm?"

"Yes, that's him. He's… he's planning to mine for scandium. And he's been very dismissive of the environmental concerns."

He leaned back in his chair, the springs creaking under his weight. He folded his hands across his stomach, a classic posture of polite dismissal. "Well now, Miss Vance, I've heard a fair bit of chatter about Mr. Vance. Seems like a man with a vision. And mining, well, that's been a part of Harmony Creek's history, hasn't it? We had the coal mines, back in the day. Brought prosperity, didn't it?"

"This is different, Mr. Abernathy. This isn't just about digging for coal. His operation… it's going to be massive. And he's not being transparent about the risks." Eleanor's frustration was beginning to bubble. She'd expected this, but it still stung.

"Risks, you say?" He steepled his fingers, his gaze unwavering. "What kind of risks are we talking about? Environmental impact studies are standard practice, I assume. Mr. Vance seems like a man who knows his business."

"He knows his business, yes, but he's not sharing the full picture. The scandium is found in a very specific type of shale, and disturbing it could have catastrophic consequences for the groundwater. Not to mention the impact on the prairie ecosystem." Eleanor opened her notebook, her fingers tracing over her diagrams and notes. "My grandmother, she was a botanist and a deeply knowledgeable farmer. She taught me about the interconnectedness of this land. She taught me how the native grasses, with their deep root systems, hold the soil in place. She taught me about the hidden springs, the delicate balance of the aquifers that feed our wells."

Mr. Abernathy remained impassive, his silence a subtle challenge.

"He plans to use heavy machinery, large-scale excavation. The dust alone will be a problem, but that's the least of it. He's overlooking the fragility of the soil in certain areas, particularly on the western slopes where erosion is already a concern. My grandmother mapped those areas, marked them as sensitive. His drills will disturb that, and the rain will wash it all away, carrying sediment into the creek, into our water supply." Eleanor's voice was gaining passion now, the words tumbling out faster. She flipped to a page with detailed sketches of plant roots. "These aren't just pretty flowers, Mr. Abernathy. This little prairie rose, and the yucca plant? Their roots are essential for anchoring the soil on those slopes. Vance's machines won't care. They'll just dig."

He leaned forward slightly, a flicker of interest in his eyes. "You seem to know a great deal about the land, Miss Vance."

"I've learned from the best," she said, meeting his gaze directly. "My grandmother, and the land itself. It communicates, Mr. Abernathy. It tells you where it's strong, and where it's vulnerable. And Mr. Vance is choosing to ignore those warnings." She pointed to another section of her notebook. "He's particularly interested in a certain lichen, one that grows on the north-facing slopes. It's an indicator species, yes, it tells him about the microclimate. But there are other indicators. The flight patterns of migratory birds, the seasonal bloom of specific wildflowers, even the behavior of burrowing animals – they all tell a story. And Mr. Vance, in his pursuit of profit, is deaf to it all."

She could see him weighing her words, his ingrained skepticism battling with a dawning curiosity. He picked up a pencil, tapping it against his desk. "So, you're saying Mr. Vance's operation, if undertaken carelessly, could contaminate the water table and cause significant soil erosion. And you have evidence of this… delicate balance, as you call it?"

"I have my grandmother's research, her field journals. And I have my own observations. I've spent years walking this land, learning its secrets. I know where the springs are that aren't on any map, where the soil is thin and prone to slumping. I know which plants signal good soil and which signal depleted or contaminated ground. This isn't guesswork, Mr. Abernathy. This is ecological knowledge, passed down and observed firsthand." Eleanor's voice was firm, unwavering. She was no longer just a desperate young woman; she was a witness.

He leaned back again, his gaze drifting to the window, as if seeking answers in the fading sunlight. "Mr. Vance is a respected businessman, Miss Vance. He's invested heavily in this community. He's promising jobs, economic growth."

"At what cost?" Eleanor pressed. "Jobs that will be temporary, if the land is poisoned? Growth that will be short-lived if it destroys the very foundation of our community – our water, our soil?" She took a breath, trying to control the rising tide of emotion. "He plans to reroute parts of Harmony Creek, to dam sections for his water supply. Those old cottonwood trees by the creek beds, their root systems are vital for preventing bank erosion. Disturbing them, altering the creek's flow… it's a reckless gamble."

Mr. Abernathy's eyes narrowed slightly. He picked up a well-worn copy of the Chronicle, flipping through its pages. "I've always believed in reporting the facts, Miss Vance. And the facts, as I understand them, are that Mr. Vance is bringing investment and opportunity to Harmony Creek. Your… theories, while compelling, lack concrete proof that would stand up to public scrutiny. I can't just print accusations without substantial evidence."

"The evidence is in the land itself!" Eleanor exclaimed, her voice rising. "It's in the way the grass grows, the way the water flows. It's in my grandmother's meticulous notes. I have proof of the soil composition in certain areas, its susceptibility to erosion. I have documentation of the specific flora that indicates the health of the water table. I'm not asking you to print accusations. I'm asking you to investigate, to send someone out there with an open mind, someone who understands that the land has a language, if you're willing to listen."

She slid her notebook across the desk. "These are my grandmother's findings, cross-referenced with my own. I can show you the specific locations. I can take you to the places where the prairie roses grip the soil, where the yucca stands firm. I can show you where the lichen thrives, but also where other, more sensitive plants struggle because of changes in the soil that your geological surveys might miss."

Mr. Abernathy's fingers brushed against the worn leather of the notebook. He didn't pick it up, but his gaze lingered on it, a silent acknowledgment of the effort she had put forth. He finally looked back at her, his expression thoughtful. "You're very passionate about this, Miss Vance. And you've clearly put a lot of thought into it."

"It's not just passion, Mr. Abernathy," Eleanor said, her voice softening but losing none of its intensity. "It's a sense of responsibility. My family has been connected to this land for generations. We've learned to respect it, to work with it. Mr. Vance sees it as a resource to be exploited. I see it as a living system that needs to be protected. And if I don't speak up, who will?"

He picked up a pencil and a fresh pad of paper. "Alright, Miss Vance. Tell me more about these 'hidden springs.' And these 'indicator species.' Perhaps you can explain them in a way that a layman, someone who hasn't spent years deciphering the whispers of the prairie, can understand." He gestured for her to continue, his skepticism still present, but now laced with a grudging respect. The dusty office, usually a place of quiet pronouncements, now held a fragile tension, the nascent spark of an investigation ignited by a young woman's fierce conviction and the undeniable wisdom of the land itself. Eleanor began to speak, her voice steady, weaving a narrative of ecological interdependence, of the land's quiet resilience, and the looming threat of its potential destruction. She would make him listen. She had to.

The air in the Chronicle office, once merely thick with the scent of paper and ink, now vibrated with an almost palpable tension. The late afternoon sun, which had earlier cast shafts of golden light, had been swallowed by a bruised, purpling sky. Outside, the wind had begun its mournful song, a low moan that escalated into a guttural howl, rattling the windowpanes like insistent, unseen knuckles. Eleanor, her heart hammering a frantic rhythm against her ribs, felt a primal fear, a recognition of nature's immense, indifferent power. This wasn't just a storm; it was a harbinger, a force that could either sweep away the truth or bury it forever.

"Mr. Abernathy," she began, her voice tight, "the sky… it's turning. That's not just a thundercloud; that's a wall of dust. It's coming faster than I thought." She glanced back at the window, her eyes scanning the horizon with a mixture of dread and urgency. The familiar, placid landscape of Harmony Creek was rapidly transforming, a vast, ochre smear blotting out the distant fields.

Abernathy, his usual placid demeanor replaced by a grim focus, stood by the window, his spectacles glinting in the dim light. He'd pushed aside the papers, the clattering press momentarily forgotten. The notebook Eleanor had left on his desk lay open, its pages filled with her grandmother's precise script and her own earnest annotations. He'd spent the last hour absorbed in it, his skepticism slowly eroding with each carefully documented observation, each sketch of root systems and fragile soil strata.

"You're right, Eleanor," he said, his voice low and grave. "This is worse than the forecasts predicted. A severe one. And if it hits with the force you're describing, it could be days before anything is visible again, let alone passable." He turned from the window, his gaze locking with hers, the weight of their shared concern settling between them. "We're not just racing against Sterling Vance now. We're racing against the elements."

The urgency was no longer a mere concept; it was a physical presence, a tightening in the chest, a quickening of the pulse. The land that Eleanor held so dear was under siege, not just from Vance's machinery, but from this primal force of nature. And Vance, oblivious or perhaps dismissive of the impending fury, was likely pressing forward with his plans, his bulldozers and drills deafening to the world's subtle warnings.

"We have to act now," Eleanor stated, her resolve hardening. "If that dust storm hits before we can alert people, before we can present what we have… it will all be for nothing. The evidence could be buried, literally. And people will be trapped, cut off. They won't hear about the dangers." She thought of her neighbors, the families who relied on the creek, who farmed the land that Vance so carelessly intended to desecrate. They deserved to know.

Abernathy nodded, a decisive movement that banished any lingering indecision. "The Chronicle has a responsibility, Eleanor. A greater one than I've perhaps acknowledged until today. My instinct is to verify, to be cautious. But sometimes, caution can be a luxury we cannot afford." He gestured to the notebook. "Your grandmother's work, combined with your own observations, presents a compelling, even alarming, picture. It's not just theory; it's a deeply rooted understanding of this place."

He walked over to a large, old map of Harmony Creek county tacked to the wall, its edges frayed and yellowed. He pointed to the area around the old Miller farm, Vance's proposed mining site. "This land… it's always been considered stable, if a little unforgiving. But your notes about the specific shale formations, the water table… and the sensitivity of those western slopes… it paints a different story. A story of vulnerability."

"Vulnerability that Vance is actively exploiting," Eleanor added, her voice laced with a bitterness that surprised even herself. "He sees dollar signs, Mr. Abernathy. He doesn't see the ancient prairie grasses that bind the soil, the delicate network of roots that prevent erosion. He doesn't see the aquifer that sustains us all." She thought of the specific lichen her grandmother had documented, a tiny organism that thrived only under precise conditions, a sentinel of the ecological health of the region. Vance's drills, indiscriminate in their pursuit, would likely obliterate

it, along with the very conditions that allowed it to
flourish.

"My immediate thought is to get this information
out to the community," Abernathy said, his mind
already working through the logistics. "We need to
print a special edition, an emergency bulletin. But
with this storm… getting it distributed will be a
challenge."

"We can't wait for the press to run," Eleanor
insisted, the wind outside reaching a new crescendo,
a shriek that seemed to pierce the very walls of the
building. "We need to go door-to-door, as many
people as we can reach before the worst of it hits.
We need to warn them directly. We need to tell them
to protect their wells, to consider what Vance is
planning, to look at the evidence themselves."

Abernathy looked at the darkening sky, then at
Eleanor, a flicker of admiration in his eyes. She was
not the timid young woman who had first entered
his office. The weight of her knowledge, the fierce
protection she felt for the land, had forged a new

strength in her. "You're right. The printed word is important, but immediate action might be even more so. The Chronicle can be a signal fire, but we need people to see it before the inferno."

He moved with a sudden, unexpected briskness, pulling out drawers, gathering supplies. "I'll need to get the most crucial information from your notes — the specifics about the water contamination, the erosion risks, the location of those sensitive areas. We'll need to condense it, make it clear and understandable for everyone." He grabbed a ream of paper, a few extra ink pens, and a worn canvas satchel.

"I can help with that," Eleanor said, already pulling out her notebook, her fingers flying across the pages, highlighting key passages, sketching quick diagrams to accompany the text. She knew precisely which of her grandmother's entries were most critical, which observations would carry the most weight with the practical farmers and residents of Harmony Creek.

"We'll also need to contact Mayor Thompson,"

Abernathy continued, his brow furrowed in thought. "He needs to be made aware. And Sheriff Brody. If Vance is truly acting without proper oversight, then the authorities need to be involved. But with this storm, reaching them… it will be difficult."

"I can try to reach Sheriff Brody's office," Eleanor offered. "I know Deputy Miller; he's usually at the station house until dusk. If I can get there, perhaps I can leave a message, or even speak with him directly if he's still on duty." The thought of venturing out into the rapidly deteriorating weather sent a shiver down her spine, but the stakes were too high to hesitate.

Abernathy's gaze softened. "You're willing to go out there? Eleanor, it's dangerous. That wind… the visibility will drop to near zero before long."

"It's more dangerous to do nothing," she replied, her voice firm. "My grandmother always said that true courage wasn't the absence of fear, but the willingness to act in spite of it. And right now, this land needs someone to act." She clasped her notebook tighter, a quiet determination settling on her features. "I know these roads, even in the dark. And I believe Deputy Miller will listen. He's always struck me as a man who cares about this community."

Abernathy considered her for a moment, then nodded slowly. "Very well. I'll focus on preparing a summary for distribution, and I'll try to get a message to the Mayor. You do what you can with Sheriff Brody. And Eleanor," he met her gaze, his eyes earnest, "be careful. This is more than just a storm; it's a fight, and it's just beginning."

As Eleanor stepped out of the relative quiet of the Chronicle office, the full force of the approaching storm slammed into her. The wind, now a solid, roaring entity, tore at her clothes, whipping dust and debris into her face. The sky had turned an angry, uniform brown, the sun utterly extinguished. Visibility was already dropping, the familiar landmarks of Harmony Creek dissolving into a hazy, swirling chaos. She pulled her scarf tighter, shielding her face as best she could, and began to walk, her steps measured against the growing fury of the elements. Each gust was a reminder of the limited time they had, a stark testament to the race against time that had begun in earnest.

She thought of Vance, likely still sheltered in his temporary accommodations, unconcerned by the encroaching darkness. He saw the storm as an inconvenience; she saw it as a critical, dangerous ally to her cause, a factor that could either disrupt or accelerate their efforts. The dust, the grit, the sheer overwhelming force of it all was a tangible manifestation of the forces she was up against. But it was also a symbol of the land's own power, a power that Vance had underestimated, a power that she and Abernathy were now trying to harness, to wield as a shield for Harmony Creek.

Her grandmother's voice echoed in her mind, not with words of caution, but with a steady, unwavering resolve.
*"The land remembers, Eleanor. And it can teach."* She needed that memory, that teaching, to guide her now. She needed the resilience of the prairie grasses, the deep-rooted strength of the cottonwoods, to

fortify her own spirit against the daunting task
ahead.

As she navigated the increasingly treacherous streets,
the wind buffeting her, threatening to knock her off
her feet, Eleanor understood the true meaning of
Abernathy's earlier words. This was no longer just
about presenting evidence; it was about awakening a
community. It was about rallying them to protect
their shared home before it was irrevocably
damaged. The storm was a ticking clock, but it was
also a catalyst, a dramatic unveiling of the
precariousness of their existence, a stark illustration
of how quickly things could be lost.

She reached the Sheriff's office, a small, unassuming
building that seemed to shrink under the immense
power of the wind. Inside, the air was cooler, thick
with the smell of coffee and the low murmur of the
radio. Deputy Miller, a burly man with a kind face,
looked up from his desk, a flicker of surprise
crossing his features as he saw her battered
appearance.

"Miss Vance! What in tarnation are you doing out in this?" he exclaimed, rising from his chair.

"Deputy Miller, sir," Eleanor began, her voice still ragged, "I need to report something… something urgent about Mr. Sterling Vance's proposed mining operation. And I need to warn everyone I can before this storm truly settles in." She quickly explained the essence of her findings, Abernathy's agreement, and the critical need for immediate awareness. She presented a few key passages from her notebook, focusing on the most immediate threats to their water supply and soil stability.

Deputy Miller listened intently, his initial surprise giving way to a growing concern. He recognized the seriousness in Eleanor's demeanor, the palpable fear and determination that radiated from her. He also knew her family, and respected the Vance name, but he also knew Eleanor, and the meticulous nature of her late grandmother.

"Vance's operation, you say? And potential

contamination?" Miller echoed, rubbing his chin thoughtfully. "I've heard some talk, but nothing concrete. Sterling Vance has been putting out a good word, talking about jobs, progress."

"He's hiding the risks, sir," Eleanor pressed, her voice gaining strength. "He's ignoring the ecological impact. And this storm… it could be a disaster if people aren't prepared, if they don't know what he's really planning to do to the land."

Miller glanced at the window, where the fury of the wind was now a visible spectacle of swirling dust. "You're right about that storm, Miss Vance. It's coming on fast. I can radio the Sheriff, but he's out on the county line and might not get through. And getting any kind of warning out to the outlying farms will be near impossible once this hits." He looked back at Eleanor, a decision forming in his eyes. "Tell you what. I've got a couple of extra flyers Abernathy's boys put out last week about community safety. I'll jot down the most critical points from what you've told me, as a supplement. I'll also make sure the Sheriff knows the moment he checks in."

He quickly scribbled a concise summary of Vance's plans and the potential environmental dangers onto a piece of paper, appending it to the existing safety notices. "Take these," he said, handing Eleanor a small stack. "Go to the homes closest to you, hand them out. Knock on doors. Make sure people see them. The Chronicle office is your best bet for getting wider distribution if you can make it back before the worst."

Eleanor took the flyers, her heart filled with a renewed sense of purpose. It wasn't as comprehensive as she'd hoped, but it was a start. Every piece of information, every informed resident, was a step in the right direction. As she left the Sheriff's office, the wind seemed to press in on her, a tangible adversary. The dust was now so thick that the world outside was reduced to a matter of feet.

She clutched the flyers, her breath coming in ragged gasps, and turned towards the nearest cluster of houses. The race against time had not only begun; it was now being fought in the heart of the storm, a desperate scramble against the encroaching darkness and the destructive power of both man and nature. The fate of Harmony Creek rested on these frantic moments, on the courage of a few to speak out against overwhelming odds, and on the willingness of its people to listen before the truth, like the land itself, was buried beneath a rising tide of dust. Abernathy was back at the Chronicle, preparing to ignite his own beacon of truth, while Eleanor, a lone figure against the tempest, became a messenger of warning, a harbinger of the fight to come.

# Chapter 5: The Eye of the Storm

The wind was no longer a mournful song; it was a banshee's shriek, clawing at the Chronicle building, each gust a violent tremor that seemed to shake the very foundations of Harmony Creek. Eleanor, her face still grimy from the initial foray into the street, felt a desperate urgency settle deep in her bones. Abernathy, his usually stoic demeanor etched with a new, almost feverish intensity, was meticulously sifting through the contents of her grandmother's old leather-bound journals, his fingers tracing the faded ink with a reverence that belied the dire circumstances. The meticulously drawn cross-sections of shale deposits, the detailed notes on water tables, and the precise descriptions of the unique soil composition were now more than just historical curiosities; they were the bedrock of their counter-offensive.

"This section, Eleanor," Abernathy murmured, his voice nearly lost in the rising cacophony outside, "your grandmother's observations on the porosity of the 'Whispering Shale' formation. She noted how it could leach minerals into groundwater under stress. Combined with your own findings about the proximity of the aquifer to Vance's proposed drilling sites…" He trailed off, shaking his head. "It's damning. Truly damning."

Eleanor leaned closer, her gaze fixed on the elegant, yet precise, script. Her grandmother, Clara Vance – no relation to Sterling, a fact that often caused mild confusion – had possessed an almost preternatural understanding of this land. Her decades of study weren't just academic; they were an intimate conversation with the earth, a deciphering of its subtle language. Eleanor felt a pang of guilt, a sense of inadequacy, as she tried to match her own more recent, frantic observations to Clara's profound, long-term understanding. But her grandmother's legacy was their weapon, a carefully curated arsenal of facts against Sterling Vance's brute-force ambition.

"And these sketches," Eleanor pointed to a series of delicate drawings depicting the root structures of native prairie grasses. "She documented how they held the topsoil even on these steeper slopes. Without them, the erosion will be catastrophic, especially after a disruption like Vance's machinery." She recalled her own walk to the Sheriff's office, the way the wind had already begun to whip the dust into blinding sheets. She'd seen firsthand how fragile the exposed earth already was in places where Vance's preliminary surveying had cleared away the native vegetation.

Abernathy carefully dog-eared a page. "We need more. We need something tangible, something that directly contradicts Vance's assurances about minimal impact. He's been circulating pamphlets, painting a rosy picture of economic prosperity, of responsible extraction. We need to show the reality." His eyes, usually filled with the quiet calm of a seasoned editor, now held a spark of dangerous excitement, the thrill of a journalist on the cusp of a major expose.

"The survey sites," Eleanor said, her mind racing. "Vance's crew has been working near the old quarry, and along the ridge that overlooks Willow Creek. My grandmother marked those areas as particularly sensitive. The shale there is… I don't know how to describe it, it seems almost… brittle." She remembered her grandmother's frustration with official geological surveys that treated all shale formations as monolithic. Clara had insisted on the subtle, crucial differences, the variations in composition that dictated their behavior under stress.

"Brittle is precisely what we need to document," Abernathy declared, his decision made. He pulled a large, folded map of the county from his desk, its creases worn deep from frequent use. "If we can get samples from those specific areas, juxtapose them with your grandmother's analysis and our own observations of Vance's activities… it could be enough. Enough to make people stop and think. Enough to galvanize opposition before the storm makes any further investigation impossible."

The wind outside intensified, a low rumble building into a thunderous roar. Rain began to lash against the windows, not in individual drops, but in solid sheets, blurring the already obscured view. The air inside the office grew heavy, charged with an unspoken dread. The storm was no longer a distant threat; it was an encroaching presence, a physical manifestation of the forces they were up against, both natural and man-made.

"It's dangerous, Mr. Abernathy," Eleanor cautioned, her voice barely a whisper. "The wind… it's already picking up. And with Vance's men likely still out there, working as long as they can before the worst of it hits…"

"Precisely," Abernathy interrupted, his gaze unwavering. "That's our window. They'll be focused on securing their equipment, on getting back to their temporary camp. They might not be paying as close attention to anyone else venturing out. And in this weather, any unauthorized presence will be quickly dismissed as someone trying to secure their own property." He began gathering a small collection of sturdy canvas bags, a trowel, and a geologist's hammer that Eleanor recognized from her grandmother's old field kit.

"We'll need to be quick, and we'll need to be unseen," Abernathy continued, his voice low and steady. "I'll take the lead. You guide me to the most critical locations based on your grandmother's notes and your own reconnaissance." He paused, meeting

Eleanor's eyes. "Are you ready for this, Eleanor? This is no longer just about reporting. This is about direct action. It's about putting ourselves at risk to uncover the truth."

Eleanor felt a surge of adrenaline, a potent mix of fear and determination. The image of her grandmother, a woman of fierce intellect and unwavering conviction, flashed in her mind. She'd often spoken of the land's silent pleas, of the responsibility of those who understood to speak for it. This was that moment. "I'm ready, Mr. Abernathy," she affirmed, her voice gaining a newfound strength. "For Harmony Creek. For my grandmother."

They stepped out into the maelstrom. The wind immediately assailed them, a solid wall of air that tore at their clothes and buffeted their bodies. The rain, driven by the gale, stung their faces like a thousand tiny needles. Visibility was reduced to mere yards, the landscape dissolving into a chaotic blur of churning earth and water. Abernathy, surprisingly agile for his age, kept a steady pace, his eyes scanning the ground, his movements purposeful. Eleanor, clutching her grandmother's notebook tightly, navigated them through the increasingly treacherous terrain, her knowledge of the local paths, even in these dire conditions, proving invaluable.

Their first objective was a survey marker Abernathy had spotted during his earlier scouting, located near a section of the ridge Clara Vance had described as having "unusually friable shale." As they approached, the wind seemed to intensify, funnelling through the gullies and ravines, creating a terrifying symphony of howling sounds. Through the sheeting rain, Eleanor could make out the faint, metallic glint of the marker. Nearby, several deep gouges in the earth indicated where Vance's equipment had recently been.

"Here," Abernathy breathed, his voice strained against the wind. "This is it." He produced the trowel and began to carefully excavate the soil around the marker. Eleanor, her gloved hands clumsy in the driving wind, knelt beside him, trying to shield the immediate area from the rain. The earth here was strangely loose, a fine, gritty silt that seemed to crumble at the slightest touch.

"My grandmother noted this specific stratum," Eleanor recalled, flipping through the notebook with frantic speed. "She called it 'paper shale.' She theorized it was highly susceptible to water infiltration and could destabilize significant sections of the hillside if disturbed." She found the relevant passage, a detailed sketch of the shale layers with annotations about its potential for 'calving' or sloughing off. "Look," she pointed to the exposed earth, where thin, almost papery layers of rock were visible, already beginning to soften and disintegrate under the onslaught of the rain.

Abernathy carefully chipped away a sample, placing it into one of the canvas bags. "This is good, Eleanor. Very good. It directly contradicts Vance's claim that his operations will only disturb 'competent rock formations'." He bagged the sample, his movements efficient and precise. "Now, for the Willow Creek area. Your grandmother mentioned a specific concern about the water table there, didn't she?"

Their journey to Willow Creek was even more harrowing. The terrain was steeper, the wind more unpredictable, and the ground slick with mud and debris. They had to use trees and outcroppings for support, inching their way forward with agonizing slowness. As they drew closer to the creek, they could hear the unmistakable roar of Vance's machinery, even above the storm's fury. They were working late, pushing the boundaries of what was safe, driven by a desperate need to complete their task.

Peeking through a screen of dripping branches, Eleanor and Abernathy saw them: a crew of Vance's men, their faces illuminated by the harsh glare of portable floodlights, operating a large drilling rig. The drill bit plunged deep into the earth, sending up plumes of muddy water and rock fragments. Eleanor's heart sank. The site was perilously close to the creek bed, much closer than any responsible operation would allow, especially given the known vulnerabilities of the local geology.

"They're drilling directly into the saturated zone,"

Abernathy whispered, his voice laced with disbelief and a growing anger. "The water table. Eleanor, look at the discharge. It's not just water; there are visible sediment and… is that oil?"

Eleanor squinted, her eyes straining in the dim light. Indeed, a dark, viscous substance was swirling in the water being pumped from the drill site, mixing with the runoff from the rain-soaked earth, and flowing directly towards Willow Creek. "My grandmother tested samples from this creek years ago," she said, her voice trembling. "She found traces of naturally occurring heavy metals, but nothing like this. This looks like a contaminant."

Suddenly, a rough voice cut through the din. "Hold up, boys! Vance wants us to secure the boreholes for the night. Storm's getting too bad."

Abernathy and Eleanor instinctively ducked lower, pressing themselves against the wet earth, the sound of their own ragged breaths seeming deafening. They watched as the drill rig was partially covered with a tarp, and the men began to pack up their portable lights. As they moved away, one of the workers muttered, loud enough for Eleanor and Abernathy to hear, "This whole operation feels wrong. Vance keeps saying there's no risk to the water, but look at this muck coming out. It stinks."

This was it. Direct evidence, not just from her grandmother's historical records and her own observations, but from the very men employed by Sterling Vance. The overheard conversation, combined with the visual evidence of the contaminated discharge, was invaluable. Abernathy, with practiced stealth, edged closer to the abandoned drill site, his trowel in hand. He carefully scooped up a sample of the oily residue pooling near the borehole, along with some of the surrounding mud. The task was fraught with danger; one wrong move, one stray beam of light, and they could be discovered. The knowledge that Vance's men were armed and likely not inclined to gentle persuasion added a potent layer of fear to their already perilous undertaking.

As Abernathy worked, Eleanor kept watch, her eyes scanning the darkness, her ears straining to detect any approaching sounds over the roar of the storm. The wind was a constant threat, whipping debris into their faces and making it difficult to maintain their footing. The rain had turned the ground into a slick, muddy morass, threatening to swallow their footprints. Yet, the urgency of their mission, the sheer weight of the evidence they were gathering, fueled their resolve.

Once Abernathy had secured the samples, they began their treacherous journey back to the Chronicle office. Each step was a struggle against the elements, a testament to their commitment. The samples, carefully sealed in their bags, felt like heavy weights, not just in their hands, but in their conscience. They represented not just geological data, but the potential ruin of Harmony Creek's water supply, the desecration of land that had been nurtured for generations.

Back in the relative safety of the Chronicle office, the air thick with the smell of damp paper and Abernathy's strong coffee, they laid out their findings. The brittle shale, the oily residue, the documented proximity of the drilling to Willow

Creek – it was a potent, damning collection. Abernathy carefully photographed each sample, meticulously labeling them with the location and date. Eleanor, her hands still trembling slightly, transcribed her grandmother's relevant passages into a separate notebook, creating a clear, undeniable link between historical understanding and present danger.

"This is what we needed, Eleanor," Abernathy said, his voice filled with a quiet triumph that resonated through the small office. "This isn't just speculation anymore. This is concrete proof. Vance can't spin this away. He can't dismiss it as 'emotional objections' or 'misinformation' when we have this – the physical evidence of his negligence, and the historical understanding of
*why* it's so dangerous." He looked at the samples, then at Eleanor, his eyes conveying a deep respect. "We've gathered the evidence. Now, we have to get it to the people, before this storm buries it, and us, along with it." The storm outside continued to rage, a relentless reminder of the ticking clock, but within the Chronicle office, a different kind of storm was brewing, one of truth and awakening, fueled by courage and the silent testimony of the land itself.

The biting wind, a banshee's shriek now, clawed at the Chronicle's windows, each gust a violent tremor that seemed to shake the very foundations of Harmony Creek. Eleanor, her face still grimy from her earlier foray into the streets, felt a desperate urgency settle deep in her bones. Abernathy, his usually stoic demeanor etched with a new, almost feverish intensity, was meticulously sifting through the contents of her grandmother's old leather-bound journals, his fingers tracing the faded ink with a reverence that belied the dire circumstances. The meticulously drawn cross-sections of shale deposits, the detailed notes on water tables, and the precise descriptions of the unique soil composition were now more than just historical curiosities; they were the bedrock of their counter-offensive. "This section, Eleanor," Abernathy murmured, his voice nearly lost in the rising cacophony outside, "your grandmother's observations on the porosity of the 'Whispering Shale' formation. She noted how it could leach minerals into groundwater under stress. Combined with your own findings about the proximity of the aquifer to Vance's proposed drilling sites…" He trailed off, shaking his head. "It's damning. Truly damning." Eleanor leaned closer, her gaze fixed on the elegant, yet precise, script. Her grandmother, Clara Vance – no relation to Sterling, a fact that often caused mild confusion – had possessed an almost preternatural understanding of this land. Her decades of study weren't just academic; they were an intimate conversation with the earth, a deciphering of its subtle language. Eleanor felt a pang of guilt, a sense of inadequacy, as she tried to match her own more recent, frantic observations to Clara's profound, long-term understanding. But her grandmother's legacy was their weapon, a carefully curated arsenal of facts against Sterling Vance's brute-force ambition. "And these sketches," Eleanor pointed to a series of delicate drawings depicting the root structures of native prairie grasses. "She documented how they held the topsoil even on these steeper slopes. Without them, the erosion will be catastrophic, especially after a disruption like Vance's machinery." She recalled her own walk to the Sheriff's office, the way the wind had already begun to whip the dust into blinding sheets. She'd seen firsthand how fragile the exposed earth already was in places where Vance's preliminary surveying had cleared away the native vegetation.

Abernathy carefully dog-eared a page. "We need more. We need something tangible, something that directly contradicts Vance's assurances about minimal impact. He's been circulating pamphlets, painting a rosy picture of economic prosperity, of responsible extraction. We need to show the reality." His eyes, usually filled with the quiet calm of a seasoned editor, now held a spark of dangerous excitement, the thrill of a journalist on the cusp of a major exposé. "The survey sites," Eleanor said, her mind racing. "Vance's crew has been working near the old quarry, and along the ridge that overlooks Willow Creek. My grandmother marked those areas as particularly sensitive. The shale there is… I don't know how to describe it, it seems almost… brittle." She remembered her grandmother's frustration with official geological surveys that treated all shale formations as monolithic. Clara had insisted on the subtle, crucial differences, the variations in composition that dictated their behavior under stress. "Brittle is precisely what we need to document," Abernathy declared, his decision made. He pulled a large, folded map of the county from his desk, its creases worn deep from frequent use. "If we can get samples from those specific areas, juxtapose them with your grandmother's analysis and our own observations of Vance's activities… it could be enough. Enough to make people stop and think. Enough to galvanize opposition before the storm makes any further investigation impossible."

The wind outside intensified, a low rumble building into a thunderous roar. Rain began to lash against the windows, not in individual drops, but in solid sheets, blurring the already obscured view. The air inside the office grew heavy, charged with an unspoken dread. The storm was no longer a distant threat; it was an encroaching presence, a physical manifestation of the forces they were up against, both natural and man-made. "It's dangerous, Mr. Abernathy," Eleanor cautioned, her voice barely a whisper. "The wind… it's already picking up. And with Vance's men likely still out there, working as long as they can before the worst of it hits…" "Precisely," Abernathy interrupted, his gaze unwavering. "That's our window. They'll be focused on securing their equipment, on getting back to their temporary camp. They might not be paying as close attention to anyone else venturing out. And in this weather, any unauthorized presence will be quickly dismissed as someone trying to secure their own property." He began gathering a small collection of sturdy canvas bags, a trowel, and a geologist's hammer that Eleanor recognized from her grandmother's old field kit. "We'll need to be quick, and we'll need to be unseen," Abernathy continued, his voice low and steady. "I'll take the lead. You guide me to the most critical locations based on your grandmother's notes and your own reconnaissance." He paused, meeting Eleanor's eyes. "Are you ready for this, Eleanor? This is no longer just about reporting. This is about direct action. It's about putting ourselves at risk to uncover the truth." Eleanor felt a surge of adrenaline, a potent mix of fear and determination. The image of her grandmother, a woman of fierce intellect and unwavering conviction, flashed in her mind. She'd often spoken of the land's silent pleas, of the responsibility of those who understood to speak for it. This was that moment. "I'm ready, Mr. Abernathy," she affirmed, her voice gaining a newfound strength. "For Harmony Creek. For my grandmother."

They stepped out into the maelstrom. The wind immediately assailed them, a solid wall of air that tore at their clothes and buffeted their bodies. The rain, driven by the gale, stung their faces like a thousand tiny needles. Visibility was reduced to mere yards, the landscape dissolving into a chaotic blur of churning earth and water. Abernathy, surprisingly agile for his age, kept a steady pace, his eyes scanning the ground, his movements purposeful. Eleanor, clutching her grandmother's notebook tightly, navigated them through the increasingly treacherous terrain, her knowledge of the local paths, even in these dire conditions, proving invaluable. Their first objective was a survey marker Abernathy had spotted during his earlier scouting, located near a section of the ridge Clara Vance had described as having "unusually friable shale." As they approached, the wind seemed to intensify, funnelling through the gullies and ravines, creating a terrifying symphony of howling sounds. Through the sheeting rain, Eleanor could make out the faint, metallic glint of the marker. Nearby, several deep gouges in the earth indicated where Vance's equipment had recently been. "Here," Abernathy breathed, his voice strained against the wind. "This is it." He produced the trowel and began to carefully excavate the soil around the marker. Eleanor, her gloved hands clumsy in the driving wind, knelt beside him, trying to shield the immediate area from the rain. The earth here was strangely loose, a fine, gritty silt that seemed to crumble at the slightest touch. "My grandmother noted this specific stratum," Eleanor recalled, flipping through the notebook with frantic speed. "She called it 'paper shale.' She theorized it was highly susceptible to water infiltration and could destabilize significant sections of the hillside if disturbed." She found the relevant passage, a detailed sketch of the shale layers with annotations about its potential for 'calving' or sloughing off. "Look," she pointed to the exposed earth, where thin, almost papery layers of rock were visible, already beginning to soften and disintegrate under the onslaught of the rain. Abernathy carefully chipped away a sample, placing it into one of the canvas bags. "This is good, Eleanor. Very good. It directly contradicts Vance's claim that his operations will only disturb 'competent rock formations'." He bagged the sample, his movements efficient and precise. "Now, for the Willow Creek area. Your grandmother mentioned a specific concern about the water table there, didn't she?"

Their journey to Willow Creek was even more harrowing. The terrain was steeper, the wind more unpredictable, and the ground slick with mud and debris. They had to use trees and outcroppings for support, inching their way forward with agonizing slowness. As they drew closer to the creek, they could hear the unmistakable roar of Vance's machinery, even above the storm's fury. They were working late, pushing the boundaries of what was safe, driven by a desperate need to complete their task. Peeking through a screen of dripping branches, Eleanor and Abernathy saw them: a crew of Vance's men, their faces illuminated by the harsh glare of portable floodlights, operating a large drilling rig. The drill bit plunged deep into the earth, sending up plumes of muddy water and rock fragments. Eleanor's heart sank. The site was perilously close to the creek bed, much closer than any responsible operation would allow, especially given the known vulnerabilities of the local geology. "They're drilling directly into the saturated zone," Abernathy whispered, his voice laced with disbelief and a growing anger. "The water table. Eleanor, look at the discharge. It's not just water; there are visible sediment and… is that oil?" Eleanor squinted, her eyes straining in the dim light. Indeed, a dark, viscous substance was swirling in the water being pumped from the drill site, mixing with the runoff from the rain-soaked earth, and flowing directly towards Willow Creek. "My grandmother tested samples from this creek years ago," she said, her voice trembling. "She found traces of naturally occurring heavy metals, but nothing like this. This looks like a contaminant." Suddenly, a rough voice cut through the din. "Hold up, boys! Vance wants us to secure the boreholes for the night. Storm's getting too bad." Abernathy and Eleanor instinctively ducked lower, pressing themselves against the wet earth, the sound of their own ragged breaths seeming deafening. They watched as the drill rig was partially covered with a tarp, and the men began to pack up their portable lights. As they moved away, one of the workers muttered, loud enough for Eleanor and Abernathy to hear, "This whole operation feels wrong. Vance keeps saying there's no risk to the water, but look at this muck coming out. It stinks."

This was it. Direct evidence, not just from her grandmother's historical records and her own observations, but from the very men employed by Sterling Vance. The overheard conversation, combined with the visual evidence of the contaminated discharge, was invaluable. Abernathy, with practiced stealth, edged closer to the abandoned drill site, his trowel in hand. He carefully scooped up a sample of the oily residue pooling near the borehole, along with some of the surrounding mud. The task was fraught with danger; one wrong move, one stray beam of light, and they could be discovered. The knowledge that Vance's men were armed and likely not inclined to gentle persuasion added a potent layer of fear to their already perilous undertaking. As Abernathy worked, Eleanor kept watch, her eyes scanning the darkness, her ears straining to detect any approaching sounds over the roar of the storm. The wind was a constant threat, whipping debris into their faces and making it difficult to maintain their footing. The rain had turned the ground into a slick, muddy morass, threatening to swallow their footprints. Yet, the urgency of their mission, the sheer weight of the evidence they were gathering, fueled their resolve. Once Abernathy had secured the samples, they began their treacherous journey back to the Chronicle office. Each step was a struggle against the elements, a testament to their commitment. The samples, carefully sealed in their bags, felt like heavy weights, not just in their hands, but in their conscience. They represented not just geological data, but the potential ruin of Harmony Creek's water supply, the desecration of land that had been nurtured for generations.

Back in the relative safety of the Chronicle office, the air thick with the smell of damp paper and Abernathy's strong coffee, they laid out their findings. The brittle shale, the oily residue, the

documented proximity of the drilling to Willow Creek – it was a potent, damning collection. Abernathy carefully photographed each sample, meticulously labeling them with the location and date. Eleanor, her hands still trembling slightly, transcribed her grandmother's relevant passages into a separate notebook, creating a clear, undeniable link between historical understanding and present danger. "This is what we needed, Eleanor," Abernathy said, his voice filled with a quiet triumph that resonated through the small office. "This isn't just speculation anymore. This is concrete proof. Vance can't spin this away. He can't dismiss it as 'emotional objections' or 'misinformation' when we have this – the physical evidence of his negligence, and the historical understanding of
*why* it's so dangerous." He looked at the samples, then at Eleanor, his eyes conveying a deep respect. "We've gathered the evidence. Now, we have to get it to the people, before this storm buries it, and us, along with it."

The storm outside continued to rage, a relentless reminder of the ticking clock, but within the Chronicle office, a different kind of storm was brewing, one of truth and awakening, fueled by courage and the silent testimony of the land itself.

Abernathy, his fingers flying across the typewriter, began to craft the exposé. The ink flowed like a river, carrying with it the weight of generations, the wisdom of Clara Vance, and the tangible evidence of Sterling Vance's reckless ambition. He knew the power of the press in Harmony Creek; it was more than just a source of news, it was the community's conscience, a beacon in the often-murky waters of progress. A single, well-crafted article in the Chronicle could ripple through the town, igniting conversations, sparking questions, and, most importantly, awakening the collective will of the people. Vance, with his smooth pronouncements and carefully constructed veneer of progress, had underestimated the enduring strength of local journalism, and more importantly, the deep-seated connection the people of Harmony Creek felt to their land. He had spoken of prosperity, of jobs, of a brighter future, but his words were like chaff in the wind compared to the solid, undeniable truths Eleanor and Abernathy had unearthed. The exposé wouldn't just detail the geological dangers; it would dissect Vance's manipulative tactics. It would remind the drought-stricken community of their hard-won resilience, the quiet strength they had always possessed, and highlight how Vance was exploiting their desperation for his own gain. The articles would paint a stark contrast: Vance's promises of progress against the grim reality of the contaminated discharge, his assurances of minimal impact against the visual evidence of drilling too close to vital water sources, his claims of responsible extraction against the very samples Abernathy held in his hands. The narrative Abernathy intended to weave would be one of stewardship versus exploitation, of community well-being versus corporate greed. He would draw parallels between Vance's current actions and historical instances where unchecked industrial ambition had scarred the landscape and poisoned communities, painting Vance not as a visionary, but as a predator, a speculator whose only true concern was profit, regardless of the cost to the land or its people. Abernathy's prose was sharp, incisive, and imbued with a quiet fury. He didn't shy away from the technical details – the 'Whispering Shale,' its porosity, its potential for leaching – but he translated them into language that any resident of Harmony Creek could understand. He described how the very earth, weakened by drought and now threatened by Vance's drills, could crumble and wash away, carrying with it the poisons of the industry. He spoke of Willow Creek, the lifeblood of the valley, now visibly tainted, its future uncertain. The article would be a testament to Eleanor's grandmother's legacy, weaving her scientific observations seamlessly with the immediate, alarming evidence gathered under the cover of the storm. Abernathy understood that Vance's power lay in his ability to control the narrative, to present a polished, reassuring image to the outside world and to the less informed members of the community. His exposé would be a direct assault on that carefully constructed facade, a mirror held up to Vance's true intentions. The newspaper, the Chronicle, was more than just paper and ink; it was a voice for the voiceless, a platform for dissent, and in that era, a powerful tool for galvanizing public opinion. In a time before widespread television and instant communication, local newspapers served as the primary conduit for information and the central forum for community debate. A story placed in the Chronicle could shape perceptions, influence decisions, and ultimately, mobilize action. Abernathy, a seasoned journalist who had seen the impact of his words firsthand, knew that this article had the potential to be a turning point. He would strategically detail the environmental risks, presenting them not as abstract scientific theories, but as tangible threats to the wells that supplied water to their homes, the creeks where their children fished, and the soil that sustained their farms. He would highlight Vance's disregard for the very community he claimed to be helping, portraying him as an outsider who saw Harmony Creek not as a home, but as a resource to be plundered.

The article would meticulously detail how Vance had deliberately targeted areas with known geological instabilities, information that he likely possessed but chose to ignore in his pursuit of profit. Eleanor's grandmother's research, proving the fragility of the shale and its proximity to crucial water systems, would be presented as definitive proof of Vance's calculated risk-taking. The journalist would emphasize the irony of Vance's public pronouncements about bringing prosperity to a drought-stricken region, juxtaposed with the very real threat of contaminating their already scarce water resources. The exposé would likely include a verbatim account of the overheard conversation among Vance's workers, lending an almost eyewitness quality to the report and further undermining Vance's carefully crafted image. The mention of the oily residue, a visible sign of contamination flowing directly into Willow Creek, would be described with stark clarity, leaving no room for interpretation or denial. Abernathy planned to run a series of photographs, painstakingly taken by himself and Eleanor, that would visually corroborate the written accounts – the crumbly, paper-like shale, the dark, viscous ooze near the drill site, the precarious proximity of the operation to the creek itself. These images, more than any words, would speak to the heart of the matter, illustrating the destructive reality beneath Vance's smooth promises. The power of the press, in these days, was a palpable force. A front-page story in the Chronicle could reach every household, sparking hushed conversations around kitchen tables and heated debates in the general store. It could turn neighbors against Vance's venture, fostering a sense of shared purpose and collective action. Abernathy aimed to ensure that the people of Harmony Creek understood that their very way of life was at stake, that Vance's drilling was not just a commercial enterprise, but an existential threat to their land, their water, and their future. He would implore the citizens to look beyond Vance's silver tongue and recognize the truth that lay beneath the surface, a truth unearthed by diligent research, brave investigation, and the unwavering commitment of a local newspaper dedicated to serving its community. The article would be a call to arms, a plea for the community to stand together, to demand accountability, and to protect the precious resources that had sustained them for generations. Abernathy knew that the storm outside was a formidable adversary, capable of obscuring roads and isolating communities, but he also understood that the storm of public opinion, once unleashed by the truth, could be far more powerful and far more difficult for Sterling Vance to weather. The exposé would be published not just as a news report, but as a historical document, a testament to the enduring power of truth and the vital role of a free press in safeguarding the well-being of a community. He envisioned the reactions: the dawning realization on farmers' faces as they read about potential groundwater contamination, the concern from mothers whose children played by Willow Creek, the anger from those who felt deceived by Vance's promises. This wasn't just about reporting a story; it was about awakening a community to the dangers it faced and empowering them to act. Abernathy meticulously reviewed the layout, imagining the headlines, the bold typeface that would grab attention, the placement of the photographs that would shock and inform. He saw the article as a weapon, honed by evidence and sharpened by truth, ready to be deployed against the encroaching threat. He knew Vance would fight back, would issue denials and threats, but Abernathy was prepared. He had the truth on his side, and in the quiet heart of Harmony Creek, that was a force to be reckoned with. He imagined Eleanor reading the published article, her grandmother's legacy finally brought to light, her efforts vindicated. The thought fueled his determination. Vance's smooth facade was about to be peeled back, layer by layer, revealing the ruthless speculator beneath, a man who saw the land not as a living entity to be cherished, but as a commodity to be exploited, a resource to be drained for personal gain. Abernathy's exposé would shatter that illusion, exposing the true, destructive nature of Vance's geological ambitions and, he hoped, turning the tide of public opinion irrevocably against him. The storm outside, though fierce, was merely a prelude to the tempest that would soon erupt in the pages of the Chronicle, a tempest of truth that could either save Harmony Creek or leave it irrevocably scarred.

The Chronicle office, usually a quiet sanctuary of ink and thought, now crackled with a palpable energy, a shared unease that seemed to seep from the pages of Abernathy's latest draft. Eleanor, her earlier exhilaration from their clandestine mission muted by the storm's relentless assault, watched as Abernathy worked. He wasn't just typing; he was weaving a narrative, a tapestry of facts and warnings that would soon be unfurled before the eyes of Harmony Creek. The storm outside, a deafening roar of wind and rain, had become a physical manifestation of the turmoil brewing within the community. Every gust that rattled the windows felt like a tremor of anticipation, a harbinger of the reckoning to come. The carefully gathered samples, the damning photographs, Abernathy's incisive prose – they were the ammunition in a battle for the soul of their valley. But as Abernathy's words took shape, Eleanor felt a growing awareness that the real fight wasn't just against Sterling Vance and his despoiling machinery; it was against the apathy, the fear, and the desperation that had made many in Harmony Creek so susceptible to Vance's promises in the first place.

The storm had done more than just obscure the landscape and make their investigative journey perilous; it had also amplified the whispers that had been circulating through Harmony Creek for weeks. What began as hushed rumors about Vance's drilling operation, dismissed by many as just another boom-and-bust cycle, had begun to coalesce into a tangible dread. Ellie's warnings, once brushed aside as the ramblings of an overly concerned young woman, now echoed in the minds of those who had heard her speak at the town hall meeting. People who had initially been swayed by Vance's talk of jobs and prosperity, of a lifeline in these hardscrabble times, were now starting to question the cost. The memory of the drought, the parched fields, the worry lines etched on their neighbors' faces — it all made them vulnerable. Vance had tapped into that vulnerability, offering a seemingly simple solution, a way out of their persistent struggles. But Eleanor knew, and Abernathy's meticulous work was proving, that Vance's solution was a poison disguised as a cure.

As Abernathy continued to type, the clatter of the keys a steady counterpoint to the storm's fury, Eleanor imagined the scenes playing out across Harmony Creek. She pictured farmers, their hands calloused from years of coaxing life from recalcitrant soil, their faces etched with the same weariness she saw in her own reflection, reading the Chronicle's front page. She envisioned the shopkeepers, their livelihoods precarious, their hopes for a stable future pinned on the land's bounty, poring over the words with growing alarm. And she thought of her grandmother, Clara Vance, her dedication to understanding this land, her quiet strength. Clara had understood that the true wealth of Harmony Creek lay not in what could be extracted from its depths, but in the health of its soil, the purity of its water, and the resilience of its ecosystem. Vance, in his relentless pursuit of profit, seemed to see only the former, blind to the irreparable damage he was inflicting.

The storm served as a brutal, undeniable reminder of the land's power, and its fragility. It had amplified the concerns about Vance's operations, transforming abstract fears into concrete anxieties. The very earth, so recently dry and cracked, was now being churned and disturbed by heavy machinery, its delicate balance threatened. Eleanor remembered her grandmother's impassioned lectures about the interconnectedness of all things in the valley – how the prairie grasses held the soil, how the creeks fed the aquifers, how the very rock formations dictated the flow of water. Vance's operations, tearing at the earth's surface and probing its depths, threatened to unravel this intricate web, with consequences that would extend far beyond the immediate drilling sites.

The initial dismissiveness that had greeted Ellie's concerns was slowly eroding, replaced by a collective apprehension. The townspeople, initially divided by Vance's promises and their own desperate hopes, were beginning to find common ground in their shared fear. The overheard conversation of Vance's own workers, captured by Abernathy and Eleanor, had been a critical turning point. The casual admission of unease, the acknowledgment of the "muck" and the "wrongness" of the operation, had lent a human voice to the growing unease. It was no longer just an abstract environmental concern; it was a tangible, visible problem, one that even the men on Vance's payroll couldn't entirely ignore.

Eleanor felt a profound sense of responsibility settling upon her shoulders. The legacy of her grandmother, a woman who had dedicated her life to understanding and protecting this land, now rested heavily upon her. Abernathy's exposé, she knew, was not merely a journalistic endeavor; it was a continuation of that legacy, a defense of the valley's inherent value against the forces of exploitation. The article would serve as a beacon, illuminating the hidden dangers and reminding the community of what they stood to lose. It would be a testament to the fact that true prosperity was not measured in dollars extracted, but in the sustained health and vitality of their home.

The wind howled, a mournful lament that seemed to echo the unspoken fears of Harmony Creek. Rain lashed against the windows of the Chronicle, each droplet a tiny hammer blow against the fragile peace Vance had attempted to impose with his promises. Inside, however, a different kind of force was at work – the force of truth, painstakingly gathered and eloquently presented. Abernathy's typing became more urgent, his fingers flying with a renewed sense of purpose. He knew that the window of opportunity was closing. The storm, while perilous for their investigation, was also the very thing that could galvanize the community. It made the abstract threat of environmental damage visceral, immediate, and undeniable. Vance had gambled that the drought would make the people of Harmony Creek desperate enough to accept any solution, no matter the cost. He had underestimated the deep, abiding love and respect the community held for their land, a love that had been nurtured over generations. He had also underestimated the power of a free press, of a dedicated journalist, and of a young woman determined to honor her grandmother's memory.

The growing unease within Harmony Creek was more than just a reaction to the encroaching storm or the revelations in the Chronicle; it was a deep-seated anxiety about the future, a fear that their way of life, so intrinsically tied to the land, was being irrevocably altered. The drought had already tested their resilience, forcing them to adapt, to conserve, to hope against hope. Vance's drilling, however, presented a different kind of threat — one that was not simply a matter of waiting for the rains to return, but of actively confronting a force that sought to undermine the very foundations of their existence. Ellie's warnings about the "paper shale" and its susceptibility to water infiltration, once dismissed as technical jargon, were now being replayed in the minds of farmers and ranchers who understood the implications for their well water, for the health of their livestock, and for the long-term stability of the land itself.

The evidence Abernathy and Eleanor had gathered was not merely scientific data; it was a narrative of neglect and potential devastation. The samples of brittle shale, the visual proof of oily discharge flowing into Willow Creek, the overheard conversations of Vance's disgruntled workers — these were pieces of a larger story, a story of corporate ambition trampling over community well-being. The Chronicle, in publishing Abernathy's exposé, was not just reporting the news; it was serving as the community's conscience, a voice for the land that could not speak for itself. Vance had attempted to control the narrative, to paint a picture of progress and prosperity, but the truth, as unearthed by Eleanor and Abernathy, was far more sinister. His actions were not about bringing prosperity; they were about extracting wealth, regardless of the environmental and social cost.

The community's unease was a collective awakening, a slow dawning of realization that the sacrifices they had made during the drought had not prepared them for this particular threat. This was not a natural disaster to be weathered, but a man-made danger to be confronted. The storm, in its ferocity, had stripped away any lingering complacency, forcing the residents to confront the harsh realities of Vance's operations. The carefully constructed facade of corporate responsibility was beginning to crack, revealing the predatory nature of Vance's enterprise.

The conversations happening around Harmony Creek were no longer about the weather, but about the future of their valley, about the legacy they would leave for their children, and about the fundamental right to a clean environment and a healthy way of life.

The growing apprehension was fueled by a deep understanding of the land, an intimate knowledge passed down through generations. Farmers knew how easily the topsoil could erode, how vital the watershed was, and how interconnected the ecosystem truly was. Vance's assurances of minimal impact were met with skepticism born of experience. They knew that disturbing the earth, especially the fragile shale formations Eleanor had documented, would inevitably have consequences. The drought had made them acutely aware of the preciousness of water, and the sight of oily residue flowing into Willow Creek was not just an environmental concern; it was a profound violation, a direct threat to their very survival. The whispers had indeed turned into worried conversations, and the skepticism had given way to a shared, palpable concern. The storm had washed away the pretense, exposing the raw vulnerability of Harmony Creek to the destructive ambition of Sterling Vance. The community was no longer merely a passive observer; it was beginning to stir, to question, and to recognize the grave danger that lay dormant beneath the surface, waiting to be unleashed. Eleanor felt a surge of hope amidst the dread. This dawning awareness, this collective unease, was the first step toward resistance, toward protecting the land they loved. The Chronicle would be the spark that ignited the flame of community action, transforming apprehension into a force for change. The storm outside, though fearsome, was a catalyst, an amplifier of the truth that Abernathy was now so meticulously laying bare. Harmony Creek was on the cusp of a profound reckoning, and the storm, in its own wild way, was helping to bring it about. The people of Harmony Creek were beginning to understand that their resilience, forged in the crucible of the Depression and the drought, would now be tested in a far more dangerous arena – one where the battle was not just for survival, but for the very soul of their home. Vance's project was no longer an abstract promise of progress, but a concrete threat, and the community's unease was the first tremor of a coming earthquake.

Vance paced the confines of his temporary office, a hastily erected structure of corrugated metal and salvaged lumber that offered little respite from the storm's encroaching symphony of chaos. Each gust of wind that buffeted the flimsy walls seemed to carry with it the mocking laughter of the valley itself, a sound that grated on his nerves with increasing intensity. The meticulously crafted edifice of his ambition, built on a foundation of empty promises and veiled threats, was showing alarming cracks. Abernathy's continued diligence at the Chronicle, coupled with Eleanor's relentless pursuit of the truth, had become more than an annoyance; they were a tangible threat, a corrosive agent eating away at the carefully constructed illusion of legitimacy he had so painstakingly cultivated. He slammed his fist against a steel filing cabinet, the metallic clang swallowed by the tempest's roar. The samples they'd managed to procure, the damning photographs of the oily sheen on Willow Creek, the overheard conversations – each piece of evidence was a barb, embedding itself deeper into the fabric of his control.

His usual veneer of cool, calculated authority was beginning to fray, revealing the volatile core of a man who had always equated power with brute force and unyielding will. He had anticipated resistance, of course. He'd factored in the predictable hand-wringing of a few sentimental fools clinging to their agrarian past. But he hadn't accounted for the quiet persistence of Abernathy, nor the unexpected fire in young Eleanor's eyes. They were an unforeseen variable, a glitch in his otherwise flawless algorithm of acquisition and exploitation. He'd expected the drought to soften them, to make them pliable, desperate for any lifeline. He'd expected the storm to further isolate them, to sow seeds of fear and dampen any nascent spirit of defiance. Instead, it seemed to have acted as a catalyst, a fierce herald of the very truths he sought to bury.

He grabbed a half-empty bottle of whiskey from his desk, the amber liquid sloshing precariously as he took a long, hard swallow. The burn did little to quell the simmering rage that threatened to consume him. His meticulously laid plans, his projections, his financial backing — all of it was now at risk. He had promised his investors a swift and profitable extraction, a tidy sum before any serious scrutiny could take hold. Abernathy's exposé, if it gained traction, would mean delays, investigations, and a host of inconvenient questions that could unravel the entire venture. The paper shale, that treacherous, easily destabilized stratum he was so keen to exploit, was also his undoing. Any significant water infiltration, any prolonged period of saturation caused by this infernal storm, could compromise the structural integrity of his drilling sites, rendering them unusable, dangerous, or at the very least, prohibitively expensive to maintain.

A sudden, violent gust of wind tore at the canvas flap of the office entrance, momentarily revealing the heaving, rain-lashed landscape beyond. It was a stark, unforgiving tableau, a mirror of the chaos raging within Vance himself. He could almost feel the earth groaning under the strain of the storm, a primal sound that resonated with his own internal turmoil. He saw Eleanor, her face etched with grim determination, handing Abernathy another batch of notes, her voice, though unheard over the wind, somehow projecting a quiet conviction. He saw the faces of the farmers, their earlier hopefulness curdled into suspicion, their eyes mirroring the anxious clouds overhead. They were beginning to understand. That was the most infuriating realization of all. They were beginning to connect the dots, to see the oily residue not as an anomaly, but as a symptom of a deeper sickness.

Desperation gnawed at him, a cold, sharp hunger that demanded to be fed. He couldn't afford to wait for the storm to pass, for the dust to settle. He had to act, decisively and ruthlessly. The window of opportunity was closing, not just because of Abernathy's words, but because of the very elements themselves. He needed to accelerate his operations, to push through the critical phases before the full weight of public opinion, amplified by Abernathy's damning report, could crush him. He needed to solidify his position, to make the damage irreversible, to present the community with a fait accompli.

He reached for the heavy-duty radio, its dial glowing ominously in the dim light. "Get me the foreman at Site Three," he barked into the microphone, his voice tight with suppressed fury. "Tell him to double the crew. I want full twenty-four-hour drilling. No breaks, no delays. And get me security detail down to the Chronicle. I want eyes on Abernathy and that girl, Eleanor. Discreetly, mind you. No heavy-handedness. Just… keep them occupied. Find a way to slow them down." He paused, the static on the line a crackle of his own frayed nerves. "And if any of those samples are still accessible, any of them… make them disappear. Quietly."

His order was not born of reasoned strategy, but of raw, unadulterated panic. He was a cornered animal, lashing out at the perceived threats that sought to expose his predatory nature. He had always operated under the assumption that money and influence could bend any situation to his will, that the desperation of others was a lever to be exploited. He had never truly comprehended the power of conviction, the quiet strength of a community bound by shared values and a love for their land. He saw their adherence to principles as a weakness, their connection to the soil as a quaint anachronism. Now, those very qualities were proving to be his undoing.

He imagined Abernathy, hunched over his typewriter, his brow furrowed in concentration, translating the raw data into a narrative that would resonate with the people of Harmony Creek. He pictured Eleanor, perhaps poring over geological maps, her young mind piecing together the intricate, fragile ecosystem that he was so carelessly disrupting. The thought of them working together, fueled by a shared purpose, sent a fresh wave of venom through him. He had underestimated them, and underestimation, he was learning, was a fatal flaw in the high-stakes game he played.

He crushed the whiskey bottle in his hand, the glass shards biting into his palm. The sting was a welcome distraction from the gnawing anxiety. He needed to control the narrative, to preempt Abernathy's article, to sow seeds of doubt, to manipulate public opinion before the truth could fully take root. He considered a direct confrontation, a public denouncement of Abernathy and Eleanor as agitators, as threats to the valley's economic future. But he knew that would be too crude, too obvious. His strength lay in subtlety, in the manipulation of perception.

He ordered his driver to prepare the vehicle. He would drive to the nearest town, to the regional office, to rally support, to exert pressure from a higher echelon. He needed to bring more resources to bear, to overwhelm any nascent opposition with a show of force, both financial and, if necessary, legal. He envisioned the town council meeting, the hushed whispers turning into murmurs of dissent, the carefully planted questions designed to discredit Abernathy's findings, to highlight the supposed economic benefits of his operation. He would paint himself as a benevolent force, a bringer of prosperity, and paint Eleanor and Abernathy as obstructionist nuisances, driven by personal vendettas or misguided idealism.

But even as he formulated these desperate strategies, a tremor of doubt ran through him. The storm, this relentless, untamed force of nature, was a constant, audible reminder of the power that lay beyond his control. It was a force that could dismantle his temporary office, flood his drill sites, and render his carefully laid plans irrelevant. He had always believed he could conquer nature, bend it to his will, just as he bent people. But the wind and the rain were a humbling, terrifying counterpoint to his hubris. They spoke of a power far older, far more enduring than his fleeting ambitions.

He pulled on his oilskin coat, the rough material a

poor shield against the tempest. He knew, with a sickening certainty, that this was not just a battle for profit; it was a battle for the very soul of Harmony Creek, and for the last vestiges of his own tarnished reputation. His carefully constructed facade was crumbling, his desperation manifesting in reckless impulses. He was no longer the cool, calculating magnate; he was a cornered predator, desperate to escape the trap he had so confidently walked into. He would deploy every weapon at his disposal – deception, intimidation, and a desperate gamble to accelerate his destructive enterprise before the truth could fully illuminate the damage he was inflicting upon this fragile valley. The storm was his enemy, Abernathy and Eleanor his immediate tormentors, but his greatest adversary, he was beginning to realize, was the unyielding truth, a truth that was as potent and as uncontainable as the tempest raging outside.

The wind, a mournful banshee, wailed through the skeletal branches of the cottonwoods lining Palo Alto Creek. Dust, whipped into a frenzy from the parched earth, swirled and eddied, a gritty shroud that began to obscure the already muted afternoon light. For Vance, standing beside his hulking, mud-splattered drilling rig, the increasing ferocity of the storm was a vulgar intrusion, a crass interruption to his meticulously orchestrated dominion. He'd chosen this spot, the very heart of his expansion, precisely for its isolation, its remoteness from the prying eyes of Harmony Creek. Yet, even here, the encroaching tempest seemed to carry the whispers of dissent, the accusing murmurs of those who clung to the dying embers of their pastoral ideals.

He watched, his jaw tight, as a small group emerged from the swirling dust, figures coalescing against the turbulent backdrop. Abernathy, his coat flapping like an ungainly wing, led the way, his gait purposeful despite the treacherous ground. Beside him, Eleanor. Even from this distance, Vance could discern the set of her jaw, the unwavering gaze that seemed to pierce through the gloom. He'd underestimated her, he knew. He'd seen her as a naive girl, easily swayed by romantic notions of preservation. He'd been wrong. Terribly wrong. She was a force, a quiet, relentless storm unto herself, and her presence here, at this critical juncture, was an affront he would not tolerate. A few other figures, indistinct shapes against the swirling earth, trailed behind them, their intentions as opaque as the heavens above.

"What in God's name do you think you're doing?" Vance's voice, amplified by the biting wind, cracked like a dry twig. He'd expected them, of course. His men had reported Abernathy's relentless digging, his persistent inquiries. But he hadn't anticipated this – a direct, public challenge at the very nexus of his operation. This was not the subtle discrediting he had planned; this was a frontal assault.

Abernathy stopped a respectful distance away, the wind tugging at his hat. He held up a sheaf of papers, the edges already frayed and damp. "We're here to see what you're doing to this land, Vance. To Willow Creek. To everything you're poisoning." His voice was steady, imbued with a quiet authority that Vance found infuriatingly effective.

Eleanor stepped forward, her movements economical and sure. She didn't raise her voice, but her words carried a chilling clarity that cut through the wind's roar. "You promised this wouldn't affect the water table, Mr. Vance. You promised no spills. But the evidence is undeniable. The sheen on the creek, the dead fish… and now this." She gestured vaguely towards the drilling rig, a metallic leviathan poised to tear into the earth's secrets. "This storm is only exacerbating the problem. You're drilling into unstable shale, and you know it. The saturation will destabilize the entire hillside, not to mention what it's doing to the water."

Vance scoffed, a harsh, disbelieving sound. "Unstable shale? Nonsense. My geologists assure me it's perfectly safe. And as for the creek, that's an unfortunate but isolated incident. These things happen with industrial operations." He flicked a dismissive glance towards the small cluster of onlookers. "This is about progress, about bringing jobs and prosperity to this valley. You people are just trying to hold back the tide of the future."

"The future shouldn't come at the cost of the present," Abernathy retorted, his voice gaining an edge. "The present is what we have, Vance. And you're destroying it." He took a step closer, the dust momentarily obscuring him. "We have samples, Vance. Samples of the creek water, samples of the soil. Samples that show clear contamination from your operations."

Vance's gaze narrowed. The samples. He'd ordered them destroyed, but he knew the risks. Abernathy, with his dogged persistence, might have secured more. And Eleanor, with her intimate knowledge of the land, would know exactly where to look. "Fabricated evidence," Vance sneered. "You can't prove a thing. You're just a sensationalist journalist looking for a story, and she's a starry-eyed idealist caught up in your fervor."

Eleanor's eyes flashed. "I'm not an idealist, Mr. Vance. I'm a resident. I grew up on this land. I know its rhythms, its vulnerabilities. And I can see the damage you're doing. The shale here, it's a delicate sedimentary layer. It's prone to landslides, especially when saturated. Your drilling process, the vibrations, the potential for underground fractures… it's a recipe for disaster. This storm, this heavy rainfall, is the worst possible condition for your operation. You're not just polluting the creek; you're risking a catastrophic collapse."

She pointed to the creek bed, a dry scar in the earth

that was now, thanks to the storm's advance, beginning to show a muddy trickle. "See that? That's Palo Alto Creek. It feeds into Willow Creek downstream. And that oily sheen you've been so dismissive of? It's starting to appear even here, miles away from your primary site. That means the contamination is spreading, seeping through the soil, finding its way into the groundwater. Your 'isolated incident' is anything but."

Vance shifted his weight, his boot grinding against a loose stone. The wind buffeted him, and he felt a primal urge to lash out, to assert his dominance. But Abernathy and Eleanor stood their ground, their conviction a shield against his bluster. The few other figures who had accompanied them, farmers from the community, their faces etched with a mixture of fear and anger, watched with a silent intensity that was more potent than any shouted accusation. They were the silent witnesses, the jury he hadn't anticipated.

"You're exaggerating, girl," Vance said, forcing a patronizing smile. "This is just weather. The land settles. It's natural. You can't blame my company for every gust of wind or every drop of rain." He gestured towards the drilling rig. "This is progress. This is opportunity. We're bringing jobs, revenue. You're asking us to stop all that for a few dead fish and some sentimental notions about preserving a creek that barely flows half the year."

"The creek might barely flow half the year *now*, Vance," Abernathy interjected, his voice rising with the storm's intensity, "but that doesn't mean it isn't vital. It's a water source, a habitat, a lifeline. And your operation is systematically killing it. The shale, Eleanor's right. It's a geological hazard waiting to happen. And when it does, it won't just be your rig that's buried. It'll be the fields, the houses. The entire valley will pay the price for your greed."

The wind intensified, whipping Eleanor's hair across her face. She didn't flinch. "My father tried to warn them about the shale years ago, Mr. Vance. He was a geologist, you know. He mapped this entire area. He saw the potential for instability. He advised against any heavy industrial development here. He said it was too fragile." Her voice trembled, not with fear, but with a profound sorrow that resonated in the raw, elemental power of the storm. "You're ignoring his warnings. You're ignoring all the warnings."

Vance felt a prickle of unease. He knew of Eleanor's father. A respected local geologist, an old guard who had served the valley's agricultural needs for decades. His son, a disgraced academic, had been sniffing around the periphery of Vance's operation, a minor nuisance he'd easily dismissed. But Eleanor… she had inherited her father's knowledge, his understanding of the land. And she was using it against him.

"Your father was a good man," Vance conceded, attempting a more conciliatory tone, "but times change. We have new technologies, better understanding. We're not the same as we were when he was surveying. And as for the shale, we have safety protocols. State-of-the-art safety protocols."

"Protocols that are failing," Abernathy said, stepping closer, forcing Vance to meet his gaze. "The proof is right there, Vance, in the contamination you're trying to hide." He held up a small, clear plastic bag. Inside, a few gray, slick pebbles were visible, coated with an oily residue. "These are from the creek bed, Vance. Samples taken just this morning. The sheen isn't just on the surface; it's in the sediment. And it's coming from your operation. We have the lab reports. We have the photographs."

Vance's composure began to crack. The meticulously constructed edifice of his influence was being chipped away, not by brute force, but by simple, undeniable truth, amplified by the fury of nature itself. The storm, which he had hoped would isolate and intimidate, was instead providing a dramatic backdrop to their confrontation, a wild, untamed force that mirrored the raw power of the land they were fighting for.

"This is a misunderstanding," Vance said, his voice losing its smooth veneer, a hint of desperation creeping in. "I'm willing to discuss this. We can reach an agreement. I can offer compensation for any… inconvenience."

Eleanor stepped forward again, her presence a quiet

but formidable bulwark. "Compensation? You can't compensate us for a poisoned aquifer, Mr. Vance. You can't compensate us for a valley that's been irrevocably damaged. What you've done here is not just illegal; it's immoral. You're gambling with our lives, with our future, for profit."

The other farmers, emboldened by Eleanor and Abernathy's defiance, began to murmur. Their initial fear seemed to be giving way to a simmering anger. They looked at Vance, at the immense drilling rig that stood like a monument to his avarice, and then at the creek, their creek, the lifeblood of their land, now marred by his carelessness.

"What about the reports you submitted to the county, Vance?" Abernathy pressed, his questions sharp and pointed. "Did they mention the unstable shale? Did they mention the potential for groundwater contamination? Or did you conveniently omit those details in your pursuit of permits?"

Vance felt a bead of sweat trickle down his temple,

despite the chill in the air. He knew Abernathy had been digging into the permit applications, poring over the bureaucratic minutiae he'd so carefully manipulated. "My company followed all regulations," Vance stated, his voice a little too firm, a little too loud. "We are in full compliance."

"Compliance or not," Eleanor said, her voice now carrying the weight of generations, of a deep, abiding connection to this earth, "you're destroying it. This land has sustained us for generations. It's not just soil and rock; it's our heritage. And you're treating it like a disposable commodity." She looked at the sky, where the clouds were darkening ominously, the wind whipping the cottonwood leaves into a frenzy. "This storm… it's a warning, Mr. Vance. Nature is telling you to stop. It's telling you that you can't control everything."

Vance glanced at his men, stationed a short distance away, their faces impassive but their stance wary. He had the power here, the physical presence. He could order them to disperse this unwelcome gathering, to remove Abernathy and Eleanor from his property. But the storm, the growing unease among the farmers, the undeniable truth in Eleanor's words… it was creating an atmosphere that was becoming increasingly volatile. A forceful dispersal now, under the watchful eyes of the community, could backfire spectacularly. It could turn a difficult confrontation into a full-blown scandal.

"You people are letting your emotions get the better of you," Vance said, trying to regain control, his voice hardening. "This is about economics, about jobs. You want to throw away the prosperity I'm bringing to this valley for a few sentimental tears over a creek?"

"It's not sentiment, Vance," Abernathy shot back. "It's survival. And it's justice. You're polluting our water, you're destabilizing our land, and you're lying about it. We have the proof. And we're not going to let you get away with it." He gestured to the small group of farmers. "These people know what's at stake. They've seen the changes. They've tasted the fear."

Eleanor nodded, her gaze fixed on Vance. "You

can't bury the truth under layers of shale, Mr. Vance. And you certainly can't hide it from a storm like this." She paused, the wind momentarily snatching her words away, only to deposit them back with renewed force. "This is our home. And we will protect it."

Vance felt a cold dread creep into his gut. He had underestimated them, both Abernathy and Eleanor, and the quiet, unyielding strength of the community they represented. He had believed his wealth, his influence, and his carefully crafted narrative of progress would be enough. But here, at Palo Alto Creek, with the storm gathering its full might, he was facing an opposition that was rooted not in financial gain or political maneuvering, but in a deep, abiding love for the land and an unwavering commitment to truth. The confrontation was far from over, but he knew, with a chilling certainty, that the ground was shifting beneath him, not just geologically, but in a way far more profound and far more dangerous. The eye of the storm was upon them, and he was caught in its increasingly violent embrace. He could feel the earth itself beginning to tremble, not just from the wind, but from the weight of the truth that was about to be unleashed.

# Chapter 6: The Black Blizzard

The wind, which had been a persistent whisper, a gritty companion to their heated exchange, suddenly found its voice. It wasn't a mournful cry anymore, but a violent, exultant roar that seemed to rise from the very bowels of the earth. Vance, Eleanor, and Abernathy, along with the cluster of grim-faced farmers, found themselves momentarily silenced, caught in the sudden, ferocious crescendo. The sky, a bruised purple a moment before, was now an angry, churning mass of umber and ochre.

Then, it came. Not as a gradual darkening, but as an abrupt descent. The horizon, already blurred by dust, simply ceased to exist. A monstrous wall of blackness advanced with terrifying speed, an unstoppable tide of earth and grit. It wasn't merely dust; it was the pulverized essence of the plains, ripped from the soil by the gale and hurled with malevolent intent. The light, already struggling against the storm's advance, was extinguished as if a colossal hand had slammed shut the lid of the world.

Visibility vanished. Utterly. The familiar forms of the drilling rig, the scattered mesquite, even the figures of the people standing mere yards away, dissolved into the impenetrable gloom. It was as if the world had been painted over, erased, replaced by a suffocating, all-consuming void. The wind, no longer a mere force, became a tangible entity, a solid wall of abrasive particles that clawed at exposed skin, stung the eyes, and filled the mouth with the taste of desolation.

Eleanor gasped, her hand flying to her mouth, not to stifle a scream, but to try and keep the choking dust at bay. The air, moments before still breathable, however unpleasantly, was now a thick, viscous substance. Each inhalation was a battle, a desperate struggle against the grit that coated the throat and lodged in the lungs. It felt like breathing in sandpaper. The roar of the wind was deafening, a continuous, annihilating blast that drowned out all other sounds, including the frantic thumping of her own heart.

Vance cursed, his bravado momentarily forgotten in the face of this elemental fury. He instinctively shielded his face with his arms, his expensive suit already a sodden, grimy mess. His men, who had been watching the confrontation with stoic detachment, now began to mill about nervously, their faces taut with a dawning, primal fear. The machinery, the symbol of his control and dominion, was being swallowed whole by this wrathful deluge.

Abernathy, his earlier defiance now tempered by a chilling respect for the storm's power, coughed violently, spitting a mouthful of dust onto the ground. He turned towards Eleanor, his voice strained and hoarse, barely audible above the din. "Inside, Eleanor! Now!"

The farmhouse, their destination, was no longer a visible landmark. It was a memory, a hope, a sanctuary somewhere within the swirling, churning abyss. The ground beneath their feet was a treacherous terrain, the earth no longer solid but a shifting, unstable mire of dust and mud, made treacherous by the storm's relentless assault. Every step was a gamble, a lurch into the unknown, where the next breath could be the last, or the next gust could sweep them off their feet and into the devouring maw of the black blizzard.

The sheer scale of it was overwhelming. It wasn't just a dust storm; it was a cataclysm. The sky, the vast, eternal canvas, had been ripped apart and replaced by a churning, infernal chaos. The familiar world of rolling hills, of creek beds and cottonwoods, had been utterly annihilated, replaced by a hostile, alien landscape. Every sense was assaulted. The darkness was absolute, a crushing weight that pressed in on all sides. The sound was a continuous, agonizing shriek, a symphony of destruction. The taste was gritty, metallic, the taste of raw, untamed nature unleashed. And the feel… the feel was the abrasive caress of a million tiny daggers, sandblasting the very flesh from bone.

Eleanor stumbled, her ankle turning on a hidden rut. Abernathy's hand shot out, a strong grip on her arm, pulling her upright. "Careful!" he yelled, his words swallowed by the gale. They pressed on, a small, vulnerable knot of humanity against the overwhelming might of the storm. The wind seemed to mock their efforts, snatching at their clothes, trying to rip them apart, to scatter them like so many discarded leaves.

She could feel the very structure of the land groaning under the assault. The shale that Eleanor had spoken of, the geological vulnerability Vance had dismissed, was now being tested in ways she could scarcely imagine. The storm wasn't just a visual and auditory assault; it was a physical one, a force that seemed intent on unmaking everything, from the grandest geological formation to the most fragile human endeavor.

They were moving, but it felt like they were wading through an invisible, viscous liquid, each step an agonizing effort. The air was so thick that it felt like swimming. The dust, fine as flour yet sharp as glass, found its way into every crevice, every opening. It coated their eyelids, their nostrils, their ears. It seeped through the fabric of their clothing, clinging to their skin like a second, suffocating skin.

The confrontation with Vance, his pronouncements of progress and prosperity, seemed like a relic from another lifetime, a fragile, insignificant human drama played out against the backdrop of an indifferent universe. Here, in the heart of the black blizzard, all human constructs, all aspirations of control and dominance, were laid bare as utterly futile. Vance's drilling rig, a symbol of his industrial might, was now a ghost, a memory swallowed by the immensity of the storm.

Eleanor risked a glance back, or rather, she tried to. There was nothing to see. No Vance, no Abernathy's followers, no rig, not even the ground they had stood on. Just the swirling, impenetrable darkness. They were utterly alone, adrift in a sea of oblivion. The fear, a cold, primal terror, began to coil in her gut, a stark contrast to the defiant fire that had burned within her just moments before. This was not a battle she could fight with words or evidence. This was a force of nature, raw and unyielding.

She focused on Abernathy's hand, still clasped firmly around her arm, a small anchor in the chaos. He was muttering words, too low to discern, perhaps prayers, perhaps reassurances, perhaps just a desperate attempt to impose some semblance of order on the pandemonium. His presence, his shared struggle against this suffocating tide, was a small comfort.

They were heading towards where the farmhouse
should be. Logic dictated it was in front of them, but
logic had no place here. The storm had rewritten the
rules of reality, turning the familiar landscape into an
unrecognizable, terrifying void. She imagined the
farmhouse, its sturdy timbers, its sheltering roof, and
clung to that image like a drowning person to
flotsam.

The wind seemed to intensify, a physical blow that
made them stagger. It was as if the storm itself was
trying to dislodge them, to tear them apart and
scatter their atoms across the plains. Eleanor
stumbled again, Abernathy pulling her forward with
renewed urgency. They were almost there, she told
herself. Almost to the fragile shelter of home. But
the intervening distance felt like an eternity, an
insurmountable chasm of darkness and fury. The
world had ended, or at least, the world as they knew
it had. All that remained was the roar, the darkness,
and the desperate, gasping fight for survival. The sky
had not just darkened; it had descended, and it was
threatening to bury them all.

The churning maw of the storm had swallowed them whole. Inside the cramped confines of the farmhouse, a different kind of darkness pressed in. The windows, usually portals to the endless prairie sky, were now opaque sheets of churning dirt, obliterating any semblance of the outside world. The wind's howl, a monstrous entity that had threatened to tear the very foundations from the earth, was now a muffled, omnipresent roar that seeped through every crack and crevice, a constant reminder of the elemental fury raging beyond their fragile sanctuary.

Ellie, Abernathy, and the handful of farmers who had managed to reach the relative safety of the farmhouse were huddled together, a small, breathing island in a sea of unleashed chaos. The air inside was thick with the coppery tang of fear and the ever-present grit that had found its way in despite their frantic efforts to seal off every opening. Every inhalation was a reminder of the storm's pervasiveness, a dry, rasping scrape against the back of the throat. The kerosene lamp cast a weak, flickering pool of light, illuminating a tableau of strained faces, eyes wide with a mixture of awe and terror. They were united not by choice, but by the sheer, unyielding force of the storm.

Abernathy, his face etched with a weariness that went beyond mere physical exhaustion, moved among the small group, his voice a low rumble that struggled against the cacophony outside. He clapped a man on the shoulder, offered a quiet word of reassurance to a woman clutching a tightly bundled babe, his presence a steadying force in the swirling uncertainty. Ellie watched him, a flicker of admiration in her own weary gaze. He had been right, and in his rightness, they had all found themselves staring into the abyss.

The tension in the small room was a palpable thing, a coiled spring of unspoken anxieties. Each gust of wind that shook the farmhouse walls, each rattle of a loose shutter, sent a fresh wave of unease through the assembled group. They were trapped, waiting, their fate held hostage by the whims of the sky. The hope that had spurred their dash for shelter, the conviction that their actions, their exposure of Vance's predatory practices, would ultimately prevail, now felt like a fragile, distant thing, a flickering ember threatened by the tempest.

"We did what we could," Abernathy said, his voice barely carrying over the wind's lament. He looked at Ellie, his eyes conveying a shared understanding of the precariousness of their situation. "We warned them. We showed them the truth."

Ellie nodded, her throat tight. The confrontation with Vance had been a pyrrhic victory, a moment of defiant clarity that had been immediately overshadowed by this cataclysm. She thought of the fine dust that now coated everything, the invisible enemy that could choke the life out of them just as surely as the visible storm. "He dismissed it all," she murmured, her voice raspy. "He said it was just… weather. Just a bit of dust."

A grim chuckle rippled through the room, a sound devoid of humor. "He'll have a hard time calling this 'a bit of dust' now," a grizzled farmer named Silas said, his voice rough as the soil he worked. He was one of the few who had initially voiced his doubts about Vance's methods, his quiet observations often drowned out by the louder pronouncements of progress.

The confinement, the forced proximity, began to chip away at the edges of their fear, revealing a deeper, more potent undercurrent of shared resilience. In the dim lamplight, faces that had been strangers just hours before began to blur into a collective portrait of hardship and quiet determination. The storm, in its terrible impartiality, had stripped away their individual anxieties and forged them into a common bond.

"My grandmother," Ellie began, her voice soft, drawing the attention of those closest to her. She hesitated, the words catching in her throat. She hadn't planned to speak, hadn't planned for this intimate sharing in the face of such elemental fury. But the shared vulnerability, the palpable sense of being at nature's mercy, unlocked something within her. "My grandmother used to say the land always spoke. You just had to learn to listen."

She saw a few heads nod in recognition. Many of them carried their own echoes of ancestral wisdom, the quiet teachings passed down through generations, lessons learned not from books or charts, but from the feel of the earth beneath their feet, the scent of rain on dry soil, the subtle shifts in the wind's temper.

"She said the prairie had a memory," Ellie continued, her voice gaining a quiet strength. "It remembered every footprint, every seed planted, every drop of rain that fell. And when it was angry, it didn't just get angry. It remembered everything that had been taken from it, everything that had been carelessly broken."

She looked at Silas, his weathered face a map of a life lived in harmony with the land. "She taught me to read the clouds," Ellie said, a faint smile touching her lips. "Not just the shapes, but the color, the way they gathered. She could tell if a storm was just passing through, or if it meant business. She said you could feel it in your bones, the coming of a truly bad blow."

Another farmer, a younger man named Thomas, who had lost his entire crop to an earlier drought, spoke up. "My pa always said you can't cheat the soil. It gives, but it also takes. And if you push it too hard, it'll take back everything you ever thought you owned."

The whispered stories, the shared memories, became a kind of balm against the roaring wind. They were not just recollections of the past; they were affirmations of a deeper truth, a truth that Vance, in his relentless pursuit of profit, had utterly disregarded. Ellie's grandmother's teachings weren't just about reading the weather; they were about understanding the intricate, often harsh, but ultimately sacred relationship between humanity and the earth.

"She taught me about the grasses," Ellie went on, encouraged by their rapt attention. "How the buffalo grass, the short, tough stuff, could go dormant for years, just waiting for the right rain, the right conditions to come back. It didn't give up. It just… endured." She thought of the deep, resilient roots of the native grasses, a stark contrast to the shallow, easily eroded soil that Vance's operations were so carelessly churning up. "She said that kind of strength, that kind of deep-down knowing, was what the prairie was made of. And that we, who lived on it, had to learn it too."

Abernathy listened, his gaze fixed on Ellie. He saw the quiet fire in her eyes, the reflection of a wisdom that transcended the immediate danger. He recognized in her words the very essence of what they were fighting for – not just a patch of land, but a way of life, a connection to something ancient and enduring. He knew that the information they had gathered, the evidence of Vance's destructive practices, would need to be presented with more than just facts and figures. It would need to carry the weight of this shared understanding, this reverence for the land that was being desecrated.

"My grandmother," a woman named Martha chimed in, her voice trembling slightly, "she used to tell us to leave a little something for the earth when we took from it. A prayer, a handful of grain. A way of saying thank you, and a way of asking for forgiveness." Her gaze drifted to the sealed-off window, as if she could see through the swirling dust to the wounded land beyond. "I wonder… if we hadn't forgotten that, if we hadn't stopped thanking it… if this would be happening."


The question hung in the air, heavy with the unspoken regret of generations. They had become disconnected, so focused on extracting, on conquering, that they had forgotten the fundamental principle of reciprocity. Vance embodied this disconnection, this belief that the earth was merely a resource to be exploited, an obstacle to be overcome.


As the storm continued its relentless assault, the shared stories began to weave a tapestry of collective memory and shared purpose. The fear, though still present, was being tempered by a growing sense of solidarity, a recognition of their shared vulnerability and their shared strength. Ellie's grandmother's teachings, once private whispers passed down through the generations, were now being amplified, resonating within the storm-battered walls of the farmhouse, offering not just comfort, but a profound sense of belonging and a quiet promise of resilience. They were sheltering the truth, not just in their words, but in their very being, in the deep, abiding connection to the land that the black blizzard, in its fury, could never truly extinguish.

The night wore on, a seemingly endless cycle of wind's fury and the unnerving quiet that sometimes followed a particularly violent gust. Inside the farmhouse, the atmosphere remained charged, a low hum of anxious energy punctuated by the soft murmur of voices. Ellie found herself leaning against Abernathy's shoulder, the shared exhaustion and the sheer intensity of the experience having blurred the lines of formality between them. His presence was a silent, steady anchor in the swirling uncertainty.

"Do you think… do you think anyone else made it?" Thomas asked, his voice barely audible. The question was for everyone, but it seemed to hang most heavily in the air around Silas and the other older farmers who had witnessed the storm's initial onslaught and knew how quickly it had descended.

Silas shook his head slowly, his gaze fixed on the flickering lamplight. "We did what we could, Thomas. We helped who we could. But that… that was like nothing I've ever seen. Not in all my years." His voice trailed off, the unspoken weight of those who might have been left behind heavy in the small space. The reality of their situation was stark: they had found shelter, but the fate of others remained a terrifying unknown.

Ellie's mind replayed the final moments before they had plunged into the suffocating darkness. Vance, his face contorted with rage, his men looking bewildered and frightened. Had they managed to find shelter? Or had they, blinded by their own hubris, been caught in the open? The thought sent a fresh shiver of dread down her spine. This storm was indiscriminate; it cared nothing for Vance's wealth or his pronouncements. It was a force that demanded respect, a force that was now dictating the terms of their existence.

"My grandmother," Ellie began again, her voice a little stronger now, as if the act of speaking itself was a form of defiance against the overwhelming power outside, "she always said that the prairie could be a harsh teacher. It taught you humility. It taught you that you were just a small part of something much bigger." She glanced around at the faces illuminated by the lamp, each one a testament to a life intertwined with the land. "And it taught you that sometimes, the most important thing you could do was just… endure. To hold on. To wait for the sun to break through again."

Martha, who had spoken of leaving offerings for the earth, nodded slowly. "She said the land remembers. It remembers the good, and it remembers the bad. And maybe, just maybe, this… this is the land's way of remembering everything Vance has done." Her words, spoken with a quiet conviction, resonated with a profound sense of justice, a belief that the natural world itself possessed a moral compass.

Abernathy cleared his throat. "We have the proof, Ellie. The records, the soil samples, the testimony. Vance can't ignore that forever. He can't make this storm disappear with a wave of his hand." His words were meant to be reassuring, but even he, a man who had dedicated his life to scientific inquiry and the pursuit of truth, could not deny the raw, untamed power that they were currently experiencing. The storm was a testament to the very forces he sought to understand, forces that often defied easy explanation or simple control.

"He'll try," Silas grumbled, his voice laced with a weary cynicism. "He'll find a way to spin it. He'll say it was just bad luck, a freak occurrence. He'll blame it on the weather, not on what he was doing to the land."

Ellie met Silas's gaze, a spark of determination rekindling within her. "But we know. And the people who are suffering, who are losing everything, they know too. This isn't just about Vance anymore. It's about all of us, and what kind of future we want to build on this land." She thought of her grandmother's words, the lessons of resilience and deep connection, and felt a surge of renewed purpose. They had sought to expose a specific wrong, but now, caught in the heart of this ecological upheaval, the fight felt larger, more profound.

The wind continued its mournful song, but within the farmhouse, a different kind of strength was taking root. It was the strength born of shared adversity, of whispered stories that connected them to a wisdom older than human memory. It was the quiet, stubborn resilience of the prairie grass, dormant but not defeated, waiting for its season of renewal.

Ellie closed her eyes for a moment, picturing her grandmother's face, the gentle lines around her eyes, the serene smile that always accompanied her stories. She remembered the feel of the earth under her bare feet, the scent of wild sage after a rain, the vast, silent expanse of the prairie stretching to the horizon. These were the truths that Vance's machines and his greed could not erase. These were the truths that would endure, long after the dust had settled and the wind had finally ceased its destructive dance.

As the hours stretched into an indistinguishable blur of wind and grit, the farmhouse became more than just a shelter; it became a repository of shared experience, a crucible in which their collective will was being forged. The truth they were trying to bring to light was no longer just a matter of legal recourse or scientific evidence; it was a truth etched into the very fabric of their lives, a truth amplified by the devastating power of the black blizzard. They were weathering the storm, not just physically, but spiritually, clinging to the enduring lessons of the land, finding strength in their shared vulnerability and the quiet, persistent whisper of hope. The memory of her grandmother's teachings, the inherent wisdom of the earth, was the shelter they truly sought, a sanctuary that no storm, however violent, could ever breach.

The wind, a relentless sculptor, had reshaped the prairie overnight, burying the scars of human ambition beneath a thick, suffocating shroud of dust. For Silas Vance, this was not just an inconvenience; it was an affront. His meticulously planned operation, the culmination of months of calculated maneuvering and financial investment, was now as inaccessible as the moon. His convoy of heavy machinery, designed to traverse the toughest terrain, was entombed. The diesel tractors, the hulking earthmovers, the specialized drilling rigs – all were swallowed by the maelstrom, rendered inert by a force that owed no allegiance to profit margins or corporate directives.

Vance, stranded in his reinforced motorhome, the opulent sanctuary he had driven out to his new expansion site, felt the familiar prickle of irritation morph into a cold, gnawing dread. The storm had descended with a ferocity that defied his projections, overriding even the most pessimistic meteorological forecasts he had consulted. His state-of-the-art communication array, a marvel of modern engineering designed to keep him connected to his empire, was reduced to a crackling, spitting ghost of its former self. The electromagnetic interference, or perhaps the sheer physical displacement of atmospheric particles, had rendered his satellite link useless. He was adrift, a captain whose ship had been instantly dismantled by an invisible enemy.

He paced the confined space of the motorhome, his expensive leather soles crunching on the fine grit that had, despite every seal and gasket, found its way inside. It coated the plush carpeting, dusted the polished mahogany surfaces, and clung to the air with a dry, rasping persistence. Each breath was a reminder of his impotence. He ran a hand over his impeccably tailored suit, now bearing the faint, mocking sheen of the dust, a stain on his carefully cultivated image. This was not how it was supposed to be. He was the architect of these landscapes, the one who bent nature to his will, not its victim.

The storm was an anomaly, an inconvenient deviation from the predictable patterns he understood. His algorithms, his predictive models, had all pointed to a manageable weather event. This… this was an act of primal, untamed rage. He had always viewed the land as a resource, a canvas upon which to paint his ambitions, to extract his wealth. He had never truly appreciated its power, its capacity to shrug off human endeavors with a careless sweep of its arm. Now, the prairie was pushing back, and he was caught in its unforgiving embrace.

He tried the radio again, fiddling with the knobs, twisting the antenna in a futile attempt to coax a signal from the ether. Static hissed back, punctuated by the mournful howl of the wind, a sound that seemed to mock his efforts. His drivers, his engineers – where were they? Had they found shelter? Or were they, too, lost in this suffocating immensity? The thought was a sour note in the symphony of his self-importance. He had always surrounded himself with competent, replaceable men; their fate was of secondary concern to the disruption of his project. Yet, even that thought felt hollow now, the usual buffer of detachment eroded by the sheer overwhelming reality of his isolation.

He peered out of the reinforced window, the thick, multi-paned glass offering a distorted, sepia-toned view of a world utterly transformed. The horizon, a familiar, comforting line that had always represented opportunity, was now an indistinguishable blur. There were no landmarks, no signs of civilization, only a churning, suffocating sea of dirt. He had chosen this site precisely for its remoteness, its untouched potential. Now, that remoteness was his prison.

His vision of progress, of harnessing the untapped resources beneath this seemingly barren earth, was in ruins, at least for the moment. The drills, the extraction equipment, the trucks that would ferry the valuable minerals away – all were effectively gone, buried deep. He could almost feel the weight of the earth pressing down on his ambitions, a physical

manifestation of nature's rebuke. He had dismissed
the concerns of the locals, their talk of respecting the
land, of understanding its rhythms. He had seen
them as superstitious, backward. Now, their ancient
wisdom felt like a haunting prophecy.

He sank onto the plush leather sofa, the silence in
the motorhome a stark contrast to the tempest
outside. It was a heavy, oppressive silence, broken
only by the occasional groan of the vehicle settling
under the relentless wind. He felt a profound sense
of unease, a disorientation that went beyond the
physical confinement. His entire identity was tied to
his ability to control, to command, to extract.
Without the tools of his trade, without the visible
manifestations of his power, he was something else
entirely. He was just a man, stripped bare by the
elements, vulnerable and utterly alone.

He thought of the meeting he had with Abernathy
and Ellie, their defiant stand, their accusations of
environmental damage. He had brushed them aside
with contempt, secure in his perceived invincibility.
He had believed that money, influence, and sheer
force of will could overcome any obstacle, including

the whispers of those who sought to impede his progress. But this storm was a force that recognized no currency, no influence. It was a primal equalizer, and it had caught him unawares.

He had planned to oversee the initial stages of extraction himself, to be present, a visible symbol of his dominance. He had envisioned a triumphant arrival, a clear signal to the land and to anyone who dared to question him that he was here to stay. Instead, he was marooned, his grand pronouncements silenced by the sheer volume of the wind. His sophisticated machinery, a testament to human ingenuity and his own financial prowess, was now just expensive scrap metal, buried beneath an indifferent blanket of soil.

He reached for his personal tablet, hoping to access some stored data, some semblance of order in the chaos. But even here, the dust had found its way in, smudging the screen, making the once-sharp display blurry and indistinct. He tried to log in to his secured files, but the network connection, already tenuous, had completely failed. Every attempt to reassert control, to connect with the world beyond his immediate, suffocating reality, ended in failure.

The realization dawned on him, cold and absolute: he was powerless. The very elements he had sought to dominate had turned on him, rendering his wealth and his influence meaningless. He was trapped, not just by the physical barriers of the storm, but by his own hubris, his utter failure to comprehend the true forces at play. He had underestimated the land, and in doing so, he had underestimated himself. The prairie, in its silent, overwhelming power, had delivered a lesson he would not soon forget, a lesson etched not in profit and loss, but in the suffocating embrace of the black blizzard. His carefully constructed world had been reduced to dust, and he, Silas Vance, was left to contemplate his own insignificance in the face of nature's unyielding might. He was stranded, defeated, his ambitions buried as surely as his machinery, a stark testament to the folly of defying the earth's ancient, immutable laws. The storm raged on, a testament to the land's memory and its power to reclaim what had been taken, leaving Vance a prisoner of his own making, utterly alone with his useless wealth and his shattered illusions of control.

The world outside had dissolved into an indistinguishable, suffocating roar. Ellie, huddled with her family in the relative shelter of their storm cellar, could feel the very bones of the earth vibrating beneath them. The wind, a monstrous, unseen beast, clawed at the surface, a relentless hand attempting to pry open their refuge. Yet, within the cramped, earthy confines, a different kind of force was at work—a quiet, unyielding strength that emanated from Ellie herself.

The darkness was absolute, thicker than any night sky. It pressed in, a physical weight that threatened to steal the air from their lungs. But Ellie didn't cower. Instead, she drew a slow, steady breath, the familiar scent of damp soil and stored grains a strangely comforting anchor. This was the earth, her earth, in its most violent expression. And she understood it, not as an enemy, but as a force that demanded respect, a force that, in its fury, was merely asserting its ancient dominion.

She thought of the journey that had brought her to this moment, to this storm, to this fight. The dusty roads of her childhood, the relentless sun on her back as she worked the fields alongside her father, the quiet wisdom passed down through generations – it all coalesced within her now. It wasn't just a memory; it was a deep wellspring of resilience, a testament to a life lived in harmony with the land, not in opposition to it. Vance, with his gleaming machines and his insatiable appetite for profit, represented a profound desecration of that legacy. He saw only resources to be plundered, a canvas to be scarred. He understood nothing of the intricate web of life, the delicate balance that sustained them all.

The howling outside intensified, a symphony of destruction that could have easily shattered her composure. But Ellie's resolve was a different kind of sound, a low, steady hum that vibrated beneath the din. It was the quiet certainty of knowing one's place, of understanding one's purpose. This wasn't just about protecting their farm, their home. It was about safeguarding a way of life, a philosophy rooted in stewardship and a profound reverence for the natural world. The black blizzard was Vance's ultimate weapon, designed to break the spirit of the land and those who depended on it. But for Ellie, it was a crucible. It was burning away any lingering doubts, any weakness, leaving behind only the unshakeable core of her conviction.

She recalled the conversations, the pleas, the outright warnings she had tried to impress upon Vance. His dismissive sneer, his arrogant pronouncements of progress, his utter contempt for the local way of life – it had all fueled her fire. She had seen the insidious nature of his ambition, the way it threatened to smother the very soul of the prairie. He saw profit; she saw a living, breathing entity that deserved to be nurtured, not exploited. This storm, in its destructive power, was a tangible manifestation of the earth's own resistance to his kind of violation.

Her hands, calloused from years of labor, rested on the rough-hewn wood of the cellar wall. She could feel the grain, the imperfections, the history embedded within. Each touch was a reaffirmation of her connection. The storm raged, a tempest of dust and fury, but within Ellie, a calm clarity had settled. She was not a victim of this storm; she was a part of the land that was enduring it. Her strength wasn't born of defiance, but of deep, abiding kinship.

She began to murmur, her voice a soft counterpoint to the wind's fury, sharing stories, fragments of lore, tales of resilience passed down from her grandmother. These were not just words; they were an invocation, a way of remembering who they were and what they stood for. The storm might bury their fields, might silence their tractors, might even threaten their very lives, but it could not touch the spirit that was woven into the fabric of their existence. Vance could control machinery, could manipulate markets, but he could never control the quiet, enduring power of a people who understood that their prosperity was inextricably linked to the health of the land.

Ellie's inner strength wasn't a sudden revelation; it was a slow, steady growth, nurtured by seasons of hardship and moments of profound connection. The black blizzard, in its terrifying totality, was merely accelerating that growth, forging her resolve into something unbreakable. She closed her eyes, envisioning not the chaos outside, but the promise of renewal that always followed the storm. The dust would settle, and the land, though wounded, would begin its slow, determined journey back to life. And she, with her quiet determination, would be there, a guardian of that fragile, enduring hope, a testament to the power of a spirit that refused to be buried. The earth had given her life, had shaped her very being, and in this darkest hour, she understood that her deepest strength lay in her unwavering commitment to protecting that sacred trust. This was not merely a fight for survival; it was a fight for the soul of the prairie.

The clamor outside was a ceaseless, abrasive entity, a physical manifestation of the land's agony. Inside their makeshift sanctuary, the air, though thick with the scent of damp earth and stored provisions, was also charged with a palpable tension. Yet, even as the dust – the very enemy that had forced them underground – continued its relentless siege, something unexpected began to unfurl. It started with the sharing of a single, precious apple, its crisp sweetness a startling contrast to the prevailing desolation. Old Man Hemlock, his face a roadmap of seasons weathered and trials endured, offered it to young Timmy, whose wide, fearful eyes had scarcely left the cellar door since the storm's inception. It was a small gesture, almost insignificant against the backdrop of such immense destruction, but it was a spark.

Ellie watched, her heart swelling with a quiet recognition. This was the true harvest of the prairie – not the bushels of grain that Vance's machines might yield, but the deep-rooted connections that held them together when all else threatened to blow away. Across the packed-earth floor, Sarah Jensen, her normally cheerful demeanor subdued but not extinguished, was carefully portioning out a meager supply of dried beans, ensuring that each family, even those who had arrived with nothing, received their share. Her voice, though a little hoarse from the dust that had seeped even into their refuge, carried a steady reassurance. "We'll see this through, together," she promised, her gaze meeting Ellie's. "We always have."

It was in these quiet acts of mutual support that a different kind of resilience began to take root. The initial fear, the stark terror of the unknown, was slowly giving way to a shared determination. They were no longer isolated individuals caught in a cataclysm; they were a community, bound by the common thread of their shared ordeal. The whispered conversations weren't of blame or despair, but of practicalities, of shared memories, and of tentative plans for what might come *after*. The storm, in its brutal impartiality, had stripped away the superficialities, leaving only the essential – the need for human connection, for shared strength.

Ellie found herself recalling instances where her own knowledge, once viewed with a degree of skepticism by some of the more mechanically-minded farmers, was now being sought with a renewed earnestness. She had always believed in the land's own wisdom, in the intricate network of life that sustained it. Her understanding of native plants, of their hardiness, their ability to survive drought and harsh conditions, had been a subject of gentle teasing. Now, as the meager supplies dwindled and the possibility of prolonged isolation loomed, those same plants, the ones she had carefully cultivated in her small herb garden, were being discussed with a serious consideration.

"Ellie," called out Mr. Henderson, his voice rough but earnest, "you said those purslane shoots… they're edible, right? And good for you?" He gestured vaguely towards a small pouch she had brought with her, filled with dried herbs and carefully labeled seeds. "My youngest is complainin' of a sore throat. Anything you got…?"

Ellie nodded, her hands already moving to the pouch. "Purslane is excellent, Mr. Henderson. Packed with vitamins, and yes, it can help soothe a sore throat. I also have some dried elderflower. We can make a tea." She felt a quiet satisfaction, not in being proven right, but in being able to contribute to their collective well-being. Her grandmother's lessons, the hours spent learning to identify, gather, and prepare the bounty of the wild, were no longer just cherished memories; they were vital tools for survival. The very things Vance dismissed as "scrub" and "weeds" were, in fact, nature's own provision, a testament to her enduring generosity.

The storm had a way of simplifying things, of stripping away the artifice and revealing the core truths of existence. In the dim, flickering light of a single oil lamp, families huddled together, their differences dissolving in the shared experience. The talk wasn't of market prices or government subsidies, but of the children's coughs, the dwindling water supply, and the faint, hopeful possibility that the wind might abate by morning. These were the immediate, pressing concerns of life, the fundamental realities that Vance, with his grand schemes and abstract theories, seemed to have entirely forgotten.

Ellie's own father had always said that the prairie demanded respect, a willingness to work *with* its rhythms, not against them. Vance's approach was one of dominance, of bending the land to his will, of extracting its wealth without regard for its inherent capacity to sustain itself. The black blizzard was, in a terrible way, the land's response to that violation, a violent assertion of its own power. But even in the midst of that fury, the human spirit, when united, possessed its own formidable strength.

She saw it in the way the men, despite their own anxieties, took turns checking the integrity of the cellar's supports, their movements slow and deliberate, a shared rhythm of mutual reliance. She heard it in the hushed lullabies sung to frightened children, a soft defiance against the howling chaos outside. She felt it in the shared warmth of bodies pressed together for comfort, a silent acknowledgment of their interconnectedness.

There was a palpable shift in the atmosphere, a subtle but profound transformation. The initial shock had given way to a quiet stoicism, and from that stoicism, a nascent hope was beginning to bloom. It wasn't a naive optimism, not a belief that the storm would simply vanish and everything would return to normal. It was a deeper, more resilient hope, born from the knowledge that they had faced hardship before, and that they had the strength within themselves, and within their community, to face it again.

Ellie found herself sharing more than just her knowledge of plants. She spoke of the resilience of the prairie grasses, how they bent with the wind, seemingly surrendering, only to spring back upright when the storm passed. She recalled stories of her ancestors, of how they had endured blizzards and droughts, their lives interwoven with the very land that now tested them so severely. These stories weren't meant to distract from their current plight, but to ground them, to remind them of the deep wellspring of courage that ran through their lineage, a heritage etched into the very soil beneath their feet.

The oppressive darkness of the cellar, which had initially felt like a tomb, began to feel more like a womb. It was a place of shared vulnerability, yes, but also a place where new life, in the form of strengthened community bonds, could begin to emerge. The storm, a destructive force on the surface, was inadvertently cultivating something precious below. It was forging a shared identity, a collective understanding that their survival depended not on individual might, but on their ability to act as one, to draw strength from each other.

As the hours wore on, and the deafening roar outside continued its assault, a different kind of sound began to fill the small space: the murmur of shared strength. The fear hadn't entirely vanished, but it was now tempered by a quiet resolve. They were weathering the storm, not just physically, but emotionally and spiritually. The black blizzard, Vance's intended weapon of subjugation, was inadvertently becoming a catalyst for unity, a harsh but effective forge for a community that was beginning to understand the true meaning of resilience. The land was testing them, pushing them to their limits, but in doing so, it was also revealing the enduring strength of the human spirit when it found solace and solidarity in the shared struggle for survival. And in that shared struggle, a profound and unshakeable hope began to take hold, a quiet promise that even after the darkest blizzard, life would find a way to endure, and to rebuild, stronger than before.

# Chapter 7: The Reckoning

The relentless roar that had pressed down on their very souls had finally begun to recede. It was not a sudden cessation, but a gradual, almost reluctant withdrawal, like a spent beast retreating into the wilderness. The oppressive weight in the air lifted, replaced by a silence so profound it felt almost alien. For hours, the world had been a symphony of destruction, a cacophony of wind and grit that had assaulted every sense. Now, only the faint, mournful sigh of a dying gale whispered through the cracks and crevices of their temporary sanctuary.

Slowly, tentatively, the inhabitants of the cellar began to stir. There were hushed movements, the creak of tired joints, the soft murmurs of relief that rippled through the huddled figures. Ellie felt a prickling sensation on her skin, a phantom echo of the countless particles that had invaded every inch of their being. She, like the others, breathed deeply, the air still thick with the familiar scent of damp earth and stored provisions, but now overlaid with the faintest, lingering trace of the dust – a ghost of the fury that had driven them underground.

It was Old Man Hemlock who first ventured towards the makeshift barrier they had erected at the cellar entrance. He moved with a caution born of long experience, his weathered hands testing the weight of the timbers. A collective breath was held by all those who watched him. The storm had tested them, not just with its physical might, but with the gnawing uncertainty of what lay beyond. Would the world they knew still exist? Would their homes, their fields, their very means of survival, have been swept away into oblivion?

With a grunt, Hemlock pushed against the wood. It resisted for a moment, then groaned in protest, revealing a sliver of the world outside. A muted, diffused light filtered in, so unlike the harsh glare they had known before. It was a light filtered through a veil of fine particulate matter, painting the air with an ethereal, golden haze. Hemlock, his eyes narrowed against the unfamiliar brightness, peered through the opening. He stayed there for a long moment, his silence more eloquent than any words could have been.

Then, he turned, his face a mask of mingled awe and devastation. "It's… it's everywhere," he rasped, his voice rough with emotion. "Buried. Everything's buried."

The words hung in the air, heavy with unspoken implications. One by one, they moved to the opening, their hearts pounding with a mixture of dread and desperate curiosity. Ellie was among the first to reach it, pushing past the hesitant forms of others, her own need to see overriding any lingering fear. She blinked, her eyes struggling to adjust.

The world that greeted her was both familiar and utterly alien. The gentle undulations of the prairie, the subtle variations in color and texture that spoke of life and growth, were gone. In their place was a stark, monochrome landscape, sculpted anew by the relentless hand of the wind. The earth, their precious topsoil, had been lifted, carried, and redeposited in vast, undulating dunes, burying fences, farm equipment, and even the lower stories of some of the more exposed homesteads. The sky, usually a vast canvas of cerulean blue, was a sickly, pale ochre,

the sun a distant, weakened disc struggling to pierce
the perpetual haze.

A profound, almost unnerving silence had settled
over the land. The absence of the storm's fury was a
palpable thing, a void that seemed to amplify the
desolation. There were no birdsong, no rustle of
leaves, no distant lowing of cattle. It was as if the
very breath of life had been stolen from the world. A
fine, gritty layer of dust coated everything, from the
splintered wood of the cellar entrance to the bent
and broken stalks of what had once been their crops.
It was a uniform, suffocating blanket, erasing the
boundaries between field and sky, between hope and
despair.

Ellie stepped out, her boots sinking slightly into the
soft, accumulated dust. The air was cool, surprisingly
so, and carried a faint, metallic tang that spoke of the
minerals churned up from the depths of the earth.
She took a hesitant step forward, then another, her
eyes scanning the altered terrain. Her own small
homestead, a familiar sight she had carried in her
mind's eye for so many hours, was barely
recognizable. The sturdy oak that had stood sentinel

beside her porch was now a ghostly silhouette, its branches laden with a thick mantle of dirt. Her carefully tended garden, a testament to her belief in working with nature, was completely obscured, its bounty lost beneath the arid drift.

A wave of sorrow washed over her, a grief for the land that had been so brutally violated. This was not merely dirt; this was the lifeblood of their community, the very substance that sustained them. Vance's machines, so powerful in their ability to churn and till, had also, in their relentless pursuit of yield, destabilized the very foundation of their existence. The deep-rooted grasses, the natural guardians of the soil, had been replaced by monocultures, their shallow roots no match for the fury of the wind.

Yet, as she stood there, surveying the devastation, a different feeling began to stir within her. It was a quiet resilience, a stubborn refusal to be overwhelmed. The storm had done its worst, had stripped away the familiar, had tested their very endurance. But it had not broken them. The community, huddled in the earth, had found a strength in their shared vulnerability, a bond forged in the crucible of fear and uncertainty.

She turned back to the cellar entrance, where the others were now cautiously emerging, blinking in the subdued light, their faces etched with the same mixture of relief and dismay. Sarah Jensen was helping her youngest son, his face streaked with dirt and tears, to brush himself off. Mr. Henderson, his brow furrowed with concern, was already scanning the horizon, as if searching for any sign of a familiar landmark.

"Ellie," Sarah called out, her voice still carrying the comforting lilt that Ellie had come to rely on, "you reckon anything's left? Our barn… it felt like it was about to lift right off its foundation."

Ellie shook her head slowly, her gaze sweeping across the vast expanse of dust. "I don't know, Sarah. It's hard to say from here. But we're out. We're alive. That's… that's something."

The "something" felt immense, a fragile seed of hope planted in the midst of utter desolation. They had survived the storm, a primal force of nature that had shown no mercy, no regard for the carefully constructed lives they had built. They had emerged from the darkness, blinking into a world that was alien, yet undeniably their own. The fight, as Ellie knew, was far from over. The dust had settled, but the challenge of rebuilding, of coaxing life back from this barren expanse, was a task that would test them even more profoundly than the storm itself.

The silence, which had initially been so unnerving, began to be punctuated by the soft sounds of the community stirring back to life. A child's tentative whimper, quickly soothed by a parent's gentle murmur. The scrape of a boot against the packed dirt. The low thud of someone testing the integrity of a partially buried fence post. These were the sounds of survival, of a fragile rebuilding commencing against all odds.

Ellie walked slowly, tracing the outline of what she remembered as the path to her own home. The dust shifted and swirled around her ankles with each step, a constant reminder of the event that had reshaped their world. She noticed a single, hardy prairie flower, somehow still clinging to life, its delicate petals dusted but not defeated. It was a small thing, almost insignificant against the backdrop of the widespread destruction, but it ignited a flicker of recognition within her. These were the plants she had spoken of in the cellar, the ones with deep roots, the ones that endured.

She reached the approximate location of her house. The structure was still standing, a testament to its solid construction, but it was partially buried, a ghostly outline against the ochre sky. The porch was gone, swallowed by the drifts. The windows were opaque, encrusted with layers of dirt. She walked around to what she knew to be the side of the house, her heart a tight knot of apprehension.

The shed, where she kept her gardening tools and the seeds she had so carefully saved, was completely gone. Nothing but a mound of earth marked its former location. A pang of loss, sharp and immediate, shot through her. Those seeds, those tiny packets of potential life, represented not just her own future, but a hope for the entire community.

But then, her gaze fell upon something else. Partially exposed by the shifting dust, near where the shed had been, was a familiar shape. It was a sturdy, wooden crate, one she had used to store her more robust gardening equipment. She hurried towards it, her boots crunching on the unfamiliar surface. With trembling hands, she began to dig, pushing away the heavy dust.

And there they were. Her heirloom seeds, carefully preserved in watertight bags and nestled within the crate. Beans, corn, squash, and importantly, the packets of native prairie grass seeds she had been so determined to reintroduce. A wave of relief, so potent it made her knees weak, washed over her. The storm had taken so much, but it had not taken everything.

She sat back on her heels, cradling the crate, a small, battered symbol of resilience. The sun, a pale disc in the dusty sky, cast long, distorted shadows. The silence remained, broken only by the sounds of her community beginning their own tentative reckonings with the aftermath. She looked at the vast, transformed landscape, at the endless expanse of dust. It was a daunting sight, a challenge that seemed almost insurmountable.

But as she clutched the seeds, she felt a quiet strength return. Her grandmother's words echoed in her mind:

*"The land remembers, child. It remembers how to grow, even after the harshest winter, even after the deepest drought."* This was not a drought, not in the conventional sense, but it was a profound upheaval, a violent disruption of the natural order. Yet, the land's capacity for renewal, for life to find a way, was a truth Ellie had always believed in.

She stood up, her gaze firm. The world was changed, irrevocably so. The familiar contours of their lives had been buried, obscured by the relentless dust. But the spirit of their community, forged in the shared ordeal of the storm, remained. And in her hands, she held the promise of a new beginning, a testament to the enduring power of nature and the unyielding resilience of the human heart. The fight was indeed not over, but for the first time since the wind began to howl, Ellie felt a true sense of readiness for the battles that lay ahead. She looked towards the cellar entrance, where the figures of her neighbors were slowly, tentatively, beginning to emerge into the strangely muted daylight, ready to face whatever the dust had left behind.

The silence that had fallen over the land was a heavy shroud, but for Vance, it was the clamor of his shattered ambitions that truly deafened him. The storm had been a brutal, uninvited arbiter, a force of nature that had judged his grand pronouncements and rendered them meaningless. Abernathy's exposé, a venomous viper he'd thought he could outmaneuver, had already poisoned the well of public opinion, leaving him exposed and vulnerable. Now, the wind and the dust had delivered the final, crushing blow, burying not only the land but also his meticulously crafted dreams beneath a suffocating blanket of earth.

He stood on the edge of what had once been a promising outcrop, now a jagged scar choked with debris, his hands balled into fists, his jaw clenched so tight it ached. The colossal metal beasts, his pride and joy, his instruments of conquest, lay scattered and broken, their once gleaming surfaces dulled and gouged by the tempest. He'd envisioned them taming the wilderness, extracting its hidden wealth, and ushering in a new era of prosperity, an era that would bear his name. Instead, they were grotesque monuments to his hubris, twisted metal carcasses swallowed by the very earth they were meant to conquer.

The preliminary dig sites, mere whispers of his intentions, were now indistinguishable from the surrounding desolation. He'd poured resources, energy, and a frightening amount of his own conviction into those nascent excavations, believing he was on the cusp of a monumental discovery. Now, any evidence of his presence, any hint of the valuable minerals he'd been so certain lay hidden beneath the surface, was buried under feet of topsoil, sifted and rearranged by the indifferent fury of the wind. The sheer scale of the task required to even begin to assess the damage, let alone resume operations, was a mountain he had no desire to climb.

The faces of the community, etched with suspicion

and resentment even before the storm, now seemed to hold a grim satisfaction. He'd seen it in their eyes as they'd emerged from their shelters, their gaunt faces a testament to their endurance, their stoic silence a damning indictment of his intrusion. They had weathered the storm, literally and figuratively, and in doing so, had weathered him. His charisma, his carefully cultivated aura of foresight and leadership, had evaporated like dew under a scorching sun, leaving behind only the bitter taste of frustration and impotent rage.

There was no rallying them now, no spinning this catastrophe into a triumph. Abernathy's words, amplified by the visible destruction, had sunk deep, finding fertile ground in the hearts of people who had already seen enough of his kind. He was no longer the visionary developer, but a reckless interloper, his machines the instruments of their potential undoing. The land itself had become his accuser, its scarred surface a stark, undeniable truth.

The decision, when it finally solidified, was not a moment of brave capitulation, but a desperate, ignominious retreat. He couldn't salvage his equipment without immense cost and effort, resources he now understood he wouldn't be able to secure. The community would never welcome him back, their trust irrevocably broken. The Texas Hill Country, once a canvas for his grand designs, had become a graveyard for his aspirations.

He barked orders to his few remaining, equally demoralized men. The goal was simple: pack what little could be salvaged, abandon the rest, and leave. There was no dignity in this departure, no measured dismantling of a grand enterprise. It was a scramble, a hurried evacuation, a desperate attempt to escape the suffocating weight of his failure. His normally immaculate attire was caked in dust, his sharp features contorted by a potent cocktail of anger and humiliation.

He watched as a battered truck, its suspension groaning under the weight of hastily loaded crates, was prepared for the journey. The mechanical heart of his operation, the very symbol of his drive and ambition, was being reduced to scrap and sentimentality. He could almost hear Abernathy's smug laughter echoing in the desolate air, a phantom soundtrack to his defeat.

As the first rays of a weak, dust-filtered sun began to creep over the horizon, painting the ravaged landscape in hues of muted gold and sickly brown, Vance climbed into the cab of his own truck. His men, their faces grim, followed suit. There were no backward glances, no lingering farewells to the land that had both promised so much and taken everything. The air was thick with unspoken accusations and the acrid scent of defeat.

The rumble of the truck's engine was a pathetic contrast to the powerful roar of the machines he had brought here with such fanfare. Each mile they put between themselves and this place was a step further away from the ghost of his shattered dreams. He gripped the steering wheel, his knuckles white, his eyes fixed on the road ahead, though his mind was still trapped in the dust-choked ruins behind him. He had come to conquer, to exploit, to build an empire. He was leaving as a vanquished foe, a cautionary tale whispered on the wind, a man who had dared to challenge the resilience of the land and been utterly, unequivocally broken by it. The Texas Hill Country had spoken, not with words, but with the unforgiving force of its wind and earth, and Vance had finally been forced to listen. His ambition, once a blazing inferno, had been reduced to smoldering embers, buried deep beneath the relentless, indifferent dust. He was not merely leaving; he was fleeing, a defeated man carrying the heavy burden of his own undoing. The silence of the land was now his silence, a hollow echo of the promises he had made and the dreams he had lost.

The suffocating blanket of dust had begun to lift, not entirely, but enough to reveal the contours of what remained. The sky, once a sickly, opaque yellow, now offered glimpses of a bruised, watery blue. It was a fragile dawn, but it was a dawn nonetheless, and with it came a stirring in the scattered homesteads. The silence that had reigned supreme during the storm, a silence broken only by the tempest's own furious roar, was gradually being replaced by the sounds of life reasserting itself. The frantic scramble of Vance and his men to depart had left a vacuum, not of emptiness, but of a potential for a different kind of rebuilding.

For Ellie, the aftermath was a peculiar blend of

exhaustion and a dawning clarity. The wind had stripped away the veneer, revealing the raw, unvarnished truth of the land and, more importantly, of the people who called it home. The fear that had once clouded some of their interactions, the suspicion that had shadowed her own deep connection to the soil, seemed to have been scoured away by the grit and fury of the storm. People emerged from their storm cellars and reinforced rooms blinking in the diminished light, their faces gaunt, their clothes dusted and worn, but their eyes – their eyes held a new light. It was a flicker of shared understanding, a silent acknowledgment of what they had endured together, and what Vance's departure truly signified.

Old Man Hemlock, his arthritic hands trembling as he surveyed the splintered remains of his porch railing, found himself nodding as Sarah Jenkins approached, her own face smudged with grime but her stride purposeful. She carried a coil of sturdy rope and a small toolkit. "Thought you might be needing a hand with that, Silas," she said, her voice raspy but warm. Silas, who had always been a proud, self-reliant man, a man who rarely asked for assistance, found himself accepting the offer without a moment's hesitation. There was no shame in it now, only necessity and a shared purpose. The storm had leveled more than just fences and outbuildings; it had dismantled the invisible barriers of pride that had, at times, kept them at arm's length from one another.

Further down the lane, where the wind had ripped a gaping maw through a section of barn wall, the Miller family and the Rodriguezes were already at work. Young Billy Miller, barely sixteen, was wrestling with a warped beam, his muscles straining. Maria Rodriguez, her usually immaculately braided hair now escaping in wisps around her face, was helping his younger sister, Clara, clear away the smaller debris, their movements surprisingly coordinated, a silent rhythm born of mutual understanding. They didn't speak of Vance, not directly. His name hung in the air, a ghost of ambition thwarted, but their focus was on the tangible, on the immediate task of mending what had been broken. The damage was extensive, undeniable, but it was also manageable, especially now that the threat of his machines and his avarice had been removed.

Ellie watched this quiet rebuilding unfold from her own porch, the small, sturdy structure that had, thankfully, weathered the storm with only minor damage. She saw her neighbors not as individuals struggling against the vast indifference of nature, but as a collective, a tapestry woven from shared hardship and resilience. The skepticism that had once followed her, the hushed whispers about her "peculiar ways" and her uncanny ability to predict the shifts in weather and the moods of the land, seemed to have evaporated with the dust. Suddenly, her knowledge wasn't a source of unease, but a beacon. People recalled her warnings, her quiet counsel about reinforcing structures, her insistence on planting certain cover crops to protect against erosion – warnings that had, in many cases, proven prescient.

"You were right, Ellie," Mrs. Gable said as she passed, her voice thick with emotion. She had lost a significant portion of her prized rose garden, the delicate blooms scattered like fallen petals, but her gaze met Ellie's with a newfound respect. "About the storm's intensity. And about… about him." The unspoken accusation against Vance hung between them, acknowledged but not dwelling. Ellie simply nodded, a small, sad smile gracing her lips. "We all did what we could, Agnes."

What followed was not a grand pronouncement or a formal assembly, but a series of small, significant gestures. A shared bucket of well water when one family's pump was damaged. An offer to help rebuild a collapsed chicken coop. A meal brought over for a neighbor too weary to cook. The shared ordeal had stripped away the pretenses and the petty grievances, leaving behind the fundamental human need for connection and mutual aid. The land, though scarred, had become a shared project of restoration, not a battleground for exploitation.

Ellie found herself drawn into the work, not as an authority, but as a fellow laborer. She helped Silas Hemlock shore up his porch, her knowledge of timber and stress points proving as valuable as his weathered experience. She worked alongside Maria Rodriguez, pointing out the best places to place temporary supports for the barn wall, her understanding of how the wood would settle and shift guiding their efforts. She showed young Billy

Miller how to properly brace a weakened joist, a technique she'd learned from her grandfather, explaining the principles of load distribution as they worked.

There was a profound beauty in this collective effort, a quiet dignity that far surpassed any ambition Vance had harbored. It wasn't about profit or conquest; it was about survival, about community, about the simple, enduring act of helping one's neighbor. The shared sweat, the grunts of exertion, the occasional shared laugh that broke through the grimness of the task – these were the new sounds of the Hill Country, sounds that resonated with a deeper truth than the roar of machinery.

The land itself seemed to respond to this renewed care. As the dust settled, and the sun, though still weak, began to warm the earth, there was a subtle shift in the atmosphere. The raw, exposed soil, so recently ravaged, began to feel less like a wound and more like a canvas awaiting new life. Ellie, walking the perimeter of her own land later that day, felt it. The wind, though still present, was no longer a destructive force, but a gentle breath, carrying the scent of damp earth and the faint, hopeful promise of rain. She noticed how the resilient native grasses, though flattened, were already beginning to lift their heads, their roots holding firm. This was the true strength of the land, its capacity for recovery, a strength that was mirrored in the people who were now actively tending to its wounds, and to each other's.

The days that followed were filled with a determined, almost quiet industriousness. There were no parades, no grand declarations. The efforts were organic, driven by necessity and a burgeoning sense of shared responsibility. Vance's departure had been the cleansing fire, the reckoning that, in its destructive wake, had paradoxically cleared the ground for a more authentic growth. The skepticism towards Ellie had been replaced by a quiet admiration, a recognition that her deep understanding of the land, which some had once feared as an oddity, was in fact their greatest asset. It was a wisdom born not of conquest, but of communion, a knowledge that now served to bind them together rather than divide them. The storm had been a test, a brutal, unforgiving one, but in its aftermath, the community of the Hill Country was not broken; it was re-forged, stronger and more united than before. The shared ordeal had revealed their vulnerabilities, but in doing so, it had also illuminated their collective strength, a resilience that ran as deep as the roots of the ancient oaks that still stood, weathered but unyielding.

The oppressive silence that had held sway during the storm was now a distant memory, replaced by a low hum of activity, the murmur of voices carrying on the wind, and the creak of timbers being secured. The dust, though still a persistent presence, no longer choked the air but rather swirled in lazy eddies, catching the nascent sunlight. For Ellie, it was a period of quiet observation, a time to witness the subtle reweaving of the community's fabric, thread by thread. The fear that had once been a palpable entity, a shadow cast by Vance's imposing presence and his disregard for their lives, had receded, replaced by a burgeoning sense of self-reliance and, more importantly, a deep-seated reliance on one another. The storm had been a crucible, burning away the dross of suspicion and indifference, leaving behind the pure metal of shared experience. Old Man Hemlock, his hands now steady as he worked alongside Sarah Jenkins to mend a broken fence post, no longer felt the weight of his years as a burden, but as a testament to his endurance. The rope Sarah provided, taut and strong, was more than just a tool; it was a symbol of the renewed bonds of trust that now spanned the small valley.

Down by the damaged barn, the collaborative efforts of the Miller and Rodriguez families were a testament to a different kind of progress. Young Billy Miller's youthful strength, guided by Maria Rodriguez's quiet competence, was transforming chaos into order. They worked with an unspoken language, anticipating each other's needs, their movements fluid and efficient. The damaged barn, once a symbol of vulnerability, was becoming a testament to their combined effort, a structure being rebuilt not just with wood and nails, but with shared sweat and mutual respect. Ellie, watching them from her porch, felt a swell of pride that was distinct from her own efforts. It was the pride of seeing the community, her community, finding its own voice, its own strength, in the absence of the domineering presence that had sought to silence it.

Mrs. Gable's acknowledgment, the simple words "You were right, Ellie," carried a weight far heavier than the storm's fury. It was an admission, an apology, a recognition that Ellie's understanding of the land, her intuitive connection to its rhythms and its warnings, was not a quirk, but a gift. The storm had been a harsh tutor, but its lessons were now etched into the collective consciousness of the Hill Country. The whispered doubts about Ellie's abilities had been silenced by the undeniable truth of her foresight. Her advice on reinforcing structures, her insistence on buffer crops, had proven not just prudent, but essential. The gentle way she showed Billy how to brace the joist, explaining the physics of load distribution with a quiet clarity, was a stark contrast to the blustering pronouncements of Vance, who had seen the land only as a resource to be exploited, not a living entity to be understood.

The days that followed were not marked by grand pronouncements or official pronouncements, but by the quiet, persistent work of healing. A shared bucket of water, a neighborly meal, a helping hand extended without a second thought – these were the building blocks of their recovery. The land, so brutally assaulted, was responding not just to the physical labor of repairs, but to the care and attention being lavished upon it. The native grasses, flattened by the wind, were already beginning to stir, their roots a testament to their resilience, a resilience that was now mirrored in the people who were tending to them, and to each other. Ellie felt it in the air, a subtle shift, a lightness that had been absent for so long. The land was breathing again, and with it, so were the people.

This quiet resurgence was not lost on Thomas Abernathy. He had been a constant presence during the crisis, his small printing press in town churning out updates, warnings, and reassurances. While Vance had been focused on his grand plans for industrial exploitation, Abernathy had been focused on the immediate needs of the people. His newspaper, the
*Hill Country Chronicle*, had become more than just a source of information; it had become a lifeline. He had meticulously documented Vance's actions, his disregard for environmental impact assessments, his heavy-handed tactics, and his ultimate, destructive ambition. Abernathy, a man of quiet conviction and unwavering dedication, had seen the potential for disaster long before the storm had arrived.

As the dust settled, and the immediate threat of the

tempest receded, Abernathy's focus shifted from warning to revelation. He continued to print, his ink-stained fingers a testament to his tireless efforts. He detailed Vance's abandoned machinery, the environmental damage that had been narrowly averted, and the extent of the disruption Vance's presence had caused. He published personal accounts from residents, their voices amplified by his careful reporting. He printed letters of gratitude, of shared hardship, and of a newfound resolve. His prose, always precise and evocative, now carried the added weight of lived experience. He didn't shy away from the grim realities, the loss and the damage, but he framed it within the context of their collective strength and their ability to endure.

One particularly impactful piece detailed the clandestine meetings Vance had held with county officials, the hushed discussions about rezoning and permits that had occurred well before the storm. Abernathy had acquired copies of these documents, obtained through a network of informants who had grown increasingly uneasy with Vance's methods. The
*Chronicle* laid bare Vance's attempts to circumvent local ordinances, his promises of economic

prosperity that masked a blatant disregard for the ecological balance of the region. It was a meticulously researched exposé, a testament to the power of investigative journalism in the face of powerful, often opaque, interests.

The reaction to Abernathy's reporting was immediate and profound. People who had been too afraid, too overwhelmed, or simply too busy with survival, now had a clear, concise account of what had transpired. The *Chronicle* became the focal point for shared understanding, a tangible artifact of their collective experience. It was passed from hand to hand, its pages dog-eared and smudged, read aloud in kitchens and on porches. Abernathy, who had always been a respected figure in town, now found himself a bona fide hero. Residents, their faces etched with the recent ordeal, would stop him on the street, not just to offer condolences for the minor damage to his own property, but to express their profound gratitude for his unwavering commitment to truth.

"Thomas," Silas Hemlock said one afternoon, his voice rough with emotion as he leaned on his mended fence, "you've given us back our voice. We were just… muddling through. You showed us what was really happening, what was at stake."

Sarah Jenkins, her hands still bearing the calluses from the storm's aftermath, echoed his sentiment. "Your paper, Thomas, it's the reason we understand why things were so bad. It's not just the wind and the rain, is it? It's what men do, too."

The victory wasn't just for Abernathy; it was a victory for the very idea of local journalism, for the principle that an informed community is an empowered community. Abernathy's newspaper had served as a bulwark against misinformation and manipulation, a beacon of truth in a landscape that had been, for a time, obscured by both dust and deception. He had faced the immense challenge of reporting on a crisis of both natural and man-made origins, and he had emerged not only unscathed, but triumphant. His reporting had validated the community's fears, confirmed their suspicions about Vance, and, most importantly, given them the information they needed to begin rebuilding on solid ground, both literally and figuratively.

The
*Hill Country Chronicle* had demonstrated that even in
the face of overwhelming natural forces, the power
of the pen, wielded with integrity and courage, could
hold those who sought to exploit or harm a
community accountable. Abernathy's win was a quiet
one, fought not with machinery or brute force, but
with ink and paper, with diligent research and an
unwavering belief in the public's right to know. He
had championed transparency and accountability,
proving that a dedicated journalist could indeed
serve as a powerful advocate for the well-being of
their community, even when pitted against the
destructive ambitions of powerful figures. The storm
had been a reckoning, and in its wake, Thomas
Abernathy and his newspaper had emerged as
undeniable victors, not for themselves, but for the
enduring spirit of the Hill Country. His name was
spoken with a new reverence, not as a mere
tradesman, but as a guardian of their collective truth,
a testament to the vital, and often underestimated,
power of the local press. The community, in turn,
rallied around him, their subscriptions increasing,
their letters of support pouring in, a testament to
their understanding that Abernathy's continued
success was intrinsically linked to their own

resilience and their ability to maintain vigilance against future threats. The *Chronicle* became more than a newspaper; it was a living document of their shared history, a chronicle of their enduring fight for self-determination, and a constant reminder that even in the darkest of times, truth, when pursued with diligence and courage, could ultimately prevail. The air, still thick with the scent of damp earth and broken wood, carried a new undercurrent: the tangible weight of assessment. For Ellie, this was the true reckoning, the quiet dawn after the tempest's rage. The farm, her sanctuary, her life's work, lay before her not as a scene of utter devastation, but as a landscape altered, wounded, yet stubbornly enduring. Her gaze swept across the fields, a familiar ache settling in her chest as she took in the flattened expanse where vibrant lavender had once stood, a sea of purple whispering promises of harvest and income. The storm had been a brutal sculptor, its fury carving new contours into the very soul of her land.

The rows of lavender, the pride of the Dawson farm, were a disheartening sight. Stalks lay broken, stripped of their fragrant blooms, a testament to the sheer force of the wind. It wasn't the gentle caress of a spring breeze that had nurtured them, but a violent upheaval that had torn at their very roots. Each fallen stem represented a lost bloom, a lost day of labor, a lost contribution to the delicate tapestry of their livelihood. The vibrant hues were muted, smudged by mud and debris, a somber echo of their former glory. Ellie knelt, her fingers tracing the bruised petals of a crushed flower. It was a visceral reminder of the fragility of their existence, of how quickly nature, in its untamed power, could reshape fortunes.

Yet, even as her heart mourned the loss of the lavender, a deeper, more resilient part of her began to catalog the intact. The core structure of their home, a testament to generations of care and craftsmanship, stood firm. The sturdy stone walls, the foundation laid with deep-set purpose, had weathered the storm's onslaught. The roof, though needing immediate attention, had largely held, preventing the catastrophic water damage that could have rendered it uninhabitable. The barn, a vital hub for their agricultural life, bore scars, but its essential framework remained. The troughs were overturned, the feed bins scattered, but the beams, the strong arms of the structure, still reached for the sky.

She walked the perimeter, her eyes a discerning observer, noting the bent posts of the fence line, the uprooted saplings that had been meant to one day provide shade and sustenance. The windbreak of pines, planted years ago with Vance's dismissive pronouncements still echoing in her memory, had performed admirably, their sacrifice a testament to her foresight. While some lay toppled, their mighty forms humbled by the gale, they had absorbed a significant portion of the wind's fury, diverting the worst of it from the more vulnerable fields and structures. It was a bittersweet victory, their strength purchased at the cost of their own well-being.

The loan Vance had so magnanimously – and suspiciously – offered now felt like a phantom limb, an irrelevant echo of a threat that had dissipated not through his intervention, but through the community's collective fortitude and Ellie's quiet preparedness. The promised capital, tainted by Vance's exploitative intentions and his blatant disregard for their welfare, was no longer a desired salvation. Instead, a different, more profound form of capital had emerged, forged in the crucible of shared crisis.

This was the capital of renewed respect, the currency of solidarity that had blossomed in the storm's aftermath. It was in the shared glance with Silas Hemlock as they surveyed the damage to his own property, a silent acknowledgment of mutual understanding. It was in the offer of extra hands from the Miller family to help secure her outbuildings, a gesture that transcended mere neighborliness and spoke of a deeper commitment to each other's survival. It was in the quiet competence of Sarah Jenkins, whose skilled hands, accustomed to mending, now reached out to help mend fences, both literal and metaphorical.

Ellie's botanical wisdom, once a quiet, almost solitary pursuit, had been thrust into the light, its intrinsic value suddenly, undeniably apparent. The subtle preparations she had made — the strategically placed buffer crops, the reinforced irrigation ditches, the knowledge of which native plants could withstand severe weather — were no longer viewed as the eccentricities of a woman too close to the earth. Instead, they were recognized as essential strategies, the hard-won knowledge of someone who understood the land's capricious nature and had prepared accordingly.

Her conversations with the neighbors now carried a different tenor. Where once her advice might have been met with polite skepticism or a dismissive nod, it was now sought with a genuine desire for understanding. Young Billy Miller, his youthful energy now directed towards practical tasks, would linger, asking about the best way to prune a damaged fruit tree, his eyes wide with a newfound respect for Ellie's knowledge. Maria Rodriguez, usually reserved, had openly praised Ellie's foresight in reinforcing the wellhead, a measure that had protected their precious water supply from contamination.

"We didn't think… well, we didn't think it would be that bad, Ellie," Mrs. Gable confessed, her voice still a little shaky as she helped Ellie clear debris from the path leading to the house. "Vance, he made it sound like it was just a bit of rough weather, a chance to get some modern improvements in. But you, you understood what the land was saying."

Ellie's response was gentle, a quiet affirmation of her deep-seated connection to the natural world. "The land always speaks, Mrs. Gable," she replied, her gaze drifting towards the distant hills, their contours softened by the morning mist. "We just have to learn to listen. And sometimes, it has to shout to be heard."

The damaged lavender fields, though a heavy loss, were not an insurmountable one. Ellie's mind, ever practical, began to envision the path forward. The very resilience of the plants, their ability to recover from severe stress, offered a glimmer of hope. With careful pruning, fertilization, and protection, the lavender could, in time, return. But more than that, her understanding of the soil, of the microclimates, of the plants best suited to this specific land, offered a broader vision.

Perhaps this was an opportunity to diversify, to re-examine the crops they cultivated. The storm had been a harsh lesson, a stark reminder of the risks associated with relying too heavily on a single commodity, especially one as sensitive to weather extremes as lavender. Her knowledge of drought-resistant native grasses, of hardy herbs that could thrive in less-than-ideal conditions, now felt like a treasure trove. She thought of the wild rosemary that clung to the rocky outcrops, the tenacious sage that graced the sun-baked slopes, plants that asked little and gave much.

This realization was not a sudden epiphany, but a gradual unfolding, a slow dawning of understanding that resonated with the quiet strength she had witnessed in her neighbors. The community, stripped bare by the storm, was now rediscovering its own innate resilience, its capacity for adaptation. The shared experience had forged a new sense of collective purpose, a mutual reliance that transcended individual hardship. The absence of Vance, and his destructive influence, had created a vacuum, but it was a vacuum that the community was now filling with its own ingenuity and interdependence.

Ellie knew the rebuilding would not be swift, nor would it be easy. The physical labor would be immense, the financial strain significant. But as she stood amidst the lingering scent of damp earth and the faint, lingering perfume of crushed lavender, she felt a profound sense of hope. It was a hope rooted not in the fleeting promises of external saviors, but in the enduring strength of the land itself, and in the unwavering solidarity of the people who called it home. The reckoning had come, and in its wake, a new foundation was being laid, built not on the shifting sands of Vance's ambitions, but on the bedrock of community, resilience, and a deep, abiding respect for the earth. The damaged fields were a wound, but they were also an invitation – an invitation to rebuild, to reimagine, and to emerge stronger, more connected, and ultimately, more in tune with the rhythms of the land that sustained them. The path ahead was uncertain, but for the first time in a long time, Ellie felt truly prepared to walk it, not alone, but as part of something larger, something that had weathered the storm and was now ready to bloom anew. The capital of trust, of shared knowledge, and of mutual support, was a far more valuable inheritance than any loan Vance might have offered. It was the currency of survival, and the promise of a truly resilient future. Her own farm, her beloved lavender, would eventually recover, perhaps in a new form, perhaps with a wider array of companions, but the spirit of the place, the spirit of the community, had been irrevocably strengthened. The storm had been a devastating blow, but it had also been a profound awakening.

# Chapter 8: Roots of Resilience

The scent of the storm, still clinging to the air like a damp shroud, was slowly giving way to the invigorating aroma of freshly turned earth. Ellie, her hands already calloused from the initial clearing, felt a familiar sense of purpose settle over her. The devastation of the past weeks had been a brutal teacher, revealing the vulnerabilities of a landscape too reliant on a single, delicate bloom. Now, a new lesson was unfolding: the profound strength found in diversity, in listening to the land's deeper whispers, and in the wisdom passed down through generations. The lavender, though resilient in its own right, had been a beautiful risk, one that the recent tempest had starkly exposed. The time for a broader, more robust approach had arrived, and it began with the soil itself.

Her grandmother's journals, once a source of quiet comfort and personal reflection, had transformed into an invaluable blueprint. Those faded pages, filled with meticulous observations on soil types, microclimates, and the subtle language of native flora, were now her guide. She remembered sitting by the hearth, a small girl with perpetually smudged knees, listening as her grandmother spoke of the hardy prairie grasses, the tenacious wildflowers that could draw sustenance from seemingly barren ground, and the deep-rooted wisdom of plants that had adapted to the land's inherent challenges long before any human hand had attempted to shape it. Vance's dismissive remarks about her "old-fashioned notions" now seemed as hollow as the wind that had whipped through the damaged fields. It was her grandmother's legacy, her deep understanding of the earth's unyielding rhythms, that was truly valuable.

The focus of their immediate efforts was the northernmost field, the one that had borne the brunt of the wind's fury and where the lavender's flattened stalks lay like a mournful carpet. This was not a field to be simply replanted with more lavender, not yet. This was a field that needed to be reborn, to be coaxed back to health with a more forgiving hand. Ellie gathered the neighbors who had volunteered their time and strength. Silas Hemlock, his own fields showing the scars of the storm but his spirit unbent, brought his team and sturdy plows. The Miller family, their younger sons eager to contribute, arrived with shovels and wheelbarrows. Even Mrs. Gable, her hands now steady, joined in, her knowledge of mending fences extending to the patient work of preparing the earth.

"We're not just clearing debris today," Ellie announced, her voice carrying across the quiet field. "We're preparing a new beginning. We'll be turning over this soil, but we'll be doing it with a different intention." She explained her plan, referencing her grandmother's notes. "My grandmother always said that the strongest roots are grown in soil that's been allowed to breathe, to recover, and to be nourished by its own natural strength. We'll be incorporating what organic matter we can salvage, and then, we'll be sowing seeds that have proven their resilience here for centuries."

The process began with a careful assessment of the soil itself. Ellie, with her trowel, dug into the earth, examining its texture, its moisture content, and its apparent fertility. She pointed out the compacted areas, the places where the wind had scoured away the topsoil, and the sections that, thankfully, still held promise. "This is clay loam," she explained to young Billy Miller, who watched her with rapt attention, holding a bucket of water. "It holds moisture well, but it can become heavy if not managed properly. See these dark flecks? That's good organic matter, some of it from the fallen lavender, which will break down and feed the soil. But we need to aerate it."

The plowing was a communal effort. The earth, still heavy with moisture from the storm, yielded grudgingly at first. The metal of the plowshare sliced through the soil, turning over dark, rich layers. It was a physical, demanding task, each turn of the plow a testament to their collective will to heal the land. Ellie, working alongside Silas, guided the horses, her understanding of their temperament honed by years of shared labor. The rhythmic creak of the plow, the snorting of the horses, the low murmur of conversation as neighbors shared stories and encouragement – it was a symphony of recovery, a stark contrast to the violent chaos of the storm.

As the soil was turned, Ellie instructed them on the careful removal of any remaining damaged plant material that could hinder new growth or introduce disease. This wasn't a hasty cleanup; it was a thoughtful, deliberate process of discernment. They were not simply removing the broken; they were nurturing the potential.

With the soil prepared, the next crucial step was the selection of seeds. Ellie had spent hours poring over her grandmother's meticulously labeled packets, many of them carefully stored in cool, dark places and miraculously untouched by the storm's wrath. There were seeds for coneflowers, their tough petals designed to withstand harsh sun and wind. There were packets of wild rye, a native grass known for its ability to stabilize soil and prevent erosion, its deep root system a natural anchor. She had also unearthed seeds for native sunflowers, their robust stalks and cheerful faces a symbol of endurance, and for bee balm, a hardy perennial that not only attracted vital pollinators but also possessed medicinal properties, a nod to her grandmother's holistic approach to the land and its bounty.

"These aren't flashy like the lavender, perhaps," Ellie said, holding up a small packet of dark, slender seeds. "But they are honest. They ask for less and they give more. They are the true heartwood of this land, the plants that have always known how to survive and thrive here, even when things get difficult."

The sowing was a slower, more delicate affair than the plowing. Ellie showed them how to create shallow furrows, spacing the seeds according to her grandmother's precise instructions. She spoke of the importance of depth, of covering the seeds with just the right amount of soil to protect them yet allow them to reach for the light. Each seed represented a promise, a tiny spark of life entrusted to their care. There was a reverence in the way they moved, a shared understanding of the immense responsibility they held.

The community's involvement was not just about muscle; it was about shared knowledge and a collective commitment. Maria Rodriguez, whose family had long cultivated herbs in their own small garden, offered her expertise on companion planting, suggesting that the bee balm would not only benefit the sunflowers but also deter certain pests. Mr. Henderson, a retired agronomist who lived a few miles west, stopped by, not to offer unsolicited advice, but to share his own observations of how certain native species had fared in past droughts. His presence, a quiet affirmation of Ellie's approach, was a welcome addition.

"It's about building resilience from the ground up, Ellie," Mr. Henderson had said, his weathered hand resting on the fence post. "You're not just planting flowers; you're planting an ecosystem. You're giving the land the tools it needs to weather whatever comes next."

The process wasn't confined to that one field. Ellie, with the help of a growing cadre of volunteers, began to assess and plan for other areas of the farm. The windbreak of pines, though damaged, had served its purpose. Now, she considered interplanting them with hardy, low-growing shrubs that could provide additional protection and habitat for beneficial insects. The areas near the creek, prone to occasional flooding, were designated for moisture-loving native plants, like certain types of iris and sedges, that could not only tolerate wet conditions but also help to filter runoff and prevent erosion.

Ellie's grandmother had often spoken of the interconnectedness of all living things on the farm, a concept that Vance had scoffed at as sentimental nonsense. Now, it was becoming the guiding principle of their recovery. They were not just restoring individual crops; they were rebuilding a functioning, balanced landscape. The damaged lavender fields, while a significant loss, were becoming a catalyst for this deeper understanding. It was an opportunity to move beyond the fragility of a monoculture and embrace the robust strength of a diverse, self-sustaining system.

The rhythm of planting became a familiar cadence in the days that followed. Mornings were dedicated to preparing the soil and sowing seeds. Afternoons were spent clearing, repairing fences, and securing damaged structures. Evenings were often filled with quiet conversations, planning sessions in Ellie's restored farmhouse, where the scent of drying herbs now mingled with the faint, lingering aroma of possibility. The younger generation, inspired by the tangible work and the sense of purpose, was deeply involved. They learned the names of plants, the feel of different soils, the satisfaction of contributing to something larger than themselves.

Ellie found herself frequently referring to her grandmother's practical advice, not just on plant selection, but on the very philosophy of farming. "The land doesn't give freely," her grandmother had written in one passage. "It demands respect, patience, and a willingness to work with its nature, not against it. A wise farmer understands that their greatest harvest is not always in the quantity of what they pick, but in the health and vibrancy of the soil that will sustain them for years to come."

This was precisely the ethos that was taking root in the community. The storm had stripped away the superficial, the easy gains, and revealed the fundamental truths of their connection to the land. Vance's offer of financial assistance, once a tempting lifeline, now seemed like a shallow attempt to impose an external solution onto a problem that required an internal, organic response. The real capital, the true investment, was being made in the soil, in the seeds, and in the shared commitment of the people working side-by-side.

As the last of the selected seeds were carefully placed into the prepared earth, a sense of quiet accomplishment settled over the fields. The work was far from over. There would be weeks of watchful waiting, of tending to the new sprouts, of protecting them from any lingering threats. But as Ellie surveyed the newly sown rows, she felt a profound sense of hope, a hope as deep and as tenacious as the roots she was nurturing beneath the surface. This was not just replanting; it was a reclamation, a testament to the enduring power of resilience, diversity, and the timeless wisdom of the land itself. The scars of the storm would remain, a reminder of the past, but the seeds that had been sown were the promise of a future, a future rooted in the strength and adaptability that had always been present, waiting to be rediscovered.

The acrid bite of dust that had choked the air, a constant, rasping reminder of the storm's fury, began to dissipate. It yielded, slowly but surely, to a softer, cleaner atmosphere. The harsh sunlight, once an enemy reflecting off debris, now felt like a gentle hand on the land, coaxing life back into its weary bones. And with this shift in the environment, a parallel, almost imperceptible transformation began to unfold within the farmhouse walls. Thomas, nestled in his bed, the same one where he had wrestled with the fever and the suffocating cough, started to stir with a different kind of energy.

Ellie watched him with a vigilance born of weeks of gnawing anxiety. The rasping sound that had become the soundtrack to her nights was softening. His breaths, once shallow and strained, were drawing deeper into his small chest, carrying with them the newly purified air. The tightness that had etched itself onto his face, a perpetual grimace of discomfort, was easing. He still coughed, but the spasms were less violent, more like the clearing of a throat than a desperate struggle for air. Each smaller cough, each moment he slept without a fitful awakening, felt like a profound victory, a tiny, precious flag of surrender planted by the forces of healing.

She would sit by his bedside for hours, the rhythmic hum of her mending, the quiet rustle of pages as she consulted her grandmother's journals, a calming counterpoint to his fragile slumber. Sometimes, he would open his eyes, and the usual glazed look of illness was replaced by a flicker of awareness. He'd look at her, and a faint smile, a ghost of his former self, would touch his lips. "Ellie," he'd whisper, his voice a thin thread, but a voice that held the promise of return. These moments, fleeting as they were, were the ones she clung to, the ones that fueled her own weary spirit.

Her relief was a tide, washing away the accumulated stress and fear. It was a quiet, internal tide, not one of outward celebration, but of a deep, profound gratitude that settled in her bones. She saw the connection so clearly: the clearing of the fields, the careful turning of the soil, the planting of those hardy, native seeds – it wasn't just about restoring the lavender fields or securing the farm's future. It was about creating an environment where healing could take root, where the youngest and most vulnerable among them could draw strength from the land's renewed vitality. The very air they breathed, now less laden with dust and more infused with the scent of damp earth and burgeoning life, was a balm to his lungs.

Thomas's gradual recovery wasn't a sudden,

dramatic event, but a slow, steady climb. He began to ask for sips of water more frequently, not just as a desperate plea, but as a simple expression of thirst. He started to tolerate small amounts of broth, the nourishment seeping into his system and slowly, painstakingly, rebuilding his depleted reserves. Ellie would spoon the warm liquid into his mouth, watching with bated breath as he swallowed, her heart soaring with each successful gulp.

One afternoon, as the sun streamed through the window, illuminating the motes of dust that still danced in the air, Thomas stirred and sat up, a movement that seemed almost monumental. He leaned against his pillows, his gaze falling upon a small, smooth stone Ellie had placed on his bedside table, a stone she had found near the creek after the storm, its surface polished by water and time. He reached out a small, still-thin hand and traced its contours.

"It's pretty, Ellie," he murmured, his voice stronger than it had been in days.

Ellie felt a lump form in her throat. "It is, isn't it, Thomas? It's been there a long time, weathering storms, just waiting for the sun to shine again." She offered him a hesitant smile. "Just like you."

He looked at her, and this time, the smile wasn't a ghost. It was a weak, but genuine expression of recognition and affection. He reached out and squeezed her hand, his grip surprisingly firm. It was a small gesture, easily overlooked in the grand scheme of things, but for Ellie, it was a beacon, a tangible sign of his return from the precipice.

The improved air quality was, no doubt, a significant factor. The storm had stirred up so much particulate matter, so much that had settled and then been violently redistributed. The careful work of clearing the debris, the dampening of dust with water from the creek before hauling away the larger remnants, and the very act of the earth beginning to re-cover itself with a delicate fuzz of new growth — all of it contributed to a breathable atmosphere. Ellie could see it in the way Thomas's chest rose and fell more easily, in the way the persistent cough began to recede into the background of their lives.

But it was more than just the air. It was the collective effort, the palpable sense of purpose that had permeated the farm and the community. The shared labor, the communal meals of simple, nourishing food, the quiet conversations that offered solace and shared strength – these were the intangible elements that fostered healing. Thomas, even in his weakened state, could sense this shift. He could feel the lessening of tension in the house, the return of a certain rhythm to their days. The fear that had clung to the farmhouse like the scent of damp earth after the rain was slowly being replaced by a cautious optimism, a fragile but persistent hope.

Ellie's grandmother's journals, which had become her constant companions, offered not just agricultural wisdom but also insights into the human spirit. She remembered reading passages about the importance of creating a sanctuary, a space where the sick could feel safe and nurtured. Her grandmother had written about the way the scent of certain herbs, like chamomile and mint, could be soothing, and how fresh, clean linen could make a world of difference to a feverish body. Ellie had diligently followed these gentle prescriptions, brewing teas from the herbs she had managed to salvage, changing Thomas's bedding with a care that bordered on reverence.

She would sit by his window and describe the work happening outside, framing it as a grand project of renewal. "The men are bringing in the new seeds, Thomas," she'd say, her voice soft. "Big, strong seeds that have always lived here, the kind that know how to hold onto the earth, even when the wind blows hard." She'd talk about Silas Hemlock and his steady hands, about the Miller boys, their enthusiasm a bright spot, and about Mrs. Gable, her quiet competence a source of reassurance. She painted a picture of a community united, each person contributing their part to the larger task of healing, not just the land, but themselves.

Thomas, his eyes often closed, would listen intently. He didn't always understand the specifics, the agricultural terms, but he understood the feeling behind her words: the feeling of being cared for, of being part of something larger and more enduring than the immediate suffering. He understood the concept of things growing, of the earth waking up. It was a narrative of hope, woven into the fabric of his recovery.

There were days when the progress seemed to stall, when a particularly deep cough would seize him, sending a fresh wave of panic through Ellie. But these moments were becoming less frequent, less debilitating. He was beginning to eat small meals at the table with her, his appetite slowly returning. He would watch her as she worked, his gaze steady, a silent observer of the renewed activity on the farm. He'd point out a bird in the distance, or the way the sunlight fell on the newly plowed earth, his observations a testament to his re-engagement with the world around him.

One crisp morning, a week after he had first managed to sit up, Thomas asked if he could go outside, even just for a few minutes. Ellie hesitated, her instinct to protect warring with her recognition of his growing strength. She looked at his face, at the faint color that had returned to his cheeks, at the spark of desire in his eyes.

"Just for a little while," she agreed, her voice filled with a mixture of caution and joy. "And you'll need your shawl."

She helped him dress, bundling him up against the lingering coolness of the morning air. With his small hand clasped tightly in hers, they stepped out onto the porch. The world outside was transformed. The ravaged fields were still visible, the scars of the storm a stark reminder of what had happened. But now, there was also the promise of what was to come. The newly turned soil looked dark and rich, a fertile bed for the seeds of resilience. The sky was a brilliant, unblemished blue.

Thomas took a deep, slow breath, his eyes wide as he surveyed the landscape. He didn't say anything for a long moment, just absorbed the sights and sounds and smells. A robin chirped from a nearby branch, a cheerful, uninhibited sound that seemed to encapsulate the season's resurgence.

"It's… it's nice out here, Ellie," he whispered, his voice carrying the wonder of a child rediscovering a familiar world.

Ellie squeezed his hand, her heart swelling. "Yes, Thomas," she said, her own voice thick with emotion. "It is. We're coming back, aren't we?"

He nodded, a small, solemn nod. "We're coming back."

The farm was not yet fully healed, and Thomas was not yet fully recovered. There would be more days of quiet tending, more days of watchful waiting. But in those small, precious victories – the softening of a cough, the return of a smile, the first tentative steps outside – Ellie saw the profound truth of her grandmother's wisdom. Resilience wasn't just about the strength of the earth; it was about the strength of the human spirit, a spirit that found its deepest nourishment in the very land it called home, a spirit that, like the native seeds they had sown, possessed an innate ability to endure, to adapt, and to bloom again, even after the harshest of storms. Thomas's recovery was a living testament to this enduring truth, a gentle echo of the land's own slow, steady, and magnificent return to life. He was, in his own small way, a symbol of the farm's own dawning resilience, a fragile sprout pushing through the soil, reaching for the light.

The whisper of the wind through the surviving lavender stalks, a sound that had once spoken of summer abundance, now carried a different message. It was a melody of survival, a subtle yet persistent hum that Ellie attuned herself to. The storm had tested their resolve, stripped away the familiar, and in its aftermath, demanded a reevaluation of everything they thought they knew about their land. The instinct to recoil, to retreat from the exposed vulnerability, was strong. But it was a whisper against the louder call of the earth, a call for adaptation, for a deeper understanding of its inherent strengths. Her grandmother's journals, once a guide to cultivating a specific, cherished crop, now became a testament to a more profound principle: resilience forged through diversity.

The very act of clearing the fields, a task that had

initially felt like an excavation of their losses, had inadvertently revealed a hidden potential. Beneath the wind-scoured surface, the soil, though bruised, was still alive. And the native plants, those hardy, often overlooked denizens of the plains, had weathered the tempest with a stoicism that Ellie now recognized as a powerful lesson. They hadn't been coddled; they had simply endured, drawing strength from the very conditions that had threatened to annihilate the more delicate lavender. It was a revelation that shifted her perspective, transforming the daunting task of rebuilding into an opportunity for reinvention.

She began to envision a new landscape, not one that merely restored the past, but one that embraced the lessons of the present. The lavender, a symbol of their family's legacy and their commitment to a particular kind of beauty, would remain. But it would no longer stand alone, a solitary sentinel against the elements. It would be interwoven, integrated, its ethereal fragrance mingling with the earthy aromas of prairie grasses and the subtle, medicinal notes of wild herbs. This was not a surrender of their heritage, but an expansion of it, a recognition that true strength lay in embracing the full spectrum of the land's offerings.

Her consultations with Silas Hemlock took on a new urgency, a deeper collaborative spirit. Silas, his hands weathered and calloused from decades of working the soil, possessed an intuitive knowledge of the native flora. He spoke of plants that could draw moisture from deep within the earth, of grasses that held the soil firm against the wind, of wildflowers that bloomed with tenacious beauty even in the harshest seasons. He showed Ellie how certain native shrubs could provide windbreaks, not just for the lavender, but for the entire farm, creating microclimates that would foster growth and mitigate future damage.

"These here," Silas explained, gesturing to a patch of sturdy, silver-green foliage, "they're called 'Silverleaf.' Tough as old boots. Don't need much water once they're established, and their roots, Ellie, they go down, down, down. They're the anchors we need." He then pointed to a cluster of vibrant purple blooms, still resilient despite the recent trials. "And this little beauty? That's Coneflower. Attracts the pollinators, even the ones that'll visit your lavender, and it can handle the dry spells like nothin' else."

Ellie absorbed his words like a thirsty plant drawing in rain. She began to see the farm not as a static entity to be preserved, but as a dynamic ecosystem to be nurtured. The meticulous rows of lavender, while beautiful, had represented a monoculture, a vulnerability that the storm had so cruelly exposed. Now, she envisioned a more complex tapestry, a mosaic of plants working in concert, each contributing to the overall health and resilience of the farm. It was a vision that honored the legacy of her grandmother, who had believed in the power of the earth, but also embraced a more evolved understanding of that power, one informed by the harsh realities of a changing climate.

The process of integrating these native plants was a delicate dance. It involved carefully selecting the right species, understanding their specific needs, and finding the optimal balance between the established lavender rows and the wilder, more robust newcomers. There were challenges, of course. Some of the native plants were aggressive spreaders, and

Ellie and Silas had to work diligently to ensure they didn't overwhelm the more delicate lavender. Others required a different approach to cultivation, a less interventionist touch, allowing them to find their own place within the farm's structure.

Ellie spent hours poring over her grandmother's journals, searching for any mention of companion planting, of natural pest deterrents, of techniques that might have been passed down through generations but had been overshadowed by the pursuit of a single, profitable crop. She found fragmented notes, hints of a time when the farm's biodiversity was not a threat, but a source of strength. Her grandmother had written of the benefits of "wild neighbors," of how the presence of certain native species could naturally enrich the soil and ward off harmful insects. It was as if the journals themselves were urging her toward this new path.

The community, too, played a vital role in this reimagining. The shared experience of the storm had forged a deeper bond, a mutual understanding of their interdependence. Neighbors offered advice, shared cuttings of hardy native plants they had in their own gardens, and lent a hand with the labor-intensive task of preparing the soil for this new, diverse planting. Mrs. Gable, with her innate understanding of natural remedies and her well-tended herb garden, became an invaluable resource, identifying plants that could act as natural fertilizers or attract beneficial insects.

"You're not just planting flowers, Ellie," Mrs. Gable had said, her eyes twinkling as she surveyed a patch of newly prepared ground, ready for a mix of lavender and native wildflowers. "You're planting a future. A future that knows how to bend without breaking."

Thomas, his health fully restored and his youthful energy now focused on the farm's renewal, became an enthusiastic participant in this transformation. He loved the wilder parts of the new design, the less structured plantings where nature was allowed a freer hand. He would run through the emerging meadows, his laughter echoing through the fields, pointing out the burgeoning wildflowers and the busy bees that now frequented a wider array of blossoms. He was, in his own way, embodying the spirit of resilience, a testament to the enduring power of life.

The impact of this hybrid approach was soon evident. The newly established native plants, with their deep root systems, began to stabilize the soil, reducing erosion and improving its water retention. The diverse flora attracted a wider variety of pollinators, creating a more robust and self-sustaining ecosystem. The lavender, benefiting from the protection of the native windbreaks and the improved soil health, began to show signs of renewed vigor, its delicate blooms promising a return of the farm's signature fragrance.

Ellie's vision extended beyond the fields themselves. She began to consider how the farm's narrative could also be reimagined. The story of a lavender farm, while beautiful, was limited. The story of a resilient agricultural haven, one that had learned to adapt and thrive in the face of adversity, was far more compelling. She started to talk about the farm as a living laboratory, a testament to the power of embracing change, of finding strength in diversity. She began to document the process, not just for her own records, but as a shared learning experience for the community and, perhaps, for others who might face similar challenges.

The lavender legacy was not being abandoned; it was being enriched. It was evolving, adapting, much like the land itself. The farm was becoming a living embodiment of her grandmother's wisdom, a wisdom that transcended the cultivation of a single crop and embraced the fundamental principles of ecological balance and enduring strength. The scent of lavender would still drift on the breeze, a familiar comfort, but it would now be accompanied by the wilder, more complex perfumes of the prairie, a symphony of resilience played out across the fields. The Dawson farm was no longer just a lavender farm; it was a testament to the enduring spirit of life, a vibrant tapestry woven from the threads of heritage and the enduring wisdom of the land itself. It was a redefinition of abundance, a profound understanding that true prosperity lay not in exclusivity, but in integration, in the tenacious beauty of a life that refused to be diminished, a life that, when faced with the storm, chose to bloom anew, in a thousand different, breathtaking ways.

The scent of drying herbs hung heavy and sweet in the air of Ellie's small cottage, a far cry from the sharp, invigorating fragrance of lavender that had once defined her farm. Sunlight, filtered through the dusty panes, illuminated motes dancing in the stillness, and landed on worn pages of botanical texts scattered across her table. The transformation hadn't been immediate, not a sudden blooming, but a slow, steady unfurling, much like the native plants she now championed. Her initial solitary pursuit of understanding the land's recovery had, quite unexpectedly, drawn others in.

It had started subtly. A neighbor, Mrs. Henderson, whose prize-winning roses had succumbed to a blight that seemed to spread with the very winds that had battered Ellie's lavender, had hesitantly knocked on her door. Mrs. Henderson, a woman who prided herself on her manicured perfection, was in despair. She'd heard whispers of Ellie's work with the wild plants, her uncanny ability to coax life from seemingly barren soil. Could she, perhaps, offer some advice for her struggling garden? Ellie, surprised by the request, had invited her in, offered her a cup of chamomile tea brewed from her own drying plants, and spent an hour sketching out a simple plan. It involved companion planting with native wildflowers known to deter pests, and a particular mix of compost enriched with native leaf litter to improve soil structure. She'd even gifted Mrs. Henderson a small packet of coneflower seeds.

The result was, to Mrs. Henderson's astonishment, remarkable. The blight receded, and new growth, stronger and more vibrant, began to emerge. More importantly, the native wildflowers, with their cheerful resilience, seemed to draw beneficial insects, creating a natural balance that her previous chemical interventions had disrupted. Word, as it always did in these close-knit rural communities, began to spread.

Soon, the trickle became a steady stream. Farmers grappling with soil erosion sought her out, not for the lavender's yield, but for her knowledge of deep-rooted grasses and their ability to bind the earth. Mothers brought their children, afflicted with persistent coughs and fevers, hoping for the gentle remedies Ellie was said to concoct. Elias Thorne, whose farm had been particularly hard-hit by the drought that followed the storm, arrived one sweltering afternoon, his face etched with worry. His corn was wilting, his well was running low, and he was facing ruin. He'd heard Ellie had found ways to make plants thrive with less water.

Ellie led him out to her fields, not just the lavender rows, but the wilder sections where she'd integrated prairie clover and native grasses. She showed him the silvery sheen of silverleaf, its shallow, widespread roots capturing dew. She pointed out the tenacious little blue grama grass, its fine roots creating a dense mat that conserved moisture. "It's about working *with* the land, Elias," she explained, her voice calm and steady. "Not against it. These plants, they've evolved here. They know how to survive the lean times. They can teach us."

She explained the concept of mulching with native ground cover, of capturing and retaining every drop of moisture. She shared her knowledge of drought-tolerant herbs like echinacea and yarrow, their medicinal properties as valuable as their ability to withstand dry spells. She even showed him how to create natural windbreaks using rows of hardy native shrubs, which would not only protect his crops but also reduce evaporation. Elias, initially skeptical, was captivated by her deep, intuitive understanding, a knowledge that seemed to flow directly from the land itself. He returned to his farm with a handful of seeds and a notebook filled with Ellie's careful, handwritten instructions.

Her home, once a place primarily dedicated to the solitary cultivation of lavender, became a hub. The small parlor, with its comfortable, if worn, furniture, was often filled with the hushed murmurs of conversation. Neighbors would arrive with wilting houseplants, their leaves browned and curling, seeking Ellie's touch. She'd examine them with a gentle reverence, diagnose the problem – usually a combination of poor soil and insufficient light – and prescribe a remedy, often a simple infusion of dandelion root or a repotting with a specially prepared soil mix.

Even the local doctor, Dr. Albright, a man steeped in the traditional practices of Western medicine, found himself referring patients to Ellie. When a mysterious rash began to affect children in the town, a rash that defied his usual treatments, he remembered Ellie's keen eye for identifying local flora. He hesitantly approached her, explaining the symptoms. Ellie, after a few quiet days of observation and consultation with her grandmother's journals, identified a specific type of milkweed that, when prepared correctly, could create a soothing poultice. The rash cleared within days. Dr. Albright, humbled and impressed, began to view Ellie's botanical knowledge not as an eccentric hobby, but as a valuable, complementary form of healing.

The transformation of Ellie's own perception was as profound as the change in how others saw her. What had once felt like a solitary, even isolating, dedication to a demanding crop had blossomed into a shared wisdom. The quiet hours spent in research and experimentation were no longer just about preserving her family's legacy; they were about contributing to the well-being of her entire community. Her understanding of the land, honed by necessity and deepened by an unwavering respect for nature's intricate balance, had become a source of strength for everyone.

She found a quiet joy in seeing the results of her shared knowledge. The vibrant splash of coneflowers blooming in Mrs. Henderson's garden, attracting buzzing bees and iridescent dragonflies, was a small victory. Elias Thorne's corn, standing tall and healthy against the late summer sun, was another. The children's laughter, free from the discomfort of the rash, was perhaps the sweetest music of all.

Ellie's reputation as a skilled herbalist and botanist grew organically, rooted in the tangible results of her advice. People began to seek her out not just for remedies, but for guidance on how to cultivate gardens that were both beautiful and resilient. They wanted to learn how to coax life from their own patches of earth, how to create havens that could withstand the unpredictable whims of the weather. Her home became more than just a cottage; it was a sanctuary of shared knowledge, a place where the wisdom of the land was valued and nurtured. The perceived eccentricities of a woman who spoke to plants and preferred the company of wildflowers to society gatherings had, in the crucible of environmental change, been transmuted into essential wisdom for a region grappling with new challenges. The subtle perfume of lavender still lingered, a whisper of the past, but it was now interwoven with the earthy, resilient scents of native blooms, a testament to a new kind of abundance.

The quiet hum of a community awakening, fueled by shared necessity and burgeoning hope, began to fill the valley. The Dawsons, their farm slowly but surely showing the first signs of recovery after the devastating storm and subsequent drought, became an unwitting beacon. Their methodical approach, their quiet determination to work *with* the land rather than fight it, resonated deeply with their neighbors, many of whom were still reeling from the losses they had endured. It wasn't just about the lavender anymore; it was about a fundamental shift in understanding, a recognition that the old ways, reliant on external inputs and often unsustainable practices, were no longer sufficient.

Ellie found herself at the forefront of this quiet revolution, not through any grand declaration, but through the simple act of sharing what she had learned. The conversations that had once begun hesitantly on her doorstep now flowed more freely, spilling out into the communal spaces of the town. The small, sun-drenched parlor of her cottage, once a sanctuary for her solitary study, transformed into a vibrant hub of shared learning. It started with a request from Sarah Jenkins, a young mother whose usually bountiful vegetable patch had yielded little more than withered leaves and stunted growth. Sarah, having heard of Ellie's success with coaxing life from the soil, approached with a basket of her failed produce.

"Ellie," she'd begun, her voice laced with a mixture of desperation and a newfound respect, "I don't know what I'm doing wrong. Everything's just… giving up."

Ellie, accustomed to these hesitant appeals, invited Sarah in, her hands still dusted with dried earth from her morning's work. She offered Sarah a cup of her own herbal tea, a blend of mint and lemon balm, and sat with her, patiently listening. She didn't offer quick fixes or magical solutions. Instead, she spoke of the soil itself, of its depleted state, and the critical need for replenishment. She shared insights from her grandmother's worn journals, detailing methods of composting that went beyond mere kitchen scraps. She spoke of the importance of incorporating native plant matter, of allowing fallen leaves and decaying wood to return their nutrients to the earth, creating a richer, more resilient foundation.

"It's not just about feeding the plants, Sarah," Ellie explained, her gaze soft but knowing. "It's about feeding the soil. Think of it like this – you can't expect a child to grow strong on just one kind of food. The soil needs a diverse diet too." She drew diagrams on a spare sheet of paper, illustrating the process of creating a layered compost heap, emphasizing the inclusion of nitrogen-rich materials like grass clippings and manure, balanced with carbon-rich elements like dried leaves and straw. She also introduced Sarah to the concept of cover cropping, suggesting hardy native legumes like vetch and clover that could be planted in the off-season to enrich the soil with nitrogen and prevent erosion.

Sarah, initially overwhelmed, found herself captivated by Ellie's patient explanations and the tangible, common-sense approach. Ellie didn't just speak; she demonstrated. She showed Sarah how to build a simple compost bin from salvaged wood and how to turn it effectively to ensure aeration. She even gifted Sarah a small starter culture of worms for vermicomposting, explaining their remarkable ability to break down organic matter into nutrient-rich castings.

The results were not immediate, but Sarah was a diligent student. By the following spring, her garden, once a testament to her frustration, was transformed. Rows of healthy, vibrant vegetables, from robust tomatoes to leafy greens, thrived. She had learned to observe her plants, to notice the subtle signs of stress or deficiency, and to respond with the appropriate natural remedies. More importantly, she had learned to foster a healthy ecosystem within her own small plot of land.

This success, like ripples spreading across a pond, encouraged others. The idea of communal gardening began to take root, not as a formal, organized initiative, but as a natural extension of shared experience and mutual aid. Neighbors began to pool resources, sharing seeds and cuttings from their own successful plantings. Old Mrs. Gable, whose arthritis made extensive tilling a painful ordeal, found herself with a steady supply of fresh vegetables from a shared plot near the town hall, tended by younger, stronger hands. In return, she offered her decades of experience in preserving and canning, her kitchen a constant source of delicious jams and pickles that sustained the community through the leaner months.

The old schoolhouse, long since abandoned by its younger pupils who now travelled to the larger town down the river, became a makeshift meeting place. Ellie, at the gentle urging of her neighbors, agreed to lead informal workshops. Her hands, once accustomed to the delicate handling of lavender sprigs, now expertly guided others in the art of seed saving, the crucial step in ensuring self-sufficiency and preserving heirloom varieties. She explained the principles of cross-pollination and the importance of isolating different varieties to maintain genetic purity. She meticulously demonstrated how to harvest, dry, and store seeds for optimal viability, drawing on her grandmother's extensive notes on the subject.

"Think of these seeds," she'd say, holding a small, papery packet of wild bee balm, "as little packets of the future. Each one holds the promise of a plant, a meal, a medicine. We must treat them with the respect they deserve."

She also began sharing her knowledge of water conservation, a critical skill in the increasingly unpredictable climate. She spoke of the ingenious methods employed by ancient civilizations, of rain catchment systems and the use of natural swales to guide and retain water on the landscape. She showed them how to create "hugelkultur" beds – raised mounds of decaying wood, soil, and compost that acted like sponges, slowly releasing moisture to surrounding plants. She demonstrated how to mulch deeply with organic materials, not only suppressing weeds but also significantly reducing evaporation from the soil surface.

"The rain we receive, we must learn to hold onto," Ellie would explain, her voice resonating with the quiet authority of experience. "It's a gift, and we must be good stewards of it. Every drop matters."

Her workshops weren't just about practical techniques; they were about fostering a deeper connection to the natural world. She'd bring in samples of native plants, their diverse forms and functions laid bare for examination. She'd identify the deep, fibrous root systems of prairie grasses that could penetrate compacted soil and draw moisture from deep underground. She'd point out the silvery, downy leaves of plants like Artemisias and Salvias, adapted to reflect sunlight and minimize water loss. She encouraged her students to observe the subtle cues of the environment, to understand the language of the plants and the soil.

One particularly memorable workshop focused on the creation of "pollinator gardens" – small, intentionally planted areas designed to attract and support bees, butterflies, and other beneficial insects. Ellie shared her grandmother's recipes for seed mixes, combinations of native wildflowers that bloomed throughout the growing season, providing a continuous source of nectar and pollen. She explained the vital role these insects played in the pollination of many food crops, a crucial element of a resilient agricultural system. She even showed them how to create simple "bee hotels" from hollowed-out logs and bundles of reeds, providing safe nesting sites for solitary native bees.

The response was overwhelming. People brought

their own forgotten seeds, the ones passed down through generations but often overlooked in favor of more commercially available varieties. They shared stories of plants their grandparents had grown, varieties that were once common but had all but disappeared. This rediscovery of heritage seeds became a vital part of the community's resilience, a way of reclaiming their agricultural identity and safeguarding biodiversity.

The collective effort extended beyond individual gardens. A group of farmers, led by Elias Thorne, began organizing working bees to help each other with larger tasks, like building new fencing or mending irrigation systems damaged by the storm. These weren't just about labor; they were about shared purpose and camaraderie. The air during these workdays was filled with laughter, the clinking of tools, and the comforting exchange of practical advice. They discussed crop rotation strategies, experimented with intercropping different species to deter pests naturally, and shared observations about soil health and moisture levels.

Ellie's role evolved from that of a solitary expert to a

facilitator of collective wisdom. She didn't hoard her knowledge; she cultivated its spread. She encouraged neighbors to teach each other, to recognize that everyone possessed a unique skill or understanding that could contribute to the whole. Mrs. Gable's expertise in foraging for wild edibles, for instance, became a valuable addition to the community's food security, and Ellie helped her document and share her knowledge of identifying safe and nutritious wild plants. Young Tommy Miller, who had an uncanny knack for understanding animal behavior, began advising local farmers on more humane and effective ways to manage their livestock, reducing stress on the animals and improving their overall health.

The establishment of a small community seed bank, housed in a cool, dry corner of the town library, was a testament to this growing collaborative spirit. Members contributed their saved seeds, meticulously labeled with the plant variety, the date of harvest, and any relevant growing notes. This shared resource ensured that no single farmer's efforts would be lost if their own harvest failed, creating a safety net of agricultural diversity.

This burgeoning network of shared knowledge and mutual support began to weave a stronger fabric for the community. The lessons learned from the land, about resilience, adaptation, and the interconnectedness of all living things, were mirrored in the human relationships that were being nurtured. The isolation that had followed the storm, the individual struggles for survival, began to recede, replaced by a sense of collective agency and shared responsibility.

The communal gardens, whether they were small plots tended by individual families or larger shared spaces, became more than just sources of food. They became gathering places, informal classrooms, and vibrant symbols of the community's renewed commitment to the land. Children learned alongside their parents, their hands digging in the soil, absorbing the lessons of patience and interconnectedness from an early age. They learned to identify native plants, to understand the cycles of nature, and to appreciate the quiet beauty of a well-tended garden.

Ellie found a profound sense of fulfillment in this transformation. The quiet dedication that had once felt like a burden, a solitary path through challenging times, had blossomed into a shared journey. The scent of drying herbs in her cottage still held a special significance, but it was now mingled with the earthy aroma of compost, the sweet fragrance of blooming wildflowers, and the palpable sense of shared purpose that permeated the valley. The resilience of the land, she realized, was intrinsically linked to the resilience of the community, and that resilience was most powerfully cultivated when rooted in shared wisdom and mutual support. The future, once shrouded in uncertainty, now felt as promising as a field of newly sprouted seedlings, nurtured by the collective care and understanding of a community that had learned to truly work with the earth, and with each other.

# Chapter 9: Whispers of the Future

The quiet hum of community awakening, fueled by shared necessity and burgeoning hope, began to fill the valley. The Dawsons, their farm slowly but surely showing the first signs of recovery after the devastating storm and subsequent drought, became an unwitting beacon. Their methodical approach, their quiet determination to work *with* the land rather than fight it, resonated deeply with their neighbors, many of whom were still reeling from the losses they had endured. It wasn't just about the lavender anymore; it was about a fundamental shift in understanding, a recognition that the old ways, reliant on external inputs and often unsustainable practices, were no longer sufficient.

Ellie found herself at the forefront of this quiet revolution, not through any grand declaration, but through the simple act of sharing what she had learned. The conversations that had once begun hesitantly on her doorstep now flowed more freely, spilling out into the communal spaces of the town. The small, sun-drenched parlor of her cottage, once a sanctuary for her solitary study, transformed into a vibrant hub of shared learning. It started with a request from Sarah Jenkins, a young mother whose usually bountiful vegetable patch had yielded little more than withered leaves and stunted growth. Sarah, having heard of Ellie's success with coaxing life from the soil, approached with a basket of her failed produce.

"Ellie," she'd begun, her voice laced with a mixture of desperation and a newfound respect, "I don't know what I'm doing wrong. Everything's just… giving up."

Ellie, accustomed to these hesitant appeals, invited Sarah in, her hands still dusted with dried earth from her morning's work. She offered Sarah a cup of her own herbal tea, a blend of mint and lemon balm, and sat with her, patiently listening. She didn't offer quick fixes or magical solutions. Instead, she spoke of the soil itself, of its depleted state, and the critical need for replenishment. She shared insights from her grandmother's worn journals, detailing methods of composting that went beyond mere kitchen scraps. She spoke of the importance of incorporating native plant matter, of allowing fallen leaves and decaying wood to return their nutrients to the earth, creating a richer, more resilient foundation.

"It's not just about feeding the plants, Sarah," Ellie explained, her gaze soft but knowing. "It's about feeding the soil. Think of it like this – you can't expect a child to grow strong on just one kind of food. The soil needs a diverse diet too." She drew diagrams on a spare sheet of paper, illustrating the process of creating a layered compost heap, emphasizing the inclusion of nitrogen-rich materials like grass clippings and manure, balanced with carbon-rich elements like dried leaves and straw. She also introduced Sarah to the concept of cover cropping, suggesting hardy native legumes like vetch and clover that could be planted in the off-season to enrich the soil with nitrogen and prevent erosion.

Sarah, initially overwhelmed, found herself captivated by Ellie's patient explanations and the tangible, common-sense approach. Ellie didn't just speak; she demonstrated. She showed Sarah how to build a simple compost bin from salvaged wood and how to turn it effectively to ensure aeration. She even gifted Sarah a small starter culture of worms for vermicomposting, explaining their remarkable ability to break down organic matter into nutrient-rich castings.

The results were not immediate, but Sarah was a diligent student. By the following spring, her garden, once a testament to her frustration, was transformed. Rows of healthy, vibrant vegetables, from robust tomatoes to leafy greens, thrived. She had learned to observe her plants, to notice the subtle signs of stress or deficiency, and to respond with the appropriate natural remedies. More importantly, she had learned to foster a healthy ecosystem within her own small plot of land.

This success, like ripples spreading across a pond, encouraged others. The idea of communal gardening began to take root, not as a formal, organized initiative, but as a natural extension of shared experience and mutual aid. Neighbors began to pool resources, sharing seeds and cuttings from their own successful plantings. Old Mrs. Gable, whose arthritis made extensive tilling a painful ordeal, found herself with a steady supply of fresh vegetables from a shared plot near the town hall, tended by younger, stronger hands. In return, she offered her decades of experience in preserving and canning, her kitchen a constant source of delicious jams and pickles that sustained the community through the leaner months.

The old schoolhouse, long since abandoned by its younger pupils who now travelled to the larger town down the river, became a makeshift meeting place. Ellie, at the gentle urging of her neighbors, agreed to lead informal workshops. Her hands, once accustomed to the delicate handling of lavender sprigs, now expertly guided others in the art of seed saving, the crucial step in ensuring self-sufficiency and preserving heirloom varieties. She explained the principles of cross-pollination and the importance of isolating different varieties to maintain genetic purity. She meticulously demonstrated how to harvest, dry, and store seeds for optimal viability, drawing on her grandmother's extensive notes on the subject.

"Think of these seeds," she'd say, holding a small, papery packet of wild bee balm, "as little packets of the future. Each one holds the promise of a plant, a meal, a medicine. We must treat them with the respect they deserve."

She also began sharing her knowledge of water conservation, a critical skill in the increasingly unpredictable climate. She spoke of the ingenious methods employed by ancient civilizations, of rain catchment systems and the use of natural swales to guide and retain water on the landscape. She showed them how to create "hugelkultur" beds – raised mounds of decaying wood, soil, and compost that acted like sponges, slowly releasing moisture to surrounding plants. She demonstrated how to mulch deeply with organic materials, not only suppressing weeds but also significantly reducing evaporation from the soil surface.

"The rain we receive, we must learn to hold onto," Ellie would explain, her voice resonating with the quiet authority of experience. "It's a gift, and we must be good stewards of it. Every drop matters."

Her workshops weren't just about practical techniques; they were about fostering a deeper connection to the natural world. She'd bring in samples of native plants, their diverse forms and functions laid bare for examination. She'd identify the deep, fibrous root systems of prairie grasses that could penetrate compacted soil and draw moisture from deep underground. She'd point out the silvery, downy leaves of plants like Artemisias and Salvias, adapted to reflect sunlight and minimize water loss. She encouraged her students to observe the subtle cues of the environment, to understand the language of the plants and the soil.

One particularly memorable workshop focused on the creation of "pollinator gardens" – small, intentionally planted areas designed to attract and support bees, butterflies, and other beneficial insects. Ellie shared her grandmother's recipes for seed mixes, combinations of native wildflowers that bloomed throughout the growing season, providing a continuous source of nectar and pollen. She explained the vital role these insects played in the pollination of many food crops, a crucial element of a resilient agricultural system. She even showed them how to create simple "bee hotels" from hollowed-out logs and bundles of reeds, providing safe nesting sites for solitary native bees.

The response was overwhelming. People brought their own forgotten seeds, the ones passed down through generations but often overlooked in favor of more commercially available varieties. They shared stories of plants their grandparents had grown, varieties that were once common but had all but disappeared. This rediscovery of heritage seeds became a vital part of the community's resilience, a way of reclaiming their agricultural identity and safeguarding biodiversity.

The collective effort extended beyond individual gardens. A group of farmers, led by Elias Thorne, began organizing working bees to help each other with larger tasks, like building new fencing or mending irrigation systems damaged by the storm. These weren't just about labor; they were about shared purpose and camaraderie. The air during these workdays was filled with laughter, the clinking of tools, and the comforting exchange of practical advice. They discussed crop rotation strategies, experimented with intercropping different species to deter pests naturally, and shared observations about soil health and moisture levels.

Ellie's role evolved from that of a solitary expert to a facilitator of collective wisdom. She didn't hoard her knowledge; she cultivated its spread. She encouraged neighbors to teach each other, to recognize that everyone possessed a unique skill or understanding that could contribute to the whole. Mrs. Gable's expertise in foraging for wild edibles, for instance, became a valuable addition to the community's food security, and Ellie helped her document and share her knowledge of identifying safe and nutritious wild plants. Young Tommy Miller, who had an uncanny knack for understanding animal behavior, began advising local farmers on more humane and effective ways to manage their livestock, reducing stress on the animals and improving their overall health.

The establishment of a small community seed bank, housed in a cool, dry corner of the town library, was a testament to this growing collaborative spirit. Members contributed their saved seeds, meticulously labeled with the plant variety, the date of harvest, and any relevant growing notes. This shared resource ensured that no single farmer's efforts would be lost if their own harvest failed, creating a safety net of agricultural diversity.

This burgeoning network of shared knowledge and mutual support began to weave a stronger fabric for the community. The lessons learned from the land, about resilience, adaptation, and the interconnectedness of all living things, were mirrored in the human relationships that were being nurtured. The isolation that had followed the storm, the individual struggles for survival, began to recede, replaced by a sense of collective agency and shared responsibility.

The communal gardens, whether they were small plots tended by individual families or larger shared spaces, became more than just sources of food. They became gathering places, informal classrooms, and vibrant symbols of the community's renewed commitment to the land. Children learned alongside their parents, their hands digging in the soil, absorbing the lessons of patience and interconnectedness from an early age. They learned to identify native plants, to understand the cycles of nature, and to appreciate the quiet beauty of a well-tended garden.

Ellie found a profound sense of fulfillment in this transformation. The quiet dedication that had once felt like a burden, a solitary path through challenging times, had blossomed into a shared journey. The scent of drying herbs in her cottage still held a special significance, but it was now mingled with the earthy aroma of compost, the sweet fragrance of blooming wildflowers, and the palpable sense of shared purpose that permeated the valley. The resilience of the land, she realized, was intrinsically linked to the resilience of the community, and that resilience was most powerfully cultivated when rooted in shared wisdom and mutual support. The future, once shrouded in uncertainty, now felt as promising as a field of newly sprouted seedlings, nurtured by the collective care and understanding of a community that had learned to truly work with the earth, and with each other.

As the seasons turned, and the valley gradually healed, a new rhythm settled over the land and its people. It was a rhythm dictated not by the frantic demands of an unsustainable past, but by the patient, enduring pulse of nature. Ellie, in her quiet moments, found herself drawn back to her grandmother's legacy, not just in the shared practices she now disseminated, but in the act of solitary, deliberate observation. The initial fervor of community learning, while vital and deeply satisfying, was a collective song. Now, a different kind of music beckoned, a more intimate melody played out in the meticulous documentation of the land itself.

She acquired a new journal, its pages thick and creamy, designed to withstand the test of time and the occasional splash of rainwater. This wasn't a ledger for garden yields or a diary of daily chores. This was a deliberate, almost sacred, undertaking to capture the essence of the Texas Hill Country, to translate its subtle whispers into a tangible form. It began with the small things: the particular shade of green on a dew-kissed sprig of Texas Lantana, the rough texture of the limestone bedrock that underpinned so much of the region's topography, the way sunlight fractured through the canopy of a mature Live Oak.

She walked the familiar contours of her own land, and then ventured further afield, into the wilder

spaces that had always held a certain allure. Each plant was an individual, deserving of its own careful rendering. She'd sketch the delicate, star-shaped bloom of the Four-Nerve Daisy, noting its preference for well-drained soil and its remarkable drought tolerance. Beside it, she'd meticulously record the botanical name,
*Tetraneuris linearifolia*, and then her own observations: "Thrives in gravelly soil, blooms prolifically after light rains, attracts numerous native bees, particularly the carpenter bee, which seems to favor its sturdy stems for nesting."

Her grandmother's journals had been a source of practical knowledge, but Ellie's own endeavor went beyond simple utility. She began to weave in the geological context, understanding that the very composition of the soil – the limestone, the clay, the subtle mineral deposits – dictated which plants could flourish. She'd describe the porous nature of the limestone, how it facilitated excellent drainage but also meant that moisture could be quickly lost. She noted how certain plants, like the prickly pear cactus with its succulent pads, had evolved to store water, while others, like the robust Indian Grass, possessed deep, extensive root systems capable of tapping into subterranean moisture reserves.

The climate, too, became a central theme. She chronicled the erratic rainfall patterns, the scorching summers, and the occasional, unseasonably cold snaps. She observed how native species adapted to these extremes, their resilience a testament to millennia of evolutionary refinement. The smoky scent of mesquite wood burning in the distance would prompt her to document the plant's tenacious ability to sprout from deep root crowns after fire, and its pods, rich in nutrients, providing sustenance for both wildlife and, in leaner times, for people. She recorded how the mesquite's deep taproots also played a crucial role in breaking up compacted soil and accessing water that lay far beyond the reach of shallow-rooted plants.

This meticulous cataloging wasn't merely an academic exercise. It was an act of deep communion, a way of solidifying her connection to a place that had, in many ways, saved her. She felt a profound responsibility to translate her intuitive understanding, the knowledge passed down through generations and honed through personal experience, into a language that others could access and build upon. Her grandmother's writings had been like scattered seeds; Ellie's journal was intended to be a carefully cultivated garden of information.

She dedicated entire pages to the intricate relationships between species. She documented how certain wildflowers, like the Bluebonnet, fixed nitrogen in the soil, enriching it for subsequent crops or native grasses. She observed the symbiotic relationship between specific plants and pollinators, noting how the Gulf Fritillary butterfly was exclusively attracted to the Passionflower vine, its larvae feeding on its leaves. She sketched the intricate network of roots underground, recognizing it as a hidden ecosystem, a silent conversation happening beneath the surface. She wrote about the importance of fallen leaves, not as a mess to be raked away, but as a vital mulch layer, protecting the soil from erosion, retaining moisture, and slowly decomposing to return essential nutrients.

Ellie understood that her own life, like the land, was a tapestry woven from countless threads. Her work with lavender had taught her about the power of focused cultivation, about coaxing a specific essence from the earth. But now, her gaze had expanded, encompassing the wilder, untamed beauty of the Hill Country. She meticulously detailed the medicinal properties of plants that her grandmother had only hinted at. She described how the sap of the Cedar Elm could be used to soothe skin irritations, how the leaves of the Texas Sage could be brewed into a calming tea, and how the berries of the American Beautyberry offered a valuable source of antioxidants, especially during the winter months.

She wasn't aiming to create a definitive scientific treatise, though the precision of her observations would have impressed any botanist. Her intention was more personal, more deeply rooted in the desire to preserve a way of knowing, a way of being that was becoming increasingly rare. She filled pages with descriptions of soil composition – the loam, the clay, the sandy loam – and how each affected water retention and nutrient availability. She noted the optimal planting times for various native seeds, based not just on calendrical dates but on observable environmental cues like soil temperature and the presence of certain insect species.

She began to categorize plants by their function within the ecosystem: nitrogen-fixers, erosion control, wildlife attractors, medicinal species, edible resources. For each entry, she would include not only a detailed description and sketch, but also a brief narrative of her experience with it – a memory of her grandmother explaining its use, a recent observation of its behavior in the wild, or a successful cultivation technique she had developed. This infusion of personal narrative gave the journal a unique warmth, transforming it from a mere collection of facts into a living document, imbued with her own journey and her deep affection for the land.

The act of writing itself became a form of meditation, a way to process the overwhelming influx of knowledge and sensory experience. As she sat in her sun-drenched parlor, the scent of drying herbs mingling with the earthy aroma of the paper and ink, she felt a profound sense of purpose. She was not just recording; she was transcribing the wisdom of the earth. She was creating a reservoir of ecological memory, a testament to the enduring power of native flora and the intricate web of life that sustained them.

She imagined future generations poring over these pages, perhaps during times of hardship or uncertainty, finding in them not just information, but inspiration. She hoped her detailed notes on seed saving, for instance, would empower them to maintain biodiversity in the face of unforeseen challenges. Her observations on water conservation techniques, honed through years of watching the landscape respond to drought and rain, would hopefully provide practical solutions for a changing climate.

This journal became more than just a personal project; it was an offering. An offering to the land that had given her so much, and to the community that was learning to embrace its profound wisdom. It was a silent promise, a commitment to ensure that the lessons she had learned, the deep understanding she had cultivated, would not be lost to the wind or washed away by the next flood. It was her way of ensuring that the whispers of the future, carried on the breath of the Hill Country, would find a steady, enduring voice.

Abernathy's gaze, once fixed solely on the immediate needs of his printing press and the circulation of his modest newspaper, had begun to widen, encompassing the broader landscape of the Texas Hill Country. The near-catastrophe of the recent drought, coupled with the stark realities of Vance's ill-fated, resource-intensive venture, had served as a powerful catalyst. It wasn't merely the local economy that was at stake; it was the very character of the land, the enduring spirit of the people who called it home, that he felt compelled to protect and nurture. His newspaper, 'The Hill Country Herald,' had always been a chronicle of local events, a voice for the community's joys and sorrows. Now, Abernathy felt an undeniable call to elevate its purpose, to transform it into a more potent instrument for education and advocacy.

He recognized that the collective awakening he witnessed, the quiet revolution unfolding on farms and in gardens across the valley, was fragile. It needed to be nurtured, documented, and disseminated. Ellie Dawson's meticulous work, her quiet wisdom shared through informal workshops, was a potent example of what was possible when knowledge was cultivated and passed on. Abernathy saw the potential for 'The Hill Country Herald' to become the conduit for such wisdom, a central hub where the lessons learned from hardship could be preserved and amplified.

With a renewed sense of purpose, Abernathy began to outline a series of articles, a deliberate campaign to illuminate the path towards a more sustainable and resilient future for the region. He envisioned a multi-part series that would not merely report on the changes occurring, but actively champion them. The first few installments would focus on profiling individuals and families who had embraced innovative, environmentally conscious practices. He imagined detailed accounts of how neighbors were successfully implementing water conservation techniques, from the simple elegance of mulching with native grasses to the more complex engineering of rainwater harvesting systems. He wanted to showcase the ingenuity born of necessity, the ways in which the community was learning to work *with* the natural rhythms of the land, rather than against them.

He spent hours in conversation with Ellie, her quiet
insights proving invaluable to his planning. He was
particularly struck by her detailed descriptions of soil
enrichment methods, the intricate dance of
composting, cover cropping, and the reintroduction
of native plant matter. He envisioned an article
dedicated solely to these practices, illustrating them
with clear diagrams and accessible language, aiming
to demystify concepts that might seem daunting to
those less familiar with agricultural science. He
planned to highlight the revival of heirloom seed
saving, a practice that ensured not only a diverse
food supply but also a connection to the region's
agricultural heritage. The stories of families
rediscovering and cultivating varieties that had been
all but forgotten resonated deeply with him,
representing a powerful act of cultural and ecological
preservation.

Beyond individual farms and gardens, Abernathy
intended to broaden his scope, addressing the vital
role of pollinators and the importance of creating
welcoming habitats for bees, butterflies, and other
beneficial insects. He planned to feature the creation
of "pollinator gardens," sharing practical advice on

plant selection and habitat design, emphasizing how these small, intentional spaces could have a significant impact on the health of the wider ecosystem. He also wanted to address the often-overlooked issue of soil erosion, detailing how practices like contour plowing and the planting of deep-rooted native grasses could protect the precious topsoil from being washed away by the infrequent but intense rains.

But Abernathy's vision extended beyond mere practical advice. He felt a profound obligation to foster a deeper understanding of the interconnectedness of all living things. He aimed to weave narratives that illustrated the delicate balance of the Hill Country ecosystem, highlighting how the health of one species directly impacted the health of others. He wanted to convey the quiet beauty of the landscape, the resilience of its native flora and fauna, and the wisdom embedded within generations of living in harmony with this unique environment. He planned to include excerpts from Ellie's grandmother's journals, not just for their practical advice, but for the lyrical descriptions of the land and the deep respect for nature they conveyed.

These were the stories that would truly capture the spirit of the community's transformation.

He also recognized the need to address the economic implications of sustainable land use. He envisioned articles that would explore the market potential for locally grown, organically produced goods, highlighting how consumers were increasingly seeking out products that were not only healthy but also ethically and environmentally produced. He planned to feature local farmers' markets and community-supported agriculture (CSA) initiatives, showcasing how these direct-to-consumer models could foster stronger local economies and create a more resilient food system. He believed that demonstrating the economic viability of these practices would be crucial in encouraging wider adoption.

The failures of the past, particularly Vance's unsustainable agricultural experiment, would also be a recurring theme, not as a point of condemnation, but as a valuable learning opportunity. Abernathy intended to analyze *why* Vance's approach had ultimately proven disastrous, focusing on the environmental costs of excessive water usage, reliance on synthetic fertilizers, and the disregard for the natural resilience of the Hill Country landscape. He wanted to ensure that the community learned from these mistakes, recognizing that true prosperity was not about short-term gains achieved through exploitation, but about long-term health and sustainability.

He understood that change often required a shift in perspective, a willingness to question established norms and embrace new ways of thinking. Therefore, his articles would also delve into the philosophical underpinnings of environmental stewardship. He planned to explore the ethical considerations of land management, the responsibility that individuals and communities held towards the natural world, and the profound satisfaction that came from living in balance with nature. He hoped to inspire a sense of ownership and pride in the land, fostering a deep-seated commitment to its preservation for future generations.

To facilitate ongoing dialogue and encourage

community participation, Abernathy decided to dedicate a regular section of 'The Hill Country Herald' to reader submissions. He invited readers to share their own experiences, their successes and challenges, their observations and insights. This would create a dynamic, interactive platform, ensuring that the conversation about sustainability and resilience was inclusive and community-driven. He envisioned this section as a virtual gathering space, where knowledge could be exchanged, support could be offered, and new ideas could be born.

He anticipated that some might be resistant to these new approaches, clinging to familiar but ultimately destructive practices. Abernathy was prepared for this, understanding that education and consistent, positive reinforcement would be key. He planned to use the success stories as powerful evidence, demonstrating tangible benefits that would speak louder than any argument. The vibrant gardens, the thriving farms, the cleaner waterways – these would be the irrefutable testament to the wisdom of working with nature.

His writing style would remain accessible and engaging, infused with the same warmth and sincerity that had characterized his earlier reporting. He would avoid jargon and overly technical language, opting instead for clear, relatable prose that would resonate with readers from all walks of life. He understood that the message of sustainability needed to be delivered in a way that was both informative and inspiring, fostering a sense of hope and empowerment rather than fear or discouragement.

The transformation of 'The Hill Country Herald' into a champion for environmental awareness and responsible land use was not merely a professional undertaking for Abernathy; it was a personal commitment. He saw it as his contribution to the enduring legacy of the Hill Country, a way to ensure that the lessons learned from recent hardships would not fade with time. He believed that by consistently highlighting successful adaptation strategies, by fostering a community of shared knowledge, and by promoting a deep respect for the natural world, he could help secure a more prosperous and sustainable future for generations to come. The newspaper would become more than just a source of news; it would become a guiding light, illuminating the path towards a future where the land and its people thrived in harmony. He was already envisioning the next steps, the possibility of organizing workshops directly through the newspaper's offices, or even collaborating with local schools to incorporate environmental education into their curricula. The ripple effect of his decision to embrace this broader purpose was already beginning to spread, promising to reshape the very landscape of thought and practice in the Hill Country. His printing press, once a tool for disseminating information, was now poised to become an engine for ecological and social change.

The sheer volume of emerging sustainable practices, the quiet innovations blossoming in backyards and on remote acres, demanded more than just sporadic reporting. Abernathy recognized the need for a sustained, organized effort to document and share this burgeoning wisdom. He began to conceive of 'The Hill Country Herald' not merely as a weekly publication, but as the central nervous system of a growing movement. His ambition was to create a platform that would not only report on success but actively facilitate it, fostering a network of knowledge exchange that would be as robust and resilient as the native grasses he admired.

He planned to dedicate a substantial portion of each edition to "The Sustainable Hill Country," a regular feature that would delve into specific aspects of ecological land management. One week, it might be an in-depth exploration of drought-resistant native plant species, complete with profiles of their unique adaptations and practical advice on their cultivation. The following week, he might focus on the benefits of integrating livestock with crop production, showcasing how thoughtful animal husbandry could enhance soil fertility and natural pest control. He envisioned a rotating cast of contributors, from farmers and ranchers who had successfully implemented these strategies to local ecologists and botanists who could provide deeper scientific context.

Abernathy was particularly keen to highlight the work of individuals like Ellie Dawson. He wanted to shine a spotlight on her meticulous documentation, her understanding of the delicate balance within the

Hill Country ecosystem. He planned a feature article that would showcase her newly acquired journal, presenting excerpts of her detailed observations on native flora, soil composition, and the intricate relationships between plants and pollinators. He believed that by giving her work a prominent platform, he could inspire others to engage in similar acts of observation and documentation, fostering a culture of deep ecological understanding. He saw her journal as a living testament to the potential for human beings to become keen observers and stewards of their environment, a stark contrast to the superficial exploitation he had witnessed in the past.

Moreover, Abernathy planned to leverage the newspaper to organize tangible community initiatives. He envisioned "Seed Swap Saturdays," where local gardeners and farmers could exchange saved seeds, ensuring the preservation and propagation of diverse heirloom varieties. He also considered hosting "Erosion Control Workshops," inviting experts – and perhaps even Abernathy himself, armed with the knowledge gleaned from Ellie and others – to demonstrate practical techniques for preventing soil loss, such as building swales and planting cover crops. He saw these events as crucial for translating the knowledge disseminated through the newspaper into real-world action, solidifying the community's commitment to proactive environmental stewardship.

The concept of a community-wide composting initiative began to take shape in Abernathy's mind as well. He envisioned 'The Hill Country Herald' spearheading the establishment of accessible composting sites, perhaps in partnership with local municipalities or community centers, making it easier for residents to divert organic waste from landfills and create valuable soil amendments. He planned to publish detailed guides on building and maintaining compost bins, demystifying the process and encouraging widespread participation. He believed that such an initiative would not only reduce waste but also foster a deeper understanding of the nutrient cycle and the importance of returning organic matter to the earth.

He also recognized the power of visual communication. Abernathy decided to invest in better photographic equipment for his reporters, aiming to capture the beauty and resilience of the

Hill Country in stark, compelling images. He wanted to accompany his articles with vibrant photographs of native wildflowers in bloom, of healthy, productive farmland, and of community members actively engaged in sustainable practices. These images, he believed, would serve as powerful visual arguments, conveying the tangible benefits of their collective efforts and inspiring a sense of shared pride in their land.

The newspaper would also serve as a vital clearinghouse for information on government programs and grants available to landowners who were implementing conservation practices. Abernathy planned to dedicate a regular section to these resources, ensuring that the community had access to the financial and technical support needed to transition to more sustainable methods. He understood that economic incentives could play a significant role in driving widespread adoption of these practices and wanted to make this information readily accessible to all.

In planning his editorial calendar, Abernathy deliberately wove in themes that directly addressed the lessons learned from the recent drought and Vance's cautionary tale. He would feature articles that explored innovative water management techniques, such as drip irrigation, rainwater harvesting systems, and the cultivation of water-wise native plants. He would also delve into the importance of soil health, explaining how practices like no-till farming and the use of cover crops could improve soil structure, increase water retention, and reduce the need for chemical inputs. He saw this as a way to ensure that the community's newfound awareness was not a fleeting response to a crisis but a fundamental shift in their relationship with the land.

Furthermore, Abernathy intended to create a sense of continuity and long-term vision. He planned to establish a "Hill Country Futures" section, where he would periodically feature essays and opinion pieces from community leaders, educators, and environmentalists, discussing the long-term challenges and opportunities facing the region. This would encourage ongoing dialogue about the future of the land, fostering a collective responsibility to ensure its continued health and vitality. He envisioned this section as a forum for forward-thinking discussion, a place where the community could collectively imagine and work towards a sustainable future.

Abernathy's ambition was clear: 'The Hill Country Herald' would become more than just a newspaper. It would be an educator, an organizer, and a chronicler of a community's journey towards ecological wisdom and resilience. He was driven by the conviction that informed, engaged citizens were the most powerful agents of change, and his newspaper would be the tool that empowered them. He understood that the whispers of the future were already in the wind, carried on the rain and nurtured in the soil, and he was determined to give them a clear, resounding voice. His printing press was about to embark on its most significant chapter yet, one dedicated to the enduring strength and sustainability of the land he called home.

The faintest tracing of ink on brittle parchment, a legacy of her grandmother's careful hands, guided Ellie's steps. The maps, more memory than navigation, whispered secrets of the land, of places that time and neglect had begun to efface from common knowledge. Abernathy's articles, burgeoning in his mind and soon to grace the pages of 'The Hill Country Herald,' spoke of a future built on sustainable practices, on a renewed respect for the earth. But Ellie knew that such a future was intrinsically tied to the most fundamental of all resources: water. The recent drought had seared that truth into the collective consciousness of the Hill Country, a stark reminder of their vulnerability. Yet, her grandmother's journals hinted at a deeper wellspring of resilience, of a time when the land, unburdened by the excesses of modern ambition, provided more reliably.

Ellie's quest, born from a quiet conviction that the land held its own solutions, began with the oldest of these ancestral charts. It depicted a series of meandering lines, not of rivers or creeks as she knew them, but of subtle undulations in the terrain, marked with symbols that spoke of moisture, of lifeblood seeping from the earth. These were not the prominent, seasonal creeks that swelled and receded with the whims of the sky, but whispers of water, hidden veins that pulsed beneath the surface. The drought had left the familiar watercourses cracked and parched, a landscape of dusty memories. It was in these forgotten places, the forgotten geographies

of her own lineage, that she sought a different kind
of sustenance.

Her journey led her through dense thickets of Ashe
juniper, their gnarled branches reaching like
supplicating arms, and across sun-baked prairies
where the very air seemed to shimmer with heat.
The common wisdom dictated seeking water where
it was most obvious, along the low-lying creek beds
and in the shaded ravines. But Ellie's grandmother's
maps pointed her towards the higher ground,
towards the subtle depressions in the landscape, the
places where certain mosses clung with an unnatural
tenacity to the rocks, even in the driest of seasons.
These were the subtle indicators, the silent testament
of hidden moisture, that only a deep intimacy with
the land could reveal.

The first discovery was almost accidental, a reward
for sheer persistence. Pushing aside a curtain of
overgrown Texas mountain laurel, its leathery leaves
a testament to drought resistance, Ellie found herself
in a small, shaded alcove. The air here was noticeably
cooler, carrying a faint, earthy scent that promised
more than just shade. There, nestled amongst a

cluster of smooth, grey stones, was a patch of vivid green grass, improbably lush against the prevailing parched earth. And from beneath the roots of a venerable Live Oak, a thin, glistening trickle of water emerged, coalescing into a small, clear pool no larger than a dinner plate. It wasn't a gushing fountain, but a steady, inexorable seep, each drop a precious gift. She knelt, cupping her hands, and tasted the water. It was cool, clean, and carried the faint minerality of the earth from which it sprang. This was a spring, a true, year-round spring, a secret kept by the land itself.

Her grandmother's markings on the map, a series of small dots clustered around this very area, now made perfect sense. They weren't just random annotations; they were pointers to the lifeblood of this landscape. With a surge of exhilaration, Ellie began to meticulously document her find. She sketched the surrounding vegetation, noting the specific species of plants that thrived in the vicinity, their dependence on this constant, albeit small, water source. She observed the way the water collected, the subtle slope of the land that guided its flow, and the small, hardy ferns that unfurled their fronds in its perpetual, life-giving mist. This was not just a source

of water; it was an ecosystem in miniature, a
testament to the land's enduring ability to sustain
life.

The rediscovery ignited a fervor within her. The
drought had fostered a sense of scarcity, of desperate
measures and uncertain futures. But this spring,
however small, was a tangible counterpoint, a
symbol of enduring abundance. It spoke of
resilience, of a wisdom inherent in the land that
predated human intervention, a wisdom that could
be rediscovered and revered. It was a beacon of
hope, not in the form of grand engineering projects
or reliance on dwindling reservoirs, but in the quiet
persistence of nature's own provisions.

Buoyed by this success, Ellie turned to another
section of her grandmother's meticulously drawn
maps. This one indicated a broader area, a seemingly
unremarkable hillside dotted with scrub oak and
mesquite. The conventional wisdom would dismiss it
as yet another dry expanse, susceptible to the
vagaries of rainfall. But her grandmother's notations,
a series of faint, crossed lines near a cluster of
ancient-looking rocks, suggested something more. It

was a gamble, a journey into the less accessible parts of the land, places that few bothered to explore anymore.

The trek was arduous. The sun beat down relentlessly, and the dry, brittle vegetation offered little shade. Yet, as she neared the rocky outcrop, Ellie noticed a subtle shift in the air. A faint, almost imperceptible coolness, a dampness that clung to the very air. She pressed on, her eyes scanning the rocky faces, searching for any sign that mirrored her previous discovery. And then she saw it. Tucked beneath an overhang, sheltered from the direct sun and wind, was a collection of smooth, water-worn stones. And from a fissure in the rock face, a steady, cool stream of water cascaded, forming a shallow, clear pool that mirrored the impossibly blue sky above. This was not a seep, but a small, flowing spring, its source hidden deep within the earth.

The volume of water was greater here, a refreshing testament to the subterranean network her grandmother's maps had alluded to. Ellie spent hours at this second spring, observing the life it supported. Dragonflies with iridescent wings hovered over the water's surface, their delicate forms a vibrant contrast to the stark landscape. Small amphibians, unseen during the dry periods, now basked in the moist air near the water's edge. The vegetation around the spring was remarkably different, too. Lush ferns, delicate wildflowers, and a variety of water-loving shrubs flourished, creating a pocket of vibrant life in the midst of arid surroundings. This was a vital hub, a place where the very essence of the Hill Country's resilience was concentrated.

Her grandmother's journals had often spoken of these hidden springs, referring to them as "earth's tears," places where the land wept forth its bounty even in times of great thirst. They were more than just sources of water; they were sacred places, imbued with a spiritual significance that connected the people to the very heart of the land. Ellie felt this connection deeply as she sat by the spring, the gentle murmur of the water a soothing balm to her spirit. It was a profound affirmation of her grandmother's legacy, a validation of her own intuitive understanding of the natural world.

The implications of these discoveries were immense. Abernathy's newspaper was already a catalyst for change, fostering a community dialogue about sustainability. But these springs, these tangible sources of life, offered a more immediate and practical solution. They were not merely curiosities; they were vital resources, capable of sustaining small gardens, providing reliable drinking water for livestock, and offering a buffer against the devastating effects of prolonged drought. They represented a rediscovered heritage, a way of living in harmony with the land that had been nearly lost.

Ellie began to consider how to share this knowledge responsibly. She knew that indiscriminate exploitation could quickly deplete these precious sources. Her grandmother's journals contained notations on how to manage these springs, emphasizing the importance of allowing the water to flow naturally, of respecting the surrounding vegetation, and of never taking more than was needed. It was about stewardship, about becoming a guardian of these hidden treasures, not a consumer.

She envisioned establishing a network of these rediscovered springs, carefully managed and maintained, providing a distributed and resilient water supply for the community. This would require careful planning, a deep understanding of the watershed, and the cooperation of her neighbors. She could imagine 'The Hill Country Herald' playing a crucial role in this endeavor, not just reporting on her findings, but facilitating the collaborative effort needed to protect and utilize these resources.

Her thoughts turned to Abernathy and his vision for the newspaper. He was already championing the idea of a community focused on self-sufficiency and ecological wisdom. These springs were the perfect embodiment of that vision. They offered a practical, accessible path towards a more secure and sustainable future, a future rooted in the deep, inherent strengths of the Hill Country itself.

Ellie returned from her explorations with more than just the knowledge of water sources. She carried with her a renewed sense of purpose, a conviction that the answers to their challenges lay not in grand, external solutions, but in the quiet, enduring wisdom of the land itself. Her grandmother's maps had led her to a wellspring of hope, a tangible promise that even in the harshest of times, life, in its most essential form, could always find a way to flow. The whispers of the future, for Abernathy and for the entire Hill Country, were now intertwined with the gentle murmur of these rediscovered springs, a testament to the enduring power of connection, observation, and a deep, abiding respect for the earth. The meticulous charting of these hidden water sources was not just an act of mapping; it was an act of reclamation, a reawakening of a forgotten relationship between the people and the life-giving pulse of their land. This was the sustenance her grandmother had understood, the quiet strength that had always been there, waiting to be found, waiting to be remembered, waiting to nourish the future.

She carefully documented each spring's location on a new, more detailed map, one that would serve as a communal resource, a guide for responsible use. She noted the subtle variations in flow rate, the quality of the water, and the surrounding flora, compiling a comprehensive understanding of each unique source. Her grandmother's emphasis on the interconnectedness of the ecosystem around these springs was paramount. She understood that disturbing the delicate balance of plants and soil could easily compromise the spring's continued viability. Therefore, her approach was one of gentle integration, of learning to live alongside these natural water features, not to dominate them.

She began to identify patterns in her grandmother's notations that suggested the existence of several more such sources, scattered across the wider expanse of the Hill Country. Some were marked with symbols indicating a stronger flow, others with notations about medicinal properties of plants found nearby, hinting at a rich tapestry of ecological interdependence. This was not just about finding water; it was about understanding the intricate web of life that these springs supported. It was about recognizing that these seemingly small, hidden sources were in fact crucial anchors for the entire local ecosystem, providing a lifeline during the dry months for countless species of plants, insects, and animals, many of which might also be overlooked or forgotten.

The rediscovery of these springs was more than just a practical solution to water scarcity; it was a philosophical shift. It challenged the prevailing notion that progress meant conquering nature, imposing human will upon the land through brute force and extensive resource extraction. Instead, it offered an alternative: a path of partnership, of listening to the land's own wisdom, of uncovering the inherent resilience that lay dormant, waiting to be recognized. Ellie's quiet dedication to deciphering her grandmother's legacy was, in essence, a reclamation of a lost ecological knowledge, a knowledge that was vital for the long-term survival and prosperity of the Hill Country.

As Abernathy prepared to publish his series on sustainable practices, Ellie's findings would provide a powerful, tangible example, grounding his broader vision in the concrete reality of the land's own provisions. The stories of gardens thriving with water from a hidden seep, of families securing their water needs from a small, perennial stream, would resonate deeply with a community that had recently faced the stark realities of scarcity. It was a narrative of hope, grounded in the very soil and stone of their home, a testament to the enduring power of nature and the profound wisdom that could be found by those willing to look, and to listen. Her grandmother's legacy, etched in ink and spirit, was now poised to become a cornerstone of the Hill Country's sustainable future, a future that flowed, clear and steady, from the heart of the land itself. The rediscovery was not an end, but a beginning, a reopening of ancient pathways to sustenance and resilience.

The parched earth, once a testament to the Hill Country's vulnerability, now whispered of a different future, a future intricately woven with the lessons learned from hardship. The years of drought, a crucible that had tested the very resolve of the community, had also forged a deep and abiding understanding of sustainability. It wasn't merely an abstract concept bandied about in academic circles; it had become a lived reality, a necessity etched into the daily routines of every household. The communal well, once a source of anxiety, was now managed with a reverence born from near-deprivation. Rainwater harvesting, once a fringe practice, had become as commonplace as tending to one's livestock. Rooftops across the landscape were adorned with an array of cisterns, catching every precious drop that fell from the sky. These weren't elaborate, industrial-scale systems, but often simple, elegantly designed structures that integrated seamlessly with the aesthetic of the homes, a quiet testament to ingenuity and respect for every molecule of water. The sound of water trickling into these reservoirs during even the briefest of showers was a comforting melody, a reassuring pulse of life returning to the land.

Ellie's role in this transition had been pivotal, her deep understanding of the region's flora becoming the bedrock upon which many of these new practices were built. Her expertise in xeriscaping, once dismissed by some as a preference for the less vibrant, had proven to be a revelation. She moved through neighborhoods, her hands stained with soil, guiding neighbors in the selection and placement of native plants. These weren't just aesthetically pleasing choices; they were ecological linchpins. She spoke of the deep, tenacious root systems of the Texas sage, its ability to anchor soil and retain moisture far beyond the reach of superficial rainfall. She highlighted the drought-resistant beauty of the prickly pear, not just as a food source for wildlife, but as a water-storing marvel, its pads holding precious reserves within their fleshy depths. The robust blue grama, with its delicate seed heads that swayed like dancers in the slightest breeze, became a symbol of resilience, a ground cover that choked out invasive weeds and reduced the need for constant irrigation. Ellie's gentle guidance, her patient explanations of how each plant contributed to the overall health of the landscape, fostered a sense of stewardship. It was a profound shift in perspective, moving from a desire to impose order on the land to a willingness to collaborate with its inherent strengths.

This collaboration was most evident in the careful management of water resources. The rediscovered springs, once Ellie's secret hope, had become communal treasures. Guided by her grandmother's meticulous notes and Ellie's own observations, the community established a system for their responsible use. Small, strategically placed stone channels diverted water for essential needs, such as watering kitchen gardens and providing drinking troughs for livestock. The emphasis was always on minimal intervention, on allowing the water to flow as naturally as possible, respecting the delicate ecosystems that had evolved around these hidden sources. Ellie had tirelessly explained the interconnectedness of these springs. She showed how the ferns and mosses clinging to the damp rocks weren't mere embellishments, but indicators of a healthy water table, essential components of the spring's ability to sustain itself. Damaging these plants, she warned, could disrupt the delicate microclimate, leading to reduced flow or even the spring's eventual demise. This understanding fostered a sense of collective responsibility. Neighbors took turns monitoring the springs, ensuring no one over-tapped them, and meticulously clearing away any debris that might obstruct the flow.

The transition wasn't without its challenges. There were still those who harbored a lingering nostalgia for the lush, water-thirsty lawns of the past, for gardens that demanded constant attention and frequent watering. But the memory of the drought, the stark reality of cracked earth and thirsty livestock, was a potent teacher. Ellie's botanical expertise became an invaluable asset in these conversations. She would patiently explain the energy expenditure required to maintain a water-intensive landscape in such an arid climate, comparing it to the minimal needs of native flora.

She demonstrated how a xeriscaped garden, once established, required far less labor and provided a habitat for beneficial insects and pollinators, contributing to a more vibrant and self-sustaining ecosystem. Her knowledge of the medicinal properties of certain native plants also began to gain traction. For instance, she shared how the infusion of desert willow bark could soothe fevers, and how the sap of the cenizo, known for its vibrant purple blooms that often appeared after rainfall, had antiseptic qualities. These were practical, tangible benefits that resonated deeply with a community focused on self-reliance.

The shift in mindset was palpable. The community began to see their landscape not as a canvas upon which to impose their desires, but as a partner in their survival and prosperity. They learned to read the subtle signs of the land: the way certain grasses turned a particular shade of golden-brown just before a rain, the specific calls of birds that indicated a nearby water source, the types of insects that thrived in a healthy, moisture-balanced environment. Ellie's efforts had cultivated not just sustainable practices, but a deeper ecological literacy, a renewed respect for the intricate, often invisible, web of life

that sustained them all. This was the true inheritance of the drought – not just the scars it left, but the profound lessons it etched into their collective consciousness. The resilience they had found was not born from conquering nature, but from a humble, profound understanding of how to live in harmony with it, to listen to its whispers, and to honor its delicate, life-giving balance. The bounty they now experienced was not a gift from above, but a reward for their newfound wisdom, a testament to their ability to adapt, to learn, and to thrive by working
*with* the land, not against it. This was the enduring legacy of those difficult years, a future built not on the exploitation of resources, but on the mindful stewardship of them, a future where sustainability was not a choice, but a way of life.

The lessons of the past few years had indeed been profound, seeping into the very fabric of daily life in the Hill Country. The community, once accustomed to a more profligate use of resources, now approached every action with a mindful consideration of its impact. This was particularly evident in their embrace of rainwater harvesting. Beyond the practicalities of cisterns and collection systems, there had been a cultural shift. Children learned about the water cycle not just in textbooks, but by actively participating in the conservation efforts at home. They understood that the water collected from their rooftops was a precious commodity, one that needed to be used wisely. This ingrained understanding extended to their interaction with the land itself. The practice of xeriscaping, championed by Ellie and her deep botanical knowledge, had transformed many of the local landscapes. Gone were the sprawling, thirsty lawns that had once demanded constant attention and immense quantities of water. In their place, a tapestry of native plants had taken root. Ellie's guidance was instrumental in this transformation. She meticulously selected species known for their resilience, their ability to thrive in the region's often-challenging climate. She introduced neighbors to the beauty of the Lindheimer's muhly, a graceful grass that produced delicate, airy seed heads, and the vibrant splashes of color provided by the Engelmann daisy, its cheerful yellow petals a beacon of enduring life. She explained how the deep root systems of these native plants not only helped retain moisture in the soil but also prevented erosion, a crucial benefit on the often-steep slopes of the Hill Country.

This careful selection of flora was more than just an aesthetic choice; it was a fundamental aspect of working

*with* nature, rather than against it. Ellie's expertise extended to understanding the intricate relationships between plants, soil, and water. She taught that by choosing species that were naturally adapted to the local conditions, the community was reducing its reliance on artificial inputs like irrigation and fertilizers. This, in turn, minimized the potential for runoff that could carry pollutants into the precious water sources. She spoke of the subtle intelligence of the land, of how native plants had evolved over millennia to efficiently capture and utilize the available moisture, and how by mimicking these natural strategies, humans could achieve a more harmonious and less resource-intensive way of life.

The management of water resources had also taken on a new dimension, moving beyond mere conservation to a deeper understanding of watershed health. The rediscovery and careful stewardship of the hidden springs, guided by Ellie's grandmother's maps and her own careful observations, had become a central focus. The community had established a system of small, strategically placed weirs and check

dams, not to impede the flow of water, but to slow it
down, allowing it to percolate into the soil and
replenish the underground aquifers. These were not
monumental constructions, but humble, earth-toned
structures designed to blend seamlessly with the
natural landscape, a testament to their commitment
to minimal impact. Ellie's understanding of the
riparian zones surrounding these springs was crucial.
She emphasized the importance of maintaining the
native vegetation along the banks, recognizing that
these plants acted as natural filters, purifying the
water and providing vital habitat for a diverse array
of wildlife. She would often take groups out to these
locations, pointing out the delicate ferns that
unfurled in the perpetual mist, the resilient
wildflowers that bloomed in the shaded alcoves, and
the myriad of insects and amphibians that called
these areas home. This hands-on education fostered
a profound respect for these fragile ecosystems,
reinforcing the understanding that the health of the
springs was inextricably linked to the health of the
entire watershed.


The lessons learned were not confined to individual
households or specific locations; they had fostered a
sense of collective responsibility and shared purpose.

Community meetings, once focused on more immediate concerns, now frequently revolved around discussions of water conservation strategies, the benefits of native landscaping, and the ongoing efforts to protect and monitor their shared water resources. Abernathy's newspaper, 'The Hill Country Herald,' had become an invaluable platform for disseminating this knowledge, publishing articles on drought-resistant gardening techniques, profiles of families who had successfully adopted sustainable practices, and updates on the health of the local springs. Ellie herself frequently contributed, sharing her insights on plant identification, soil health, and the importance of biodiversity. Her clear, accessible explanations demystified complex ecological concepts, making them understandable and actionable for everyone in the community.

This shift towards working
*with* nature had not only made the community more resilient in the face of environmental challenges but had also fostered a deeper sense of connection to their land. The act of tending to a native garden, of observing the subtle changes in the landscape throughout the seasons, of participating in the collective effort to safeguard their water sources, had

cultivated a profound appreciation for the delicate ecological balance that sustained them. It was a realization that true prosperity wasn't measured in material wealth alone, but in the health and vitality of their environment, in the ability of the land to provide for them, and in their capacity to reciprocate that provision through careful stewardship. Ellie's expertise, honed through years of study and a deep, intuitive connection to the land, had been the catalyst for much of this transformation. She had shown them that resilience wasn't about building higher walls or digging deeper wells, but about understanding the inherent wisdom of the natural world and aligning their actions with its rhythms. The whispers of the future, once tinged with the anxiety of scarcity, now resonated with the quiet confidence of a community that had learned to live in harmony with the earth, proving that true sustainability was not a burden, but a pathway to a richer, more enduring existence.

The dust, a persistent specter of the recent past, had begun to settle, not just on the physical landscape, but within the collective consciousness of the Hill Country inhabitants. The raw, visceral fear that had gripped them during the relentless drought and the terrifying spectacle of the dust storms had slowly, painstakingly, given way to a more tempered, yet deeply ingrained, sense of respect for the land's power. It wasn't a forgetting of the hardships, but a re-framing of them, a recognition that the very forces that had threatened to break them had also, paradoxically, taught them invaluable lessons. This newfound understanding was woven into the fabric of their daily lives, manifesting in subtle yet profound shifts in their interaction with the environment. The whispers of the future, once laced with desperation, now carried a melody of cautious optimism, a quiet affirmation that survival, and indeed prosperity, could be found not in conquering nature, but in a graceful, informed partnership with it.

Ellie, more than anyone, felt this palpable shift. Her days were no longer consumed by a desperate search for solutions, but by a steady, patient cultivation of the practices she had helped introduce. Her walks through the community, once filled with the urgent need to advise and correct, now felt more like a communion. She'd see the shimmering blues and purples of the native verbena cascading over stone walls, a stark contrast to the parched earth it once struggled to survive in. She'd observe the careful placement of rain barrels, their utilitarian forms now softened by the tendrils of climbing vines, a visual testament to their integration into the home and the landscape. There was a quiet pride in these scenes, a satisfaction that came from witnessing the slow, steady healing of the land, mirroring the healing within the people themselves. The xeriscaping, initially seen by some as a somber aesthetic, was blooming into a vibrant testament to resilience. The Texas sage, with its silvery foliage and occasional bursts of rose-purple flowers, stood as a stoic sentinel against the arid conditions. The agaves and yuccas, with their architectural forms, provided structure and visual interest, their drought tolerance a reassuring presence.

The collective memory of the dust storms, however, remained a potent reminder of nature's formidable power. The choking grit that had infiltrated homes, stung eyes, and coated everything in a suffocating layer of brown was not easily forgotten. This memory had spurred a renewed commitment to soil conservation, a practice that Ellie had championed from the outset. The communal efforts to stabilize slopes with native grasses and groundcovers had intensified. Abernathy, in his role as a local leader and editor, frequently featured stories about these initiatives in 'The Hill Country Herald.' One article detailed the successful efforts of the Miller family, who had transformed a steep, erosion-prone hillside behind their home into a series of terraced wildflower meadows using techniques inspired by Ellie's teachings. They had painstakingly incorporated compost and mulch, and planted deep-rooted native grasses like Little Bluestem, whose fibrous root systems formed a living net to hold the soil in place. The visual impact was striking – a riot of color that not only prevented erosion but also provided a vital habitat for pollinators and beneficial insects. The accompanying photographs, often taken by Abernathy himself, showcased the before-and-after transformation, serving as a powerful visual argument for the efficacy of these methods.

This commitment to soil health extended beyond individual properties to the broader community landscape. The town's central park, once a patch of struggling Bermuda grass that required constant irrigation, was undergoing a gradual transformation. Under Ellie's guidance, large sections were being replanted with native grasses and drought-tolerant wildflowers. The process was slow, deliberate, and required considerable volunteer effort. Neighbors would gather on Saturday mornings, armed with shovels and trowels, and work alongside Ellie, learning to identify invasive species that needed removal and carefully planting plugs of native vegetation. The sounds of their labor were often accompanied by the chirping of newly arrived songbirds, drawn to the burgeoning habitat, and the hum of busy bees. The children, too, were actively involved, learning to distinguish between beneficial and harmful insects, and understanding the role each played in the larger ecosystem. This shared endeavor fostered a profound sense of ownership and pride in their communal spaces.

The management of the rediscovered springs had become a cornerstone of their sustainable living. The near-deprivation had instilled a deep reverence for these hidden sources of life. The small, carefully constructed check dams and weirs, designed to slow water flow and encourage infiltration, were meticulously maintained. Ellie often led educational excursions to these sites, her explanations bringing the often-unseen processes to life. She would point out the moisture-loving ferns and mosses that thrived along the spring edges, explaining how their presence indicated a healthy, consistent water table. She showed how the slower-moving water allowed sediment to settle out, naturally filtering the water before it reached the deeper aquifers. She also emphasized the importance of riparian vegetation — the cottonwoods, willows, and sycamores that grew along the watercourses. These trees, she explained, not only provided shade, which kept the water cooler and reduced evaporation, but their deep root systems helped stabilize the banks, preventing erosion and contributing to the overall health of the watershed.

The community's relationship with water had evolved from one of fear and scarcity to one of mindful stewardship. The cisterns, once symbols of last resort, were now seen as integral components of a well-managed water system. Beyond the simple collection of rainwater, there was a growing interest in more sophisticated water harvesting techniques. Some families were exploring the use of swales — shallow, broad ditches on contour — to capture and infiltrate storm runoff on their properties, especially on gently sloping terrain. Others were experimenting with small, infiltration basins designed to mimic natural depressions that collect and absorb rainwater. These weren't large-scale, engineered solutions, but rather subtle interventions that worked in concert with the natural topography of the land. Ellie's role in this was primarily as an educator and advisor, sharing information and facilitating workshops where community members could learn from each other's experiences.

The economic implications of these shifts were also beginning to be recognized. The reduced need for purchased water, fertilizers, and pesticides translated into tangible savings for households. Furthermore, the increasing popularity of xeriscaped gardens and the abundance of native plants had begun to attract a different kind of visitor to the region – those who appreciated the natural beauty and ecological integrity of the Hill Country. Local artisans were incorporating native plant motifs into their work, and small businesses were emerging that specialized in native plant nurseries and sustainable landscaping services. Abernathy dedicated significant space in his newspaper to profiling these new ventures, highlighting the economic opportunities that arose from embracing an environmentally conscious approach. He wrote about the success of a local couple who had started a small business selling heirloom seeds of drought-tolerant vegetables and native wildflowers, their venture rapidly gaining a loyal customer base.

Yet, the memory of hardship was not entirely erased. It served as a constant, subtle reminder of the land's inherent limitations and the potential for nature's fury. There were still those who occasionally spoke of the lush, green lawns of yesteryear with a wistful sigh, a yearning for a time that seemed less constrained. But these sentiments were increasingly met with reasoned arguments about water conservation and ecological responsibility. Ellie would often address these lingering nostalgic desires with gentle, factual explanations. She would describe the ecological footprint of maintaining a water-intensive lawn in an arid climate, detailing the sheer volume of water required, the energy consumed by pumps and irrigation systems, and the potential for nutrient runoff into local waterways. In contrast, she would highlight the lower maintenance, higher ecological value, and inherent beauty of native landscapes. She'd show how a well-designed xeriscape could be just as, if not more, visually appealing than a traditional lawn, offering a richer tapestry of textures, colors, and seasonal changes, all while supporting a greater diversity of wildlife.

The community's newfound harmony with the land was not a static state but an ongoing process of learning and adaptation. There were always new challenges, new observations to be made, and new refinements to be implemented. The scars of the drought and the dust storm, while visible in the memories and in the occasional stark landscape that had yet to fully recover, were now overlaid with a tapestry of hope and resilience. The whispers of the future were no longer whispers of fear, but confident pronouncements of a community that had learned to listen to the land, to respect its rhythms, and to find enduring peace and prosperity in a life lived in sincere, committed harmony with the natural world. The land, in turn, seemed to respond to this newfound respect, offering its bounty not in abundance that led to waste, but in a steady, reliable provision that nourished both body and soul. This was the deep, quiet wisdom that had been forged in the crucible of hardship, a testament to their enduring spirit and their capacity for change. The Hill Country was not just surviving; it was thriving, reborn through its understanding and embrace of its own inherent, resilient nature. The careful stewardship, the mindful practices, and the collective commitment to living in balance had transformed the very essence of their existence, creating a sustainable future rooted in the enduring strength of the land itself. The air, once heavy with the threat of desiccation, now carried the scent of resilient wildflowers and the promise of a future cultivated with care and understanding.

# Chapter 10: Echoes of the Past, Seeds of Tomorrow

The cool, morning air, still carrying a hint of the night's dew, felt like a balm on Ellie's skin as she walked the familiar path towards the old, stone cottage. It wasn't just a cottage; it was a sanctuary, a repository of memories, and now, the site of a nascent dream. The drought, though vanquished in its most destructive form, had left its indelible mark, a constant reminder of the fragility of their existence and the profound importance of understanding the land. This understanding, Ellie felt more keenly than ever, was a legacy, not just hers, but one that belonged to the entire Hill Country, a legacy deeply rooted in the wisdom of her grandmother.

Her grandmother, Eliza, had possessed an almost mystical connection to the plants that thrived in this often-unforgiving landscape. Her knowledge wasn't confined to dusty botanical texts; it was alive, breathed into her by the very soil she tended, whispered to her by the wind rustling through the mesquite and oak. Ellie remembered countless afternoons spent at Eliza's side, learning to identify the subtle differences between native grasses, understanding the medicinal properties of herbs that grew wild along the creek beds, and marveling at the resilience of wildflowers that seemed to burst forth with defiant beauty after even the slightest rain. Eliza's garden, a riot of color and texture, was a testament to this innate understanding. It wasn't manicured in the conventional sense, but rather a thriving ecosystem in miniature, where each plant had its place, contributing to the overall health and vitality of the whole.

The idea to formalize this legacy, to create a space where Eliza's teachings could be preserved and shared, had been germinating within Ellie for years. The recent trials had only amplified its urgency. It felt like a moral imperative, a way to honor the woman who had shaped her understanding of the world and to ensure that future generations wouldn't be left adrift, disconnected from the deep ecological wisdom of their heritage. The cottage, inherited from Eliza, with its sturdy stone walls and shaded veranda, was the perfect setting. It was a place steeped in Eliza's presence, a tangible link to the past that would anchor the future of this endeavor.

Ellie envisioned more than just a memorial; she saw

a living, breathing center for learning and preservation. An educational garden, meticulously designed to showcase the diverse flora of the Hill Country, would be the heart of this new initiative. It would be a place where visitors could walk amongst the native plants, experiencing their textures, their scents, and their subtle beauties firsthand. Signage, thoughtfully crafted and informative, would explain the ecological roles of each species, their traditional uses, and the best practices for their cultivation and conservation. This wasn't about creating a static museum, but a dynamic, interactive space that encouraged exploration and discovery.

The initial work had been challenging, a labor of love that demanded both physical exertion and a deep well of patience. The land surrounding the cottage, while possessing the inherent beauty of the Hill Country, had also borne the brunt of neglect during the extended dry spells. Ellie, with the help of a small group of dedicated volunteers – neighbors who, like her, felt a profound connection to Eliza's memory and a growing commitment to the principles of sustainable land management – began the arduous task of transforming the overgrown acreage. They cleared away invasive species that had taken root, not with harsh chemicals, but with careful hand-pulling and strategic pruning, always mindful of preserving the native undergrowth. They amended the soil with compost generated from local organic waste, enriching it with the nutrients necessary to support a thriving ecosystem.

The design of the garden itself was a collaborative effort, guided by Ellie's deep knowledge and Eliza's established principles. Instead of rigid rows and formal beds, they opted for a more naturalistic approach, mimicking the patterns found in the wild. Gentle, winding paths, mulched with shredded bark, would guide visitors through different ecological zones. There would be a section dedicated to drought-tolerant wildflowers, a vibrant tapestry of blues, purples, and yellows that would attract pollinators and bring a splash of color even in the driest of times. Another area would feature native grasses, their varied textures and heights creating a sense of movement and providing crucial habitat for birds and small mammals. A small, shaded corner would be reserved for medicinal herbs, their familiar scents evoking memories of Eliza's kitchen and her healing remedies.

The establishment of the research center itself was a crucial element. Ellie wanted this to be a place where scientific inquiry and traditional ecological knowledge could converge. She envisioned a small, well-equipped laboratory space within the cottage where studies could be conducted on native plant propagation, soil health, and the impact of various land management practices. She planned to collaborate with local universities and agricultural extensions, bringing in experts to conduct workshops and share their findings with the community. This wasn't about pitting science against tradition, but about finding synergy, about using modern tools to validate and expand upon the centuries-old wisdom passed down through generations.

The grandmother's legacy was not merely about plants; it was about a way of life, a profound respect for the interconnectedness of all living things. Eliza had taught Ellie that the health of the soil was directly linked to the health of the water, the health of the air, and ultimately, the health of the community. This holistic perspective was something Ellie was eager to impart. The educational garden would serve as a living classroom, demonstrating these principles in action. Children, in particular, would be a focus. Ellie planned to develop curriculum materials and organize field trips for local schools, allowing students to get their hands dirty, to plant seeds, and to observe the life cycles of native plants and the creatures they supported. She wanted to foster a new generation of land stewards, individuals who understood the importance of conservation not as a burden, but as a joy and a responsibility.

The commitment to preserving Eliza's specific botanical knowledge was paramount. Eliza had kept meticulous journals, filled with detailed observations, hand-drawn illustrations, and notes on the cultivation and uses of countless native species. These journals, weathered and fragile, were a treasure trove of information. Ellie carefully cataloged and digitized them, ensuring their long-term preservation. She planned to create a comprehensive database of Eliza's findings, cross-referencing her notes with modern scientific research. This would not only safeguard Eliza's unique contributions but also make her insights accessible to a wider audience of researchers, gardeners, and conservationists.

The 'Hill Country Herald,' under Abernathy's continued guidance, became an invaluable partner in disseminating information about the burgeoning center. He dedicated a regular column to 'Eliza's Garden,' featuring articles on the progress of the garden, profiles of the native plants being cultivated, and practical tips for home gardeners interested in xeriscaping and native planting. He highlighted the volunteer efforts, celebrating the community's collective investment in this endeavor. These articles served not only to inform but also to inspire, drawing in more people who were eager to contribute their time and skills. Abernathy's photographs, capturing the vibrant beauty of the garden and the dedication of the volunteers, were a powerful visual narrative of the project's growth.

The initial phase of establishment saw the creation of several key features. A small, rustic greenhouse was constructed, providing a controlled environment for propagating delicate native species and nurturing seedlings. Rainwater harvesting systems were integrated into the cottage's design, channeling water into storage cisterns that would supplement the irrigation needs of the garden, further demonstrating the principles of water conservation. Raised beds, constructed from reclaimed timber, were built to showcase specific plant groupings and to allow for easier accessibility for educational purposes. Stone pathways were laid, using locally sourced rocks that blended seamlessly with the natural landscape, creating a sense of timelessness.

One of the most significant undertakings was the restoration of a small, natural spring that had been choked with invasive weeds for years. Ellie and her team worked diligently to clear the area, carefully replanting native riparian vegetation along its banks – hardy ferns, moisture-loving wildflowers, and young cottonwood saplings. The goal was to not only revive the spring itself but to create a healthy buffer zone that would protect its water quality and provide a haven for wildlife. Observing the return of dragonflies and damselflies to the clear water, and the increased presence of birds and small animals drawn to the revitalized habitat, was a deeply rewarding experience, a tangible sign of the land's capacity for healing when given the proper care.

The community's response was overwhelmingly positive. People who had once been hesitant about embracing xeriscaping or native planting found themselves drawn to the beauty and resilience of Eliza's Garden. They saw it as a living testament to the possibility of thriving in the Hill Country without depleting its precious resources. Conversations at the local market and at community gatherings frequently turned to discussions about the garden, about specific plants, and about the shared commitment to environmental stewardship. Ellie often found herself fielding questions, sharing her grandmother's insights, and guiding neighbors towards resources that could help them implement similar practices on their own properties.

The research center component began to take shape as well. With the help of a grant secured through Abernathy's connections, Ellie was able to purchase essential laboratory equipment. She began collaborating with a botanist from the nearest university on a study of native seed viability, comparing germination rates of seeds collected from different microclimates within the region. She also initiated a long-term project to document the seasonal changes in the garden's insect populations, focusing on the diversity and abundance of pollinators. These research efforts, rooted in practical observation and scientific inquiry, aimed to provide data that could inform conservation strategies and sustainable land management practices throughout the Hill Country.

The cottage itself underwent a subtle transformation, becoming the administrative and educational hub of the center. One room was dedicated to a small library, filled with books on botany, ecology, and traditional land management, with a special section devoted to Eliza's personal collection. Another room served as a meeting space, where workshops and study groups could convene. The veranda, with its sweeping views of the evolving landscape, became a popular spot for quiet contemplation and informal discussions, fostering a sense of community and shared purpose.

Ellie's grandmother had always spoken of plants as living libraries, each species holding within it a unique history and a wealth of information. Eliza's

Garden was intended to be a physical manifestation of that idea, a place where those libraries could be accessed, explored, and appreciated. It was a tribute to a woman who understood that true wealth lay not in accumulation, but in connection – a connection to the land, to its rhythms, and to the enduring wisdom that sustained it. The legacy, once whispered in the intimate confines of Eliza's garden, was now being broadcast, shared, and nurtured, promising to bloom and flourish for generations to come, a testament to the enduring power of traditional ecological knowledge and its vital relevance for the challenges of tomorrow. This garden was more than just a collection of plants; it was a living monument to resilience, a sanctuary of knowledge, and a beacon of hope for the future of the Hill Country.

The scent of sun-baked earth and blooming lavender, a fragrance as familiar to Ellie as her own breath, now drew visitors from far beyond the immediate county. What had begun as a personal endeavor, a deeply felt obligation to her grandmother's memory, had blossomed into something far larger – the Dawson farm, a living testament to the quiet strength and enduring wisdom of the Hill Country. It had become, to her surprise and quiet satisfaction, a recognized model of resilience, a beacon of sustainable agriculture in a region often battered by drought and economic uncertainty. The whispers of Eliza's legacy, once confined to the stone cottage and the intimate circle of dedicated volunteers, now echoed through the valleys, carried on the very winds that swept across their fields.

People came, not in droves, but with a steady, earnest purpose, drawn by the stories that began to circulate. They arrived in dusty sedans and worn pickup trucks, their faces etched with the same hopes and anxieties that had once spurred Ellie's own transformation. They sought not just a glimpse of what was possible, but a deeper understanding, a practical education in how to coax abundance from a land that demanded respect and careful stewardship. Ellie, often found with a smudge of soil on her cheek and a patient smile, became the de facto guide, sharing the hard-won lessons learned from her grandmother and the ongoing experiments that defined their farming life.

The core of their success, Ellie explained, was a deliberate turn towards the native. It wasn't a rejection of conventional agriculture, but an embrace of the land's inherent genius. The days of monoculture, of vast, thirsty fields of single crops that leeched the soil and demanded constant intervention, were long past. Instead, the Dawson farm had become a vibrant tapestry of diversified agriculture, a mosaic of native grasses, drought-tolerant wildflowers, and carefully selected, regionally appropriate crops. She'd speak of the mesquite, once seen as a nuisance, now understood as a valuable nitrogen-fixer, its deep taproots accessing moisture far below the surface. The prickly pear, with its succulent pads and edible fruit, provided both food and an incredibly resilient ground cover, minimizing soil erosion even during the most punishing dry spells.

Water conservation, a lesson etched into the very bones of the Hill Country, was not merely a practice but a philosophy that permeated every aspect of their operation. The ingenious rainwater harvesting systems, integrated into the roofs of the barn and the cottage, collected every precious drop, channeling it into a network of underground cisterns. These cisterns, far from being just reservoirs, were part of a larger, closed-loop system. The water, filtered naturally through layers of gravel and sand, was used first for the most critical needs – the propagation beds in the greenhouse, the small orchard of native pecans and persimmons. Then, any excess would be carefully allocated to irrigate the more demanding crops, always with drip irrigation systems that delivered water directly to the roots, minimizing evaporation. Ellie would often demonstrate how the soil itself had been conditioned to retain moisture, a rich, dark loam, thanks to years of composting and the incorporation of cover crops like native sunflowers and certain varieties of clover, which not only added nutrients but also improved soil structure.

The visitors would walk the winding paths, their boots crunching on the decomposed granite and shredded bark mulch, and see not just fields, but a carefully orchestrated ecosystem. They'd observe the rows of heirloom tomatoes, interspersed with beneficial companion plants like marigolds and basil, a practice honed from Eliza's own garden, designed to deter pests naturally. They'd marvel at the small, meticulously managed apiary, its buzzing inhabitants crucial pollinators for the orchard and the surrounding wildflowers. They'd see fields of sorghum and millet, ancient grains that thrived in arid conditions, providing sustenance for both humans and livestock, and leaving the soil richer than they found it.

Ellie would often pull a hardy sprig of native rosemary or some of the bluebonnet seeds from her apron pocket, handing them to a visitor with a quiet instruction: "These are of this place. They know how to survive here." She'd explain the careful selection process, not just for yield or marketability, but for adaptability and ecological contribution. The corn, for instance, wasn't the tall, water-hungry hybrid of commercial farms, but a more ancient variety, smaller in stature but more resilient, its deep root system anchoring it firmly and seeking out scarce moisture. The beans, climbing the sturdy stalks of the corn, offered a symbiotic relationship, fixing nitrogen in the soil, a natural fertilization that reduced the need for external inputs.

The economic viability of the Dawson farm was a constant source of inquiry. Skeptics, accustomed to the high-input, high-output model of industrial agriculture, would question how such a diverse, naturally managed system could possibly turn a profit. Ellie's answer was always grounded in pragmatism and a long-term vision. "It's not about getting rich quick," she'd say, her gaze sweeping across the fields. "It's about building wealth that lasts. Wealth in the soil, wealth in the water, wealth in the health of our community." She'd point to the reduced costs associated with pesticides, herbicides, and synthetic fertilizers, expenses that were entirely absent from their operation. She'd speak of the premium prices their produce commanded at local farmers' markets and restaurants, where consumers actively sought out the pure, unadulterated flavors of food grown with care.

The diversified nature of the farm provided a buffer against market fluctuations. If one crop had a less-than-ideal year due to an unforeseen weather event or pest outbreak, others would likely thrive, ensuring a more stable income stream. The honey from the apiary, the seeds saved from open-pollinated varieties, the surplus of certain herbs that could be dried and sold as value-added products – these all contributed to a more robust and resilient economic model. They weren't solely reliant on the whims of a single commodity.

The farm's success story wasn't just about Ellie and her family; it was a story of community collaboration. Neighbors, inspired by the visible changes on the Dawson land, began to experiment with similar practices. The local feed store saw an increased demand for native wildflower seeds and drought-tolerant grass varieties. The community garden, once struggling, found new life as residents shared knowledge and resources, many of them drawing directly from Ellie's accessible guidance. Abernathy, through the 'Hill Country Herald,' continued to champion these efforts, featuring stories of individual farms and ranches that were successfully integrating native plants, implementing water-wise irrigation, and moving towards more diversified, sustainable agricultural systems.

One of the most impactful aspects of the Dawson farm's model was its demonstration of integrated pest management. Ellie would walk visitors through an insectary, a dedicated patch of plants specifically chosen to attract beneficial insects — ladybugs, lacewings, parasitic wasps — that preyed on common agricultural pests. She'd explain how the absence of broad-spectrum pesticides had allowed these natural predators to flourish, creating a self-regulating system that kept pest populations in check. It was a living example of nature's own balance, a stark contrast to the chemical arms race that defined much of modern farming. They learned to tolerate a certain level of insect activity, understanding that not all bugs were bad, and that a healthy ecosystem included a complex web of interactions.

The visitors were particularly captivated by the educational aspect of the farm. Ellie had established a small, open-air classroom beneath a majestic old live oak, its branches providing natural shade. Here, she and her family would lead workshops on topics ranging from seed saving to composting techniques, from identifying beneficial insects to understanding the subtle signs of soil health. Children, often accompanying their parents, were given hands-on activities, planting seeds in small pots to take home, or helping to weed and water a designated children's garden. The aim was to foster a new generation of stewards, individuals who understood that farming was not just a business, but a profound responsibility to the land.

The story of the Dawson farm offered a tangible counter-narrative to the prevailing sense of doom that often accompanied discussions of climate change and rural decline. It presented a hopeful path forward, proving that economic viability and ecological responsibility were not mutually exclusive goals, but rather two sides of the same coin. The farm wasn't just producing food; it was regenerating the land, enhancing biodiversity, and strengthening the social fabric of the community. It was a living demonstration that the wisdom of the past, when combined with careful observation and a commitment to sustainability, could provide the very seeds of tomorrow's prosperity. The visitors, as they departed, often carried not just samples of the farm's bounty, but a renewed sense of purpose, a tangible belief that a more resilient and flourishing future for the Hill Country was not just a distant dream, but a harvest waiting to be cultivated.

The spirit of shared stewardship, ignited by the quiet revolution unfolding at the Dawson farm, began to manifest in more tangible, communal ways. It was no longer enough for Ellie to simply share her knowledge through casual conversations or impromptu farm tours. The challenges faced by the

Hill Country – the capricious rainfall, the ever-present threat of drought, the subtle degradation of soil health across countless acres – demanded a more organized, a more unified response. Recognizing this, the idea of regular community dialogues on land use and conservation began to take root, a concept that resonated deeply with the spirit of collaboration that Abernathy had so diligently fostered through the 'Hill Country Herald.'

Abernathy, ever the keen observer and facilitator of community discourse, was instrumental in bringing these forums to life. He proposed using the old Grange Hall, a sturdy, weather-beaten building that had long served as a gathering place for farmers and ranchers, as a regular venue. Its central location and historical significance made it the ideal space for these crucial conversations. The first meeting, advertised through flyers posted at the general store, the feed co-op, and, of course, in the pages of the 'Herald,' drew a diverse crowd. There were seasoned ranchers with generations of land-management experience, younger farmers eager to embrace new, sustainable methods, conservationists passionate about preserving the region's unique ecology, and even a few families new to the area, seeking to understand the delicate balance of their new home.

Ellie, along with her father, Robert, and her cousin, Sarah, who had become an indispensable partner in managing the farm's burgeoning operations, were among the first to arrive. The air in the Grange Hall crackled with a mixture of anticipation and a shared sense of urgency. Abernathy, standing at the front near a worn wooden podium, opened the proceedings with his characteristic blend of warmth and gravity. "Friends," he began, his voice carrying clearly through the hushed room, "we gather today not as individuals, but as a community. We stand on land that has sustained us, nurtured us, and challenged us for generations. The lessons Eliza Dawson taught us, and that Ellie continues to embody, are not just for one farm; they are for all of us. Today, we begin a conversation, a commitment to ensuring the health and vitality of this land for the generations yet to come."

The initial discussions were broad, encompassing the immediate concerns of the attendees. Water rights and allocation were a recurring theme, particularly as the summer heat began to bear down with its familiar intensity. Old-timers spoke of past droughts, of wells that ran dry and pastures that turned to dust, sharing hard-won wisdom about how their predecessors had managed during lean times. They recalled techniques like building check dams in gullies to slow water runoff and capture sediment, planting deep-rooted native grasses that could survive on minimal moisture, and the practice of "water-wise" grazing, moving livestock frequently to prevent overgrazing and soil compaction. These were not abstract theories but lived experiences, passed down through oral tradition, and now, they were being laid bare for a new generation to learn from.

Younger farmers, armed with charts and data from university extension programs and their own on-farm trials, spoke of innovations in irrigation, the efficacy of soil moisture sensors, and the benefits of cover cropping for retaining moisture and improving soil structure. There was a palpable synergy as the accumulated knowledge of the past met the scientific advancements of the present. Abernathy ensured that these discussions remained grounded, always circling back to Eliza's foundational principles: observe, adapt, and work *with* the land, not against it. He would often interject with historical anecdotes, reminding everyone of how native flora, like the drought-resistant mesquite and juniper, had thrived for centuries with minimal human intervention, offering clues to solutions that were already present in the landscape itself.

A significant portion of the dialogue focused on land use. The pressures of development, the increasing demand for agricultural products, and the desire to conserve wild spaces created a complex web of competing interests. Conversations evolved from simple complaints to collaborative problem-solving. One farmer, whose land bordered a significant tract of undeveloped prairie, expressed concern about potential overgrazing by a growing deer population, which was impacting his ability to establish native grass pastures. Another attendee, a local biologist, suggested implementing wildlife corridors, strategically placed strips of native vegetation that would allow wildlife to move freely without concentrating damage on a single property, while also providing habitat for beneficial insects. This led to a discussion about shared fencing costs and collaborative management of buffer zones.

The 'Hill Country Herald' became more than just a source of information; it transformed into an active facilitator of these ongoing dialogues. Abernathy dedicated a regular column, simply titled "Community Roots," to summarizing the discussions from the Grange Hall meetings, posing follow-up questions to readers, and highlighting successful examples of collaborative conservation efforts from other regions. He encouraged readers to submit their own observations, their successes and failures, and their ideas for the future. This created a dynamic feedback loop, extending the conversations beyond the walls of the Grange Hall and weaving them into the very fabric of daily life in the community.

As these dialogues progressed, a shared sense of responsibility for the land began to deepen. The abstract concept of conservation transformed into a concrete commitment, a collective endeavor. When a plan emerged to restore a degraded creek bed that ran through several properties, the community rallied. Ranchers offered the use of their equipment for clearing invasive species and hauling native rocks to stabilize the banks. Ellie's farm provided compost and seedlings of riparian native plants. Volunteers, many of whom had first learned about the Dawsons' sustainable practices at the Grange Hall meetings, dedicated weekends to the restoration work. Children from the local school, involved in a program coordinated with Abernathy's newspaper and the Dawson farm's educational initiatives, learned firsthand about the importance of healthy waterways, contributing to the planting efforts with youthful enthusiasm.

The discussions weren't always smooth. There were disagreements, rooted in differing priorities and decades of ingrained practices. Some grappled with the initial investment required for water-saving technologies or the perceived loss of productivity from shifting away from conventional monocultures. However, Abernathy and Ellie, drawing on Eliza's quiet persistence and wisdom, consistently steered the conversations back to the long-term benefits: the resilience of the land, the health of the community, and the preservation of a way of life that was intrinsically tied to the natural world. They emphasized that sustainability wasn't about deprivation, but about a more intelligent, more harmonious way of living and working.

The forums also began to address the economic dimensions of conservation. Discussions arose about the potential for ecotourism, the marketing of locally sourced, sustainably grown products, and the possibility of forming agricultural cooperatives to share resources and processing facilities. The success of the Dawson farm in achieving economic viability through its sustainable practices served as a powerful example, demonstrating that ecological responsibility and profitability were not mutually exclusive. This fostered a sense of optimism, a belief that by working together, they could not only protect their environment but also build a more prosperous future for themselves.

The legacy of Eliza Dawson, therefore, was not merely confined to the practices on her family's land. It had become a catalyst for a broader movement, a fundamental shift in how the community viewed its relationship with the land. The regular dialogues, facilitated by Abernathy's newspaper and sustained by the shared commitment of the residents, ensured that the lessons of the past remained not just historical footnotes, but living, breathing principles that guided their present actions and shaped their future aspirations. The Grange Hall, once a symbol of a fading agricultural era, was reborn as a vibrant hub of innovation, collaboration, and a profound, shared responsibility for the land that sustained them all. The echoes of Eliza's wisdom were no longer solitary whispers, but a collective chorus, singing a song of resilience, foresight, and enduring community spirit.

The stark beauty of the Hill Country, often perceived as unforgiving, held a deeper truth: an ingrained, almost defiant resilience. It was a resilience etched into the very bedrock of the land, a testament to millennia of adaptation. The limestone, worn smooth by wind and water, wasn't a sign of weakness, but of enduring strength. The hardy scrub oak, its gnarled branches reaching skyward, drew life from scarce resources, its roots delving deep into the earth, anchoring it against the tempestuous whims of the Texas sky. This enduring spirit of the land, its ability to bounce back from drought, fire, and the encroaching pressures of human activity, mirrored, Ellie found, the quiet fortitude that had begun to bloom within her own soul. She saw it in the way a single wildflower could push through a crack in the parched earth after a scant rain, or how the stubborn mesquite, often dismissed as a nuisance, could survive and thrive where other plants withered. This inherent ability of the landscape to regenerate, to find a way forward even in the face of overwhelming adversity, became a profound source of inspiration for her. It was a lesson learned not from a textbook or a lecture, but from the very soil beneath her feet, from the relentless cycle of sun and storm.

Ellie often found herself reflecting on this, particularly during those solitary hours spent surveying her family's land. The vastness of the sky, often a canvas of brilliant, unblinking blue, could quickly transform into a brooding expanse of storm clouds, unleashing torrents of rain that would either replenish or devastate. It was this constant push and pull, this unpredictable rhythm, that defined the Hill Country and, by extension, the lives of those who called it home. The droughts were legendary, periods of intense scarcity that tested the mettle of every farmer and rancher. Wells would run dry, creek beds would become parched arteries, and the very earth would crack with thirst. Yet, after the suffering, after the lean years that seemed to stretch into an eternity, the land would inevitably respond to the touch of moisture. The dormant seeds, held captive within the soil, would awaken, and a vibrant tapestry of green would once again spread across the hills. This cyclical resurgence, this refusal to succumb entirely to the harshness, was the land's enduring song, a melody of survival that resonated deeply within Ellie. She understood, with a clarity that had only sharpened with experience, that hardship wasn't the end, but often a necessary precursor to renewal. The struggles she had faced, both on the farm and within herself, had not diminished her; they had forged her.

The early days of the regenerative farming practices, when she and her father were first implementing Eliza's vision, had been fraught with their own set of challenges. There were moments of doubt, times when the unconventional methods seemed too slow, too uncertain. The soil, depleted by years of conventional agriculture, was slow to respond. Cover crops struggled to take hold in the compacted earth, and the transition to rotational grazing required a discipline and foresight that felt, at times, like swimming against the prevailing current. But with each small success — a slight improvement in soil organic matter, a noticeable increase in beneficial insect populations, the gradual return of native grasses to depleted pastures — Ellie felt a surge of affirmation. These were not dramatic, overnight transformations, but subtle, incremental shifts, much like the slow weathering of the limestone that shaped the very landscape. They were whispers of the land's innate capacity to heal, and Ellie was learning to listen.

She saw this same inherent resilience mirrored in the community's response to the ongoing dialogues initiated by Abernathy. While the initial enthusiasm was palpable, the path forward was not without its detours and disagreements. Old habits, ingrained practices passed down through generations, were not easily shed. The concept of "water-wise" grazing, for instance, challenged the traditional mindset of keeping cattle on pastures for extended periods. Ranchers who had always believed in maximizing acreage for their herds found it difficult to embrace the idea of strategically resting and rotating pastures. Similarly, the initial investment in new technologies, such as improved fencing for rotational grazing or the installation of water catchment systems, presented a financial hurdle for many. Yet, as the shared discussions continued, as the successes of farms like the Dawsons' began to be more widely recognized and disseminated through Abernathy's newspaper, a collective understanding started to dawn. The younger generation, often more receptive to new ideas and scientific data, played a crucial role in bridging the gap, demonstrating through their own farms the tangible benefits of these sustainable approaches.

Ellie recognized that her own journey was a microcosm of this larger struggle and triumph. Her initial anxieties about taking on the farm, the weight of Eliza's legacy, and the sheer physical demands of the work had often felt overwhelming. There were days when the sheer volume of tasks, from mending fences to managing the compost piles, to planning the next season's planting, seemed insurmountable. The unpredictable weather, the constant battle against invasive species, and the economic uncertainties of farming in a region prone to boom and bust cycles could easily have crushed her spirit. But she had learned to draw strength from the land itself. She found solace in the quiet diligence of her work, in the tangible results that, however small, represented progress. The resilience she was cultivating within herself was directly intertwined with the resilience of the ecosystem she was tending. It was a symbiotic relationship, a feedback loop where the health of the land fostered her own inner strength, and her renewed spirit, in turn, allowed her to care for the land with greater wisdom and perseverance.

The harshness of the Hill Country, which some viewed as a barrier to prosperity, was, in fact, the crucible in which its unique character and its people's resilience were forged. The very conditions that demanded ingenuity and adaptation had fostered a deep understanding of the natural world, a respect for its limits, and a profound appreciation for the cycles of life and renewal. The sparse rainfall, the thin soils, the often-unforgiving terrain – these were not impediments, but teachers. They taught the value of every drop of water, the importance of soil health, and the necessity of working in harmony with the natural rhythms of the environment. Ellie understood that this inherent toughness of the land wasn't a flaw, but its greatest asset. It was what allowed it to endure, to heal, and to continue to provide sustenance and beauty to those who learned to listen to its whispers and respect its inherent wisdom.

The beauty of the Hill Country wasn't a manicured prettiness, but a rugged, untamed splendor that spoke of endurance. It was in the fiery hues of the sunset that bled across the vast sky, in the silhouette of cedar trees against a twilight horizon, in the sudden, breathtaking vista that opened up after navigating a winding, rocky trail. This beauty was intrinsically linked to the land's resilience. It was a beauty born of survival, of adaptation, of life finding a way against all odds. Ellie's own journey had been a similar process of discovery, of finding strength not in avoiding hardship, but in embracing it, learning from it, and ultimately transforming it. She had come to understand that the very elements that made the Hill Country challenging – the aridity, the rocky soil, the intense sun – were also the architects of its unique and enduring beauty. It was a beauty that demanded respect, a beauty that was earned through perseverance, and a beauty that, like the spirit of the land itself, would continue to thrive, generation after generation. The community's growing commitment to regenerative practices was, in essence, a deepening of this respect, a conscious decision to nurture and protect the very qualities that made their home so special, so enduring, and so uniquely beautiful. The legacy of Eliza Dawson was not just about farming techniques; it was about cultivating a profound appreciation for the tenacity of life, a lesson whispered by the wind through the live oaks and written in the enduring spirit of the land itself.

The lingering scent of lavender, a perfume that had once defined the Dawsons' endeavor, now mingled with the subtler, earthier notes of the native wildflowers that had begun to reclaim the edges of the fields. It was a new fragrance, one born of acceptance and adaptation, a testament to the land's persistent will to flourish in its own way. The immediate storm, both literal and metaphorical, had passed. The deluge of the past weeks, which had threatened to wash away not only soil but also the fragile shoots of progress, had receded. What remained was a landscape softened by rain, its colors deepened, its promise renewed. Yet, this was not a scene of pristine recovery; it was a landscape marked by the passage of hardship, bearing the subtle scars of struggle. The lavender, though battered, still stood, its purple blooms a muted testament to perseverance. But alongside it, and in places where the cultivated rows had yielded to the wilder impulses of the earth, a vibrant tapestry of native blooms had emerged. Prickly pear blossoms, a startling shock of yellow against the grey-green of the cacti, mingled with the delicate, star-like flowers of various native grasses. This intermingling of the cultivated and the wild was, Ellie mused, a perfect metaphor for their current state. They had weathered the storm, and in its wake, something new, something perhaps even more resilient, was beginning to take root.

The profound sense of accomplishment that settled over the community was not the boisterous triumph of a decisive victory, but a quieter, more deeply felt satisfaction. It was the knowledge that they had faced a significant threat, not with panicked reaction, but with collective intention and a growing understanding of the natural world they inhabited. The days of intense labor, of sandbagging against the rising waters, of anxiously watching the skies and the soil, had forged a new kind of bond between them. They had seen each other's strengths, their fears, and their unwavering commitment to protecting their homes and their shared future. Abernathy, his usual spirited pronouncements tempered by the gravity of the recent events, spoke of it not as a disaster averted, but as a hard-won lesson. "We learned," he declared at a gathering in the community hall, the air still thick with the scent of damp earth and shared relief, "that the land can be both our provider and our challenge. And we learned that by working with it, not against it, we are stronger." His words resonated, echoing the sentiment that had begun to bloom in Ellie's own heart. This was not about dominating nature, but about finding a harmonious rhythm with it.

The immediate crisis had passed, but the awareness of ongoing challenges remained. The water table, though replenished, would need careful management. The delicate ecosystem, stressed by the unseasonable weather, would require continued attention. The economic realities of farming, always present, would continue to demand vigilance. Yet, these were no longer the paralyzing fears of the unknown, but the manageable concerns of a community that had faced adversity and emerged with a clearer vision. There was a palpable shift in the air, a sense of forward momentum driven not by blind optimism, but by a deep-seated belief in their collective capacity to adapt, to learn, and to thrive. This wasn't the naive hope of a child believing in fairy tales, but the grounded hope of a seasoned farmer who understood that life, like the land, was a constant cycle of planting, tending, and harvesting, with moments of difficulty interspersed with periods of bounty.

Ellie found herself drawn to the edges of her lavender fields, where the wilder growth was most apparent. She observed how the native wildflowers, often overlooked in their focus on the cultivated crop, now thrived with an almost aggressive vitality. They had adapted to the soil, to the sun, to the very essence of the Hill Country, in ways that the imported lavender, for all its beauty and fragrance, could only mimic. These unseen blooms, often hidden beneath the more ostentatious displays of the cultivated varieties, were the true anchors of the ecosystem. They were the plants that drew the specific pollinators, that held the soil in place with their tenacious root systems, that offered sustenance to the native fauna. They were the quiet sustainers, the unsung heroes of the landscape. And in their resilience, Ellie saw a reflection of the deeper, more enduring hope that was taking root within her. It was the hope that came from understanding one's place within a larger, interconnected web of life, the hope that stemmed from recognizing the inherent strength and wisdom of the natural world.

The conversations at the community meetings had shifted, too. Gone were the anxieties about immediate survival; in their place were discussions about long-term sustainability, about water conservation strategies that went beyond mere rationing, about diversifying crops to include more drought-tolerant native species, and about building soil health as a bulwark against future environmental extremes. Abernathy, with his keen eye for narrative, had begun to document these evolving discussions in his newspaper, framing them not as concessions to adversity, but as advancements born of necessity and wisdom. He wrote of the "unseen blooms," the quiet victories in soil regeneration, the subtle shifts in farming practices that were creating a more robust and self-sufficient agricultural landscape. He highlighted the work of families who were experimenting with heritage grains, of ranchers who were meticulously managing their grazing rotations to promote native grass diversity, and of individuals who were actively restoring native plant communities on their properties.

Ellie's own father, a man who had always been more comfortable with the tangible realities of the land than with abstract pronouncements, had become an unexpected advocate for these new approaches. He spoke with a quiet authority, not of grand theories, but of practical observations. He would point to a patch of newly returned native grass, explaining how it held the moisture better than the depleted Bermuda grass it had replaced. He would show Ellie the increased activity of beneficial insects in the cover-cropped areas, a direct counterpoint to the reduced pest pressure they had experienced the previous season. His endorsement, rooted in years of hard-won experience, carried significant weight within the community. It was the quiet affirmation that the old ways, while deeply respected, were not the only ways, and that embracing change, when guided by observation and a deep understanding of the land, could lead to greater prosperity.

The challenges of the past had not been erased; they had been absorbed, transformed, and in some ways, integrated into the fabric of their lives. The lavender fields, though perhaps smaller and more intermingled with the wild, still held their beauty and their economic potential. But now, their value was understood in a broader context. They were not just a source of fragrant oil, but part of a larger, more resilient agricultural system. The hope that now pervaded the community was not a fragile thing, easily shattered by the next unexpected frost or drought. It was a hardy, deep-rooted hope, like the mesquite tree that could survive in the most arid conditions, drawing sustenance from seemingly barren ground. It was a hope that recognized the interconnectedness of all living things, that understood the vital role of the unseen blooms, the native grasses, the beneficial insects, the healthy soil.

Ellie walked through a section of the farm where the lavender had been significantly impacted by the recent rains. Some plants had been uprooted, others were showing signs of stress. But interspersed among them, vibrant and tenacious, were wildflowers she had only recently begun to identify. There were delicate bluebonnets, their petals unfurled to the sun, and the sturdy purple coneflowers, already attracting a flurry of bees. It struck her then that the true success of their endeavor wasn't in preserving the lavender at all costs, but in ensuring the overall health and vitality of the ecosystem that supported it. If the lavender thrived, it was a bonus. If the native plants flourished, the land itself was strengthened. This realization brought a profound sense of peace. It was a move away from a singular focus, towards a more holistic vision of abundance.

The collective journey had been one of slow, deliberate learning. It had involved questioning long-held assumptions, experimenting with new approaches, and, most importantly, listening to the land. The conversations were no longer just about maximizing yield, but about building long-term ecological health. The focus had shifted from controlling nature to collaborating with it. This subtle but significant shift in perspective had unlocked a new wellspring of hope. It was a hope that was rooted in the understanding that they were not merely stewards of the land, but participants in its ongoing, dynamic evolution. The unseen blooms, in their quiet persistence, were a constant reminder of this truth. They represented the inherent capacity of life to adapt, to find a way, to bloom even in the most challenging circumstances. And in that, Ellie found a deep and abiding sense of optimism, not for a return to a past idealized, but for a future built on the enduring strength of the Hill Country itself. The lavender, once the sole star of their agricultural show, now played its part in a richer, more complex, and ultimately more resilient ensemble. The fragrance that now hung in the air was a testament to

this evolving harmony, a subtle but undeniable scent
of a quiet, enduring hope.

# Chapter 11: The Unseen Bloom

The air, once thick with the anxious dampness of an overlong storm, began to shed its clinging moisture, replaced by the crisp promise of a returning sun. The earth, saturated and yielding, breathed a sigh of relief, its parched lungs filled with the sweet, clean scent of rain-kissed soil. For weeks, the community had lived under a sky that seemed intent on drowning their efforts, a relentless deluge that tested the very foundations of their existence. Now, the clouds had retreated, not entirely banished, for the memory of their power lingered, but subdued, yielding to a sky of an almost audacious blue. This was not a dramatic dawn after a single night's storm, but the slow, deliberate unfolding of a new season, one that carried the weight of past trials but also the undeniable lightness of renewed hope.

Ellie felt it most acutely when she stepped out onto the dew-kissed ground each morning. The lavender, though still bearing the marks of the recent battering, was beginning to straighten, its delicate stems finding their resolve. But it was the symphony of the wilder growth that truly captured her attention. Where the water had receded, leaving behind a rich, dark loam, the native wildflowers, once mere whispers at the periphery, were now erupting in a vibrant chorus of color. Tiny bluebonnets, like scattered fragments of the sky, carpeted the ground, their ephemeral beauty a poignant reminder of nature's fleeting yet persistent artistry. Alongside them, the hardy purple coneflowers, their petals reaching skyward, were already drawing the diligent hum of bees, their fuzzy bodies dusted with pollen. These were the plants that understood the land's true language, the ones whose roots delved deep, anchoring themselves against the very forces that had threatened to overwhelm the cultivated rows.

The shift was subtle, a gradual recalibration rather than an abrupt change. It was in the way the sunlight now slanted through the trees, longer and warmer, coaxing forth the latent energy of the earth. It was in the calls of the birds, no longer the anxious chirping of those seeking shelter, but the clear, resonant songs of territorial claims and burgeoning life. Even the wind seemed to carry a different tune, a gentle caress that rustled the leaves of the mesquite and whispered through the taller grasses, a sound that spoke not of impending chaos, but of natural rhythms reasserting themselves. The deep, almost primal need for survival, which had gripped the community during the protracted storm, was slowly giving way to a more nuanced appreciation for the land's inherent capacity for renewal. They were no longer just weathering the storm; they were beginning to dance with the returning sun.

The awareness of the persistent drought, a shadow that always loomed over the Hill Country, was undeniably present. The rain had been a blessing, a much-needed reprieve, but the underlying scarcity was a truth etched into the very landscape. Yet, this time, the presence of that knowledge felt different. It wasn't a harbinger of doom, but a reminder of the delicate balance they were learning to cultivate. The community's approach had evolved. The frantic efforts to simply keep the water out had been replaced by a more considered strategy of working with the land's natural inclinations. Conservation was no longer a matter of desperate rationing, but a deliberate practice woven into the fabric of their daily lives. They had learned to observe the subtle signs of moisture retention, to understand which native plants were most adept at drawing sustenance from deep within the earth, and to recognize the quiet efficiency of well-managed soil.

Ellie found herself spending more time in the sections of the farm where they had intentionally encouraged the proliferation of native species. The lavender, once the sole focus of her attention, now shared the stage, its fragrance still a sweet and familiar comfort, but its dominance tempered by the vibrant presence of its wilder companions. She watched, with a growing sense of awe, how the different plants coexisted, how the deep-rooted native grasses provided a protective buffer for the more sensitive lavender, preventing the soil from washing away in the inevitable, albeit less intense, seasonal rains. The biodiversity that was emerging was not a chaotic intrusion, but a harmonious symphony. The wildflowers attracted a wider array of pollinators, not just the bees that favored lavender, but a host of other insects, each playing a vital role in the intricate web of life that sustained the farm.

Her father, a man of few words but profound observation, would often join her. He wouldn't offer pronouncements, but rather gentle observations that resonated with years of lived experience. "See how

the dew lingers on these little blue flowers, Ellie?"
he'd say, pointing to a cluster of bluebonnets. "They
drink what the morning offers, and ask for no more.
The land remembers how to provide, if we only
learn to listen." His quiet wisdom, grounded in the
practical realities of the soil, was a constant anchor.
He had witnessed the folly of trying to force nature
into a mold, and now, he was a quiet champion of a
more yielding approach. He'd show her how the
native ground cover was keeping the soil cool,
reducing the need for supplemental watering, and
how the presence of certain wildflowers seemed to
deter the pests that had once plagued their crops.

The community meetings, once filled with anxious
discussions about crop failure and the looming
threat of another devastating drought, had
transformed. The conversations now revolved
around sustainable grazing practices, the cultivation
of heritage grains that were more resilient to arid
conditions, and the restoration of native plant
communities along the creek beds, which acted as
natural sponges, absorbing and filtering precious
rainwater. Abernathy, in his weekly newspaper, had
become the chronicler of these quiet revolutions. He
wrote not of grand gestures, but of the meticulous

care being taken to nurture the land's own resilience. He highlighted the families experimenting with dryland farming techniques, the ranchers implementing rotational grazing that encouraged the growth of native grasses, and the individuals dedicated to re-establishing native flora on their properties.

Ellie realized that their understanding of abundance had undergone a profound transformation. It was no longer measured solely by the volume of harvested lavender, but by the overall health and vitality of the entire ecosystem. The 'unseen blooms,' as Abernathy had so aptly termed them, were no longer an afterthought, but an integral part of their agricultural success. They were the indicators of a land that was not just surviving, but thriving. The resilience of these native plants, their ability to draw sustenance from seemingly barren ground, their tenacity in the face of harsh conditions, served as a powerful metaphor for the community itself. They, too, had weathered a severe storm, and in its wake, they were discovering a deeper, more enduring strength.

As the season progressed, the landscape responded

with an almost eager vitality. The lavender fields, though still a significant part of their endeavor, were now integrated into a richer, more diverse tapestry. The intermingling of cultivated and wild was no longer a sign of neglect, but of intentional design. The subtle fragrance of lavender still hung in the air, but it was now underscored by the earthy, sweet scent of wildflowers, the clean aroma of newly sprouted grasses, and the hint of wild herbs that had begun to reclaim the edges of the farm. This complex bouquet was the fragrance of a renewed rhythm, a testament to a community that had learned to embrace the land's own seasons, its own patterns, and its own quiet power.

The shift from mere survival to conscious cultivation was evident in every aspect of their farming practices. The water management systems were more sophisticated, incorporating rainwater harvesting, drip irrigation that minimized evaporation, and a deep understanding of soil moisture levels. The focus on soil health was paramount, with cover cropping and composting becoming standard practices, not just to nourish the lavender, but to enrich the entire soil biome. They were actively creating an environment where native plants could flourish, understanding that their presence contributed to a more stable and productive agricultural system. This wasn't about abandoning their established crops, but about creating a more robust foundation upon which all life on the farm could depend.

Ellie found herself increasingly drawn to the wisdom of the indigenous plants. She learned to identify the subtle differences in their flowering times, the specific pollinators they attracted, and their remarkable ability to thrive with minimal intervention. She saw how the Indian Blanket flowers, with their vibrant splashes of red and yellow, acted as a natural pest repellent, deterring the aphids that had once been a nuisance in the lavender. She observed how the tall, feathery stalks of switchgrass helped to hold the soil in place, preventing erosion during the occasional heavy downpours. These were not mere plants; they were living lessons, offering insights into resilience, adaptation, and the profound interconnectedness of all living things.

The community's appreciation for the seasons had

deepened, transforming from a passive acceptance of weather patterns to an active engagement with the land's cycles. They understood that each season brought its own challenges and opportunities, and that true abundance lay in working with, rather than against, these natural rhythms. The summer heat, which could once be a source of dread, was now approached with strategies designed to conserve moisture and protect the delicate balance of the ecosystem. The autumn harvest was no longer just about gathering the lavender, but about observing the subtle changes in the wildflowers, the ripening seeds of native grasses, and the gathering of late-season blooms that would provide sustenance for wildlife through the leaner months.

The winter, which had always represented a period of dormancy and quiet, was now viewed with a different perspective. It was a time for rest, certainly, but also a time for reflection and planning. The community would gather, sharing observations from the past year, discussing new experiments, and solidifying their commitment to practices that nurtured the land's long-term health. The knowledge that the drought, though currently abated, was a persistent reality, fueled their dedication to building a more resilient agricultural system, one that could withstand the inevitable lean years. They understood that true abundance was not a steady state, but a dynamic equilibrium, maintained through careful stewardship and a deep respect for the land's inherent limitations and capabilities.

The lavender, still a vital crop, was now understood in a broader context. Its value was not diminished, but enhanced by its integration into a more sustainable and ecologically sound agricultural system. The fragrance that now perfumed the Hill Country air was a complex blend, a testament to both human endeavor and nature's enduring power. It was the scent of hard-won wisdom, of community resilience, and of a quiet, deeply rooted hope that bloomed not just in the cultivated fields, but in the heart of the land itself, sustained by the unseen bloom of a thousand native wildflowers.

The sun, now a regular and benevolent presence in the sky, cast long, gentle shadows across the fields as Ellie moved among the lavender. It wasn't the urgent, hopeful tending of a young farmer anymore, nor the anxious vigilance of someone merely trying to survive. This was the practiced, almost reverent touch of a seasoned steward, her movements economical and filled with a quiet certainty. The lavender, while still a cornerstone of their livelihood, was no longer the sole focus of her gaze. Her eyes, honed by years of observation, now scanned the periphery, noting the subtle shifts in the undergrowth, the emerging patterns of native flora that interwove with their cultivated rows. It was in these spaces, the wilder edges and the carefully integrated wild patches, that her true leadership was most evident.

She had begun taking on apprentices of sorts, young men and women from the community, drawn to her deep understanding and her gentle, persuasive way. They came from families who had seen their own struggles with the unpredictable climate, who understood the precariousness of a single-crop reliance. Ellie didn't impose her will; she invited them to learn. They would walk the fields together, her voice a low murmur as she pointed out the medicinal properties of a roadside herb, or explained the symbiotic relationship between a specific wildflower and a native pollinator. She taught them to read the soil, not just for moisture, but for its composition, its history, its inherent capacity. "The land speaks," she'd often say, her hand resting lightly on the dark, rich earth, "but you have to be quiet enough to hear it."

One sweltering afternoon, young Silas, his brow furrowed with concentration, pointed to a patch of what looked like common weeds choking a struggling lavender seedling. "Should I pull these, Ellie? They're taking all the light." Ellie knelt beside him, her fingers tracing the delicate leaves of the offending plant. "This," she explained, "is Devil's Claw. Its roots go deep, deeper than most of our cultivated plants. They help break up compacted soil and bring nutrients from below. And see these flowers? They attract a particular kind of wasp that preys on the aphids that bother our lavender. It's a partnership, Silas, not a competition." Silas looked from the plant to Ellie, a slow dawning of understanding in his eyes. It was in these moments, patiently unraveling the intricate tapestry of the land, that Ellie's quiet leadership truly took root. She wasn't just teaching them about plants; she was teaching them a new way of seeing, a philosophy of coexistence.

Her influence extended beyond the farm's borders.

The community meetings, once dominated by anxious discussions about weather patterns and market prices, had evolved. Now, there was a palpable shift in the tenor of their conversations. Abernathy, still diligent with his weekly articles in the local gazette, had become a sort of informal chronicler of these emerging practices. His columns weren't filled with pronouncements or grand theories, but with detailed, often anecdotal, accounts of how families were adapting. He wrote about the Davidsons and their success with a heritage strain of sorghum, a grain that required significantly less water than their previous corn crops. He detailed how the Miller family had revitalized a section of their land by planting native prairie grasses along the creek beds, observing firsthand how these resilient plants stabilized the soil and captured precious rainfall, creating small, vital oases.

Ellie, though never seeking the spotlight, was often the unspoken inspiration behind these changes. When a new irrigation technique was discussed, or a debate arose about diversifying crops, it was often Ellie's quiet voice that offered a balanced perspective, grounded in her deep understanding of ecological principles. She didn't advocate for radical departures, but for gradual, thoughtful integration. She'd share her observations about how the native wildflowers near their lavender fields seemed to be drawing in beneficial insects that also visited their cultivated rows, suggesting that a carefully managed polyculture could offer a natural form of pest control and enhance overall plant health. Her knowledge wasn't confined to her own acreage; it was a shared resource, offered freely and without agenda.

Her home had become a quiet hub of this learning. The scent of dried herbs hung heavy in the air, mingling with the faint, sweet perfume of lavender that always seemed to cling to her. Young people, and even some of the older generations, would drop by, seeking her advice on everything from identifying a troublesome weed to understanding the best time to plant certain native species for wildlife. She had a way of listening, truly listening, that made people feel heard and valued. She'd examine a wilting plant brought to her with the same care she'd give a prized lavender bloom, her brow furrowed in concentration as she considered the conditions, the soil, the surrounding environment. Her diagnoses were rarely simple; they often involved a deeper understanding of the interconnectedness of the farm as a whole.

One evening, as the sun dipped below the horizon, painting the sky in hues of orange and deep violet, Ellie sat on her porch swing, a worn ledger open on her lap. Beside her sat young Clara, who had been helping her tend the lavender for the past two summers. Clara, usually boisterous, was quiet, her gaze fixed on the distant hills. "Ellie," she began hesitantly, "sometimes I feel like… like all this work with the wild plants, it's not as important as the lavender. The lavender sells. It pays the bills." Ellie closed the ledger, her gaze soft but steady. "Clara," she said, her voice carrying the quiet strength of conviction, "the lavender is beautiful, and it is important. But so are these wildflowers, and the grasses, and even the humble weeds that keep our soil healthy. They are the foundation. Without them, the lavender wouldn't thrive, not in the long run. They are the unseen bloom, and they are just as vital, perhaps even more so, for the health of this whole land."

She explained to Clara how the native plants helped

to retain moisture in the soil, reducing the need for supplementary irrigation, especially crucial in their often-arid climate. She spoke of how their deep root systems prevented soil erosion, protecting the valuable topsoil that was the very essence of their farming success. She pointed out the diverse array of pollinators that these wild blooms attracted – not just the bees that favored lavender, but a multitude of native bees, butterflies, and other beneficial insects that contributed to the overall health of the ecosystem. Clara listened, her eyes wide, absorbing the depth of Ellie's understanding. It wasn't just about agriculture; it was about stewardship, about recognizing the intrinsic value of every living thing.

Ellie's leadership was characterized by a profound humility. She never claimed to have all the answers, but she possessed an unshakeable faith in the resilience of nature and in the capacity of their community to learn and adapt. She would often recount her own early struggles, the moments of doubt and near despair during the prolonged droughts, as a way of reminding them that growth often came through adversity. "We learned, didn't we?" she'd say, a faint smile playing on her lips. "We learned to work with the land, not against it. We learned to listen to its rhythms, to respect its limits, and to celebrate its generosity." This acknowledgment of her own journey made her wisdom accessible, relatable. She wasn't a distant authority; she was one of them, a fellow traveler on the path of understanding.

Her commitment to the well-being of the land and its people was absolute. It was evident in the way she shared her knowledge, the way she encouraged experimentation, and the way she fostered a sense of shared responsibility. She understood that true sustainability wasn't just about environmental practices; it was about building a community that was invested in its own future. She saw the interconnectedness of everything – how a healthy ecosystem supported healthy people, and how a strong community was better equipped to care for its environment. This holistic vision was the bedrock of her quiet, yet powerful, leadership.

The lavender fields, though still a significant source of their income, were now just one vibrant thread in a much larger, more intricate tapestry. The wild flowers, once relegated to the edges, now flowed into the cultivated rows, creating a visual harmony that was as pleasing to the eye as it was beneficial to the land. Ellie had meticulously planned these integrations, understanding the specific needs of each plant, the timing of their blooms, and the roles they played within the larger ecosystem. She had experimented with companion planting, discovering that certain native species, when strategically placed, could deter pests, improve soil fertility, and even attract beneficial insects that aided in the pollination of the lavender.

The annual Lavender Festival, a cornerstone of their local economy and a symbol of their community's resilience, had begun to reflect this evolution. While the fragrant blooms remained the central attraction, the festival grounds were now dotted with educational booths showcasing native plants and sustainable farming practices. Ellie, often found at a small, unassuming table laden with samples of medicinal herbs and wildflower seeds, would patiently answer questions, her deep knowledge and calm demeanor drawing people in. She wasn't just selling products; she was sharing her passion, her philosophy, and her unwavering belief in the interconnectedness of their lives with the natural world.

Her mentorship extended to the youngest members of the community as well. She had started a small garden project at the local school, where children learned firsthand about the cycles of growth, the importance of soil, and the joy of nurturing a plant from seed to bloom. She taught them to identify common wildflowers, to understand their roles in the ecosystem, and to appreciate the subtle beauty of the land around them. "Every plant has a purpose," she'd tell them, her voice gentle, as they carefully planted tiny seeds in the earth. "Just like every one of you has a purpose. We are all part of this beautiful, living world."

This quiet leadership, born from a deep wellspring of knowledge, resilience, and an unwavering love for the land, was transforming their corner of the Hill Country. It was a leadership that didn't demand attention, but earned respect through consistent action and genuine care. Ellie had become a living testament to the strength that could be found in working in harmony with nature, in embracing the unseen blooms that sustained the visible harvest. She was a beacon, not of grand pronouncements, but of quiet, enduring change, her legacy woven into the very fabric of the land she so deeply cherished and the community she had helped to nurture. The legacy of the lavender was now inextricably linked with the legacy of the unseen bloom, a testament to Ellie's profound understanding of the land's true, enduring power. Her influence was like the deep roots of the native grasses she championed, unseen but essential, anchoring the entire ecosystem and fostering a future of sustainable abundance for generations to come.

The hum of the cicadas, a constant, resonant song of summer, was more than just background noise; it was a pulse, a testament to the vibrant life that teemed in every corner of their valley. Ellie understood this symphony, not as a random chorus, but as a carefully orchestrated movement, each creature playing its vital part. The iridescent wings of a dragonfly, a blur of emerald and sapphire, zipped past a cluster of wild aster, its delicate petals a soft violet against the deep green of the surrounding grasses. This dragonfly, she knew, was a silent guardian, a voracious predator of mosquitos that could plague both the lavender fields and the inhabitants of their homes. Its presence was not an accident; it was a consequence of the habitat they were painstakingly cultivating, a habitat that provided both sustenance and shelter for these beneficial hunters.

She walked the borders of her land, where the cultivated rows of lavender met the wilder, untamed prairie. It was here that the most profound lessons unfolded. A patch of coneflowers, their sturdy, pinkish-purple blooms reaching towards the sky, stood sentinel. Beneath them, the soil was richer, darker, teeming with the unseen labor of earthworms and mycorrhizal fungi. These fungi, an intricate network of threads invisible to the naked eye, were the unsung heroes, extending the reach of the coneflowers' roots, facilitating the uptake of water and nutrients. In turn, the coneflowers, with their deep taproots, broke up compacted soil, allowing air and water to penetrate, creating an environment conducive to the delicate root systems of the lavender. It was a silent, ancient contract, a mutual dependence that had sustained this land for millennia before any human hand had ever touched it.

Ellie paused, her gaze falling on a small, unassuming plant with tiny, bell-shaped flowers. She recognized it as vervain, a plant often dismissed as a weed by those who saw only the showier blooms. Yet, vervain held its own significance. Its nectar was a vital food source for a specific species of butterfly, one whose pollination efforts were crucial for the reproduction of several native wildflowers. These wildflowers, in turn, provided food and shelter for ground-nesting birds, whose presence helped to keep insect populations in check. Even the smallest, most overlooked plant, she mused, was a linchpin in the grand design, a crucial thread in the intricate tapestry of life.

This understanding had permeated through her apprentices, the young men and women who now worked alongside her. Young Silas, who had once seen only competition in the "weeds," now approached the margins of the fields with a different eye. He had spent an afternoon observing a queen bumblebee, its fuzzy body laden with pollen, navigate a patch of clover. He'd learned that the clover, a nitrogen-fixer, enriched the soil, benefiting the lavender that followed, and that the clover's blooms were a preferred nectar source for these crucial pollinators. He saw not just a plant, but a vital component of a system, a provider, a partner. His initial frustration with the seemingly unproductive growth had transformed into a quiet fascination with the intricate relationships at play.

The well-being of their community was, in Ellie's view, inextricably linked to the health of the land. When the soil was healthy, it yielded nutritious crops. When the water sources were clean and abundant, the people were healthy. When the wild spaces were preserved, they offered not only beauty and solace but also essential resources – medicinal herbs, game, and opportunities for quiet reflection. She saw the land not as a commodity to be exploited, but as a living entity, a partner in their sustenance, deserving of respect and care. The decisions made on their farms rippled outwards, affecting the local streams, the wildlife corridors, and ultimately, the resilience of their community.

She often spoke of the "unseen bloom" not just in terms of plants, but in the broader context of the ecosystem. The pollination of the lavender, for instance, relied heavily on a diverse array of native bees, many of which were solitary and nested in the ground or in hollow stems. Their survival depended on the preservation of these natural habitats – the undisturbed patches of soil, the stands of native grasses, the decaying wood that offered nesting sites. If these habitats were degraded or destroyed, the pollinators would suffer, and the lavender harvest would inevitably decline. It was a stark reminder that their prosperity was not solely a product of their own labor, but a gift, bestowed by a healthy and functioning ecosystem.

The extended drought, a trial they had weathered together, had served as a harsh but effective teacher. It had stripped away any illusions of human control over nature, forcing them to confront their dependence on its rhythms. Ellie had observed how the native grasses, with their deep, fibrous root systems, had held the soil together, preventing catastrophic erosion when the infrequent rains finally came. These grasses, often overlooked in favor of more productive crops, proved to be the true anchors, the silent custodians of the land's integrity. She had also noted how the presence of diverse native plants along the creek beds had helped to retain moisture, creating microclimates that allowed certain species to survive even in the harshest conditions. These were the lessons of resilience, hard-won and deeply ingrained.

When Abernathy wrote about the Davidsons' success with sorghum, he also mentioned how they had planted rows of native sunflowers alongside their fields. The sunflowers, he observed, attracted a specific beetle that preyed on the sorghum pests. It was a small detail, easily overlooked, but Ellie recognized it as a perfect illustration of her philosophy. The sunflowers were not just a visual offering; they were an active participant in the farm's defense, a natural ally in the ongoing struggle against destructive insects. This was the interconnectedness made tangible, the recognition that even the most cultivated landscapes were richer and more robust when they embraced and integrated the wild.

The community gatherings, once focused on shared anxieties, now often featured discussions about ecological observations. Farmers would share their experiences with companion planting, the benefits of cover crops, or the surprising resilience of certain native species they had incorporated into their land management. There was a growing appreciation for the subtle language of the land, an understanding that by observing and working with nature's intricate web, they could build a more sustainable and prosperous future. Ellie's quiet guidance, her ability to draw connections and illuminate the underlying ecological principles, had fostered this shift in perspective. She encouraged them to see their farms not as isolated entities, but as parts of a larger, interconnected whole.

Ellie's own home, filled with the scent of drying herbs and the quiet presence of well-tended plants, had become a living embodiment of this philosophy. Her garden was a vibrant tapestry of cultivated lavender interspersed with native wildflowers, medicinal herbs, and drought-tolerant shrubs. It was a place where beneficial insects congregated, where songbirds found refuge, and where the soil itself seemed to breathe with health. She would often invite visitors to walk through it, pointing out the symbiotic relationships, the subtle indicators of a thriving ecosystem. She explained how the native milkweed not only provided nectar for pollinators but was essential for the life cycle of the monarch butterfly, a creature that, in its own migratory journey, connected their valley to distant lands.

Her apprentices were learning to read these signs. Silas, now more confident, pointed to a cluster of ladybugs devouring aphids on a lavender stem. "They found them, Ellie," he said, a note of quiet pride in his voice. "They know where to go. The wild plants must be attracting them." Ellie smiled, her heart swelling. This was the understanding she hoped to cultivate — a deep, intuitive knowledge of the land's needs and its inhabitants' roles. It was about recognizing that the health of their farm was not an isolated achievement, but a reflection of the health of the entire ecosystem.

The success of their community, Ellie believed, was measured not just in economic terms, but in its ecological health and its capacity for resilience. When a neighboring farmer, Mr. Henderson, experienced a blight that threatened his entire apple orchard, it was the knowledge shared from Ellie's community that offered a solution. They had learned from the wild, observing how certain native plants, when planted strategically around the orchards, attracted beneficial insects that preyed on the pests responsible for the blight. Mr. Henderson, initially skeptical, had implemented the practice, and the results had been remarkable. The shared wisdom, born from observation and a deep respect for the interconnectedness of life, had saved his livelihood.

This interconnectedness extended to the very water they drank and used. The preservation of the watersheds, the protection of the riparian zones along the creeks, were paramount. Ellie advocated for planting native trees and shrubs along the watercourses, their roots helping to stabilize the banks, prevent erosion, and filter pollutants. These vegetated buffers acted as natural sponges, slowing the flow of rainwater, allowing it to infiltrate the soil, and replenishing the groundwater table. The health of the lavender, dependent on consistent, clean water, was directly tied to the health of these crucial riparian ecosystems. It was a chain of dependence, stretching from the highest ridges to the lowest valleys, linking every living thing.

The annual Lavender Festival, a celebration of their bounty, had become a microcosm of this broader understanding. Beyond the fragrant blooms and the bustling market stalls, there were areas dedicated to showcasing the region's biodiversity. Local naturalists, guided by Ellie's principles, would lead guided walks, pointing out native flora and fauna, explaining their ecological significance. Children would participate in scavenger hunts, identifying different types of bees or the seeds of various wildflowers. The festival was no longer just about celebrating lavender; it was about celebrating the vibrant, interconnected web of life that made their valley so special.

Ellie's vision was not one of a return to a pristine wilderness, but of a thoughtful integration, a conscious effort to weave human endeavor into the existing ecological fabric. She understood that their farms were not separate from nature, but a part of it. The choices they made – from the seeds they planted to the way they managed their water – had profound and lasting consequences. This awareness, this deep understanding of the interconnectedness of all living things, was the true foundation of their prosperity, the unseen bloom that nourished the visible harvest and promised a sustainable future for generations to come. It was a quiet revolution, a testament to the power of observation, empathy, and a profound respect for the delicate balance of the natural world.

The lingering scent of lavender still perfumed the air, a sweet testament to the season's bounty, but now it mingled with a new aroma – the crisp, earthy scent of anticipation. The community, having navigated the unpredictable currents of nature's temperaments, stood at a threshold, not of uncertainty, but of deliberate progression. The lessons etched into their collective memory by the sun-baked earth and the scarce rain were not fading; they were solidifying into a bedrock of understanding. This was a future rooted not in the ephemeral trends of the marketplace or the fleeting promises of quick gain, but in the enduring wisdom gleaned from the land itself, a wisdom as ancient as the bedrock beneath their feet. They had learned, through diligent observation and persistent effort, that true abundance was not a conquest, but a cultivation, an act of stewardship that nurtured the very sources from which all life flowed.

The "unseen blooms," a concept Ellie had so eloquently articulated, had ceased to be a mere poetic metaphor for the hidden workings of the ecosystem. They were now recognized as the tangible, vital components of their sustained well-being. The native prairie grasses, with their intricate, deep-root systems that had held the soil against the erosive force of wind and water, were no longer considered mere background foliage. They were appreciated for their ecological resilience, their ability to draw moisture from deep within the earth, and their capacity to host beneficial insects that lent natural protection to cultivated crops. These uncelebrated plants, often overlooked in favor of more conventionally attractive or productive species, were understood as the true anchors of their agricultural success, the silent custodians of the valley's integrity. Their persistence through drought and their ability to revitalize soil meant they were now actively integrated into farming practices, not as competitors, but as vital partners.

Similarly, the hidden springs that bubbled forth from unexpected crevices in the hillsides, sources of water that had often been taken for granted, were now treated with a reverence born of scarcity and understanding. The careful management of riparian zones, the planting of native willows and cottonwoods along the creek beds, were not viewed as arduous chores but as sacred duties. These vegetated buffers, Ellie had taught them, acted as natural filters, their roots creating a living sponge that cleansed the water, slowed its passage, and replenished the groundwater tables. The clarity and abundance of their water supply, crucial for the thriving lavender fields and the health of their families, was directly linked to the health of these unassuming, yet vital, natural systems. The community saw these water sources not as a right, but as a trust, a fragile resource that demanded their vigilant protection.

The resilient spirit of the people themselves, forged in the shared challenges and collective triumphs, was another of these unseen blooms. The drought had stripped away any vestiges of complacency, revealing a core strength that was both individual and communal. Neighbors had shared water, knowledge, and labor without hesitation, understanding that their individual survival was inextricably linked to the well-being of the entire community. This spirit of mutual support, of shared purpose, was as essential to their future as the fertile soil or the clean water. It was the unseen mortar that held the stones of their society together, enabling them to adapt, to innovate, and to persevere. They recognized that this inherent resilience, this capacity to find solutions and maintain hope even in the face of adversity, was not simply a fortunate trait, but a cultivated asset, nurtured by shared experience and a deep-seated understanding of their interdependence.

The younger generation, particularly Ellie's apprentices, had become keen observers and proponents of this philosophy. Silas, whose initial impatience with the 'wild' had long since evaporated, now spoke with a quiet authority about the migratory patterns of birds and their role in seed dispersal, or the subtle signs of soil health indicated by the presence of certain fungi. He had spent hours documenting the nesting habits of solitary bees, understanding that the preservation of undisturbed ground was critical for their survival and, by extension, for the pollination of the lavender and other essential crops. His once-skeptical gaze had been replaced by one of profound respect, an almost reverent attention to the myriad life forms that contributed to the valley's vitality. He saw the farm not as a static entity to be controlled, but as a dynamic ecosystem, a living partnership that required constant learning and adaptation.

This shift in perspective was visible in the very landscape of their farms. Where once there might have been a sterile monoculture, there were now intentional integrations of native plants. Rows of sunflowers, now recognized for their ability to attract predatory insects that protected sorghum crops, stood sentinel beside fields. Patches of wild columbine and bee balm were deliberately allowed to flourish at the edges of cultivated areas, providing nectar and pollen for a diverse range of pollinators, many of which were crucial for the success of their horticultural endeavors. The concept of "weeds" was being redefined; many plants once eradicated as undesirable were now understood for their ecological contributions, their ability to improve soil structure, fix nitrogen, or provide habitat for beneficial organisms.

The annual Lavender Festival, once a celebration primarily of the cultivated bloom, had evolved into a broader affirmation of the valley's ecological wealth. Guided nature walks, led by those who had absorbed Ellie's teachings, drew crowds eager to learn about the native flora and fauna. Children, their faces alight with discovery, would meticulously sketch the intricate patterns on a butterfly's wing or identify the calls of local birds, their understanding of the natural world deepening with each passing moment. The festival became a vibrant demonstration of the community's commitment to its heritage, a heritage that encompassed not only the lavender they cultivated but the entire intricate web of life that sustained it. It was a celebration of the seen and the unseen, an acknowledgment that their prosperity was a shared gift, a collaborative effort between human endeavor and the natural world.

Ellie, watching these developments, felt a profound sense of fulfillment, not merely for the success of her endeavors, but for the enduring wisdom that had taken root within her community. She saw that the hardship had not broken them, but refined them, clarifying their purpose and deepening their connection to the land that sustained them. They were not simply farmers or stewards; they were inheritors of an ancient knowledge, rediscovering and reinterpreting it for their own time. The future, they understood, was not a destination to be reached through conquest, but a garden to be tended, a delicate balance to be maintained through continuous learning, respect, and a deep, abiding appreciation for the unseen blooms that formed the true foundation of their enduring strength. This was the legacy they were building, a testament to the power of understanding, to the resilience of nature, and to the enduring spirit of a community that had learned to thrive by honoring the intricate, interconnected beauty of life in all its forms, seen and unseen.

The rhythm of their lives had, in essence, been recalibrated. It was no longer solely dictated by the planting and harvesting cycles of their primary crops, but by a more holistic understanding of the land's needs and its capacity. This meant embracing practices that might seem counterintuitive to an outsider, such as leaving certain areas to rewild, allowing native grasses and wildflowers to reclaim the land. These "wild" patches, far from being seen as neglected or unproductive, were recognized as vital reservoirs of biodiversity, essential havens for the myriad insects, birds, and small mammals that played crucial roles in the valley's ecological health. They understood that the health of the cultivated fields was, in large part, dependent on the well-being of these surrounding, less managed areas.

This commitment to ecological integration extended to their water management practices as well. Beyond the riparian buffers, there was a growing emphasis on water conservation techniques that mimicked natural processes. The use of swales and berms to capture and infiltrate rainwater, for instance, was becoming more prevalent, reducing reliance on irrigation and allowing the soil to absorb moisture more efficiently. They were learning to read the land's subtle cues – the way the ground held moisture after a rain, the types of plants that flourished in specific microclimates – and applying this knowledge to optimize their resource use. It was a quiet revolution in agricultural thinking, one that prioritized long-term sustainability over short-term yields.

The impact of this philosophy was also felt in the social fabric of the community. Discussions at local gatherings had shifted from concerns about market prices or weather forecasts to shared observations about local ecosystems. Farmers would exchange tips on companion planting that discouraged pests naturally, or share their experiences with using cover crops to improve soil fertility and structure. There was a palpable sense of shared purpose, a collective endeavor to build a more resilient and harmonious way of life. This communal learning and collaborative problem-solving had fostered a deeper sense of connection and mutual reliance, strengthening the bonds that held the community together.

Ellie's home had become something of a living laboratory, a testament to the principles she espoused. Her garden was a testament to polyculture, a vibrant tapestry where lavender mingled with medicinal herbs like echinacea and yarrow, interspersed with native wildflowers that provided nectar and pollen throughout the season. Here, beneficial insects were not a scarce commodity but a constant presence, their hum a familiar soundtrack to daily life. Songbirds flitted through the branches of fruit trees, their presence a natural deterrent to insect pests. The soil itself, dark and rich, teemed with microbial life, a visible indicator of its health and vitality. She would often invite visitors, apprentices and curious neighbors alike, to walk with her, pointing out the intricate symbiotic relationships, the subtle indicators of a thriving ecosystem that guests might otherwise overlook.

The success of this integrated approach was not confined to the valley. News of their methods, their emphasis on ecological stewardship and community resilience, began to spread. Visitors from other regions, facing similar environmental challenges, would come seeking advice and inspiration. They saw in the valley a model of how human ingenuity and respect for nature could combine to create not just a sustainable livelihood, but a truly flourishing community. This outward recognition validated the deep, hard-won wisdom that had been cultivated, proving that the lessons learned in their seemingly small corner of the world held universal significance.

The apprentices, now embodying this philosophy, were becoming educators in their own right. Silas, in particular, had taken on a mentorship role, guiding younger individuals who were just beginning to understand the interconnectedness of their environment. He would lead them on excursions to observe the foraging habits of native bees, explaining how the presence of certain flowering shrubs directly influenced the pollination success of the lavender fields. He taught them to identify the signs of soil health, the importance of earthworms and beneficial fungi, and the long-term benefits of minimal tillage. His own journey from skepticism to deep understanding served as a powerful example, demonstrating that true mastery of the land came not from imposing one's will upon it, but from learning to work in concert with its inherent wisdom.

The concept of the "unseen bloom" had thus expanded to encompass more than just the ecological underpinnings of their agricultural success. It now represented the collective knowledge, the shared spirit of cooperation, and the enduring resilience that had been cultivated alongside the lavender. These were the intangible assets, the true sources of their enduring strength and their capacity to overcome adversity. They were the springs that nourished the visible harvest, the deep roots that ensured their future prosperity, and the quiet blossoms that promised continued abundance for generations to come. It was a future built not on exploitation, but on a profound, unwavering respect for the intricate tapestry of life, a tapestry where every thread, seen or unseen, played its vital part.

The scent of lavender, a rich perfume that had once been the sole herald of their success, now carried within it a deeper resonance. It was more than just the aroma of blooming flowers; it was the concentrated essence of lessons learned, of resilience forged, and of a future carefully, deliberately cultivated. This enduring fragrance, a constant on the Dawson farm, had become synonymous with a profound and unshakeable hope. It was a hope not born of blind optimism or wishful thinking, but of demonstrable evidence, of a deep understanding of the land's intricate rhythms and a unwavering commitment to working in harmony with them. The very air seemed to hum with this quiet confidence, a testament to the transformation that had taken place.

The farm, once a precarious venture teetering on the edge of despair, had blossomed into a beacon of ecological wisdom. It was a living, breathing embodiment of Ellie Mae Dawson's vision, a testament to her unwavering belief in the interconnectedness of all life. The careful integration of native flora, once considered mere weeds by those who did not understand, now stood as a vibrant illustration of nature's inherent strength and its capacity for self-renewal. The wild grasses, their roots delving deep into the earth, were no longer an afterthought but active participants in the farm's ecosystem, holding the soil, nurturing beneficial insects, and contributing to the overall vitality of the land. They were the silent guardians, the unseen foundations upon which the visible abundance was built.

Ellie Mae often found herself walking the perimeter of the fields, her hands brushing against the sturdy stems of the lavender, the familiar texture a comforting anchor. Her gaze would drift to the patches of native wildflowers – the vibrant splash of Indian paintbrush, the delicate purple of coneflowers, the cheerful yellow of Black-Eyed Susans – that she had deliberately encouraged. These were the "unseen blooms" made manifest, their quiet persistence a powerful counterpoint to the cultivated beauty of the lavender. They were a constant reminder that true abundance was not a singular achievement, but a complex tapestry woven from countless, often overlooked, threads of life. The bees, a constant hum of industrious activity, seemed to understand this implicitly, flitting from the cultivated lavender to the native blooms with equal dedication, their pollination efforts a crucial bridge between the managed and the wild.

The transformation was not merely aesthetic; it was deeply ingrained in the very fabric of their farming practices. The methods that had once been viewed with skepticism had become their greatest strength. The practice of leaving certain areas to rewild, for instance, was now understood as a vital strategy for maintaining biodiversity and supporting the natural predators of common pests. These "wild" havens acted as nurseries for beneficial insects, providing them with shelter and sustenance when cultivated crops were not in bloom, ensuring their presence and efficacy throughout the growing season. Similarly, the thoughtful implementation of water conservation techniques, like the strategic placement of swales and berms, had not only reduced their reliance on irrigation but had also demonstrably improved the soil's ability to absorb and retain moisture, creating a more resilient water system that was less susceptible to the vagaries of drought.

The younger generation, those who had grown up

absorbing Ellie Mae's teachings, were now the stewards of this evolved understanding. Silas, his initial skepticism long since transformed into a profound respect, moved through the fields with a quiet competence, his knowledge of the land now intuitive. He could read the subtle signs of soil health in the growth patterns of cover crops, identify the beneficial insects by their behavior, and understand the critical role of even the smallest creatures in the intricate web of life. He had become a mentor himself, patiently guiding younger apprentices, sharing his knowledge with the same clarity and passion that Ellie Mae had once shown him. He understood that the legacy they were building was not just about growing lavender; it was about cultivating a deep, abiding reverence for the natural world.

The annual Lavender Festival, once a celebration primarily of the cultivated harvest, had evolved into something far richer and more meaningful. It had become a vibrant showcase of the valley's ecological wealth, a testament to the community's commitment to stewardship. Guided nature walks, led by those who had internalized Ellie Mae's philosophy, drew crowds eager to learn about the intricate relationships within the local ecosystem. Children, their eyes wide with wonder, would meticulously sketch the delicate patterns on a butterfly's wing or mimic the calls of native birds, their connection to the land deepening with each passing moment. The festival was no longer just about the visible blooms; it was a holistic celebration of the seen and the unseen, a joyous affirmation of the shared bounty and the collaborative effort that sustained it.

Ellie Mae often found solace in her garden, a place that perfectly encapsulated the principles she championed. It was a vibrant symphony of life, where the familiar rows of lavender were interwoven with medicinal herbs like echinacea and yarrow, and punctuated by a riot of native wildflowers. Here, the air was alive with the murmur of bees and the gentle rustle of leaves. Songbirds, their presence a natural deterrent to insect pests, flitted through the branches of fruit trees, their cheerful chirping a constant melody. The soil, dark and rich beneath her touch, teemed with unseen life, a testament to its health and vitality. She would invite visitors, from curious neighbors to visiting agriculturalists from distant regions, to walk with her, to share in the quiet magic of her garden, pointing out the symbiotic relationships, the subtle indicators of a thriving ecosystem that might otherwise go unnoticed.

The success of their integrated approach had not gone unnoticed beyond the valley's borders. Word of their innovative methods, their dedication to ecological stewardship and community resilience, began to spread like the seeds carried on the wind. Visitors from other areas, facing similar environmental challenges, would journey to their valley seeking inspiration and guidance. They saw in the Dawson farm and the surrounding community a tangible model of how human ingenuity, when coupled with a deep respect for the natural world, could foster not only a sustainable livelihood but a truly flourishing way of life. This external recognition served as a powerful validation of the hard-won wisdom that had been cultivated, a testament to the universal significance of the lessons learned in their seemingly small corner of Texas.

Ellie Mae's own journey had reached a quiet culmination, a peaceful affirmation of her lifelong connection to the land. The anxieties that had once gnawed at her, the constant worry about the whims of nature and the vagaries of the market, had been replaced by a profound sense of contentment. She had found a deeper understanding, not just of how to farm, but of how to live in harmony with the rhythms of the earth. The challenges had not broken her; they had refined her, clarifying her purpose and deepening her bond with the soil that sustained them. She saw herself not merely as a farmer, but as a caretaker, an inheritor of ancient wisdom that she had helped to reawaken and adapt for their time.

The future, as she perceived it, was not a distant destination to be conquered, but a garden to be nurtured, a delicate balance to be meticulously maintained. It was a future built on continuous learning, on unwavering respect, and on a deep, abiding appreciation for the myriad unseen blooms that formed the true, enduring foundation of their strength. This was the legacy she was building, a testament to the transformative power of understanding, to the unyielding resilience of nature, and to the indomitable spirit of a community that had learned to thrive by honoring the intricate, interconnected beauty of life in all its forms, both seen and unseen.

The final vestiges of the summer heat still lingered in the air, but a subtle coolness now presaged the approaching autumn. The lavender fields, their purple glory beginning to fade into the muted tones of seed heads, still offered a gentle fragrance, a soft whisper of the bounty they had yielded. Ellie Mae stood at the edge of the largest field, the familiar scent of dried lavender mingling with the crisp, earthy aroma of drying herbs and the sweet, subtle perfume of late-blooming wildflowers. The air was alive with the industrious hum of bees, their diligence a testament to the success of the integrated planting strategies she had championed.

Her gaze swept across the landscape, taking in the verdant patchwork of the valley. The native grasses, their tall stalks swaying gently in the breeze, stood as sentinels along the contours of the land, their deep roots anchoring the soil against any potential erosion. The wild columbine and bee balm, deliberately allowed to flourish at the edges of the cultivated areas, provided a vibrant splash of color and a vital source of nectar for the pollinators that were crucial to their agricultural endeavors. She noticed the familiar silhouette of a burrowing owl perched atop a fence post, its keen eyes scanning the fields, a natural guardian against rodent populations that could threaten the crops. Each element, from the smallest insect to the most resilient plant, played its indispensable part in the grand, interconnected tapestry of their farm.

The lessons Ellie Mae had imparted, the philosophy she had so patiently cultivated, had taken root not just in the soil but in the hearts and minds of her community. The conversations at the general store, once dominated by concerns about market fluctuations and unpredictable weather, had shifted. Now, neighbors eagerly shared observations about the migratory patterns of local birds, exchanged tips on companion planting that naturally deterred pests, or discussed the benefits of incorporating certain cover crops to enhance soil fertility. There was a palpable sense of shared purpose, a collective endeavor to build a more resilient and harmonious way of life, a life lived in concert with the land rather than in opposition to it.

Her home, a modest farmhouse that had weathered its share of storms, now stood as a living laboratory, a vibrant demonstration of the principles she held dear. The garden was a riot of polyculture, a testament to the beauty and productivity that could be achieved through careful integration. Lavender mingled with medicinal herbs, interspersed with native wildflowers that provided a continuous bloom throughout the season, supporting a diverse array of pollinators. The fruit trees, carefully pruned to encourage beneficial insect activity, offered not only their sweet bounty but also a natural defense against common garden pests. The soil itself, dark and rich, teemed with the unseen life of microorganisms and earthworms, a visual indicator of its robust health and vitality.

Silas, his presence a comforting and capable one, now often led the younger apprentices on excursions, his voice carrying the quiet authority of experience. He would point out the intricate nesting habits of solitary bees, emphasizing the importance of preserving undisturbed ground for their survival and, by extension, for the pollination of the lavender and other crops. He taught them to identify the subtle signs of soil health, the crucial role of earthworms and beneficial fungi, and the long-term advantages of minimal tillage practices. His own journey, from initial skepticism to profound understanding, served as a powerful living example of the transformative power of open-mindedness and dedication to learning from the land itself.

The annual Lavender Festival, a celebration that had once revolved solely around the cultivated bloom, had evolved into a broader affirmation of the valley's ecological wealth. Guided nature walks, led by those who had absorbed Ellie Mae's teachings, now drew significant crowds, eager to learn about the native flora and fauna that contributed to the region's unique character. Children, their faces alight with discovery, would meticulously sketch the intricate patterns on a butterfly's wing or identify the calls of local birds, their understanding of the natural world deepening with each passing moment. The festival had become a vibrant demonstration of the community's commitment to its heritage, a heritage that encompassed not only the lavender they cultivated but the entire intricate web of life that sustained it. It was a celebration of the seen and the unseen, an acknowledgment that their prosperity was a shared gift, a collaborative effort between human endeavor and the magnificent, resilient power of the natural world.

Ellie Mae, watching these developments unfold, felt a profound sense of fulfillment. It was not merely the success of her endeavors that brought her joy, but the enduring wisdom that had taken root within her community, a wisdom as deep and pervasive as the scent of the lavender that perfumed the air. She saw that the hardships they had faced had not broken them, but refined them, clarifying their purpose and deepening their connection to the land that sustained them. They were not simply farmers or stewards; they were inheritors of an ancient knowledge, rediscovering and reinterpreting it for their own time, weaving it into the fabric of their daily lives.

The future, they now understood, was not a destination to be reached through conquest, but a garden to be tended, a delicate balance to be maintained through continuous learning, unwavering respect, and a deep, abiding appreciation for the unseen blooms that formed the true, enduring foundation of their strength. This was the legacy they were building, a testament to the power of understanding, to the resilience of nature, and to the enduring spirit of a community that had learned to thrive by honoring the intricate, interconnected beauty of life in all its forms, seen and unseen. The persistent fragrance of lavender was no longer just a scent; it was the enduring symbol of their hope, a promise of continued abundance, a testament to the quiet power of nature, and the profound resilience of the human spirit. The Texas Hill Country, a landscape that had once tested them to their limits, was now a place of deep connection and enduring promise, a promise whispered on the fragrant breeze.

**Cover Crops**: Plants grown primarily to benefit the soil and ecosystem rather than for harvest. They can improve soil fertility, prevent erosion, suppress weeds, and support beneficial insects.

**Native Flora**: Plant species indigenous to a particular region, adapted to the local climate and soil conditions.

**Regenerative Agriculture**: A philosophy and set of farming practices that aim to improve soil health, biodiversity, and water cycles, moving beyond sustainability to actively restore ecological functions.

**Swales**: shallow ditches dug on contour lines of slopes to capture and slow down rainwater runoff, allowing it to infiltrate the soil and reduce erosion.

**Polyculture**: The practice of growing multiple crops in close proximity, mimicking natural ecosystems and promoting biodiversity.

**Companion Planting**: The arrangement of plants that benefit each other, often through pest deterrence, nutrient sharing, or attracting beneficial insects.

Altieri, Miguel A. *Agroecology: The Science of Sustainable Agriculture*. Westview Press, 1995.

Callicott, J. Baird. *In Defense of the Land Ethic: Essays in Environmental Philosophy*. State University of New York Press, 1989.

Fukuoka, Masanobu. *The One-Straw Revolution: An Introduction to Natural Farming*. Bantam Books, 1978.

Kingsolver, Barbara. *Prodigal Summer*. HarperCollins Publishers, 2000.

Nabhan, Gary Paul. *Coming Home to the Pleistocene*. University of Arizona Press, 1997.

Savory, Allan. *Holistic Management: A Commonsense Revolution to Restore Our Environment*. Island Press, 2016.

Thompson, Paul B. *Food, Forests, and the Future of Life: Taking Down the Industrial Food Machine*. Columbia University Press, 2021.